TIKKI SHEDS HER CLOTHES AND WILLS THE CHANGE

It takes only instants.

Her body stretches out long. Her musculature swells immense. Fur the color of blood—striped by black—rushes up her arms and body and over her face. Hands spread wide and swell into enormous paws. She drops to all fours. Claws emerge, ears arise twitching and flicking, her long tail slides out of the end of her spine. Her breathing deepens and resonates with the menacing timbre of a long, low animal growl.

"What was that?" asks Adama's chosen, voice wavering with anxiety and doubt.

"A friend," Adama says casually. "A very good friend."

SHADOWRUN: STRIPER ASSASSIN

SHADOWRUN

STRIPER ASSASSIN

NYX SMITH

A ROC BOOK

ROC
Published by the Penguin Group
Penguin Books USA Inc., 375 Hudson Street,
New York, New York 10014, U.S.A.
Penguin Books Ltd, 27 Wrights Lane,
London W8 5TZ, England
Penguin Books Australia Ltd, Ringwood,
Victoria, Australia
Penguin Books Canada Ltd, 10 Alcorn Avenue,
Toronto, Ontario, Canada, M4V 3B2
Penguin Books (N.Z.) Ltd, 182–190 Wairau Road,
Auckland 10, New Zealand

Penguin Books Ltd, Registered Offices:
Harmondsworth, Middlesex, England

First published by Roc, an imprint of New American Library,
a division of Penguin Books USA Inc.

First Printing, June, 1993
10 9 8 7 6 5 4 3 2 1

RoC REGISTERED TRADEMARK—MARCA REGISTRADA

For the Believers

Yo, ma! I'm in print.

Special thanks to Robert N. Charrette for passing along my invitation to the Dodger to come and join the party.

Thanks also to MJW and WTW, for too many things to recount, including my existence; JW and WE, for important insights; RNC, renaissance man, friend and mentor; AJF, for support; LT, for liking the short story; TZ and JF, who probably think I'm dead by now; DNZ, for grotesque unmentionables; M*A, for intriguing talks lasting till dawn; SB (are we having fun yet?); LJ, whose enigmatic smiles rival those of the Mona Lisa; PH and TD and certain other brains who unwittingly contributed to this project; DG & friend, for language tips; SR, comptech extraordinaire; LD, for a cool rendering; JCB for encouragement; & everyone at FASA & ROC who helped to get this into print.

And, of course, Ginger Ann and Oscar . . .

For various reasons.

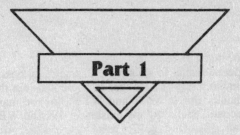

Part 1

PREDATOR

One impulse from a vernal wood
May teach you more of man,
Of moral evil and of good,
Than all the sages can.
  William Wordsworth, ''The Tables Turned''

1

Prey is prey.

Human, elk, ork, troll—it makes no difference. Two-legs or four-legs does not matter. That was the first thing she'd ever learned and she's never forgotten it. All beings are part of Nature's scheme. Each has its proper role to play in the immortal cycle of life and death, where there is only the hunter and the hunted, predator and prey.

The world of humans knows her as Striper, but her real name is Tikki and tonight Tikki hunts.

The soft hum of human technology fills her ears, and the oily scents of machinery tickle her nostrils. She wrinkles her nose and flicks her nails, patiently awaiting the moment of death, when the plotting of many hours, the study and the preparation all come together in the climax of the kill. She has tracked her prey carefully. She knows its spoor, its habits. Now the stalking is done, the trap is set. Soon the prey will enter her killing ground, and then all questions will be answered, all doubts resolved with lethal finality.

It is just like hunting in the wild.

The elevator waits, motionless. Tikki stands inside. The control panel there hangs open, showing an array of wires that connect the elevator controls to a diagnostic portacomp used by repair techs. The comp, dangling from the open panel, gives complete override control of the elevator; it has persuaded the building's central computer system that the elevator is undergoing routine maintenance. A second array of wires connects certain colored cables from the elevator control conduit to a small, palmsized monitor hanging beside the portacomp. The monitor provides a view of the area just beyond the elevator doors, courtesy of the building's own security cameras.

There are two elevators, one in service, one not. The elevator Tikki commands waits with doors closed at the level of the underground parking garage.

The moment of the kill approaches.

On her monitor, Tikki sees a long black Nissan Ultima V limousine roll into the garage and glide to a gentle halt before the elevators. An instant later she hears a soft ding from her left. That is the other elevator, the one in service, now arriving at her level, the sublevel garage. She counts off the seconds . . . one, two, three. A light flares on the portacomp. Her ears detect a soft rumbling. On the monitor, she sees the doors of the other elevator sliding open. A small group of five people steps out. The individual she awaits is a slim Asian male with the traits of old age: thin white hair, deeply wrinkled face, fraillooking hands. His name is Ryokai Naoshi and he is one of several ranking yakuza bosses targeted for assassination.

Ryokai's status among the yakuza will not save him. Tikki knows about yakuza, knows that they possess great power and many soldiers. But that is irrelevant to her and no reason to forego tonight's work. Every animal has its weapons, some possess more than others. The successful predator eludes the dangers posed by her prey, and, once committed, strikes ruthlessly to the kill.

Ryokai and his companions move toward the limo.

Tikki keys the portacomp.

When the doors in front of her trundle open, she is holding a Vindicator minigun, a large and cumbersome weapon with six revolving barrels that are already whirring. No need for her to leave the elevator. The limo is right there, barely five meters away and just slightly to her left. Ryokai, his two bodyguards, and another suit

and a stylishly attired female are just coming up alongside the limo. One of the suited bodyguards abruptly
snaps his head around and looks in Tikki's direction, but
even he is too slow, too late.

They are all in her direct line of fire.

Tikki squeezes the trigger.

The Vindicator roars, the whirling barrels spitting fire,
the weapon's rapid-fire stammer rising to thunder quick
and raw. Armor-piercing shells chew up the side of the
limo, smashing windows and flattening tires, shredding
the soft-bodied humans in-between like so much fleshly
foliage. Shattered glass and spraying blood shower the
limo and the concrete floor. The bodies twist and spin
and topple. Tikki spends the final few rounds of the Vindicator's fifty-round magazine on her primary target, Ryokai's body. It leaves the corpse looking like carrion,
shredded pulp, and that is very satisfactory.

Her contract for tonight's kill required that the hit *look*
like a hit and that it be very noisy and overwhelmingly
destructive.

Contract complete.

She stabs at the portacomp. The elevator descends to
the maintenance sublevels. From there, she will depart
via various utility tunnels.

All goes according to plan.

Null sheen, as the humans say.

2

The last thing that seems at all real to him is the sudden clenching pressure of Jennifer's hand at his elbow
and her soft, sudden exclamation, like a gasp.

Then the nightmare begins.

A roaring like thunder fills the air, fire flares in his
eyes, then comes pain, an ocean of pain, a galaxy of
pain, more pain than he had ever imagined might afflict
a single person, agony, excruciating, without end, with-

out limit. Piercing him from every direction. Pounding into his skull. Slamming through his whole body. Some part of him can't believe that one person could suffer this degree of agony and survive. He feels as if pain alone, like a tangible physical force, might split him apart, break him into pieces and crush him, smash him into atoms.

What comes next exceeds comprehension. Despite the agony, he's moving, moving fast, as if shooting down a long dark tunnel. Faster and faster. Till the speed is ripping at his flesh, tearing at his limbs, wrenching at his whole body.

The tunnel grows brighter, brilliant, blinding. He plunges into an incandescent whiteness, a searing inferno of white. Utterly overwhelming.

Without end . . .

3

By two a.m. the old road is deserted, leading north through the Blue Ridge Mountains and the Confederated American State of North Carolina. In the distance lightning sears the black vault of the night, and the sound of thunder resounds through the hills like barrages of massed artillery.

Raman stands along the shoulder of the road. Gleaming steel claws protrude from the studded black bracer sheathing his right forearm. He watches the bulging eyes of the man hanging from the razor-edged blades. The man, like his companion sprawled nearby, wears the corporate uniform of the state patrol, and he is dying for his indiscretions. Blood streams from his midsection to pool on the hard-packed ground around his feet. Before long his eyes glaze over. His body goes limp. It is a death Raman considers unfortunate for the trouble it may bring, but wholly unavoidable.

Raman lowers his arm and lets the body fall. He dislikes having to kill law enforcement officials, but these

two left him no choice. They sought to prevent his es-
·cape.

The contract cops' dark blue Nissan Interceptor sends
blips of red and blue across the face of the trees flanking
the road. Other cars and other police will soon be coming. Perhaps even airborne vehicles. Raman's recent work
in Atlanta seems to have roused half the Confederated
American States. He glances around quickly, then gives
the snapblades a shake before retracting them with a soft
snick of gleaming metal. Obviously, he must continue
his headlong rush to safety. His record is too long to risk
being snared by the authorities. Arrest would surely be
followed by conviction, imprisonment and death, and that
must never happen. It is his promise to himself.

Better to be cut down by a hail of bullets, left to die
alone in some rubbish-strewn alley or along a forgotten
stretch of highway than be confined in a prison to die like
a lamb at the hand of his executioners.

Death itself is not the issue.

Death is his brother. Raman has no fear of it. When
he dies, he will die free, as fate should have it.

Some other night, perhaps.

His stolen Harley Scorpion awaits him on the shoulder
just a few steps back. Raman sets the engine to whining
and tears out onto the pavement, hurtling up the road.
He hunches forward, shifting his weight to keep the hog's
front tire on the decaying blacktop. A few kilometers
more and he'll be across the border and into a part of
the world known as Virginia.

The irony of the name draws from him the wry flicker
of a smile. There is nothing virginal any more.

Nothing, nowhere.

4

In a room awash with a reddish haze Bernard Ohara awakens to the cozy heat of the bed and the warm, yielding pressure of a pair of female bodies, one on his left and the other on his right. The names that go with the bodies are Christie and Crystal. Both biffs are blue-eyed blondes; they look and sound and feel enough alike to be twins. Their figures are miraculous, exquisite, lush. Ohara is sure the biffs owe their extravagant proportions to Gold's Premier Salon or some other similar establishment specializing in body sculpture, but doesn't care.

His only interest is their willingness to please him. That's why he keeps them, why they came to his attention in the first place.

Lying there in the blood-hued dark, Ohara recalls with a smile his promises to get the twins into trideo, perhaps even state-of-the-art simsense productions. Those promises have since become irrelevant, much as he had expected. The biffs aren't interested in acting. All they care about is money. They will do almost anything for the right amount of nuyen, wait on him like slaves, warm his bed. That doesn't stop Ohara from wondering if having them on chip might be even more exciting than the real thing. It often works out that way—with the right emotive overlays, the right editing . . . and so forth.

Something warm and wet slips over his ear. Moist lips gently brush his cheek. Long-nailed fingers graze his neck, his chest, moving to caress him lower down. His new implant responds with a speed and resolve he still finds astonishing, but that he has come to relish. In mere moments he is hard as stone, aching for it.

One of the biffs moans and climbs onto his hips, taking him inside. Her husky pleas urge him to exuberance. The grip of her body sends an electric thrill streaking up his spine to erupt all through him with explosive delight.

It leaves the biff panting, sprawled over to his side. Ohara grunts contentedly. The other one, Christie or Crystal, whichever, begs for a turn. Ohara smiles and gives it to her hard and fast, the way he likes it.

As it ends, the telecom bleeps.

His private line.

"Drek," he grumbles.

The Hi-D telecom display set into the wall beyond the foot of the bed shifts to a muted gray. The stylized corporate logo of KFK International, Kono-Furata-Ko, appears briefly at center-screen, then swells to fill the background as the rounded features of an Asian male come into view.

It is Enoshi Ken, Ohara's corporate aide.

"Give me the remote."

One of the biffs, Crystal, or Christie, presses the remote into his hand while squirming sensually against his side, nuzzling his neck, trailing a hand across his groin.

Ohara grunts, keys the remote.

Audio only.

"I said no interruptions, dammit!"

Up on the big screen, Enoshi bows his head.

Ohara smiles acidly. At least his fool of an aide has not yet used his name, not over an open telecom line. Ohara is careful about security, and demands no less from his subordinates, what with all the neoanarchists and other radicals yearning to work out their deep-seated psychological disturbances against the upper strata of the corporate hierarchy. His condominium here in the Platinum Manor Estates is registered to his corporate benefactor, rather than in his own name. He also employs a pair of elite Birnoth Comitatus executive protectors around the clock, plus other defenses as well.

"Please excuse me, sir," Enoshi says in a typically ingratiating tone, apologizing for the interruption, as certainly he should. "In this case, however, I thought—"

Ohara isn't interested in the rationale. "Get on with it."

"Yes, sir. Excuse me, sir. I have just received word

from our chief of security that Mister Robert Neiman is dead.''

This comes as a surprise. Ohara frowns at the thought of losing a chunk of the corporate architecture he has so artfully redesigned. This is not only inconvenient, but at least briefly disturbing. Neiman was head of the Special Projects Section of Exotech Entertainment, a closely held subsidiary of KFK and Ohara's primary realm of control. Since joining KFK, Ohara had lifted Neiman from the dusty crannies of mere research to control over the special unit that has recently made Exotech a hot corporate property. He had given Neiman a taste of real power, and been well-rewarded.

"What in fragging hell happened?" Ohara growls.

"I'm told that all the details are not yet known, sir." Enoshi replies, his face ever impassive. "It appears that the police are treating the matter as a deliberate killing. A murder. They have divulged nothing specific."

"I want a full report!" Ohara snarls, but he is far less outraged than he sounds. What the police will readily divulge and what they will surrender under pressure are two different things. Obviously, they have no suspects in custody or they would have said so up front, while making the standard notifications to Neiman's next of kin, and of course, to his corporate master, Exotech.

The concept of some minor police official withholding information irks Ohara, but it's not worth getting upset about it. That is a matter for Enoshi to handle, a minor issue of intercorporate prestige.

As for the actual details of Neiman's death, Ohara has little interest. It is enough to know that the modern metroplex provides abundant opportunities for a person to get himself killed. All it takes is a single slip. Even a normally cautious individual like Neiman might commit a fatal error in judgment. The man probably had no inkling of what was coming until it was too late. Ohara has seen it happen that way.

One can never be too careful.

"Yes, sir," Enoshi says, again bowing his head. "I will get you a full report. Immediately. Is there anything else?"

It should be obvious. Even half-asleep, in bed with a pair of sex-addicted biffs, Ohara's got more on the ball than his toady senior aide and so-called chief of staff. As if there could be any doubt. He allows himself a sarcastic smile. The only problem with the Japanese, the one most serious problem, is that they have no initiative. They can't make a decision without first consulting a committee of thousands—everyone they work with, everyone they work for, right on up to the chairman of the board of directors—if Ohara let them go that far.

Unfortunately, in an organization like KFK, and a world like that of 2054, Ohara can't avoid dealing with the ''culturally challenged.'' Drones like Enoshi are too deeply embedded within the structure. They're pervasive.

''Who's Neiman's assistant? Baines?''

''Bairnes, sir.''

''Right.'' Details like that, the names of junior staff members, are what he pays Enoshi to know and know by rote, as if written into his soul. Ohara's responsibilities run more toward the big picture, the complete picture, as from atop the corporate heap.

''Tell Bairnes he's about to be promoted. I want his assessment of the Special Project Section's current strategy in my queue by tomorrow noon. And that is to include his recommendations for changes. Don't waste my time with visuals. I want hard text. Paydata. Got it?''

''Yes, sir,'' Enoshi says quickly. ''I'll notify Mister Bairnes at once.''

''See that you do,'' says Ohara, abruptly cutting the connection.

5

The name of the club is Spit's and tonight the cataclysmic fury of bruiser metal roars out from the entrance, sending a feral rhythm through the steel-and-concrete canyon whose glaring neon billboards rise to thirty and forty stories. Skyswimmers drifting far overhead blare with the audio tracks of adverts winking and flashing on ten-by-eight trideo displays. Ground traffic hums and growls and squeals along four narrow lanes of pavement. The breeds and breeders alike crowd the crumbling sidewalks: humans and metas, polis and skinheads, suits and scats, trogs and toughs, wannabe razors in studs and leather, the NeoMonochromes and tats and electrobodyware freaks, and all the other thousand sweating, swearing, shouting variants to be found in the postmodern, post-Ghost Dance, re-Awakened urban environment.

Just down the street, voices rise sharp and vicious. A flurry of fists ends with the flash of a knife and the quick, dull thumping of a semi-automatic weapon. One man slumps to the concrete, all but disemboweled. Another staggers toward the corner, bleeding copiously from the shoulder. One dies, one survives. To the victor go the spoils.

Philadelphia metroplex, downtown Saturday night.

Tikki leans back against the gleaming, wet-look front of the vibrating nightclub and lights a Dannemann Lonja cigarro, long and slim. She smiles, only to herself. She's in her element here, amid the throbbing pulse of the urban jungle, where the noise assaults the ear and the street life flows eternal. To her, the passing crowds are a single, seething herd of animals oblivious to the gaze of the hunter and to the intimate nearness of death.

They are prey without eyes.

A red and white cruiser marked for Minuteman Security Services Inc., the local law, comes rushing up the block, strobe lights flashing, siren squealing. Tikki had nothing to do with the killing just down the sidewalk, and she does not plan to hang around long enough to see whether or not the law will believe it. She turns and steps around the corner of Spits, into the alley there. Two minutes later, she's heading down a long tunnel leading to the Market Street subway. The next arriving train fires her across town toward the Schuylkill River.

She hasn't been in Philly long, but the terrain is familiar, just one more sub-sector of the vast metroplex sprawling away to the horizon, an urban nightmare that will one day blanket the globe. Cablecast trideo, the global computer networks, and the world's hopelessly interlocked economies have so homogenized the urban lands where Tikki hunts that she often has to stop and remind herself where she is. Telling one place from another is sometimes that difficult.

Of course, there are nuances to the terrain, special dangers and other distinctions, most of them rather minor, but the careful predator learns the differences with every breath, every glance, every snatch of sound.

Also, Tikki has good contacts who provide her with the most essential information.

Her fixer in Chiba steers her to the right people.

As the express roars through the dark, dank tunnels under the earth, a uniformed Minuteman cop strolls up the aisle to the end of the last car of the train. That's where Tikki stands, leaning against the car's rear wall. Her eyes take in the cop's every movement. Her nose discerns nothing unusual, no hint of either excitement or alarm, though the slag strolls right up to her, looking her over. It's easy to guess the cause for his interest. It's highly unlikely that he has spotted the Kang heavy automatic concealed at the small of her back. Rather, it's probably a question of image.

Tikki is tall for a female, tall and lean. Her eyes are covered with black Toshiba mirrorshades, and her face is a carefully painted mask of crimson red, striped with black. Her close-cropped hair, including the wispy tuft floating down over her left brow, is tinted to match her face. She wears gleaming blood-red leather—jacket, mesh blouse, slacks, fingerless gloves—all "striped" by the studded bands at her neck, wrists, waist, and on her supple boots.

All the studs are brushed steel. Tikki has sometimes worn gold studs in the past, but never anything silver. Silver is retro-skag. She hates it.

"ID?" the cop says, facing her from a step away.

Tikki lifts her special card right up in front of his face. A squeeze of one corner displays her City of Philadel-

phia, Inc., weapons permit and official bodyguard ID in
alternating sequence. The cop doesn't react except to
move his eyes like he's reading, then to compare the picture to her face. She could put a monofilament sword
straight into his gut right now and he wouldn't even notice till he felt the first searing rush of pain.

Amateurs and fools are everywhere. Her primal heart
urges her to lash out, take this prey, an easy kill, but she
resists.

Some other night, perhaps.

The train squeals to a halt in the bowels of the Thirtieth Street transit center. Tikki follows the suits out onto
the grim gray platforms and joins the herds moving slowly
toward the escalators.

The suits all wear the colors of their corporate affiliations pinned to their lapels, just like yakuza or ordinary
street gangs. Only the corporate gangs have names like
Cigna Universal, Renraku, ITT-Rand, SmithKliner, Fuchi, or Aztechnology, each with its special area of influence and interest. The only difference between the corp
gangs and the street gangs is the texture of the violence
they do and the number of bodies they leave lying around.
None really obey the law. Rather, they exert themselves
to evade the law, evade capture, evade punishment.

Tikki often wonders why humans bother making laws
at all. At best, laws provide unnecessary complications.
To her, the only laws that really matter are the ones gov-
erning survival, the struggle between predator and prey,
and the balance between the thousand species of animals
walking the planet. Nature's laws.

The herds ascending the escalators are about half white
and half black, brown, or tan. Asians account for a far
less significant share of the population here than in other
cities, but their power and influence is ubiquitous, obvious at a glance. Trogs and other metahumans maintain a
low profile. The Night of Rage still simmers. The slo-
gans of the Alamos 20,000 and various other anti-meta
policlubs cover the sides of the trains, the platforms, and
concrete columns like so much spattered gore.

Tikki has no problem with racially motivated hate and

violence. It keeps the herds looking in every direction
but the one from which she's coming.

She rides up to the ground-level concourse.

Meters-tall trideo screens climb the walls, flaring and
buzzing with adverts. The herds of suits spread out to fill
the wide floor. Subways, buses, and commuter rail lines
all converge here in the Thirtieth Street transit center.
Like the Market East station downtown, it is a main hub
for suits sluicing between Center City plazas and their
secured corporate enclaves out in the burbs. Minuteman
patrol cops and the more heavily armed and armored
Flash Point Enforcement officers keep a close scan on
the mobs pouring ceaselessly through the accessways.
The salarymen must be protected or else the city's corporate patrons will take their minions to safer quarters.

Tikki is stopped twice for ID checks. That's nothing
more than she expected.

Clusters of telecom stands turn the broad floor of the
concourse into an enormous pinball game, breaking the
rivers of hustling salarymen into hundreds of individual
streams. Tikki steps up to one of the stands and puts a
wad of chewing gum over the telecom's visual pickup.
When the time on the telecom's display shows 20:05:00,
she thrusts a certified credstik into the chrome port. Her
fingertips tingle, the telecom bleeps. The words "Enter
Telecom Code" wink on and off, on and off. Tikki leans
toward the display like a near-sighted geezer, interposing
her head between the screen and anyone who might try
to look over her shoulder. She taps at the keys. Three
times she enters the code, and three times she hears
sounds like a telecom bleeping at the other end of the
line, followed immediately by a return of call tone. She
is into and through several secured telecom systems that
quickly. Midway along she lifts a Fuchi MemoMan recorder to the telecom's audio pickup. The corder spits
out a rapid-fire electronic melody that gets her past a
specially coded protocol barrier.

The telecom's display goes blank, jet-black. A male
answers, in Japanese. Tikki's Japanese isn't fabulous, but
she gets by.

"Who's this?" he asks.

"Two guesses," Tikki murmurs.

Her reply is enough for a voiceprint analysis that clears her call through the final barrier. Call tone returns. Tikki taps in a final number. A new voice, also male, comes on the line. It is a computer-synthesized simulation of the voice of her Chiba fixer. The agent's name, translated from the Japanese, means Black Mist. He makes connections for her worldwide and performs other services, all for a fee.

"Yes?"

"Anything?" Tikki asks.

A moment's pause, then, "Several inquiries."

The phrasing there is important. The use of any descriptives, such as "several *interesting* inquiries," would mean trouble had arisen. The words as stated mean simply that two or more inquiries for Tikki's services have been received. She isn't interested, not right now. She's made a good connection here in Philly and intends to play it out.

"What else?"

"Nothing."

That's the end of the call. Tikki hits the Disconnect key. Her credstick is docked and released. Her only reason for making the call was to find out what else Black Mist might have to tell her about the main matter he's checking out for her. His info led her here to Philly. She needs to know more, but for the moment can do nothing but wait.

Somewhere in the city is a man she's going to kill, with extreme malice, just as soon as he turns up.

It's more than personal.

It's a fact waiting to happen.

6

The night outside the transit center is a flickering flashing flaring neon phosphorous halogen multi-chrome fantasy. Skyswimmers with giant trid screens fill the sky. Adstands with reverberating audio tracks line the sidewalks. Salarymen bustle along in every direction. A seething ocean of automobiles, taxis, and buses hums and snarls and roars. Emergency vehicles with glaring strobes and squealing sirens add a touch of frantic pandemonium to the ambiance of mass confusion.

An unbroken line of limos, mostly Toyota Elites, waits at curbside. The limo Tikki wants is a Mitsubishi Nightsky, sleek and black and gleaming like rainwater on wax. The double-sized door to the rear passenger compartment swings open as she approaches. Bending low, she climbs right in. The door thumps shut behind her.

The environmental seals close with a soft gush of air.

The compartment is spacious and rich. Plush synthleather seats like compact sofas face each other across a fully equipped center console replete with trideo, telecom, and refrigerated bar. The trid glows with "Suerte y Muerte," the gladiator games broadcast from Aztlan. A glass of Suntory beer sits on the bar, freshly poured. Beside the beer lies a pack of slim Sumatran cigarros. Tikki takes the rear-facing seat, glances at the trid and the beer and the cigars, then at the man in the seat facing her.

"All is well?" he inquires.

Tikki nods.

The man's name is Adama Ho. At least that's what he says. His look is Anglo, which proves nothing. He has short, thinning hair, deep-set eyes, and a neatly trimmed black mustache and beard that cover his upper lip and jawline but leave his cheeks mostly bare. In his midnight black suit, silk shirt and tie, he looks urbane and elegant.

Tikki takes nothing for granted. Some of the most dangerous men she has ever met were both soft-spoken and polite, even when confronted by the most vicious of street punks.

The Anglo look is pure deceit, she's sure of it, probably the result of body-shop alterations. Instinct is her only evidence for that, but there's also his fluent Mandarin, which he speaks like a native. Tikki knows about Mandarin. It's the tongue of China's ruling Han majority and the only way to speak it the way Adama does is to learn it growing up. That's exactly how she learned it.

Mandarin just happens to be the primary language of the Triads. That coincidence alone demands caution.

Tikki knows about Triads, too.

Very dangerous.

"Then Ryokai Naoshi is no longer a problem."

To this, Tikki says nothing. She meets Adama's gaze evenly, all the answer she need give. As she has already indicated, all is well. She would not be sitting here in the man's luxurious limo had she not completed her job. Adama should know that. Even if he hasn't already heard of Ryokai's assassination via other sources, which she seriously doubts, he should *presume* that her work is complete.

Momentarily, Adama forms a smile, a broad smile, clearly visible despite the thick mustache and neatly trimmed beard. Dimples form in his cheeks.

"Good. Very good," he says quietly. "Feel free to smoke."

A hand formed into the likeness of a blade points to the bar. The limo is armored against attack, the doors secured, so Tikki decides to accept her employer's generous offer to indulge herself. She opens the pack of Lonjas and draws out one long, slim cigarro. The leaf is the color of café au lait and promises to yield a mild, tangy smoke. Adama draws a golden lighter from the vest of his chic black suit and offers her a flame. She accepts. Adama's hand catches her eye, not for the first time. He wears a heavy gold ring with a large reddish stone. His nails are long for a male's and finely manicured. He is nothing if not meticulously groomed.

As Tikki takes a first drag, the climate controls kick in with a soft gush of air. The smoke is everything she expected. Adama passes her a certified credstick for the hit on the yakuza boss Ryokai Naoshi.

Tikki nods and slips the stick into a pocket.

"Satisfactory?" Adama inquires.

She nods. *Very* satisfactory.

Adama lights one of his big, thick soberanos, Honduran leaf, to judge by the scent. Tikki tastes her Suntory. For beer, it isn't bad. Cider is her drink of choice, but she likes a little variety now and then. She glances at the blood sport on the trid and suppresses her recurring feelings of amazement.

Tikki is used to deference, respectful treatment, even from major syndicate leaders. In the steel and concrete world of humans, she is a specialist, a technician. She rates special consideration, her skills always in demand. She can usually name her price or simply walk away if the terms of a job don't suit her. Yet her experience with Adama is unique. At times, his manner is so casual, so familiar, that an objective observer might wonder if something intimate, something owing to gender distinctions, might possibly exist between them.

"You've finished your personal business?" Adama asks.

Tikki nods again.

The question comes quietly and casually and Tikki gives only the necessary response. She has certain strategies for survival. Never give away more than necessary, never give away something valuable for nothing. What Adama knows of her personal business tonight is that she had something to do. That is all he needs to know. She has hired on with him in the dual capacity of assassin and sometime bodyguard. That does not endow him with the right to know her every move. Neither does it grant him twenty-four-hour access.

"Good, very good," Adama says, still smiling. He takes a long drag on his soberano, gently blows the aromatic smoke away. The smoke billows and curls and vanishes into a ventilation port. "I'm in the mood for some entertainment. I'd like you to come along."

"I'm on the clock," Tikki says.

"Naturally." He seems almost amused to say so. His smile broadens to the point of a grin. "Any suggestions?"

Tikki looks at him quizzically. "Why ask me?"

"You are a creature of the night, are you not?" says Adama, still smiling, looking at her as if making a quiet little joke. Tikki is used to his little jokes. They don't come all that frequently, but when they do they always slide near the truth. In another man, she might consider that dangerous. Adama, though, is not just any man. "Go ahead," he says. "Make a suggestion."

Tikki smiles vaguely, wryly. Where to go? Never the same place twice—that is the warning of instinct. "Someplace new."

Adama nods, just slightly, approvingly, and keys the limo's intercom. "Club Penumbra."

"Yes, sir," replies the voice of the chauffeur.

Adama smiles contentedly as the limo glides smoothly away from the curb, turning in the direction of Center City, just minutes away.

The club is on Tenth just north of Chinatown. Its real name is Penumbra East, alluding to the original Club Penumbra, which is located in Seattle. The crowd waiting on line at the front door extends halfway down the block toward Girard Street; in places the line is four and five deep.

The limo swings in and stops at curbside. Scanning for trouble, Tikki steps out first. Adama follows. Together they cross the sidewalk toward the club entrance. Doormen single Tikki out with their eyes and move as if to block her, possibly to conduct a search. Her red- and black-striped face paint and bodyleather might be taken for Penumbra style, but the studs and spikes are definitely not.

Adama motions the doormen back with a mere flick of the fingers. "No need," he says, smiling. "No need."

Credsticks discreetly change hands.

The doormen bow and scrape and usher them inside.

A hostess in black synthleather and glowing neon strips

waits in the dark interior. "Welcome to Penumbra East," she says. "May I have your names, please?"

"Fuchi," Adama says, smiling. He glances sideways at Tikki as if to share a private joke. "Mister Fuchi."

Adama brushes briefly at his lapel, directing the eyes of the hostess to a pin bearing the corporate colors of Fuchi I.E., the multinational electronics giant. Obviously impressed, the hostess draws a quick breath. She looks surprised, off guard, and suddenly smells very anxious.

Adama smiles.

"Of course," he explains, "you might say I'm traveling incognito tonight. *Wakarimasu-ka*?"

"Yes of course," the hostess says breathlessly. "Mister Fuchi. *Wakarimasu*." She nods, she bows, she understands completely.

"Good," Adama says amicably. "Very good."

"May I show you to a table, Fuchi-*sama*?"

"Domo arigato," Adama says, smiling, nodding faintly.

"Do itashimashite," the hostess replies, bowing deeply.

Tikki refrains from any sort of comment. This business regarding Fuchi I.E. is a farce. Adama is no more a patriarch of Fuchi I.E. than is the fawning hostess. What he is, Tikki suspects, is a ranking Triad official, probably a Red Pole, or 426, in charge of enforcement. Certain things he has said in private suggest ties with the Green Circle Gang, a particularly vicious arm of the infamous 999 Society, controlled by Silicon Ma out of Hong Kong. This is interesting because Tikki's mother once did some work for Silicon Ma himself. Perhaps the crime lord recommended Tikki to Adama . . .

As a rule, Triads rarely hire outside help—the average gang boasts thousands of members—but there are always exceptions. The one thing Tikki does know is that her assassination of Ryokai Naoshi in the parking garage, as ordered by Adama, would suit the Green Circle Gang's style just fine.

If a Triad gang was intending to move into Philly, hitting the yakuza would be a good way to start. The

Philadelphia-Camden sprawl is a kind of three-way split. Northern Philadelphia is the fractured territory, the Zone, constantly battled over by gangs: go-gangs and thrill gangs, ordinary street gangs, fleeting associations of skells and scum, humans and trogs, even elves. Strictly amateur stuff. South Philly belongs to the Sicilian mob. The mob does some serious biz down there, but the yakuza rule the sweetest territory, the casino sprawl over on the Camden side of the Delaware River.

All of the above have interests downtown. Even the Korean Seoulpa Rings have interests downtown.

If Tikki were to choose the target for a new prime player, she would definitely go for the yaks. Go for the money, the real nuyen. By far the most interesting game.

Perhaps Adama is here to scout the territory. Perhaps the Green Circle Gang is already here, but undercover. There are many possibilities, most of them basically irrelevant as far as Tikki is concerned, except as interesting speculation. No one Tikki's talked to lately has heard of any Triads coming to Philly, but that's not surprising. It's a big city, a big world, and crime lords like Silicon Ma aren't in the habit of advertising their plans. Ma in particular would be much more likely to butcher anyone stupid enough to give anything away.

Tikki follows Adama into the depths of the club.

The ceiling is lost in darkness. Sizzling bolts of laser light zigzag through the air. The walls are turning fields of stars and oversized trid displays flashing haute modern adverts and flickering scenes from the sunken dance floor. Adama's table is one of many lining the aisles ringing the dance floor like tiered balconies. The music is loud and ponderous, throbbing, vibrating. The dancers turn and bob like mannikins on strings. Tikki keeps her eyes moving. Most of the club's patrons are dressed in Penumbra-style: glowing neon over black; silvery monochrome that glints with pinpoints of light like stars; luminescent face paint. Males favor flowing shogun blouses and billowing trousers. Females tend toward kimonos and clinging gowns. Hair is samurai, cut back from the brow and knotted in back; or geisha, piled up on top in intricate weaves. Most of the bodies walking around look to

have been sculpted at the better body salons. Credsticks
are always glinting.

"What do you think?" Adama asks.

Tikki crinkles her nose in distaste, shakes her head.
The original Penumbra is not like this. There's nothing
of the wild here, and silver-infected fashions raise her
hackles.

Adama smiles apologetically.

A waiter brings food and wine. The food is grossly
overcooked and smells like burnt-out waste, but Adama
doesn't seem to mind. Probably doesn't even notice. Like
most humans, he has only a token sense of smell. Fortunately, he's the only one eating. Tikki stands to his left,
keeping her hands free. She and her employer are in the
open now and there are rules to be observed. Never compromise your hands. Never allow anyone to interfere with
your eyes. Stay alert.

Adama makes the job difficult. He talks to Tikki constantly, as if she were merely a companion rather than a
guard. Always, he insists on a reply. "What about that
one?" he inquires. "Will she be my Leandra?"

Tikki has heard the question before. Finding the man's
"Leandra" is the primary objective of a night on the
town. What he's really talking about is finding and then
playing with a suitable female, one who fits his specs. It
isn't half as odd as it sounds, and the way Adama plays
the game only enhances Tikki's estimation of him. He
doesn't simply look at the biffs strolling around, he sizes
them up, like a hunter. Not a hunter like Tikki, but a
hunter all the same. The instincts are right there for her
to see in his black marble eyes. Adama knows about
predator and prey, killing and death. He knows that killing is sometimes essential and that death is an intrinsic
part of life. He knows that humans use a word like *murder* because they lack the perspective of the hunter, not
understanding what occurs between predator and prey in
the final moment, when teeth meet flesh and the waters
of life pour out steaming and red to stain the earth.

In the wild, there is no *murder,* no laws, no moral
rights and wrongs. There is only Nature, the contest for

survival. She who kills tonight has food to eat and may thereby live to see a new dawn.

The true hunter understands this.

Even before Adama is finished eating, a curvaceous brunette brushes his shoulder with an elbow, then pauses, looking at him, smiling as if to apologize. Adama looks up and around at her and smiles, the next moment gesturing vaguely to the other chair at his table.

The brunette sits, smiles, begins a conversation. Tikki discreetly points a compact Fuchi SCX-5 ScanMan at her. The ScanMan declares the woman safe, unarmed.

"Will you be my Leandra?" Adama inquires.

The brunette laughs softly and turns to call a friend over.

That one brings another along.

Before long, Adama is surrounded by seven well-proportioned women who act as if enraptured by his talk. One by one, he escorts them onto the dance floor and back again. He buys them drinks. He compliments their hair, their clothes, their looks. He lights their cigarettes, chuckling softly when one or more of them provide a flame for his cigar.

Tikki is anything but surprised. She's seen all this before. Perhaps the Fuchi pin on Adama's lapel has something to do with it. Or perhaps, just as she has a talent for stalking prey, Adama may have a skill or an instinct for sitting and waiting, for lurking, for setting a subtle form of ambush. Or perhaps certain human females have a special sense for males who radiate power and wealth.

"Who will be my Leandra?" Adama asks.

The females all laugh.

The hour grows late.

Inevitably, a favorite emerges, a voluptuous redhead with lightly tanned skin. She wears a clinging black gown that reflects the surroundings like a mirror. Adama glances at Tikki, inclining an eyebrow in question. Tikki scrutinizes the favorite and nods. Adama always asks her opinion, one hunter to another.

Privately, intimately, Adama asks the chosen one, "Will you be my Leandra?"

The woman smiles and nods eagerly, moaning, slip-

ping her arms around Adama's shoulders and nuzzling
his neck.

Adama smiles as if satisfied. "My beautiful Leandra,"
he says. "Will you come home with me?"

The chosen one nods and croons.

"Yessss . . . Oh, yeessss . . ."

Adama gives her his arm. Tikki leads them out of the
club to the limo waiting at curbside. Tikki surveys the
terrain in crossing to the car, letting Adama and the chosen one precede her into the limo's rear compartment.

The environment seals shut with a soft gush of air.

The limo glides smoothly through the city streets. The
redhead, the chosen one, leans against Adama's side,
cooing and stroking the man as he keys the telecom.

Music begins, something loud and fierce and raw.

Tikki lights another of her slim Sumatran cigarros and
allows herself a faint smile. The game will soon get interesting.

Humans delude themselves with the belief that they are
thinking animals and therefore not animals at all. The
truth, as Tikki sees it, contrasts starkly with that view.
All animals think, to one degree or another. The human
animal is a very sophisticated animal, with complicated
thoughts and an almost endless variety of habits, but it
is still an animal and thus subject to Natural Law and the
challenge of survival.

The limo pulls up in front of Adama's five-story town
house. The redhead has yet to realize what's happening.

The clues are too obscure.

The entrance hall of Adama's town house is spacious
and broad, floored in marble and adorned with paintings
and other objets d'art. Adama shows the redhead, the
chosen one, through the door on the left, into the drawing
room. Tikki locks the door to the street. It's a heavy
door, heavy enough to be soundproof. Just like the rest
of the house.

The door to the drawing room stands slightly ajar.
From there Adama's voice carries out clearly. He offers
drinks. He pours liquids that gurgle softly as cubes of
ice ring against the glasses. He says, in a poetical tone,
"Tiger, Tiger, burning bright . . . in the forests of the

night. What immortal hand or eye could frame thy fearful
symmetry?''

"Excuse me?'' the chosen one asks.

Adama chuckles, laughs, louder and louder till he bel-
lows with hilarity. The chosen one still does not understand.

That is easily remedied.

Tikki sheds her clothes and wills the change. Her body
stretches out long. Her musculature swells immense. Fur
the color of blood—striped with black—rushes up her
arms and body and over her face. Hands spread wide and
swell into enormous paws. She drops to all fours. Claws
emerge, ears arise twitching and flicking, her long tail
slides out from the end of her spine. Her breathing deepens and resonates with the menacing timbre of a long,
low animal growl.

"What was that?'' says Adama's chosen, voice wavering with anxiety and doubt.

"A friend,'' Adama says casually. "A good friend.''

"It sounded like . . . like a lion!''

Tikki steps up to the doorway leading to the drawing
room and jabs one paw at the door as if to slash at prey.
The door whips inward, slamming into the wall. The bang
thunders through the house.

Standing near the center of the drawing room, Adama's
chosen one looks over, then shrieks and fills the air with
the stink of her terror, and that is good. Prey should
always know it is prey, and should react like prey when
faced with the hunter. Now in her natural form, her true
form, Tikki is large even for that breed she so perfectly
resembles, *Panthera tigris altaica,* the largest tigers on
earth.

Tikki growls, then *roars.*

The chosen one screams.

Adama grins.

7

The night is cool and fine.

It's so quiet that just the softest scuffing of a shoe against the gravel along the side of the road stands out starkly, sounding loud. Overhead a few stars show through the hazy clouds. A faint breeze drifts through the surrounding woods.

Sighing, she wonders how much further she's gonna get tonight. It doesn't look too good.

Her name is Neona Jaxx and she sits on a concrete block she found lying on the shoulder of the road. From time to time, she scuffs one of her florescent pink Reebok Sprinters against the ground in hopes of preventing any creepy-crawlers from climbing up her legs. The mere idea gives her shivers, and briefly distracts her from the flat rectangular presence in the bag she holds cradled in her lap, though never for very long.

The anonymous black nylon bag holds a gray macro-plast case inscribed with the Fuchi logo. Inside the protective case is a Fuchi-6 cyberdeck in mint condition. It isn't top of the line anymore, hasn't been for a while, but it's the slickest tech she's ever had in her own two hands. Almost half a million nuyen off the shelf. A deck with real power, a load rate that's pure quicksilver, and the capability to do things she's only dreamed of. She can't help but hold it tightly, squeezing the rounded edge of the safety case against her stomach till it hurts.

What she paid for the deck can't be measured in nuyen. That's really what makes it hurt.

She wipes more tears from her eyes.

None of her chums back in Miami liked either the Johnson or the job. It was she who talked them into it. The Johnson's offer of the Fuchi-6 as part payment must have blinded her to everything else. Until then she'd been creeping along with a Sony CTY-360 rebuilt so many times the internals looked like spaghetti, a silicon mish-mash that almost no one could figure out, much less re-pair. With a Fuchi-6, she figured she'd slice through the Matrix like lightning—and she did, only that didn't help her buds.

The Johnson turned out to be dirty, a real slot. The job was a setup, and her buds all got smoked. Neona would have gotten scragged too, except that she picked up and ran and never stopped.

That was six weeks ago. Since then, nothing. No more problems. Just bad memories, sleepless nights.

Rides to nowhere.

Thirty klicks short of Philadelphia, a rigger dumped her out of his cab like so much spare change. She's lonely and alone feeling the price for her newfound fortune, her Fuchi-6.

It's pretty bad, but she knows it could be worse.

Now, from a ways off, comes a distant rumbling, gut-tural and deep, kind of like thunder at first, but rising slowly and steadily in volume till she realizes it's a cycle. Not a battery-powered whiner, either, but an old-style petrochem chopper.

Disappearing into the darkness, the road is flat and narrow and flanked by trees. She looks down the two-lane to her left, the direction from which she came. That way leads back toward Miami and the chummers she left for dead, a thought that squeezes a few more tears from her eyes. She wipes them with the back of her hand and looks again. The noisy chopper sounds like it's right on top of her and she still can't see a thing.

Then, all at once, there it is—five, six meters away, roaring past her like a jet, blurring before her eyes, a phantom machine glinting in the starlight.

Caught by surprise, she sways back, catching her breath, clutching at the macroplast case in her lap.

Whoever is riding the thing is driving with no head-light, no lights at all.

The thudding roar of the engine Dopplers down, then drops like a brick from a roof, going almost silent. She hears the whispery breeze rustling the woods and the metallic rasping, almost a ringing, of the chopper's chain-link drivetrain. She squints up the road in the direction of Philly, catches a glint of starlight on chrome, but that's it. The chopper rumbles again, thudding briefly. What's happening? She's certain the hog slowed down, but is the rider going on ahead or coming back?

Abruptly, the phantom's back, gliding across the two-lane on a diagonal, coming straight toward her. That's when the headlight flares like a supernova glaring right into her eyes.

For a few seconds, ten, maybe more, her dark-adjusted eyes are too busy screaming in protest for her to do more than squeeze one forearm across the bridge of her nose trying to block out the light. The chopper stops directly in front of her, rumbling smoothly. Neona guesses she shouldn't be surprised to have gotten hit by the beam. A girl with spiky mohawk hair, wearing a black vinyl jacket, sitting here all alone in the middle of nowhere at sometime around midnight—she'd be suspicious, too. Hell, she wouldn't even have slowed down had she been riding the bike.

The glaring headlight turns aside. The rumbling chopper seems to come a little closer. She lowers her arm enough to wipe at her eyes, and gets her first decent look at the slag on the bike. From the looks of the black hair falling to his shoulders, his strong features, the bandanna around his neck, the broad shoulders and heavy build, she guesses that he must be an Amerind. Black synth-leather jacket ornamented with fringe and studs. Dark pants, heavy boots. He rolls the bike to a halt a short distance away. She can feel the heat from the engine, can almost feel him watching her through the mirrored lenses of his shades.

The shades must be low-light specs, that or two-ways, reflective on the outside, clear from within. They add to the image of power. Like this is no one to frag with, chummer.

Slowly, carefully, she stands up, struggling to find a smile. "So, hoi," she says.

In reply, he motions at her with his chin, like he wants to know what she's doing, what's going down.

"Waitin' for a ride."

"I got a ride," he says.

His voice is like a low growl, so intensely masculine
it's almost animal. It sends a quick shiver up her spine.
She tries not to show it, whatever it is that's suddenly got
her heart thumping so hard. "Yeah?"

"Come closer."

Another shiver slips up her back. She can't tell if it's
excitement or fear. Something's happening here, but
what? The urge to turn and run right into the tree line,
run for her life, careens wildly through her thoughts even
as Neona steps closer, one step, then another. She definitely gets the feeling that he's looking her over from
behind those mirrored lenses. Incredibly, she finds herself desperately hoping he likes what he sees. He could
be just what she needs right now, more than just a ride.
If nothing else, he looks like he could make the world a
lot safer for a girl who's long on programming and short
on hand-to-hand. The view from her angle is impressive.
She likes her men hard, even a little rough. This one
looks rougher than most.

From little more than a step away, she can see he's
dark for an Amerind, if that's what he is. The darker the
better. Really light-skinned people make her feel
glitched, like a cake too long in the oven, burnt almost
black.

"What's in the bag?"

A flush of anxious heat rushes up the back of her neck.
She forces a smile. "Nothin'. Just a deck."

"A good one."

How did he guess that? She deliberately mixed truth
and falsehood to try and protect the deeper truth, the
fantasy deck in her hands. She feels a gnawing of real
fear, but shrugs, struggling to keep up the act. "It's decent."

"You're a decker."

"Yeah."

"A good one."

Where is he getting this from? A rush of giddy fear
blossoms into an uncontrollable grin. Is he reading her
aura? She'll fall over dead if he turns out be a mage.
"I'm decent, too."

"You want a ride?"

Is he kidding? "Sure."

"What's your name?"

"People call me Angel."

"Get your pack, Angel."

"Okay." She's practically breathless, and grinning, as she turns back toward the shoulder of the road. This slag has got her reeling! She's never met anyone who affected her this way before. He's just scary enough to be real, but not quite so scary as to send her running. She stumbles and almost flops on her face just reaching down to pick up her small backpack. Good thing she's been traveling light. She's feeling way too muzzy to even *want* to deal with much luggage. She slings the pack from one shoulder, the Fuchi-6 from the other, and turns back to the chopper man.

She can't stop smiling.

"What do I call you?" she asks.

"Ripsaw."

More chills up her spine. The name suits him. Any handle he used would have to be hard and sharp like razor claws. Anything less menacing would seem absurd.

"Get on."

"Okay." That growly voice is turning her to butter. She lifts one leg up and over and slides onto the back of the hi-rider seat, which is just high enough for her to see over Ripsaw's shoulders. The bike never moves, never sways, like it's planted in stone, till she's settled in her seat. Then, the engine rumbles, briefly revving, and the chopper rolls around in a smooth half circle, then starts accelerating up the road, running straight as an arrow.

It's still hours before dawn when they pull into the hard-packed lot of a truck stop just off the main highway. In the light of a passing rig, Neona gets her first clear look at the back of Ripsaw's jacket. The synthleather bears the cat's head logo of the Sioux Wildcats. She's heard that name before. On the news somewhere. Something about some banger Native American Nations military unit.

She's got herself a real killer here.

A real killer chiller.
Yeah . . .

8

: : : *North Central Metroplex*
05-19-54/10:17:03

Switch on, plug in, engage . . .
This must be his lucky day!

Natch, he's got all the standard gads, and today everything seems to be working—scum damn fragging incredible as it may be, and *is*—to him at least.

His Seretech Evening Shade cybereyes with FlareGuard
and the thermographic-enhancement option provide a
crisp, direct-vision image of the crumbling tenements and
decaying sidewalks along Erie Avenue, not far from the
Frankford Creek toxic waste dump. His Eyecrafter opticam package provides a complete diagnostic readout in
the form of a direct-vision overlay right in front of his
eyes. With a touch of the Bionome tridlink controller
strapped to his right forearm, he enhances the overlay to
include data on all the rest of his hardware, both implants
and strap-ons. The datajacked Sony CB-5000 camera
in the steady-mount atop his helmet comes on-line with
a flood of snow that blinds him before clearing to
crystal-linked clarity. Even the AZT Micro25 minicam
strapped to his right wrist gives him a picture-perfect
image.

Utterly damn fragging amazed, he swings his arm up
and around, panning right, optics cued to the Micro25,
only to close-frame on a lovely thermographic image of
Sidewipe, the scrod-frakkin' nit holding the Fuchi short-
range transmitter, smiling at him and looking stupid, taking a pause from adjusting his crotch.

Dweezle dirtbrain ignoramus . . .

"Skeeter! Skeeter, *come on*!" J. B. calls impatiently.
The hell with it.

Main lens: pan left, zoom, up-focus, close-face. The
so very trid-o-genic Asian features of J. B. come clearly
through the datajacked Sony mounted atop his helmet
and the optical receptors inside his skull: onyx A-sym
hair, bangs across the brow, one long tuft curving down
over right cheek; one pointed elven ear showing; coal-
black eyes; powder-white skin; crimson lips; red serpent
tattoo on left cheek.

If she ever gets a direct network feed, she'll be deadly.
She's bad enough as it is. A real pain in the back-door
trumpet, excuse my scum fraggin' *français*!

"Am I on?"

Skeeter jabs a finger at her—*YOU'RE ON!*

"This is Joi Bang of WHAM! Independent News coming to you direct from North Central Philadelphia where
yet another victim in a series of cannibalistic mutilation
killings has just been discovered."

Yea, team.

Then of course she's running, running right out of the
frame, only looking back to wave frantically—come on!
come on! The very trid-o-genic biff never stands still for
very long. Damn blast her anyway. Skeeter hustles forward, feeling a tug from the right of his belt. That's because the dirtbrain with the Fuchi transmit dish can't stop
picking his nose long enough to wake up and smell the
poop.

Just another twerkin' newsday chasing J. B. around.

Fraggin' scrod-damn bull-hooey . . .

'Scuse my *mutha muckin' French*!

05-19-54/10:19:44

Establishing shot: J. B. and Minuteman cop standing
on the sidewalk inside a ring of shabby slummers. Zoom
in, split-view, close-focus, and hold. Main lens on cop,
direct-view cybereyes on J. B. Roll cams.

"You were the first officer on the scene?" J. B.
prompts.

"Yeah," the cop replies.

This is sum-biff news?

"What did you find?" she inquires.

"Talk to the sergeant."

Great.

Eat my sokkin' mutha chip.

J. B. smiles, glances back toward Skeeter. That's the usual signal. Skeeter realizes what's coming. Stop cam, close eyes. He briefly shuts down the Sony atop his helmet, too. When he re-engages, a faint cloud of some damn golden particulate stuff, glinting with tiny motes of light, is drifting around the cop's face. The cop is now smiling. J. B. lifts her mike.

"Is it true the victim was cannibalized?" she asks.

"What a mess," the cop says, now grinning. "I mean, there wasn't hardly nothing left. You shoulda seen it!"

"Was the victim male or female?"

"Who could tell?"

"Which way to the body?"

"Right in there." The cop points. "Have a look. But don't say I didn't warn ya."

Then of course J. B.'s running up the steps and into the tenement. Skeeter hustles forward. Another tug from his belt. Dammit to all fraggin' hell, Sidewipe.

Get your finger outta your nose!

05-19-54/10:20:07

Close-frame, close-focus: dingy tenement hall. A sprawl rat peers out from around the frame of a doorway. They call 'em devil rats. More like rodents from hell. Red glowin' eyes, wrinkly mutant skin, shiny little black claws.

J. B. pulls up abruptly, cutting short a shriek.

Heh.

05-19-54/10:22:18

"Fraggin' hell! Get the hell back! All of you! Get the hell back!"

Main lens: low-light, zoom in. J. B. heading down a dark, decrepit stairway into some blackened, garbage-strewn junkyard hell of a basement. Minuteman cop with stripes coming into the stairwell waving his arms around. J. B.'s already blabbing into her mike, "This is Joi Bang for WHAM! Independent News. Is it true, Sergeant, that you've found yet another victim in the series of mutilation cannibal killings that Minuteman Security Services seems unable to crack?''

''Get the hell outta here!'' the sergeant shouts.

Another damn cloud of glinting gold blossoms into the air. No warning this time.

Reverse and purge.

05-19-54/10:22:57

''Well, heck,'' the sergeant says. ''It ain't that bad. I mean, there's only been three so far. Three bodies. And we're workin' on it. The detectives—''

''Can we see the body?''

''Yeah, it's right over there.''

05-19-54/10:23:46

Establishing shot, slow pan. Garbage-strewn basement, ancient pipes crossing the ceiling, graffiti and unsanitary-looking moisture covering walls. What's left of the body is bloated and kinda greenish. Main lens: pull back and hold. Direct-view: close in and scan maggot-covered skull. Exposed bones. Quick thermographic sequence from the AZT microcam on his wrist.

J. B. provides voiceover.

Blah blah blah . . .

''What you're looking at is the third victim in a series of cannibal-mutilation style killings occurring within the Philly metroplex within the last month. So little of the body remains it's hard to tell if the victim was male or female, or even human. Some of the bones look gnawed. Large portions of the cadaver seem to be missing—limbs, internal organs . . . at least they don't seem to be anywhere nearby . . .''

New voice, demanding, ''What's happening here! Who are these people! Sergeant! *Sergeant!*''

Someone grabs Skeeter's shoulder and tugs. He hears a whimpery exclamation from Sidewipe while staggering around in a half circle. The line to the damn Fuchi dish is wrapping around his ankles. Fraggin' wackweed Sidewipe.

Main lens: up-angle, broad view, sharp focus. Some big slag in plainclothes with a brass detective's shield hanging out of his jacket pocket. Face mottled red with anger. J. B. steps up from his right, mike uplifted. Zoom in, split-screen.

"I'm Joi Bang from WHAM! Independent News. Do you have any comment, Detective, on this latest in a series—"

"This is a crime scene, dammit!"

"Can you explain why Helter-Shutt Inc., Minuteman's parent corporation, has called upon renowned metazoologist Doctor Marion Liss of the University City Science Center?"

"How the heck should I know *that*?"

"Isn't it true that numerous sightings of the metabeings called ghouls have been reported to Minuteman police within just the last week?"

"What! Who—?"

"Do the police intend to send out death squads in order to neutralize the threat posed by these creatures?"

"Who says it's ghouls, dammit!"

"Are you suggesting, Detective, that some other metacreature is responsible for this series of cannibalistic mutilations?"

"I didn't say that!"

"Then what are you saying, Detective?"

"Slot it outta here! And *now*!"

J. B. looks back toward the camera view.

Dust the fraggin' badge and be done with it.

Damn scrogging nithead biff.

9

At six minutes past the hour of seven a.m., Enoshi Ken steps from the elevator and makes his way briskly down Teak Row, as the corridor is known, toward the suite reserved for his immediate superior, Bernard X. Ohara, member of the board of Kono-Furata-Ko Corporation and

Chief Executive Officer of the KFK subsidiary, Exotech
Entertainment.

The day is hardly begun and already Enoshi is in a
position he dislikes intensely, that of being behind sched-
ule. Too well, he knows how swiftly small delays and
other minor problems can mount and mount, till serious
disruptions result. His job as Executive Chief of Staff to
the CEO of Exotech Entertainment is to see that, among
other things, such disruptions do not occur. It is a job
for which he considers himself well-suited. It is his firm
belief that the quality executive must find ways to cir-
cumvent trouble, regardless of circumstance, even before
it occurs, and where necessary, make silver purses from
sows' ears. Enoshi is not so naive as to believe that it is
always possible to attain such miracles, but neither is he
so self-indulgent as to imagine that fate or bad luck
should ever be blamed for personal failures.

Probably, there are those who do not share Enoshi's
determination, and may therefore consider him intolerant
or perhaps excessively devoted. It can be difficult to know
what others think. Despite this, he does his best to maintain good relations with his own subordinates, those
members of Ohara-*san*'s staff who are under his super-
vision.

Enoshi turns a corner and strides briskly into the
reception area of Ohara-*san*'s suite. Remarkably, the receptionist is not at her desk. Shocked, Enoshi checks his
watch, if only to confirm that he is not dreaming, that it
is in fact just past seven a.m. on a day when a full com-
plement of staff persons should be at their posts. He then
moves quickly through the door to the right of the reception counter and into the staff office. Here he finds his
explanation. The desks running up both sides of the room
are all empty. The entire staff of eight, including one
receptionist, one office lady, two secretary-transcribers,
a data aide, a computer aide, a statistical aide, and an
assistant manager are standing in a group midway up the
center aisle.

With them is Nigao Yorito from personnel.

Apparently, the whole group has banded together to
keep Nigao occupied, covering for Enoshi's absence.

Enoshi walks rapidly up the center aisle, apologizes for the delay. His failure to arrive at the usual time has upset the entire office and disrupted the usual morning routine. He should have been here almost thirty minutes ago. He must hasten to regain lost time. "Ms. Harrington," he says briskly, "would you please show Mister Nigao into the inner office? Thank you."

That much done, he turns to the others.

"I will be with you in just one more moment."

At the front of the room, he moves quickly behind his own desk, sets down his briefcase, and removes his pocket secretary bound in dark red synthleather. With that in hand, he steps through the connecting door leading into Ohara-*san*'s office, the "inner" office. An expansive wall of windows arcs gently around to the rear of the imposing onyx desk situated on a low dais. Enoshi pauses to exchange brief bows with the man from personnel, then also shakes hands.

Ms. Harrington goes out to summon the rest of the office staff. Enoshi takes his position in front of the onyx desk, and invites Nigao to stand beside him.

The group comes in, a mixture of Asians and occidentals of various ages, three males, five females. All are meticulously groomed and attired. All wear plastic-laminated badges identifying them as employees of Exotech Entertainment, Inc. The only one not wearing such a badge is Nigao Yorito. His badge of course identifies him as an employee of the parent corporation, KFK.

To begin, Enoshi gives a brief nod of his head and says, "Good morning."

The group responds in kind, most nodding in a casual manner or smiling in addition to saying good morning. That is quite acceptable. The only reply that really stands out is that of the statistical aide, who bows and says, "*Ohayo,* Enoshi-*san*."

Enoshi suppresses a wince. Many of the ethnic Japanese on the staff make the error of overusing familiar habits acquired in Japan or elsewhere in their youth. It is the policy of Exotech Entertainment, and its parent, Kono-Furata-Ko, to mitigate wherever possible the differences between East and West, to take the best of each and blend them together. Though Enoshi is originally from Kyoto, Japan, where traditions are greatly respected, he has made every effort to appear westernized. He expects no less of his subordinates. He must have another private meeting sometime soon with the Japanese on his staff and encourage them to "loosen up."

As he takes a moment looking from one to the next, he realizes that something more is wrong. Several of the group look distressed. Two of the women seem emotionally upset. One wipes briefly at her eyes. Enoshi opens his mouth to ask what is going on when abruptly it strikes him, hard enough to shock him.

How could he be so insensitive!

Here again, one problem threatens to compound another. In his haste to regain lost time, he has nearly missed what should have been obvious. He composes his features, striving to seem solemn, but also sympathetic.

Though of course he knows English well, he struggles to find the proper words.

"By now, I'm sure you have all heard of the tragic death of Mister Robert Neiman of Special Projects. Please be assured that Mister Neiman's family is being looked after and that the police are investigating. Unfortunately, little is known at this time of the circumstances surrounding Mister Neiman's death, other than what you may have seen on the news. However, I will keep you informed as new information becomes available, and possibly we will have some official announcement later in the day."

Several of the group smile or nod as if to thank him, and by this Enoshi perceives that what little he has said, what little he could say, is sufficient.

"For the moment, I believe our best course would be to continue per usual." He says this carefully, so as not to seem cold or unfeeling, and the group seems inclined to go along with his suggestion. He offers a tentative smile—his wife is always reminding him to smile—then turns slightly to indicate the man standing beside him.

"This morning, Mister Nigao of the Kono-Furata-Ko Personnel Department has some things to tell us." With a brief nod and a subtle bow, he invites Nigao-*san* to begin. Nigao nods to Enoshi, and also bows, subtly, then smiles and turns to the group.

"Good morning," he says, with another slight bow of the head. The group responds in kind with a few nods and a few awkward bows. Nigao begins by saying that with Enoshi's permission, they might offer a moment of silence in memory of Robert Neiman. Enoshi consents to this, of course, and silently chastises himself for not having thought of it himself. How loudly the words of his father echo inside his head throughout the quiet few moments that follow. *There is always room for improvement!* Next time he will do better. Next time he will think twice!

Nigao goes on to make his announcements, all quite routine. It is the express policy of Kono-Furata-Ko Incorporated to maintain close relations with all its employees, including those of subsidiary corporations. This is to ensure, among other things, that the employees of subsidiary corporations, such as Exotech Entertainment, remain informed about the policies and general strategies of the parent corporation. It is also desired that all employees remain informed as to their rights, obligations, and benefits.

Nigao concludes by speaking briefly of some new benefits available under the corporate health insurance plan, then hands out brochures and invites any who have questions to contact him at his office.

"Thank you, Mister Nigao."

Enoshi leads the group in a brief bow, then smiles and shakes Nigao-*san*'s hand in thanks. Hand-shaking, of course, is an essential part of daily business within the bounds of the United Canadian and American States, however extraneous the gesture may otherwise seem. Nigao departs. Enoshi consults his red synthleather-bound pocket secretary and turns to face the group.

The dark cloud conjured by Robert Neiman's death seems to have diminished, if not faded altogether, at least for the moment, and now a few smiles come out, reminding Enoshi to smile as well.

"It is my pleasure to announce," he then says, looking from one member of the group to the next, "that for the third month in a row the clerical support group assigned to Mister Bernard Ohara has achieved a significant increase in productivity. Congratulations.''

Enoshi makes a point of showing appreciation by answering a few quick, somewhat awkward bows with a bow of his own, and then by going down the line shaking hands and again offering congratulations. Several of the group seem quite delighted, and this pleases Enoshi as well. People should be happy with their own superior performance, and that performance deserves to be recognized. When everyone performs beyond expectations, the corporation excels. He does not even really mind when a few of the women, rather impulsively, given him quick hugs.

Back in front of the desk again, he says, ''Now I believe it is time to hear a few words from Ms. Stevenson.''

Enoshi leads the group in a brief round of applause, merely to encourage this morning's speaker. Laura Stevenson, the receptionist, by far the most attractive woman in the group, is always a bit a nervous about giving the morning address, though she has done it many times before. Enoshi is encouraged by such nervousness. It is rewarding to see that a woman of obvious European ancestry should be so concerned about her words that she actually gets nervous.

Stevenson joins Enoshi in front of the desk and there spends a few moments pursing her lips, adjusting her hair, her suitdress, clearing her throat . . .

Enoshi smiles and touches her shoulder. ''No need to be nervous. We're all family here.''

Smiles flare brilliantly all around, and several of the group chuckle or laugh, just as Enoshi had hoped. If he chooses his moment correctly, he is usually able to inspire just such a reaction, even if the joke is not really a joke at all, but merely kidding around.

Ms. Stevenson blushes and nods, her smile gushing wide. She seems embarrassed but not uncomfortably so. ''Well,'' she begins, consulting her notes, ''what I want to talk about, I mean what I'm going to talk about, is the importance of always trying to do your best.''

Enoshi nods, and remembers to smile, smile with approval. Ms. Stevenson's theme is one he considers of vital importance, and he is always pleased when the morning speaker chooses to expound upon it. He often does so himself when he feels the need to personally give the morning talk. A corporation is no better than the sum of its parts. Every part, every individual, must always strive to give the best performance if the corporation is to succeed in the very competitive global marketplace.

"It's so easy to get complacent," Stevenson continues. "I see myself doing it sometimes. Oh, that's good enough, I say to myself. But then I realize, no, that's not good enough. It's not as good as I can really make it, and that's how good it really ought to be . . ."

Stevenson concludes before long. A lengthy speech is not necessary. The idea is to inspire hearts or jog forgetful brain cells, not to put everyone to sleep. Enoshi leads the group in brief applause, then adds his own voice to the woman's words. "I believe it was the Italian artist-scientist Leonardo da Vinci who said, 'Details make perfection, and perfection is no detail.' "

The quote is well-received with smiles and nods of the head, even another little burst of applause. Nothing more need be said, Enoshi decides. He must remember to thank his wife, for it was she who came across the quote in her reading.

Time now for the corporate creed, the "pledge," as some of the employees call it. Enoshi takes the printed notecard bearing the creed from the inside flap of his pocket-secretary and leads the group in reciting it. He of course knows the creed by rote, backward and forward, as he has since the first day of his employment, but he does not wish to appear pretentious or in any way superior beyond his station.

That task he leaves in the able hands of his "boss."

10

The dingy little restaurant sits just off Spring Garden
Street on the fringes of Chinatown. The dining room is
about the same size as a studio doss, and boasts eight
linen-draped tables and six booths. The rear booth is
near the swinging door to the kitchen and provides a good
view of the street via the restaurant's front windows. A
pair of brass-colored fans turn slowly on the ceiling. The
lacquered wooden floor is worn.

The girl who waits tables comes by again. "More?"
she inquires.

Tikki shakes her head. The girl is already sufficiently
amazed to remember her long after she's gone, and three
plates of *yauk hae* have her feeling a little lazy. Food in
quantity has that effect. Especially *yauk hae*, also known
as steak tartar. Raw meat in sauce. Tikki regards it as
one of the rare signs suggesting that humans might be an
intelligent species after all, and considers the dish definitely one of the more interesting ones humans serve.
Tikki could eat a ton of it. Gorge herself till she feels
barely able to move. Unfortunately, this is not a good
time for her to gorge. Biz awaits.

She lights a slim Dannemann Sumatran cigarro and
blows the first flavorful drag up toward the ceiling.

"Cha."

The girl nods and gets the tea.

Tikki watches the other few people in the restaurant
and on the street out front. Those who preceded her in
here, like those who came in on her heels, finish eating
and leave. People out on the street keep moving, hustling
along the sidewalks, in and out of doorways. No one
lingers. No one does more than glance in her direction.
It appears that she is not under surveillance.

The girl returns.

"I want to see the owner," Tikki says.

"Owner not here," the girl replies.

"Kim Tae Hwan says you're wrong."

The girl stares, just for an instant, then looks at Tikki long and hard, as if trying to see through the mirrored lenses of her Toshibas. "I find out. You wait."

Tikki nods vaguely, turning her head toward the front windows as if to look out at the street again, but watching peripherally as the girl hustles through the swinging door leading into the kitchen. There is no "Kim Tae Hwan," at least not at this restaurant. The name is a password.

Tikki sips her tea and waits.

A few minutes later, the girl returns. "The owner says, how you know Kim Tae Hwan?"

Tikki replies, "Black Mist."

"You wait." The girl turns and goes off again, but is soon back.

Tikki has a last drag of her slim cigar, finishes her tea, then follows the girl through the swinging door into the kitchen. A powerfully built adolescent male waits right there, a heavy automatic tucked under the front of his belt. "You got heat?"

Tikki draws the sides of her jacket wide open. The boy gives her a quick frisk. Naturally, she isn't carrying any guns, knives, or any other tool of the trade. That would be bad form. But that does not mean she isn't armed. Even naked and empty-handed, Tikki would never be unarmed.

"You follow."

Tikki follows the boy through a door at the rear of the kitchen, and into a narrow, garbage-strewn back alley. The boy knocks on a metal door of a building opposite the restaurant, three knocks, then two more. The door opens. Tikki follows the boy through the doorway, down a dimly lit hall, through a room jammed with piles and carts of clothing, through another room occupied by a dirty man seated at a worn wooden desk, down another hall, through a door, then down a wooden stairway. The air at the bottom of the stairs smells of guns, gunpowder, and the assorted oils and other chemicals used to clean and maintain guns.

They go through a long corridor like a tunnel. Earth smells, like dirt and peat and mold, mingle with the aroma of gun metal. The boy pulls open a heavy wooden door that's about ten centimeters thick. Beyond that waits an Asian man in a gray jump suit that shows many dark stains. He looks Tikki over very briefly, before saying in heavily accented English, "Black Mist okay. I'm Chey."

That's the name.

Chey is a specialist in weapons. You don't get to see him if you ask for him by name. What you get in that case is a friendly greeting from the local Seoulpa gang. A blade in the stomach, maybe a bullet in the head. A quick burial in a garbage dumpster somewhere. No mourners, no funeral.

"You got nuyen?" Chey asks.

"You got hardware?" Tikki says.

Chey smiles. "Believe it."

They step past another thick wooden door and into another room. The front end of the room is lined with racks full of hardware: handguns, assault rifles, submachine guns, and more. Samurai swords. A grenade launcher. Demo packs. Other tools. Tikki pulls a Sandler TMP from the rack. Because the Sandler submachine gun is usually available at cheap prices, it is a favorite low-rent weapon of gangs and other amateurs. Various police organizations have been known to dismiss the possibility of a pro assassin using a Sandler. Therein lies its attraction for Tikki.

On the other hand, her upcoming job is supposed to look like a pro hit, so she exchanges the Sandler for a SCK Model-100, the favorite of Japanese Security Forces and supposedly even the elite Red Samurai guard of the Renraku arcology in Seattle.

She pulls out two of the M-100s.

"Demonstrate."

Specialists like Chey tend to be careful with newcomers. They don't just hand over loaded weapons. Too easy to kill the storekeeper and rob the store. Chey locks one of the SMGs into a wooden mount fixed to a bench facing the far end of the room. Then he hands Tikki a clip. Tikki fits the clip to the weapon, snaps the bolt, grips the grip and squeezes the trigger. Five rounds blast through the brown paper target hanging at the end of the room. The thunderous report, magnified by the confined space, briefly sets Tikki's ears to ringing.

She tests the other SMG, which also works satisfactorily. She'll buy them, but wants them cleaned before she leaves. No problem, Chey informs.

"I want slick rounds."

"Explosive?"

Tikki shakes her head. A little mix-up in the vernacular here, Chey's mistake. She's used explosive bullets on occasion, but doesn't like them. They limit options. She doesn't want to have to worry about what's going to happen to her hand and maybe her whole arm if she jams a gun into somebody's gut and lets off a round. Also, in this particular case, explosive bullets wouldn't suit the work she has in mind.

"Coated bullets. Teflon."

"Ah." Chey smiles. "Gel slick. Very good."

Tikki smiles enough to express agreement. Gel-coated armor-piercing rounds will penetrate just about anything—body armor, metal, what-have-you.

"How many?"

"Six."

"For the buzzguns?"

Tikki shakes her head. "I.M.I. SP-57 in five-millimeter. Fabrique SMP-2A silencer. Ares optical night-sight, variable magnification to 200-X. Lumex laser targeting module. Armsman matte-black finish."

Chey nods and nods, then frowns. "Uh, I.M.I. very difficult," he says. "Hard to find. Many imitations. Many badly modified. I only sell top-quality merchandise. Can get you Walther XP-700 with what you want, null sheen."

"How long?"

"To get I.M.I.? Maybe several days. No guarantee. Walther top quality. Two hours."

Tikki prefers the finely balanced I.M.I., but she's used the Walther with equal success. Either weapon will suffice, properly modified. She nods. "Walther."

Chey summons the boy from the next room, fires off

quick instructions. The boy nods and hustles out like his life depends on speed. Chey holds up two fingers. "Two hours. Have everything ready. Sights and target system precision-tuned. What else?"

"Tune it for two hundred meters."

Chey nods. "What else?"

"X-heads for the SMGs."

"Two full clips?"

"Four."

Before Tikki leaves, weapons in hand, she is impressed with Chey's ability. Good gun techs are hard to find.

Like he said, there are many imitations.

11

Ohara slips his Beretta 101-T into the flat holster at the left of his waist, then straightens and closes his suit jacket. His image reflected in the mirror is satisfactory, even pleasing. The gray custom suit is by Dunhill, the shirt a Barton & Donaldson, the tie Paul Stuart—conservatively styled, flawlessly constructed, and tailored specifically for his physique. The gun is virtually invisible, sleekly concealed.

Most pleasing of all is the knowledge of how his appearance has improved, thanks to a generous investment of nuyen. Though in his late middle age, he looks like a much younger man, with a full head of close-trimmed hair, a face reflecting confidence and strength, a trim physique. No one who had known him as little as two or three years ago would recognize him now. Even his voice is different. The change is that complete.

Christie comes out of the master bath wearing a robe of fiery orange-red satin. The robe does little to hide how voluptuously she jiggles up front, and sways further down. The seductive biff walks straight over and cozies up against his side. The scent of her perfume and the warm weight of her breasts oozing against his right arm give rise to a modest urge right where he feels such things the most.

With a smile, the biff slips a plastic carrier into his inside jacket pocket. Ohara knows what's in that, another BTL chip. *"Something special,"* she promised him. From private sources. Ohara's got sources of his own, but the chips Christie's provided in the past have been nothing short of spectacular.

"Don't stay out too late," she croons. "You *know* how hungry I get when you're gone."

Ohara restrains a smile, straightening his tie. The good thing about having a pair of biffs like Christie and Crystal, rather than just one, is that they keep each other occupied when their lord and master is away. "You can go shopping."

"We did that yesterday, lover."

"You'll think of something, I'm sure."

"Oh . . . we will. We will."

Ohara can well imagine.

"I'd just rather do it with you."

Ohara nods. "Get my briefcase."

She does, and demands a kiss before releasing it. Her petty tyrannies do not disturb him. At a word, he could have her tossed out on her well-formed buttocks. There's no doubt as to who's in charge. Ohara likes it that way, insists on it, in fact.

Briefcase in hand, he heads through the living room to the entryway. His two Birnoth Comitatus executive protectors are ready and waiting. One guard precedes him as they head out into the hall, the other following close behind. They do no more than nod in greeting. No casual banter, no chatter of any kind.

One checks the elevator, nods again. Ohara enters. They ride to the sublevel parking garage. Waiting by the elevators is Ohara's long black Nissan Ultima V limousine, today accompanied by a Ford sedan and a General Products security van and additional guards, all provided by Kono-Furata-Ko at his request.

It pays to be careful. The death of Exotech's Special Projects Director Robert Neiman has reminded Ohara of the need for care. That death was probably just another incident of random violence, but until the police confirm that, Ohara will assume the worst—that he himself might be next on the assassin's list of targets. A man like himself, who has held high posts in some of the world's leading corporations, could hardly have risen to his current level without acquiring a few enemies here and there along the way. Such is the nature of the corporate environment. To be expected. A man in his position, a member of the corporate elite, must remain aware of the realities, and aware too of his own vulnerability.

With four brisk strides, Ohara moves from the elevator and into the rear of the limo. His two Birnoth Comitatus protectors follow him in. The doors close and the limo moves out, gliding swiftly from the garage and out through the "estates," a planned community of low-rise condos and parks built and maintained by a consortium of the city's major corporations.

The ride along Highway 30 into downtown Philadelphia passes quickly, the limo taking the express lanes and moving fast. Ohara spends some time watching real estate vids on the console trideo. His success with Exotech Entertainment has put his career back on track. A few months more and he'll be in a position to demand that the board of KFK renegotiate his contract. After that, he'll begin to work on his next objective, control of the board of directors, and, eventually, the chairmanship. The investigators he's got quietly researching the board members' backgrounds have already turned up a few choice tidbits of information that should prove very useful.

Once he has his new contract, with a significant increase in salary and benefits, he'll be ready for a new home, possibly an estate in the very exclusive preserve of Villanova. Almost anything would be an improvement over the Platinum Manor condominiums. Him, in a condominium? The very thought is repugnant. Practically a slap in the face.

Will his two playmates survive the move? He'll have to decide that soon. Certainly, the board of KFK would

be more content with him if he could come up with a
wife and some children.

Perhaps a rapprochement with his ex?

Something to think on.

"Good morning, Mister Ohara."

"Enoshi and cha."

"Yes, sir. Right away."

Ohara waves a hand vaguely and continues on up the
plush carpeted hall to his office. The iconic blonde at the
reception desk knows how to react, and how to jump.
Ohara likes that. He especially likes it when people act
as if *pleased* to knock themselves out doing what he
wants. It's the kind of loyalty he's always preferred, people panting like eager puppies.

Real talent eventually gets ambitious, then greedy. Eager puppies like the receptionist are too busy wagging
their tails to concoct ways of screwing him.

The double doors at the head of the hall snap open.
His Birnoth Comitatus guards accompany him into the
office and take up positions flanking the door. Ohara steps
onto the low dais on which his desk sits before a wall of
windows. The floor-to-ceiling window panes are constructed from heavily insulated macroplast and form an
effective defense against all but the most powerful weapons. The windows are also mirrored on the outside to
prevent anyone from looking in, and have a special coating that inhibits laser-borne surveillance devices from
picking sound vibrations off the surface. A variety of
other devices prevent snooping as well.

Ohara lays his briefcase on the desk top and drops into
his chair, then switches on his computer terminal. The
keyboard slides out the back of the desk. The monitor
rises out of the desktop. Ohara snaps his fingers.

"Initiate privacy function."

"Acknowledged," says one of the Birnoth protectors.

The other one nods.

The Comitatus guards are elite in every sense of the
word. When the privacy function is initiated, implanted
headware blanks their memory of everything they see and
hear every sixty seconds. At the end of the day, they'll

remember nothing except accompanying Ohara into his office and then out of it again. Of course, that function would immediately end if an emergency occurred or if they perceived a need to declare a security alert. In either case, they would immediately inform him that the privacy function had been discontinued.

Ohara looks to his computer monitor. The stylized circular logo of KFK fills the screen. He enters his personal security code, then taps a final sensor tab and finds a number of memos in his queue, as well as the report on the Special Projects Section requested from Bairnes.

Enoshi comes in to give his morning report and ticks off the day's appointments.

The office lady delivers tea.

"Get Wyatt in here."

Enoshi bows and hustles off.

Ohara sips his tea and goes through the memos in his queue. Most require a simple yes or no. He hits Y or N and then TRANS to shoot his answers back to the appropriate parties. Nothing very complicated today. Taffy Lee, simsense star extraordinaire, still refusing to accept the terms of her eighteen-country forty-six-city tour to promote her new line of chips. Persuade her? Yes. Obviously. The biff owes everything to Exotech and she'll do the tour at the prescribed terms or spend the rest of her life fighting lawsuits over it.

Jeff Wyatt comes in.

"Look at this," Ohara says, slapping at the monitor, spinning it toward Wyatt. "Our Hermetic line's outselling practically everything else on the market and now Bairnes comes along proposing some cybernetic warrior drek. You don't change winning strategies. You enhance them. Doesn't anyone around here know anything!"

Wyatt just glances at the display, seems to clench his teeth, exhale deeply. "Bairnes is a techie. He doesn't know marketing."

Ohara compresses his lips. There is no excuse for ignorance. "*The Summoning of Abbirleth* hit number one on the charts in its first week of release and stayed there for almost nine months."

"Six months."

"Don't argue with me! *Night of the Enchanter* followed the same track. Doesn't that suggest anything to anyone but me? How do you suppose this corporation gained twenty-three percent market share in just under a year? Do you think the skag you were peddling before is what put this organization at the top of the market?"

Wyatt looks unmoved, much as Ohara expected. "You should have asked me for a recommendation, not Bairnes," Wyatt says. "I'm the V.P. for Product Development. Special Projects is in my division."

This very unnecessary reminder sends prickles of heat up the back of Ohara's neck. "Save me your territorial imperatives. This is my show. Understand?"

"I don't remember questioning that."

"Why do I always get the feeling that you're just waiting for an opportunity to usurp my authority? Is there a problem, Jeff? Do you have a problem taking instructions?"

"Just tell me what you want me to do."

"Oh, Jesus Christ." Ohara swings his chair aside, struggling to suppress his anger. Goading him to a fit of temper is one of Wyatt's foremost talents. "What do you *think* I want? I want a replacement for Neiman! You may recall that our Special Projects Section is the fire that got this corporation *going*! Without it, the Hermetic line'll get buried!"

"Do we at least wait till after Neiman's funeral to announce his successor?"

Widows and orphans wait for bodies to go into the ground—business doesn't. "Maybe you'd like to be buried along with your former director."

"Is that a threat, Mister Ohara?"

"If you can't find a replacement for Neiman, I'll find someone who can."

"I think I can handle it."

"Then get on it."

Ohara swings back to face Wyatt and makes a point of smiling his most vicious smile. Wyatt's private agenda is quite apparent to him. Wyatt wants control of Exotech. He plans to get it by making Ohara look bad in front of the directors of KFK, Exotech's parent corporation. Ohara must remain constantly on guard, take every opportunity to turn the man's treachery against him. That is why Ohara picked Bairnes to serve briefly as Neiman's heir apparent. He knew Bairnes would never do. By the time he's finished, he'll make it look like Wyatt wanted Bairnes and that only Ohara's constant vigilance prevented a debacle.

Before Wyatt can leave, another man enters, coming through the side door from Enoshi's office. The new arrival is heavily built and wears a rumpled trench coat over a rather untidy suit. Both the trench coat and the suit look like they were purchased straight off the rack. Ohara has never seen the man before. He is certainly not an Exotech employee. He isn't even wearing a visitor's ID. Ohara frowns and glances at his Birnoth executive protectors, but neither one moves except to look at the stranger.

"Sorry to interrupt," the stranger says, lifting an identity card that flashes a two-D photo of the man and, in alternating sequence, the easily recognized logo of Minuteman Security Services. "Lieutenant Kirkland," the stranger says, glancing at the Birnoth guards. "Homicide Bureau."

Ohara smiles. "Yes, Lieutenant. Is there something I can do to help you?"

With a poorly suppressed sneer, Wyatt departs.

Kirkland merely glances at him, then turns again to Ohara. "You're Ohara?"

Ohara nods, still smiling. "Bernard Xavier Ohara. Yes."

"Just want to make sure I got the right guy." Kirkland gives a quick smile, nods. "I'm sure you're busy. I'm a little short on time myself. Lemme toss you a few questions about Robert Neiman and then I'll leave."

"Of course. You're conducting the investigation into Bob's death?"

"Bob Neiman? Yeah, that's right."

"Would you care for cha?"

"A cup would go good about now. Thanks."

Ohara waves a hand. Enoshi, hovering decoratively by the side door, summons the office lady, who delivers the tea. "So you're the head honcho around here," Kirkland says.

"I'm Chief Executive Officer and a member of the board of Kono-Furata-Ko, Exotech's parent corporation.

"Nice office."

"Thank you."

"I understand Mister Neiman was your protégé."

Ohara smiles, just briefly. Toady might have been a better choice of words. "Protégé is perhaps too strong a word, Lieutenant. I recognized that Bob had management ability and so I saw to it that he found a position where he could exercise that ability."

"Isn't that what protégé means?"

"A question of emphasis, Lieutenant. I did not take a special interest in Bob's career overall. I merely corrected what I saw as a waste of resources, if you'll forgive the clinical terminology."

"Is that how you saw it? Clinically?"

"No, not at all. I was very pleased to give Bob a boost upward. I was also pleased to upgrade the structure of the corporation."

"So everybody's happy."

"Good morale is an integral part of a successful corporation."

"And Exotech's successful."

"Quite right."

"Neiman was a junior researcher and then you promoted him to head of the Special Projects Section? Sounds like quite a jump."

"I'm sure it might seem that way. But from my perspective, it was not quite so big a jump. You should realize, Lieutenant, that the S.P.S. is really a very small unit, a small subsection of a small department."

"Is that right?"

Ohara nods. It was not only right, he could prove it beyond any reasonable degree of doubt. "The bulk of our fiscal muscle goes right into product, marketing, sales. You must understand that, by and large, simsense is an established industry. The major R&D work is being done by the electronics people, such as Fuchi or Truman, who produce the sense decks by which end-users experience simsense. Exotech is primarily involved in the production of simsense chips, or what we call 'wax.' ''

"Some real hot wax, I'm told.''

Ohara nods. "Correct.''

"How did a simsense outfit like this end up in Philadelphia, anyway? I would've thought Cal Free a more likely locale.''

Ohara smiles. "Actually, Chicago is becoming the 'Dream Town' of the U.C.A.S., insofar as simsense is concerned. We maintain certain of our production facilities there as well as in Cal Free. However, Philadelphia offers excellent tax incentives.''

"I understand Exotech produces music, too. Not just simsense.''

Ohara nods. "Digitized extended-spectrum sound on MC-disk and chip, correct.''

"What was Neiman working on?''

Ohara hesitates, forming an uncertain expression. "I'm sorry?''

"He was in charge of Special Projects, right? What was he doing? Recently. Like just before he died.''

"Specifically? I'm afraid I don't have those details. I'm sure my chief of staff could steer you to the right person, probably Bob's immediate superior, the director of our research department. Or Jeff Wyatt, our vice president for product development. Both excellent people, quality executives in every respect.''

"Thanks for the suggestion. I'm a little curious, though. You're Exotech's C.E.O. Neiman's management, head of a department. You took enough interest in him to promote him. How come you don't know what he's working on?''

Ohara resists a faint smile. This lieutenant's style of questioning is so transparent it's absurd. "I'm sure that must seem odd to an outsider. However, the fact is that when I first came on board about two years ago, I conducted an intensive survey of all Exotech personnel. Part of my charge, you see, was to shape up an industry loser. I did that from the ground up. Rebuilt the entire architecture of the corporation. Once assured that I had the right people in the right places, I could afford to delegate authority properly. Now I concern myself with the corporation's overall strategies and leave the day-to-day details to my subordinates.''

"You must be pretty pleased with the results.''

"Very pleased.''

"You still don't get it, do you?''

"I beg your pardon?''

"I guess nobody filled you in. I'll be blunt. Robert Neiman didn't just die. It was a hit. Whoever did it wanted Neiman very dead, and wanted everybody to know that they wanted him that way. Your Mister Neiman obviously crossed the wrong person. Any idea who that might be?''

Ohara gazes at Kirkland for a moment, then lets his eyes drift slowly aside. The lieutenant's remarks are obviously intended to throw him off guard, with the obvious goal of tripping him into blurting something revealing. Obviously, the lieutenant takes nothing at face value. Such a quality might make him dangerous, despite his clumsy technique. "I can't really think of anyone like that. Who might have had cause to kill Bob. Of course, I really didn't know him on a personal level.''

"Uh-huh. Well, let me say this. When people get dead in ways like Neiman did, it's usually meant to serve as an example. Meaning this is what happens when you do the wrong thing. If I were you, I'd be at least a little concerned about who else in this corporation might be a target. Neiman's exec assistant and data aide were both killed with him. That could be just coincidental or it could indicate a corporate tie-in. I'd suggest you play it safe, tighten up security around here. Maybe assign bodyguards to your key people.''

"Yes, well . . . I see what you mean. I'll pass your recommendations along to our security chief. Thank you, Lieutenant.''

Ohara rises. Kirkland takes the hint and steps up to the front of the desk, reaching out to shake Ohara's hand. "As our investigation progresses,'' Kirkland says, "I may need to drop you a few more questions.''

"I'll be happy to cooperate.''

"Thanks for your time.''

The lieutenant heads out through the side door. Enoshi pauses in the doorway, looking in. Ohara waves him inside. As per usual, Enoshi pauses several steps back from the desk, face impassive, arms at his side, his posture like that of a low-ranked soldier awaiting orders.

"Order Operation Clean Sweep."

Enoshi hesitates. "Sir, this is very drastic—"

"Don't question my decisions!"

Ohara pounds the heel of his hand against the desk top and swings around in his chair to face the broad expanse of windows overlooking KFK Plaza. Dealing with one rebellious employee in his first hour of business is enough. The possibility of a police investigation turning up something best left buried pushes his tolerance to the limit.

"Just do it, *dammit*! Clean Sweep *at once*!"

"Yes, sir," Enoshi replies. "At once."

12

The room is quiet and smells of urine and sweat and the humid aromas of sex. Raman discreetly lifts his head to look around, then rises from the bed, going first to the door, then back to the window, a massive Dragon Slayer knife gripped tightly in his hand. At the door he hears nothing, and a quick look into the hallway reveals only the darkness and decay of this tenement located on Philadelphia's north side. The only window provides a view of the garbage-littered alley. Nothing moves. Twilight is fading into night.

The female sprawled naked on the bed mutters something, but does not awaken. Raman watches her for a moment. She drank enough alcohol to become extremely intoxicated and to admit things to him. She calls herself Angel, but that's only the name she goes by in the Matrix of the global computer net. Her real name is Neona, Neona Jaxx. From Dallas, though most recently of Miami.

Raman finds her appealing. He particularly admires the dark hue of her skin and its yielding softness, tempered by supple muscles. She is lively in bed and is also a decker, but that does not make her worth keeping around any longer. Deckers can be purchased when required, then discarded. Female companionship is no less disposable. Raman has had many females. Most have been like this one, hungry for the company of a male, eager to shield themselves behind his strength and power. It is a dangerous world. He supposes it is only natural that some females should barter their physical appeal for the protection offered by a strong male. Most females he has met are about as capable of defending themselves as infants or snowflakes.

What he needs now is a shower. If he had a pot of water he would plunge his head into it and wring his hair out, spill the water over his body. Failing that, he pulls on yesterday's clothes, thrusts back his hair, and ties the bandanna around his brow. Life on the move is often a matter of making do. It is the lifestyle he prefers. He travels light.

Raman pulls on his jacket, the studded, fringed jacket marked with the mountain lion logo of the Sioux Wildcats. He obtained the jacket in Atlanta, where he killed the jacket's owner in a fight. He has since worn it with the intent of encouraging the misconceptions of those he meets. With his dark skin, long black hair, and chiseled facial features, people often mistake Raman for an Amerind, and that is convenient. He would rather be taken for an Amerind than other things. For example, something that might verge on the truth. Truth could be very dangerous in the wrong hands.

He distributes his weapons about his person, and thrusts a heavy pistol into the holster built into the lining of the studded jacket. It's time to get down to biz, find his contact and make some nuyen, and that means going it alone. He throws a last look at the female sprawled on

the bed, then steps through the door, down the hall and
into the night.

Down in the alley, his Harley chopper is waiting.

13

It promises to be a nasty little piece of work, and naturally Dana hasn't stopped mouthing about it since they
got started.

"I'm not a killer," she says for the ten millionth time.
"I'm not going to just walk in and start killing people."

"Why not?" Mickey jokes. "Sounds like fun."

"It's *wrong*!" Dana exclaims.

"Who says so?" Dog Bite demands. "We got our-
selves a contract, woman! There ain't nothing wrong with
that!"

"That's not what I'm saying!"

"We don't know who these chummers be! They deserve to get smoked! Somebody's payin' to get 'em
smoked! It don't get any righter than that!"

"Dog Bite, you're not even *listening* . . ."

"I'll tell you what's wrong! You got your brain screwed
in wrong!"

Sitting in the passenger seat of the van, Hammer lights
a final Millennium Red, takes a deep drag, and checks
his watch. It's a couple minutes past twenty-two hundred
hours. Any time now.

The corpse in the driver's seat shifts position. His
name's Axle. He's got cyberoptics for eyes and black-
wired jacks stuck into the side of his skull. He can pilot
the van without even putting a hand on the wheel. That
won't be necessary tonight, though. Axle's the rigger so
he does the driving, but this job won't require much of
his special skill. This one is pure rock and roll.

"Alley's still clear," Axle murmurs.

The alley is about nine blocks away, well within the
hell zone of northeast Philly. Axle can see it because he's

got a floater in the air, an Aerodesign LDSD-23, which is like a helium balloon with a sensor pod slung underneath. The alley Axle is watching is important because it provides the only access to the place they plan to visit tonight. Hammer isn't worried about possible witnesses. There are no witnesses north of Spring Garden Street and Center City. Just gangs, crazies, thriller chillers, and bikers. Hammer simply prefers no one to get in the way. It would be inconvenient.

The argument in the back of the van starts to get loud. The problem is less Dana than Mickey. They all know about Dana, what sets her off. She and Dog Bite can go at it all day and night yet never take it beyond just butting heads. But once Mickey gets involved, things get out of hand. Mickey just doesn't care. Not about anything. That really sets Dana to mouthing.

Hammer turns in his seat, looks back, snaps the slide on his Ingram smartgun. The metallic clacking snares their attention. "Show time."

Dana gives him a look of profound appeal. Hammer takes it calmly, as calmly as the last drag of his smoke.

"Hammer," she says.

"Just do your bit. That's all."

The look in her eyes turns to resignation.

Axle rolls the van ahead.

Northeast Philly, more than any other part of the city, remembers the Night of Rage when humans and metahumans met in the streets and set the night to burning. Even after fifteen years the scars are still plain. Block after block of two- and three-story row houses bear gaping wounds, seared and cauterized by fire, many with roofs and whole walls reduced to crumbling masonry, charred timber, and ash. Debris from fallen buildings and mounds of festering garbage flow from the alleys into the streets. Incinerated autos squat along the curbs. The only streetlights are the steel-can fires of derelicts.

Against this background of devastation, tonight's little job seems like a mere drop of rain.

Clean Sweep, it's called.

Headlights off, the van turns down a broad alley. The entrance to the target site is just ten meters down, the black metal door of the building on the right. They all put on night-vision goggles with heads-up displays and wire-framed headsets with full ear coverage to guard against interference. All except Dana. The mage doesn't need that kind of protection.

They pile out. Axle keeps the van running in case they should have to stage a quick extraction. Hammer motions Mickey and Dog Bite to the left of the black metal door and takes the right side for himself. Dana steps up, standing directly in front of the door.

She lifts her hands before her face as if to pray, then begins doing things with her fingers, linking them together, folding, unfolding, forming pyramids, triangles, circles, complex knottings that rush from one configuration to the next. She calls it the emblemology of power, these finger-signs she makes. Hammer doesn't much care about that. All he knows or cares about is that whatever she does, however she does it, it works.

The dark space between Dana and the door begins to blur and waver like hot summer air shimmering above a road. The door takes on a waxy sheen. The sheen begins to run, flowing, cascading down like a shower of water, only the water is the substance of the door. The next moment there is no door, just a puddle of something black and wet oozing into the alley.

Dana sways, visibly draws a deep breath, then thrusts her hair back from her face. Turning things to ooze costs her a lot. What remains for her to do is far less taxing.

Hammer points at the dark opening of the doorway.

Dana nods, makes more finger-signs.

The music, the flaring lights, the calamitous babble of voices—screaming, shouting, swearing—begins at once. Hammer can't see or hear any of it thanks to the goggles and headset, but he knows what it's like. A thousand high-intensity lights all flashing and glaring into your eyes. A thousand maniacs screaming into your head. You can't think, you can't fight, you can't tell what the frag's going on. Hammer gestures with the Ingram smartgun. Mickey darts into the doorway and the darkness beyond. Hammer follows. Dog Bite and Dana bring up the rear.

The doorway leads into a corridor that immediately

turns and ends at a stairway, heading down. Three razorguys with heavy artillery—heavy-caliber SMGs—
stagger around on the stairs and in the corridor at the
bottom of the stairs. A few quick bursts from Mickey's
AK-97 SMG and Hammer's smartgun take care of them.

The passage at the bottom of the stairs leads past two
doors, both on the right. Dog Bite and Mickey take the
first one; Hammer takes the other. The doors aren't even
locked. Hammer enters a room outfitted like a bedroom.
A pair of hot, red-tinted bodies twist and writhe on the
bed, hands uplifted as if to cover their ears. Even as
Hammer opens fire, one of the two bodies slips from the
end of the bed and staggers around like a machine with
blown circuits, before jerking spasmodically and falling.
A pair of quick bursts is all it takes.

"One clear," Hammer says.

A gasp of static, then Dog Bite replies, "Two clear.
We're all clear. Check this out."

Hammer lowers his goggles. A long rectangular pane
in the wall opposite the foot of the bed gives a view into
the other room. Hammer tries the communicating door,
which lets him into some kind of control room, now
showing the generous damage of automatic weapons fire.
Three more bodies lay sprawled amid the debris. The
focus of the room is the long gray console that runs along
the wall beneath the large window. It looks like the kind
of equipment used for professional music recordings,
only this isn't a recording studio and the console isn't
just for sound.

"Look at this skiz," Dog Bite says. "Man oh man,
we could make some fine change selling this stuff."

Hammer takes a look. What Dog Bite says is true. The
case in Dog Bite's hand contains about twenty silicon
chips, and plenty more are scattered about. Sex-chip BTL
always sells. Like the name promises, it *is* better than
real-life sex in some ways. No mess, no fuss, no need
for a cooperative partner or partners.

Hammer wonders why their Mr. Johnson wanted some
dinky BTL lab in northeast Philly wasted, along with
everyone in it.

Who knows?

"Set the charges," Hammer says. "Torch all of it."

Dog Bite looks at him. "You sure?"

"We got a contract."

"Who's to know?"

"Don't be stupid."

"Hey! Stupid's my middle name!"

Mickey starts to laugh; Dog Bite, too. Hammer's heard the joke too often to be amused.

Five minutes later, Dog Bite's explosives go off. Axle spots the flames by remote. The entire building is soon engulfed. Mr. Johnson should be pleased.

14

The night rumbles with the sounds of traffic and the massed machinery of more than a million human beings.

Neon flickers, chrome gleams.

Voices echo through the alley.

Tikki waits in the shadows, a niche of brick and mortar that smells of piss and rancid liquor. A motorcycle buzzes past, one of those shiny aerodyne machines with sleek plastic cowlings, colored like the blood of prey. And this is one of the fastest, a Rapier. It comes to a halt nearby, just off to her right, engine whining, winding down. Tikki pulls the Kang heavy automatic pistol from under her jacket and steps from her hiding place.

Just a few paces up the alley is a basement-level bar called Numero Uno. Signs advertising beer and other attractions wink and flash above the stairs leading down to the entrance. It's a gathering place for losers, fools who imagine themselves immune to injury and death. Most of them come on cycles, which is why Tikki is here now. She walks toward the newly arrived Rapier, the Kang held back behind her right hip.

As she approaches, the big hairy ork in synthleather and studs dismounts the Rapier, turning toward her with a smile. The teeth protruding like tusks from his lower jaw give the smile a feral look. "Hoi, biff," he grunts.

Tikki sneers. She hasn't even opened her mouth and already the ork is showing her an attitude. Orks do that a lot, behaving like they can do anything they please just because they're big and strong. Tikki finds that irritating. It's not only a challenge to her—her power, her position—but a challenge against Nature, the balance of power among the many predators populating the human domain. A threat she has to meet.

She brings up the Kang, points it at the ork's face, then extends her other hand, palm-up. "Keys," she growls. "Now."

The ork frowns and stares, then grunts, "You gotta be skeekin' me, geek."

She never skeeks. "Last chance."

The ork sneers, opens his mouth.

Tikki drops her arm and squeezes the trigger. The Kang blams. A tongue of flame strokes the shadowed air. The ork howls and falls to one knee, his face contorted with pain. He's got a hole in his right boot, a big bloody hole, but that couldn't be helped. That was a necessary part of the lesson. Tikki won't be taken lightly, not by anyone. When she says something, she expects people to listen, orks included.

"Keys."

The ork shouts and curses and hands her the keys. He's also saying what he's going to do to her, how she's going to regret shooting him. Tikki doesn't like that. It's a bad attitude grown worse. She swings the Kang like a club against the side of his head, the impact telegraphing up her arm almost to the elbow. That's how she knows that the blow would have laid most humans out cold. The ork's a little too tough for that. His head jerks over sideways and he sways toward the ground, but he catches himself on one arm. Tikki swings the Kang again.

This time, the ork goes down.

Tikki points the Kang's muzzle at his head, finger tightening on the trigger, then hesitates when she sees him going slack. A part of her wants to finish the job, dust the ork, blow his head clean off, but another, calmer part of her is saying there's no need. For a moment, she could go either way. The one thing she's sure of is that Adama would laugh, even call her a fool, for leaving the ork alive. That she could not stand.

Abruptly, she points the Kang and makes it roar four times in quick succession. What's left of the ork is sufficiently dead to satisfy anyone, and that is as it should be.

That's good, very good, she decides.

She thrusts the ork back with a shove of her foot and pulls the bike upright. Tikki knows about bikes and is well-practiced in their use. They are very handy implements.

Too bad her mother couldn't stand them.

Couldn't abide the noise.

Noise is part of the machine, intrinsic. The greater the noise, the greater the bike. She jerks the Rapier's throttle, sets the engine to wailing, the rear tire to spinning, shrieking, and with one foot planted on the ground she whips the bike around in a quick half circle. A flashy but effective way to quickly reverse direction. Tikki drops her weight onto the cushioned synthleather seat, and the cycle screams, sending her hurtling up the alley and out to the street.

Traffic around Center City is dense and sluggish. Cars and trucks jam the streets. Scooters and bicycles flood the curb lanes. Tikki winds her way through the press, wrenching the throttle on full, setting the Rapier to screaming, only to jerk the brakes and make the rear tire shriek.

The siren from a Minuteman patrol cruiser wails out, and a cop waves at her through the cruiser's window, but there's no way a full-sized vehicle can pursue her through the crush.

She veers around a corner.

Minutes later, she's into the underground, the sublevel parking garage beneath KFK plaza. The platinum towers above provide office space for the Philadelphia branch of the city's leading yakuza clan, the Honjowara-gumi.

Tikki's biz tonight involves that very group—that is, a particular member of that group.

The garage ceiling is low, spanned by massive concrete struts and further supported by concrete columns. Arrays of florescent lamps affixed to the ceiling between the struts cast a stark illumination. Aisle after aisle of waiting automobiles march off into the distance. Tikki stops the Rapier, pulls a small knapsack off her shoulders. She takes out a Toshiba SC-701 graphic transceiver, and turns it on with the touch of a finger. The display comes to life with colored geometrics, giving her a detailed schematic map of her current location. The entire city is chipped into the transceiver's memory. The little red blip on the display shows the location of a particular car, a heavy Nissan Ultima V limousine, used by a member of the local yakuza. Tikki has previously attached a Tohisba SCA-7234 transponder to the car, which now communicates directly with the transceiver in her hand.

She likes to be prepared.

Soon, her target arrives via elevator with a pair of male companions. Tikki watches them through the rows of parked cars. They glance around idly, but give no indication they suspect that a hunter is watching, gauging their movements. Waiting for the moment to strike.

Taking human animals in the city is little different from taking other kinds of animals in the wild. The successful predator chooses her moment with care. A strike that fails to kill is worse than no strike at all because it alerts the prey to the hunter's presence. The prey must remain unaware until the final moment, when death comes crashing down with jaws of steel to crush and snap its neck.

The Nissan rumbles to life and rolls toward the garage exits. Tikki starts the Rapier and follows.

The moment of death draws near.

The limo takes the Franklin Bridge over the Delaware into Camden, Inc., where the night burns in garish neon and simmers with flashing strobes. The procession of dazzling megawatt façades begins. The names of the casinos and nightclubs rise up five, ten, fifteen, twenty stories: Polichrome Palace, Ritz Royale, Dragon's Loft, Rage of Mages, Four Aces, Glistening Underling, Silk

Refuge. The streets widen into boulevards. Laserdis adverts arch out over the streets. Econocars vanish among a tide of gleaming limousines and posh executive sedans. Crowds in glittering Prestigewear and the mirrored fashions of NeoMonochrome flow ceaselessly along the sidewalks and through fantastic entrance ways of glaring, flickering light.

Police are rarely seen. Yakuza run the city corporation and yakuza provide security. Standing on every corner, strolling along every block, are two or more of their *kobun* in special red, orange, or yellow jackets. Heavily armed back-up waits in marked security vans on various side streets. The ordinary citizen is treated with a respect usually accorded only to kings and queens, while disruptive individuals are dealt with immediately and without reference to any court. Incidents of violent crime are generally few and far between. All this makes Camden an interesting place to be. Especially interesting for a hunter.

The Nissan pulls up at the Gingko Club. Tikki's target comes here once or twice a week. She's scoped the layout previously. The name of the place refers to the nut-bearing gingko tree with fan-like leaves. The tree is Chinese, the name Japanese. The club is owned and operated by the local branch of the Honjowara-gumi yakuza. No surprise.

This is where it will happen.

The main entrance is closely guarded. The doormen use a Fuchi SecTech-7 scanning system to catch weapons on the way in. Tikki knows ways past such things. In fact, she's got a black box from a specialist in San Francisco that would probably walk her straight through, hardware and all. She's got other options, however, that offer higher probabilities of success.

The moon rises full and white and brilliant against the dark canopy of the night. Tikki grins just to see it. There's something about a full moon that makes her feel wild and free and even a little crazy. It's a hunter's moon, a moon to kill by.

She steers the Rapier into the dark of an alley.

The rear door of the Gingko Club is solid metal and

faces a small parking lot lit by orange spots. Tikki waits for a parking valet to head up toward the front of the club, then steps up to the back door and pounds on it with her fist.

Not a security cam in sight.

The intercom beside the door squeals. "What you want!" a male voice demands.

"Red Bullets!" Tikki says, giving the name of the local yakuza patrol. "Open up!"

A moment passes. Something inside the door clangs. An Asian man smelling of fish and wearing a stained white apron pushes the door open and looks at Tikki, first frowning as if annoyed, then going wide-eyed, and with good reason. The muzzle of her Kang automatic is right in his face. She has goaded him into error, just as planned. Only three nights ago she saw a Red Bullet patrol stop here for a quick bite to eat. Bang, shout, and the door opens.

Tikki motions with a finger: Out, step out.

The man obeys. She motions him to her left as if to walk him away from the door, then slams the barrel of the Kang across the rear of his head. The man crumbles.

Good prey.

Very good.

A short hallway takes her to a red door. She steps through and into the rear of the club. The music is loud and asynchronous, led by a bamboo flute and a geisha's keening intonations. Simulated rice-paper screens divide the place into squarish spaces for dancing and broad corridors lined with silk-curtained alcoves. Laserdis ideograms, swords, flowers, and other images of feudal Japan wax and wane, blossom into view and then fade like phantoms throughout the shadowy space.

Trid screens everywhere provide a murmuring undertone that extols the many virtues of the Honjowara-gumi. Yaks are very big on image. Many maintain official offices, publish brochures and newsletters, hold press conferences, produced their own cable shows, and even own banks. *Kambu atsukai*, the lower-ranked executives, have

been known to invite local citizens to their offices for tea
merely to encourage a favorable public image.

Triad bosses rarely attempt to seem so benign.

In search of her prey, Tikki moves through a crowd of
dancers. Those who notice give her odd looks. She isn't
dressed to the mode. Neither is she wearing her usual
streetside costume. She's dressed for a hit. Mirrorshades
conceal her eyes. A strip of black silk covers the lower
half of her face. A long dark-blue duster obscures the
rest, all but her soft-soled black boots.

She works her way toward the front of the club, but
somehow misses her mark. The place is like a maze, with
people constantly moving, changing places. She's certain
her target must still be here. He stayed for hours any time
he's ever come here in the past. She backtracks, covering
old ground, and abruptly sees him coming right at her,
approaching through a swirl of dancers. The man is a
heavyset Asian male named Saigo Jozen, the next yakuza
sub-boss targeted for assassination. Moving with him
through the crowd is a group of two males and three
females. The males all wear the lapel pin of the
Honjowara-gumi. Emerging from the press of a dance
space, the group forms into three couples.

Tikki slips a pair of fleshtone ear plugs into her ears,
then opens her long duster and brings up the twin SCK-
100 submachine guns slung from her shoulders. Saigo
never sees what's coming. One moment he's grinning at
the woman on his arm, laughing with his companions,
and in the next he's twitching and jerking under the
massed assault of Tikki's SMGs.

The distinctive staccato clattering of the SCKs slashes
through the music and the noise like razor-tipped claws.
As Saigo's face and chest turn into a mass of blood and
gore, Tikki widens her field of fire. The five people near-
est Saigo jerk and crumble. Blood sprays the air and spat-
ters over the floor. People scream and fall. Saigo is lying
in a puddle of blood and gore but still is not dead, not
quite. He's making feeble efforts to crawl away over the
body of a dead woman. Tikki gives him another burst,
but the man keeps moving. She empties the SMGs into
him.

That finishes him.

Adama will be pleased.

She tugs at the strap slung from her left shoulder and drops one of the SMGs to the floor, rams a fresh clip into the other one and snaps the bolt. People are fighting to get away from her now, struggling against the press of the herd to escape the deadly menace of the hunter. It's good, very good—not quite as close and personal as she likes it but very good all the same. Good and bloody. The screams of the prey echo in her ears, and the scents of terror and death swarm lush and hot into her nose.

A door opens in the red wall between two alcoves. Tikki points the SMG and fires. Even before the man in the dark suit can pass through the doorway, he staggers back and falls. Tikki dips into her duster pocket and pulls out a compact grenade. Concussion effects can be deadly at close range. She pulls the pin and lobs the grenade up the corridor paneled in mock rice paper. Two more men, fighting against the crowd and coming toward her from that direction fall flat to the floor in the wake of the detonation, along with others.

The blast sends people screaming toward the rear of the club. Tikki lobs another grenade in that direction, then drops a smoke bomb at her feet.

Smoke swirls up around her.

A heavily built man holding a gun up over his head comes crashing through the paper screen along the right of the corridor. Pointing the SMG, Tikki fires, smearing the man's front with red, tearing holes in the rice-paper screens, and finishing off the magazine. Even as the man goes down, she drops the SMG and pulls the Kang. More screams arise from the next corridor over, and that's good. Incidental casualties are greatly desired, an integral part of the job. Tonight, it's open season, a hunter's dream come true.

A primal grin flashes across her features.

Prey is everywhere.

"Good. Very good."

The throbbing rhythms of the multi-snythlinked band inside the Devil's Roost make mere spoken words hard to hear, but Tikki sees and hears enough, and smells enough, to guess at what Adama says. He gives a long smile of satisfaction. A wolfish light shines in his eyes. The familiar rhythm of his words, "Good . . . very good," resonates clearly in Tikki's ears. More than that, the man's smell fills with pleasure. He fingers the bright brass cap of his walking stick, then motions Tikki nearer.

"Hong Kong appreciates your efforts," he says, smiling, adding a little flick of his fingers as if brushing away the competition like a fly. "So do I."

Tikki nods.

The mention of Hong Kong brings to mind Adama's alleged ties with the Green Circle Gang, that particularly vicious arm of the infamous 999 Society ruled over by the Triad leader Silicon Ma. Pleasing someone like Ma is a good thing. His connections in North America might be limited, but his influence is growing and his power throughout eastern and southern Asia is pervasive.

Adama remarks that he is ready to start Tikki on her next hit. She wants to hear more, but before Adama can elaborate, his five glamorous female companions return from their trip to the lavatory. The females smell of fresh perfume and various hygiene products. Adama smiles broadly and invites them to rejoin him in his booth.

"Who will be my Leandra?" he asks.

One of them, a luscious redhead, croons with pleasure.

The town house is quiet, for the moment. The only light is that sifting through the drapes and curtains, a dusky gray suffusion that glows subtly against the darker shadows of the rooms. A human might have trouble seeing. Tikki can see just fine.

She lies in the ground floor entrance hall. For her, now, in this place, there are no doubts or uncertainties. She is *Were* and back in her true form, and has made this place her own.

Anyone who enters would immediately recognize her power. She lies in a hazy shaft of moonlight that enters through the skylight above. Mere skin has transformed into a dense, shaggy coat of red and black, the color of

blood and the night. Her forelegs are heavy with muscle,
her paws the size of a troll's. She could crush a man's
skull between her teeth, or lay him open from shoulder
to groin with a single pass of her claws. She knows that
because she's done it, that and more. She's even fought
a troll or two while in her natural form, and always come
out the victor.

Now, she flicks an ear and idly curls her tail, then
yawns, stretches, and rises to inspect the house.

No one could get into the town house without her no-
ticing at once, but that isn't what draws her to her feet
again. It's the character of the air, which takes on the
color of what she's doing and thinking. If Tikki just lies
around, the air takes on a lax quality. If she's up and
moving, looking, listening, testing the air, the atmosphere assumes a wary character, a scent like vigilance,
suggestive of muscle like spring-loaded steel, of a
strength and power that few creatures in the world would
dare to confront.

When she does a job, such as guarding a place, Tikki
likes to do it right. That means even the air should smell
right.

She pauses to rub the side of her face against the corner of a hallway. That leaves traces of her own body
scent, strong traces, to better color the rest of the hall,
which already smells like her. Places she defends should
smell like her. In that way, she makes them hers, her
personal territory, one she generously allows others, such
as Adama, to share.

Adama is of course a male, a human male, but still a
male, and she doesn't mind sharing territory with an
amiable male. With the right sort of male, she might
offer to share much more, if she felt so inclined.

Certain sections of the floor creak softly beneath her
weight. She pauses and lowers her head to sniff briefly
at those spots, but detects nothing of termites or rust or
rotting wood, or anything else suggestive of trouble in
the making.

Her walkabout confirms what she already knew: doors
and windows all sealed, no intruders.

No problems.

She returns to the entrance hall and stretches out on the floor. In her natural form, Tikki doesn't bother much with furniture, except maybe for sleep. Chairs and sofas aren't really large enough to accommodate her, and if she had to get up in a hurry, a chair or sofa might suddenly shift, throwing her off balance.

It was like her mother always said. Birds are meant for the sky. Monkeys are safest in the trees. Four-legs like her belong to the earth, and should stay close to it.

Abruptly, a swirl of dust set aglow by the moonlight sifting down from above whips up right in front of her nose. She tugs her head back in surprise, then grunts, grumbles. Another of Adama's little jokes, a signal, meaning he's ready for her now. She isn't sure how he made the dust move like that, but she knows it isn't magic. Adama doesn't like magic any more than she does. In all likelihood, he would agree that her own special brand of magic is all the world should allow.

Probably, it was just some weird techie effect, electromagnetic, something like that. She's used tricks like that herself. A little FX can make a rough job go smoother.

She heads down to the basement.

The room there is large, the walls, ceiling, and floor all black. The only illumination comes from the twenty flat-screen trids set into the wall on the right. Each of those screens plays and replays scenes from the end of the world, the Fifth World, and the coming of the Sixth: food riots in New York City, corp wars, devastation, death. Chaos struggling against human law for supremacy. Civilization hanging in the balance.

At the center of the room is a metal rack like a pull-up bar for exercising. Beneath the crossbar, spread-eagled, wrists and ankles secured, stands Adama's chosen one for tonight, a voluptuous female, a redhead, naked. Beside her is a black marble table. Laid out across the table is a collection of gleaming stainless steel instruments. Beside the table stands a heavily built ork named Jacklash.

Adama sits at the left of the room, in an ornately carved wooden chair facing the captive female and the wall of trideo screens. Beside him rises a gleaming black marble stand formed of delicate strands gently twining around one another. Atop the stand rests a huge gemstone, as pure to the eye as diamond, and about the size of a man's fist.

"Ah," Adama says, smiling, smelling pleased, even gratified. He extends a hand toward Tikki. "The tigress comes. Join us. Please."

The words are expressive, full of pleasure.

Tikki watches the ork.

Jacklash looks to Adama and back to Tikki again. He does not understand that she is Were, that she is a thinking creature. He imagines her to be a crude, unthinking beast. He fears her, as he should, and perhaps fears Adama too, but strives not to show it. His smell makes most of that quite clear.

Adama waves vaguely at the ork, smiles and says, "Don't be disturbed. The tigress and I have an arrangement."

"Yeah," Jacklash replies. "You said."

Adama smiles and waves.

Tikki walks forward, as far as the metal bars that hold the female in place. The many aromas in the air tell Tikki more about the captive's condition than anything she sees. The female is very tired and in much pain. She has lost some blood. She is afraid. She is afraid of dying, and now terrified to see the massive tiger standing calmly beside her, barely a step away.

Jacklash is very anxious.

"Come," Adama says amiably. "Sit by me."

Tikki turns toward the man, and in turning brushes her tail across the captive's thigh.

Terror pure and free blossoms into the air.

Good prey, very good.

Tikki walks over to Adama's big chair, a very unusual chair, like a throne. It smells like real wood, which makes it very expensive, though not terribly interesting to Tikki. What intrigues her is the large gemstone on top of the marble stand. She pauses before it, sniffs it, wonders about it, but does not touch. Adama has warned her never to touch it. She would not in any event, under any circumstances. It's too strange.

Some sort of natural phenomena, not magic, something else, has imbued the stone with unusual properties. It's a very special piece of rock. The outer facets gleam with a fiery light, but further in, the heart of the stone seems to burn with fierce white light. Tikki has never seen anything like it.

Standing very close to it, she could swear she hears a murmur of voices, a subtle babble of voices, a nearly inaudible chorus of screams and shouts and cries of pure agony.

She ignores them, the voices. It's nothing to worry about. Adama told her so. Just more FX.

She sits, haunches down, head erect.

"Does the huntress approve?" Adama says.

Tikki looks again to the captive, flicking her ears. Does she approve? Of course she does. The captive female is full-grown and full-bodied. Nothing in the female's scent so much as hints at disease or illness. This a fine one, a good specimen.

Very good.

Softly, Adama chuckles, then waves a hand vaguely at Jacklash. The trial continues.

How long will the female survive?

That's the real question.

Most humans are horrified by death. Tikki accepts it, sees it as an integral part of Nature. So does Adama. That's part of what makes him so unusual. Adama not only understands, he savors the kill, anticipates it with pleasure, relishes the coming of the final moment. Tikki has felt much the same way on many an occasion, primarily in the wild, while hunting in her natural form.

That the prey in this case suffers torture rather than the torment of flight and the agony of capture is basically irrelevant. Adama says that death makes everything equal. Tikki is not so sure about that, but is willing to play along.

"Isn't she beautiful?" Adama inquiries. "My *Leandra.*"

Tikki supposes that all prey is beautiful.

In a sense.

15

The pain comes out of nowhere, excruciating, captivating. Pounding into his body, piercing his skin. Slamming through his whole being like hammers and nails, the agonies as blunt as bricks and as sharp as spears. Shouts and screams and a strange staccato clattering fill his ears, but the sounds are oddly distant, and seem meaningless.

He remembers his mother, and begins to cry.

Through it all, he feels a tingling, an electric energy, like a zillion megawatts of static electricity enveloping his skin; and then a tugging, a yanking, as if his heart, his internal organs, are being wrenched right out of his chest.

Then, suddenly, he's flying forward as if fired out of a cannon, hurtling down a long dark tunnel at an incomprehensible speed. Faster and faster. Till the speed becomes a tangible power, flaying his body, tearing at him, threatening to break him into pieces and crush him.

The tunnel grows brighter, so bright it's blinding, and he's plunging into a sea of incandescent white, an inferno of white. The agony only swells.

Never-ending . . .

16

The Master Corporator sits behind his magnificent onyx desk in the huge main office of his luxurious private suite, at the helm of a vast multinational corporate empire. His position is one of near-omnipotence, the resources at his command virtually incalculable, and that is as it should be. Destiny has declared that he should rank high among the world's corporate elite, as in fact he does, and with good reason. His intelligence is unrivaled. His foresight borders on the uncanny. His wit, his ability to perceive opportunities and the best possible manner in which to exploit those opportunities have no parallel. All that he has achieved in his lifetime is his by right of his own superlative ability. He owes nothing whatsoever to luck or to the errors of other persons less brilliant than himself. He has proven this countless times before, and will do so again.

Naturally, the world will strive to drag him down, to topple him from his position of power, but he will reign supreme.

Few things could be more apparent.

His Birnoth Comitatus executive protectors glance past him, scanning the room. The privacy function is on. These elite protectors are necessary only because he does not choose to exert himself in the realm of mere physical violence. That would hardly be appropriate for an individual of such limitless capabilities as himself.

Softly now, Ohara laughs. His concerns over the police investigation into the death of Robert Neiman were entirely unfounded. Clearly, he has nothing to worry about, nothing at all. Once again he has demonstrated his transcendent abilities. Though a potential problem existed, he laid plans to eliminate it before the difficulty could manifest.

When he came onboard with KFK, taking charge of Exotech, he had another kind of problem, a lack of funds, no investment capital, and that was what he needed to turn an industry dog into a leader. Did he beg and plead with the KFK board for money? Of course not. He approached the problem creatively, laterally, and solved it. Solved it in a way that was almost *Better Than Life*! He set up a BTL production lab, using the profits from that venture to finance a special undertaking in Exotech's Special Projects Unit. With that money, he hired top-notch talent, produced a simsense masterpiece—still at the top of the charts—and brought Exotech to a position of dominance in the marketplace.

Now, of course, he has no more need of the "special financing" provided by the BTL lab. Clean Sweep took care of that and so eliminated a potential problem.

The Master Corporator.

Indeed . . .

Ohara smiles and removes the unmarked chip from the chipjack concealed behind his right ear. He has no further need of the artificial emotive boost from a common track-loop BTL. The truth is too obvious. No one could ever possibly come between him and the attainment of his objectives. No one.

The telecom bleeps softly. The word RECEPTION appears in block letters that wink on and off at the center of the monitor screen. "On," Ohara says with a grandiose wave of his hand, tapping a key to make the cosmetically flawless features of his receptionist immediately fill the screen.

"A Lieutenant Kirkland of Minuteman Security to see you, sir," she says.

Ohara smiles, amused. This is, what? the lieutenant's second visit this week? The man must be a complete incompetent to require another interview so soon. "Show the lieutenant in."

"Right away, sir," the receptionist replies.

This time Kirkland comes through the main office door. He does not scam his way past KFK security, slipping in through side doors, as on his last visit. Heads have rolled over that little episode. KFK Plaza is now on full terrorist alert.

Ohara's Birnoth Comitatus protectors look Kirkland over briefly as he enters the office. Kirkland wears a visitor's badge. He walks directly up to Ohara's desk, offering a hand, and saying, "How are you?"

"Quite well." Smiling, Ohara rises graciously from his chair and accepts the offered hand. One shake is enough. Ohara sits, gestures casually for the lieutenant to have a seat. "And how are you, Lieutenant?"

"Not bad," Kirkland says. He spends a moment sorting through his synthleather portfolio. His rather cheap-looking, worn, synthleather portfolio. "I'd like to show you a couple of snaps."

Ohara smiles. ''Of course.''

The lieutenant hands him a thin sheaf of twenty-by-twenty-five centimeter photos, which Ohara looks at one at a time. He has the time to do Kirkland the favor of pretending to be interested, more than that, *cooperative*. Time is his to spend as he desires. There are seven snaps in all. Each one focuses on a single individual. The quality of the shots varies. Some are blurred, variously distorted. The only one that stands out is a photo of a woman in crimson mirrorshades, red and black facepaint, and matching synthleather. She stands behind a man who kneels on a bare white floor. In one hand, she holds something, perhaps a strip of wire, wrapped tightly around the man's throat. In her other hand, she holds a gun, a huge automatic, which points straight out from the center of the picture.

The look on her face, or what can be seen of it beneath the visor-style shades, is one of inhuman resolve, a look emotionless as stone, utterly ruthless.

Ohara feels a sudden shocking rise of tension, a gnawing in his gut, a crawling up his spine. This woman with the facepaint and the gun is not unknown to him. In fact, he has encountered her in the flesh, face to face, once, just once. It was the first time in his life that he was ever forced to admit, if only to himself, that certain powers existed in the world with the potential to invalidate his plans, through the simple expedient of ending his life.

''Ever see any of them before?'' Kirkland asks.

''No.'' Ohara hands the snaps back to Kirkland. Maintaining his aura of pre-eminence is difficult now, though a lesser individual would be completely unnerved. He considers the chip safely ensconced in the plastic carrier in his inside jacket pocket. *The Master Corporator*. He could use an emotive boost right now. First, he'll have to get rid of Kirkland . . .

He struggles to maintain his composure.

''I take it that these are your suspects?''

''The major players,'' Kirkland replies. ''Some are just local kick-artists. The others are from out of town.'' Kirkland pauses, staring openly at Ohara, then says, ''The one female in the batch is an interesting case. She's been linked to assassinations in Chicago, Seattle, San Francisco, and maybe a dozen other cities scattered across Japan, Korea, China, and Southeast Asia. She's done work for just about every major criminal organization with ties to East Asia and North America, the yakuza, Triads, you name it. She's absolutely ruthless. Meaning if she got the right contract she wouldn't hesitate to kill you and everyone you've ever known. And probably would enjoy it, too. That's how vicious she's reputed to be."

Ohara swallows, breathes deeply. He knows *precisely* what Kirkland is talking about. He's seen firsthand just how vicious this female, this *creature,* can be. The knowledge is almost too much for any civilized person to bear.

"Well . . . well, I should certainly hope never to make her acquaintance," is all he says.

Kirkland nods. "Hope and pray."

Ohara forces an intemperate smile. He doesn't need some lowly police lieutenant telling him how to think or behave.

"I'm always amazed to learn, Lieutenant, that such people as you describe can so consistently evade apprehension. One would think that the police would make a priority of incarcerating such vicious creatures."

Kirkland nods, just once. "Oh, it's a priority all right," he says. "In fact, this particular case is a very hot priority. Now that we've got another killing."

Ohara drops the smile. "You're not serious."

"Maybe you knew him," Kirkland says. "Steven Jorge? I'm told he was your Deputy Director for Production."

Ohara feels a rush of heat up the back of his neck. "This isn't at all amusing, Lieutenant."

"Of course not," Kirkland says in a definite tone. "Murder's never amusing."

The lieutenant isn't kidding, isn't playing games, and the recognition engulfs Ohara in a sudden wave of vertigo. With it comes an almost unbearable tension, all born of acute anxiety. Even fear. The death of Robert Neiman might have been just random, coincidental. This new death carries far more profound implications. Sudden, shocking implications.

Kirkland lays a sheaf of hard copy on Ohara's desk, officially stamped and marked for Minuteman Security Services. The ritual notification to Steven Jorge's corporate masters. To that Kirkland adds three more notices.

"This time the killer got greedy," Kirkland says, returning to his chair. "It wasn't enough to take out just a couple of people. The perp smoked a whole bunch, eight by last count. With various corporate affiliations. Grievous bodily injury to about seventeen more."

Ohara draws a deep breath. "This . . . wasn't in the news."

"Of course it wasn't in the news," Kirkland says quietly. "And it isn't gonna get into the news until we've got some idea what's going on. You think we want the public to hear about this? The corporate fallout alone is going to be incredible."

"It's quite a *shock*."

"I'm sure," Kirkland replies. "And I'm sure you'll understand if we get down to business. Two men who are both execs in your corporation got dusted, along with a couple of personal aides, a comp-spec, and a data analyst. In the business, the police business, we call that a pattern. We think your man Jorge was the real target. The others just happened to be there. What do you think?"

"I think . . . I think you'd better begin treating this matter with the attention it deserved from the start!"

"Believe me, we're giving it all the attention it deserves. Now try answering my question."

"Just what would you like me to tell you?"

"I don't know, be creative. Why would somebody want Jorge aired out? What was he into? Did he usually frequent establishments operated by the yakuza?"

"How . . . I'm sure I have no idea!"

"Kono-Furata-Ko. Exotech's parent corp. Very Japanese organization. Got any yakuza connections?"

Kirkland's whole attitude has changed, and Ohara does not like it. The man's aggressive tone of questioning has him on edge. It's intolerable. "I *refuse* to be addressed like some *criminal*!"

Kirkland ignores this last. "You had a big blowout at one of your sites up near Germantown about a year ago. A fire, a few deaths. Some mana-types cooked up something that got a little out of hand. Think it might be related to Neiman and Jorge's deaths?"

Ohara stares for several moments, caught off guard. "That . . . that whole matter has been laid to rest."

"I read the reports."

"Then you know there could be no connection."

"I know something got out of hand. I know that some of your people got aced then, and several more just got aired out now. Everything else is conjecture. The question is why are so many of your people getting scragged?"

"That's absurd! What you're implying . . ."

"You're making inferences. So am I. What part of Exotech was that up there in Germantown? The Special Projects Unit?"

"I'll . . . I'll have to check my corporate schematic."

"You don't know?"

"As I *explained* to you previously, I've restructured the entire architecture of the corporation."

"Yeah, I remember. In the meantime, what was Steven Jorge's position a year ago? What kind of work was he doing?"

"I don't recall."

"By any chance was he another guy you boosted up the corporate ladder?"

"I don't like your tone, Lieutenant!"

"Did you *boost* Jorge up the ladder like you *boosted* Neiman? Yes or no?"

"This is impossible!"

"Yes or no, *dammit*!"

"I'll consult my records."

"Yeah, good idea. I'd like to see those records. In fact, I want complete corporate dossiers on both Jorge and Neiman, too."

"You have no authority to make those kinds of demands!"

"Hey, no problem, chummer. You don't wanna cooperate, that's fine. Of course, in that case, I might have
to talk to the media. Investigation stalled, Ohara with-
holds pertinent data."

"That's blackmail!"

"Call it leverage. Call it what you want. Just get me
the files." Kirkland rises, turns to leave and abruptly
turns back. "You had some problem in Seattle. What
happened?"

Ohara jerks involuntarily. "I . . . I was assaulted."

"Shot up, beaten, and burglarized. Lots of things
smashed, nothing stolen. That's what the police reports
say. You claimed you never got a good look at your as-
sailant. No one was ever arrested. What really happened?"

"My . . . one of my servants was killed."

"Yeah, I know. Don't forget about the files."

Kirkland turns and walks out through the main door.
Ohara waits for the door to close, then slumps in his
chair, closes his eyes, feeling weak, drained. What happened to him in Seattle was supposed to have been swept
forever from his life. He's made every effort to bury it,
to wipe the slate clean, every effort but one. Now, clearly,
the horror has risen again.

Kirkland is a fool. He has no idea what he's up against.
What the deaths of Robert Neiman and Steven Jorge im-
ply is too obvious to be missed. Ohara sees it too plainly.
The horror that shattered his life in Seattle and nearly
brought his plans to ruin has followed him here to Philadelphia, obviously with the intention of striking yet
again. The death of Neiman and Jorge is just the beginning. The precursor of an assault aimed directly at him.

It is the woman again, the one from Seattle, the one
in Kirkland's pics. The female in red and black. Striper.
She is no mere denizen of the streets. She is a creature
of the city's dark underbelly. She is neither woman nor
animal, but some creation of the Sixth World, a guileful
demon, a vicious monstrosity, the personification of evil.
His encounter with her in Seattle, the sheer violence of
their meeting, the psychic torture, the bloodletting, all
but destroyed him. He has lost precious time climbing

out of the ruin of his former life. He will not allow the demon to ravage him again. She must be destroyed. His future demands it.

Using the police as a tool to capture or kill her is not a viable option. It would require too many explanations. It would mean explaining what might have attracted the demon's attention to him in the first place.

Ohara extends a hand to the telecom, presses a tab.

When Enoshi enters, Ohara is standing before the windows, gazing out across the metroplex. He feels equal now to the challenge of issuing orders. The threat against his life will be eliminated. Not only will he survive, he will go on to build the greatest corporate empire ever assembled.

"I have something for you to take care of," he says. "I cannot over-emphasize its importance. I shall simply say that the matter is essential to the well-being of our corporate holdings. It must receive top priority. At once. You must do it at once."

Enoshi replies, "Of course, sir. At once."

The demon must die.

17

Matsushita Gardens is located just north and west of downtown, along the eastern bank of the Schuylkill River. The five towers there rise from a lush park, a gently rolling landscape of trees, hedges, and lavish gardens of flowers and flowering shrubs. Here one may also find several traditional karesansui, or dry-landscape gardens, a teahouse, and a small Buddhist temple.

One may enter the Gardens complex via any of three access points. Enoshi takes the one off Kelly Drive. The routine is familiar. Stop before the red and white striped barrier of the guardhouse, nod in acknowledgment of the bow offered by the uniformed guard. Extend an arm out the window, place his credstick in the receiving port and put his thumb to the pad. A soft bell tone sounds and the barrier begins to rise. His identity as an authorized guest of the complex is confirmed. The uniformed guard bows in acknowledgment, much deeper than necessary, no doubt a reaction to the automobile Enoshi is driving.

Until recently, he drove a Ford Americar, a common enough sedan that some might view as beneath his station, but that no one could ever consider pretentious. Besides, it was a car with an American name that also gave good fuel economy and had an adequate maintenance record. He never felt embarrassed by the car. On the contrary, it coincided with his own self-image: unassuming, efficient, task-oriented. Naturally, his superior, Bernard Ohara, took issue with this when the matter came to his attention, insisting that Enoshi lease through the company, through Exotech, a vehicle more suited to the senior aide of a director of Kono-Furata-Ko.

And so now Enoshi drives a Mercedes 200 Classic four-door sedan, equipped with a variety of wholly unnecessary options. The console portacom is just one example. Enoshi routinely carries a very serviceable Panasonic UltraThin in his briefcase.

Parked in his usual spot in the garage beneath Tower Three, he draws the UltraThin from his briefcase and taps in a telecom code. The other end rings twice, then a male voice answers, "Hello?"

"Are you free?" Enoshi says, without preamble.

The line clicks, then a new voice, exquisitely soft and fine, consummately feminine, says, "Of course I'm free."

"I'll be there in about ten minutes."

"I'll be waiting."

Enoshi marks the time on his wrist watch and lets ten minutes elapse before leaving his car. It is another five or six minutes before he exits the elevator and turns down the carpeted corridor of the thirty-ninth floor. Perhaps twenty minutes in all pass before he presses the tab beside number 3905.

It is but a moment before the door opens and she is standing there, looking as if she had spent the whole morning preparing for his arrival. Her name is Frédé-

rique, a name that Enoshi finds every bit as exotic as the
woman herself. Her eyes are blue, and naturally so. Her
golden blonde hair flows luxuriously down across her
brow, partially concealing the right side of her face. The
diaphanous white gown she wears looks like real silk,
though it is covered in places, all the special places, by
a frothy white lace. The gown is very exciting without
being overly revealing. It enhances her beauty, showing
her to be delightfully contoured and yet not excessively
styled.

Her greatest beauty, however, and the one that keeps
Enoshi enthralled, is seen only in her eyes, and in her
smile . . . and in all she says and does.

Enoshi bows, stepping in through the door. Softly
smiling, Frédérique draws back a step, then another, and
then bows like a lady of feudal Europe, lowering her
head, her whole body, briefly lifting her gown from about
the hips as if to keep the hem above the floor. Enoshi
finds himself smiling, effortlessly beaming.

Frédérique steps up and kisses his cheek, the only instant her eyes leave his. Her touch is as light as a but-
terfly's wing, and she smells of a flowery perfume, a
veritable garden of delightful scents.

"Where have you been?" she says softly, still smiling.
"I've missed you so."

It seems less a question than a soft, gentle way of
pointing out that Enoshi has not been to see her for almost a week. Perhaps she has felt a bit lonely. Half a
dozen explanations run through Enoshi's mind—his work,
his family, the house, other concerns—but to a woman
like Frédérique these would seem like mere excuses. For
her, love is paramount, and whoever she chooses to grace
with that love means more, far more, than any job, than
family, more than anything else in the world. Enoshi can
imagine only one reply.

"Forgive me," he murmurs.

"Of course," Frédérique croons, gazing into his eyes.
"How could I not?"

"You are always in my thoughts."

Softly, she whispers, "You lie."

"In my heart, then."

"That I believe."

Again Enoshi smiles, again without forethought. The moment seems right for him to present his little gift. "This is for you."

Frédérique smiles, tenderly, exquisitely, as if moved to the brink of tears. "For me?"

Enoshi nods and leans close to kiss her cheek. She rings his neck with her arms and kisses him back, then accepts the slim white box with the gold foil insert. Inside she will find a small and artfully arranged bouquet that Enoshi has personally assembled at the Kyoto Florist downtown. The small pink foil card bears ideograms that read, "Art is truth, love is more . . ."

"How beautiful," Frédérique breathes. "Thank you."

No thanks are necessary.

"Let me make you tea."

"Of course."

They share a brief kiss, then Frédérique is leading him through the apartment and into her salon, a kind of den walled on two sides by windows, full of light and plants and comfortable furnishings, equipped with a bar and immense trideo screen, and dominated by a huge hearth. Frédérique seats him along one plush sofa unit facing the windows, removes his shoes, then proceeds to make him tea, all with an artist's attention to detail.

"It's so wonderful to see you in the daytime," she says.

"Really? Why so?"

"Must there be a reason?"

"Yes, tell me."

She smiles and then slowly nods. Of course there is a reason. Why is she glad to see him in the daytime? "Because of the sun," she says. "Because I love you. Because the two go together so well."

Enoshi smiles with pleasure.

After tea, after more talk, when the proper moment finally arrives, he takes her hands in his and says, regretfully, "There is something I must ask of you."

Of course, she smiles, smiles and looks at him with eyes that gently inquire what it is that he might possibly desire. "Anything," she whispers. "Ask me anything."

"I must meet with Sarabande again."

The look in her eyes turns curious, but that is all the inquiry she makes. Without another word, she rises and goes down the hall toward her bedroom. Enoshi hears the quiet tapping of telecom keys. Then Frédérique returns, padding quietly across the floor on naked feet. She sits beside him on the sofa, shaking back the soft thick hair that hides the side of her face. She smiles at him, saying simply, "Done."

Enoshi lifts her hands to his lips.

18

The sun is little more than a smoldering red-orange globe hanging low over the vast suburban expanse to the west of the city when Enoshi pauses on the bustling sidewalks around the Thirtieth Street transit center. He checks his watch and tries to maintain his focus on the biz immediately before him.

The brief time he spent with Frédérique served only to distract him from his mounting concerns about his superior, Bernard Ohara. The man's continued reliance on methods at variance with prevailing social values—covert, illegal methods—can only be viewed by any rational person as most dangerous. The extraterritorial nature of multinational corporations might prevent local government entities from preferring criminal charges or launching lawsuits, but that would never protect a corporation's image.

Immunity to prosecution could never save face.

Now, a sleek silver Rolls Royce Phaeton limousine swings toward the curb and glides to a halt as smoothly as a maglev train pulling into Kyoto station, stopping precisely in front of Enoshi. He waits, hands at his sides. The door to the passenger section immediately opens. A man in a black synthleather trench coat steps out. His long white hair and pale complexion suggest the elven

metatype, but this is of no special significance. The elf
is merely a servant of the personage whom Enoshi has
come to meet. The elf consults a small scanning device,
but Enoshi is carrying no weapons.

"*Está bien. Entre.*" The elf nods toward the limousine.

Enoshi nods, gets in. The elf follows on his heels. The
limousine is swinging away from the curb and moving
off even as Enoshi settles into the rear-facing seat. The
elf sits at his left. Facing him across the center console,
fully equipped with portacom/stereo/wetbar and possibly
a satellite uplink, is the woman known as Sarabande. She
is *kuromaku*, a fixer, one who arranges matters from behind the scenes. She appears to be pure human, European, Spanish, or possibly Italian—Enoshi is not sure
which. Her black hair is drawn back sleek and flat from
her face and brow. Dark, visor-style shades conceal her
eyes, but clearly visible is the black wire-lead of a datajack descending from her right temple. She wears a black
jacket adorned with swirls of gold over a tight-fitting
black blouse and matching slacks. Her low-heeled black
boots shine like mirrors.

Seated to her left is an enormous ork and to her right
a huge Asian male. Both wear mirrored shades, sharply
tailored suits, and show the massive builds of weight lift-
ers or *sumotori*.

"Your business?" Sarabande says.

"Yes," Enoshi replies, with a nod. "I have the details
here." He extends his left arm fully, then draws back the
sleeve of his jacket and dress shirt to display the chip-
carrier case strapped to his arm just above the wrist. He
opens the case and passes the chip carrier to the elf, who
inspects it before handing it to Sarabande. Experience
has taught Enoshi never to make any sudden moves or
do anything that might be perceived as threatening. In
his first meeting with Sarabande, he suddenly found himself staring into the muzzle of a gun, an extremely large
automatic pistol, merely because he had reached rather
suddenly toward his inside jacket pocket.

Without further comment, Sarabande slots the chip
carrier into the computer deck set into the center console,

then sits back, briefly lifting a hand to the datajack at her right temple. Several minutes pass. The limousine seems to pick up speed. Enoshi glances out the dark-tinted windows to his right and sees that they are riding up onto a highway, the section of I-76 that loops around the southern end of the central city.

Abruptly, Sarabande is asking him, "What is your interest in the person referenced on this datafile?"

"The person must be invalidated."

"What are you willing to pay?"

"What price do you ask?"

"The shadows are very busy. Talent is coming at premium prices. How much talent are you willing to buy?"

"Whatever will be adequate for the work to be done."

"First-rate talent serves the global market, is always in demand, and is unlikely to be available on short notice."

"Time is of the essence."

"The price will then be approximately double what you paid for your last run."

Price is not a major concern. The funds generated by Ohara-*san*'s illegal BTL production lab were significant, in the millions of nuyen, and provided Exotech with a much-needed infusion of cash. The cost to destroy that same lab, to do all that was required by Operation Clean Sweep, was trivial by comparison. Enoshi's only concern regarding the price of the run he is now trying to arrange is that the *kuromaku*, the fixer Sarabande, should not think him foolish or gullible.

"The price you suggest seems somewhat high," he says. "The task in this case seems much simpler. I would expect the price to be lower."

"Then you do not realize what you are asking."

Enoshi hesitates a moment, then catches himself, suppresses a rush of irritation. Sarabande's manner has always been rather curt, in his limited experience. His impression is that she is merely *to the point,* rather than intentionally rude. He composes himself, and says, "Please explain."

"The individual in question is extremely dangerous. And known to be eccentric. Unpredictable. What you want will therefore entail a high risk. The individual must also be found. Locating the SINless takes time.''

And time takes money. Enoshi had presumed that this new run would cost more than the last, more than Clean Sweep, but had wanted to hear the fixer's reasons for quoting higher fees. ''You will guarantee completion?''

''I will guarantee only that the attempt will be made,'' Sarabande replies. ''If it fails, the loss is yours.''

''You guaranteed success on the last run.''

''The point is not open to negotiation.''

''May I have some reason?''

''I've already given you the reason. The individual who is the focus of this new run is extremely dangerous. Eliminating that person will entail a high degree of risk.''

Enoshi nods. Fortunately, he had some idea of what to expect during this meeting and was able to decide on possible contingencies ahead of time. ''I believe I must split my options.''

''Continue.''

''I would like to go ahead, arrange for the run as we have discussed, for immediate execution and using available talent. At the same time, I would ask that you make inquiries, ascertain whether first-rate talent is available, and when, so that if the first attempt fails, another first-rate individual or team will be ready to act at once.''

''You want back-up.''

''Quality back-up. Yes.''

''That is no problem. However, first-rate talent will require compensation merely to open a window of availability. This may increase your cost by a factor of four. I will act on your behalf to obtain an equitable price, but where elite skills are concerned, the room for negotiation is limited.''

''That is understood.''

That first-rate talent should require such a premium is no surprise to Enoshi, and the point would not sway him in any event. Time is the critical element. Ohara-*san* had said, ''At once.''

To Enoshi, that meant, *''Now!''*

''Then our negotiation is concluded,'' Sarabande says.

"I will require an immediate payment of one hundred-kay nuyen."

That is easily arranged.

19

The glaring trid screen set into the wall at the rear of the booth jammers about some suit chewed up by a machine gun inside a parking garage. Neona ignores it. The bar is Humphrey's Jack Zone, and from her booth near the street entrance it has the wild-eyed ambiance of an arcade. A billion multicolored lights flash and flare from the mirrored ceiling, walls, tables, and bar, and from at least half the people crowding the place, all wearing mirrored NeoMonochrome. The band is wired for sound and playing frantic-time from the semicircular stage up behind the U-shaped bar. Holographic images of impossibly proportioned naked and semi-naked women dance along the top of the bar, in alcoves along the walls, and on top of the few unoccupied tables. Every table has a bowl of Nerps, a paycom, a Matrix port of deckers, and headsets for those who want to sample the bar's 1,000+! Dir-X! Theatrical! Masterpiece! simsense recordings, including *Monochrome Dreams* and *The Summoning of Abbirleth,* looping twenty-four hours a day. The roaring music, the jammering trids, and the bells, buzzers, and sirens of the games being played everywhere blend into a deafening electronic babble that threatens Neona's head with static.

That static is about all that's keeping her from a babble all her own. Her chiller thriller Amerind biker dude, Ripsaw, got her into the city, then just bugged out. She can understand that. In the short time they spent together, she wasn't anything but baggage. Neona never had a chance to show him what she could do, except in bed, and that's never enough by itself. Getting dumped might not be so bad if she hadn't found him so exciting, so totally massively intensely male that she couldn't help herself. At least he saved her a long goodbye. Slot and run. It hurts less like that.

Between her and the wall at the back of the booth is the black nylon bag holding her Fuchi-6 cyberdeck in its gray macroplast case. If she's gonna eat anytime soon, she's gonna have to put the Fuchi to work.

She wipes at her eyes, and glances around.

Walking toward her is a group just emerged from the crowd at the rear of the bar. They go straight past her table, heading for the door to the street. Three of them look like razorguys. One has gleaming silver cybereyes to go with his cool, smirky smile and NeoMonochrome duster. Another has an Ingram smartgun dangling from one hand down along his side. Another of the slags has razorcut hair sliced into fins and a datajack in his right temple. The one girl with the group could be a mage. She wears a lot of dull metal jewelry—necklaces, pins, bangles, and rings—and once, just once, she lifts a hand and does something funny with her fingers.

They gotta be runners, shadowrunners. Neona's sure of it. She scrambles out of her booth, hustling after them, calling, "Yo, chummers! Hoi! *Hey,* hoi!"

Her voice seems totally drowned by the thundering noise of the club. Yet, suddenly, the shadowrunners turn to face her, and the one with the Ingram smartgun is pointing it directly at her. The mage girl has both hands raised and flickering with blue energy like eldrich lightning. Neona freezes, wide-eyed, heart pounding, but manages a shaky smile—what she hopes is a *friendly-looking* smile.

"Uhh . . . hoi."

The slag with the Ingram watches her a moment, then leans the smartgun back against his shoulder. The mage lowers her hands. They all turn away.

"Hey, *wait*!" Neona calls. "WAIT A SEC!"

This time the guy with the Ingram turns around and steps right into her face, glaring. The Ingram presses lightly into her left ribs. "What's your beef?" he growls.

Neona swallows. What she'd give right now for some

heavy-duty back-up. "I'm just . . . I'm new in the plex. Tryin' to make a connection."

The guy tilts his head, studying the side of her head where she's got her datajack, her right temple. "Yeah? So what?" he says.

"Know anybody who needs a decker?"

"You a ramjammer or a chiphead?"

"I'm burning chrome on a hotjack!" she blurts adamantly. The slag just watches her for a moment, glancing down at her bag, then says, "Hardwired?"

"Neu . . . neuromantically radical," she stammers.

The slag opens his mouth to say something, but doesn't get any further than that. A troll built like the front end of a bus comes up behind the group and brawls, "Hammer! Cloak da iron, *dammit*! 'Fore I count zero on you!"

Hammer, the slag glaring into Neona's face, lifts a hand to his mirrorshades, and shouts back, "I'm talkin' biz with a Mona Lisa!"

The guy with the silver eyes and smirky grin nods at Neona and says, "Let's try 'er, Hammer."

"HAMMER!" the troll roars.

Hammer's face turns a furious red, but then the mage puts a hand to his right shoulder and says, "Let's go outside and talk." With a glance at Neona, then a glance back at the troll, she adds amiably, "We're not looking for grief."

"Yeah, *right*!" Hammer looks at Neona, then nods curtly toward the main entrance. Neona follows the group outside.

It's looking like maybe she's made a connection.

That would make it a good night.

20

The digital display on Tikki's wrist chronograph reads 00:56:29 as she steers the stolen Volkswagen Superkombi III into the southwest parking field of the Ardmore

Royal Residence Plaza. She notes with satisfaction that, as usual, a minimum of a half-dozen other personal-use commuter and cargo vans are scattered about the parking field, along with a wide variety of standard autos, everything from executive sedans to basic econocars. Maybe a thousand vehicles in all. The Volkswagen will blend in just fine.

The sprawling apartment complex lies just off Route 30, just beyond the Philadelphia city limits. Nine tall towers rise from the orange-vapor glare of the parking fields. At this hour, the only other illumination is from the desolate ground-floor lobbies and the flaring red strobes of aircraft warning lights stroking the dark night sky.

All very, very good.

Tikki steers the Volkswagen around the parking field. Position is important. There are no empty parking spaces close to Tower Seven, but that is no problem. She planned to park at a distance. Tikki finds a space where she can park the van with the rear window facing the southwest façade of Tower Seven at a range of about two hundred meters. She cuts the engine and waits, waits and watches, then gets down to business.

Tonight's work requires that she carry an unusual amount of gear. That meant careful planning and now requires methodical execution. Tikki takes her time, spends a few moments adjusting the fit of her gloves, black plastic ones that fit like a second skin. She moves to the rear of the van and takes a Walther XP-700 semiautomatic pistol from her compartmentalized duffel bag. The XP-700 is one of the few match-grade precision weapons that load more than one bullet at a time—five rounds via an integral magazine, and one directly into the firing chamber. The weapon is loaded and ready to go.

Tikki kneels on the back bench seat and takes another look around. Except for the vehicles parked there, the parking field is deserted.

With a touch of a sensor tab, Tikki lowers the van's rear window, then braces her arms on the back of the bench seat and sights in on the southwest face of Tower

Seven. The pistol's flat-black finish absorbs light rather than reflects it. The Ares optical night sight brings the distant rectangle of a fire door so close it seems only an arm's length away. Tikki inclines the muzzle of the XP a bit, bringing the security cam mounted just above the door clearly into view, seeming close enough to touch. The Lumex laser targeting module puts a sharply focused red dot on the upper surface of the downward-angled cam to indicate her exact point of aim.

When she pulls the trigger, there is only a quiet thump, thanks to the Fabrique silencer.

Through the optical sight, Tikki sees a hole appear in the top surface of the security cam. That is exactly as planned. She also glimpses what seems to be a quick shower of sparks. Better and better. She touches the tab to raise the van's window, returns the Walther to the duffel bag and crouches down to wait.

In about three minutes, according to her wrist chrono, a car comes squealing into the parking field, amber strobes flashing as it races through the turn, then rushes across the lot toward the southwest fire door. The timing is important, suggestive. The first time she gave Ardmore security a reason to respond, a car showed up in about thirty seconds. That was two weeks ago. Response times, on average, have been growing progressively slower even since.

The car slows abruptly in approaching the fire door, then races off across the lot, then returns, then races around some more—back and forth, back and forth—and finally comes to a halt by the fire door.

A uniformed guard gets out and looks around, then up at the security cam. He tugs on the fire door, which does not open. He glances back and forth, then again, and again, then gets into his car and lifts something to his mouth, probably the mike from the dashboard com.

Twenty minutes pass. A police cruiser rolls into the lot and pulls up beside the security car. The guard gets out. The contract cops do not. This is the sixth night in just under two weeks that someone has shot at the complex, or committed other acts that might be taken as mere vandalism. The targets on other nights included parking field lights, lobby windows, and the cardkey lock on one of the automated booths at the entrance to the complex. One of the private vehicles that patrol the complex was also vandalized, forcibly entered, and stripped of various equipment.

The guard puts on a good show, but the response times tell the story. No one gets very excited about a busted security cam. Their voices carry across the parking field, in through the van's side windows, to Tikki's ears. Audibly enough for her to discern tones and emotive inflections, even if she doesn't catch every word.

It's just one more incident of malicious property damage, they seem to decide. Probably it's all random.

"So call repair," says one of the cops.

Good, very good.

The cops soon depart.

The guard stands around a while, then drives around a while, then finally goes away and doesn't come back. Tikki spends a few moments in preparation, then pulls on a knee-length lightweight black duster. She has no further use for the Volkswagen van and abandons it where it sits.

Duffel bag in hand, she walks across the parking field to the fire door. The second floor of the apartment tower projects out over the ground floor and casts moderate shadows over the door. That provides some useful cover.

She takes a pair of Zeiss Optik CFS-49 goggles from the duffel bag and slings the unit around her neck. That's so she can bring them quickly into use when the moment arrives. She could have put them on in the van, but preferred not to walk across the parking field with a military-grade vision-enhancement device dangling from her neck.

Under the duster she wears a nylon-reinforced web belt and harness. From a clip at the front of the belt, she pulls out a passkey marked for Ardmore security. She presses the On tab. Something like a standard cardkey slides out the business end of the device. She fits that to the fire door's cardkey port, and the unit engages automatically.

The door buzzes and clicks.

Tikki pulls the door open, returns the passkey to her belt, then lifts the Zeiss goggles over her eyes. A pair of blue laser beams cross the doorway, one at chest-height, the other just below the level of her knees. The beams spring alarms if interrupted, but Tikki can easily by-pass them. She removes the duster, tosses it between the beams, then follows the duster, bending under one laser and stepping over the other. Still carrying the duffel bag, she enters the stairwell, then eases the fire door shut behind her.

Penetrating supposedly secure civilian facilities is generally no problem. What Tikki has encountered so far— guard patrol, security cam, hi-tech lock, laser-activated alarm—is about standard for apartment complexes. Enough to deter the average felon. For her, a casual slide. All it takes is preparation.

No further use for the duster. She kicks it into the dark space beneath the final flight of stairs descending to ground level. No basement access here, but that's no problem, either. She pulls on a black ski mask that covers her whole head, but with openings for ears, nose, and mouth, and a wide gash for her eyes that allows for full peripheral vision. Even though Tikki often relies heavily on her ears and nose and even her mouth for data about her surroundings, vision is her primary perception, just as it is for humans. Sometimes she wonders if that might be all she has in common with the breeders.

To the left of the fire door, set into an inside wall, is a large metal panel marked Danger High Voltage. She knew it would be here because she's consulted the building plans. The panel was pivotal in her planning. Now, she pulls the panel open and hooks a small diagnostic comp over the lower flange, then draws out a section of white- and orange-striped wire. Using an Armalite multitool, she strips a short section of its insulated plastic coating, connects two leads from the Telex comp to the stripped section of wire, then cuts the wire between the two leads. This effectively disables the motion detectors monitoring each of the stairway landings above her.

The Ardmore complex relies on strategic placement of security elements, rather than blanket coverage. Security cams watch all external entrances and selected internal locations. Tikki has to worry about only three, those located on the second-, fourth-, and sixth-floor landings directly above her. She connects a second device to three colored wires from the panel. This device, purchased locally, is called a line-looper. She's tested it to make sure it works. What it does is record what a security cam sees over the course of, say, a millisecond, then feeds that recording endlessly to the central monitoring station. That effectively blinds the cams to what's really passing by.

Tikki knows that a decker could have been of help in this operation, but she avoids using them unless absolutely necessary. Deckers rank among the class of things she considers to be perverse. Projecting one's consciousness into the electronic realm of the global computer net is perverse. Animals have meat bodies because they were meant to live in a world of meat bodies. Abandoning one's flesh and blood like a tool no longer needed strikes her as grotesque. She mistrusts anyone who would do that, all deckers, nearly as much as she mistrusts all mages.

She mistrusts computers too, just generally.

There is also the fact that a decker would demand a minimum of several thousand nuyen to do electronically what she has accomplished with just a few simple tools in just a few seconds. At this stage in her operation, she can spare both the time and the effort.

She heads up the stairs.

The unexpected occurs as she nears the third-floor landing. The stairway door suddenly bursts open with a thump, letting a skinny male adolescent in a tee and shatjeans onto the landing. He doesn't seem to notice Tikki until he's reaching for the handrail and starting down the steps, coming right at her. He merely glances at her, his face showing no expression. Hurrying on, he goes right past her.

None of that fools Tikki. The boy's physical reaction to the sight of her is immediate and telling. The scent that floods the air shouts of surprise and chilling fear. The young one knows that something is wrong. From her black ski mask and the gear on her belt, he's got to know she means trouble. That compels her to respond.

Adama would be very displeased if she let this young animal live, placing her mission in jeopardy. Her mission is maximum destruction, and only her own survival rates higher than that. She puts the duffel bag on the steps, then leaps to the landing immediately below. The youth turns and looks up, wide-eyed, filling the air with terror, even as she descends.

It's over quickly. She slams him back bodily against the stairwell wall, jams her left forearm across his throat. At a precise movement of her right fist, a supple black spike snaps out of the mount on her right forearm. The prey realizes what's coming and floods the air with the stink of excrement. Tikki bares her teeth, suppresses a growl, and drives the spike into the juncture of throat and jaw, right up into the brain.

Death is instantaneous.

Tikki retrieves her duffel bag and continues up the stairs. Going up twelve flights or even fifty or a hundred with only occasional pauses to listen or test the air is no problem. She's in excellent condition, always has been. Tikki can push herself to the point of collapse before exhaustion finally sets in. Her mother could do that, too.

As she nears the fifteenth-floor landing, the air takes on an aroma like cigarette smoke and a subtler scent suggestive of soykaf. She pauses and wonders about that, but when nothing untoward occurs, she continues up onto the landing.

She puts the duffel bag down and steps to the hallway door. Set into the door at about eye-level is a small reinforced transparex window. She puts her back to the door to the right of the window, then lifts a small smoked mirror up to the lower-left corner. Once she gets the angle right, the mirror provides a view of the hallway leading directly away from the door. The smoky pane minimizes the chance of the mirror catching the light. Her view of the corridor elaborates on her scent-impressions. At the end of the hall, which extends perhaps thirty meters, are a pair of over-size males in suits. One on the left, one on the right. They are standing guard, Tikki supposes. At least that seems to be the idea. One guard holds a disposable cup. The other holds a cigarette in one hand and an ashtray in the other.

It's amateur hour.

Never compromise your hands.

Tikki pulls the Walther XP-700 from her duffel bag, puts the passkey to the door lock, then turns her back to the door again, lifting the smoky mirror.

The door buzzes and clicks. Maglocks generally give a person ten, maybe fifteen seconds, before the lock automatically resets. The passkey will keep the door open till it's disengaged.

Through the mirror, Tikki sees one of the guards look in her direction, then look back to his partner. They converse. One shrugs. Tikki drops the mirror, yanks the door wide open and braces her left forearm against the inside of the doorway, aiming the XP-700 straight up the hall. The weapon's laser targeting system and optical sight have been zeroed in for two hundred meters exactly. She's now taking aim at close to one-eighth that range, which changes the geometry. Tikki's no mathematician, but she knows certain bits of math through long experience. She worked out the degree of error in point-of-aim a few days before. It's a matter of several centimeters. She's got the number in the back of her mind, but what she thinks right now is almost subconscious, intuitive, instinctive: *aim low*. She knows how much lower is right by how it looks, how it feels.

The guard on the right notices her.

"Yo!" he says, turning toward her, providing a broader target. Just so things should be clear, he shoots a look at his partner and blurts, "Contact!"

If you have to be told . . .

Stupid.

Tikki puts the red dot of the targeting laser just under his sternum, and squeezes the trigger. The Walther thumps and a red blotch appears almost dead center between where she guesses the guard's pecs should be. He staggers back, the cup of soykaf falls. Tikki immediately shifts her point of aim. By then, the guard on the left has thrown down his cigarette and ashtray and is thrusting one hand under his jacket. A pro caught so badly off guard would simply have moved his or her hands as the situation required without wasting the time to throw any-

thing anywhere. When the game is for real, milliseconds
count. Tikki puts the red dot on his chest and fires again.
The Walther thumps and a red blotch appears right over
where the guard's heart should be. The man spins back
and sprawls, his heavy automatic clattering to the floor.

Both guards down.

Tikki retrieves the passkey and grabs the duffel bag,
then hustles up the corridor, taking long strides, but not
running. Not quite. She has two shells remaining in the
Walther. She puts one each into the heads of the fallen
guards, just to be sure neither comes up on her rear.

No longer needing the Walther, she drops it onto the
body of one of the dead guards and reaches into the duffel
bag. From it she takes a Fabrique National MAG-5, a
medium machine gun that resembles an ordinary assault
rifle but is more heavily constructed. Its one-hundred-
round disintegrating-link ammo belt is already locked and
loaded. She braces the butt of the FN's shoulder stock
against her right hip and drapes the belt over her shoulders.

Just a step away is the door to apartment 1510. Tikki
puts the passkey to the door's maglock. The passkey
winks. The door slides open. Tikki steps inside.

The foyer is flanked by sliding closet doors and
expensive-looking antique furniture. Two large males in
suits sit in dark red armchairs. One looks up at Tikki
with an expression of surprise. Two quick bursts from
the FN slam both men from their seats.

Beyond the foyer is a large, open room finished mostly
in hues of gold and outfitted with an extensive entertainment system that includes a huge, wall-mounted trideo
screen. About a dozen humans in flashy Neo-
Monochrome and various non-reflective fashions deco-
rate the plush sofa units and chairs scattered about the
room. Two of them scream and several more exclaim and
shout as the FN machine gun fires and the two males in
the foyer fall.

Pandemonium breaks out as Tikki enters the main
room, the living room. Everyone is screaming and shouting, standing up, sitting down, throwing themselves flat

to the wall, the sofas, the floor, turning as if to run every which way, run and run. Terror fills the air. Tikki bares her teeth and squeezes the trigger, swinging the machine gun's muzzle back and forth. The FN roars like thunder. Armor-piercing shells chew everything in the room between the gun muzzle and the walls, including the furniture, the decor, and especially the humans present. Two of the males draw guns and shoot in the instants before they themselves are cut down. One shot goes wide and the other merely punches at Tikki's Kevlar V-insulated shoulder. The FN stammers. People spin and fall and bleed. Tikki grins. It's just what Adama ordered. An outright massacre. She can almost hear him laughing.

Her primary target is Tomita Haruso, a portly Japanese with a penchant for wearing white suits. Haruso is *shatei*, a "younger brother" of the ranking oyabun, a kind of senior yakuza underboss. Joining him at tonight's casual meeting, according to Tikki's info, are several *wakashira-hosa* and *kambu atsukai*, lower-ranked leaders and executives of the Honjowara-gumi.

Tikki finds Tomita Haruso sprawled on the floor by the mirrored bar. Big, bloody stains stand out starkly against the man's white suit, but she realizes the he is still struggling to move. Several holes in him and he's still not dead? Unusual. This demands her immediate attention.

She lowers the muzzle of the FN and rips at the man with burst after burst until the body is no more than a torn-open bag of jiggling, splashing gore. The man dies then, like he should. That ends her need for the FN—she drops it. From the right side of her belt, she takes a DM-105 demo pack, sets the timer, and drops that too. She could drop a DM-105 from orbit and it wouldn't go off unless she set it to go off that way.

She draws her Kang automatic pistol from the holster at the left of her waist and looks around. The walls are splashed with red. The floor is strewn with bodies and shattered bits of ceramic, plastic, glass, and more red. None of the bodies seem to be moving. That's good.

Very good.

* * *

Tikki walks through the apartment to the master bed-room. The window overlooking the bed is about three meters across. At fifteen stories above the ground, the pane is probably impact-resistant plastic. Tikki holsters the Kang, takes a small packet from her belt. In it is a two-meter-long strip of zip tape, which she smoothes across the lower half of the window. An ordinary butane lighter is sufficient to ignite it. Holding a hand across her eyes, Tikki applies the flame, then turns her back as the tape flares. She hears a hissing sound, like high-voltage electricity, followed by a bright flash of light. At the same time, an alarm bell begins to clang. Probably keyed to the window.

Tikki turns back to the window to find a two-meter-long gash melted right through the lower half of the pane. She picks up a chair, gives it a really good heave. The weakened pane fractures, breaks into shards, and falls away. The chair goes with it.

Now comes the exciting part. She steps up onto the bed, puts one leg out the window, sits on the empty still. Attaches a steel hook to the climber's winch at the front of her harness. Seats the hook securely over the window-sill. Slips outside.

The windowsill is all steel and set into a reinforced concrete wall, so the hook should hold.

She thinks about that as she falls.

Abruptly, the winch cuts her speed, nine or ten stories down. The straps of her harness grab her hard about the hips. She could get bruises if she did this often enough. The ground is suddenly there, smacking into her feet, her body, the side of her head, but nothing breaks, so the winch must have done its work. She pops the belt and harness, draws the Kang, and rises to a crouch. She can still hear that clanging bell far above, but otherwise the night is quiet. No sirens, no security cars, no cops.

Not yet anyway.

She steps across a meter of grassy turf, a sidewalk, and then down to a Nissan Jackrabbit, the multifuel IC model, which she parked here earlier in the day.

She keys the lock, gets in. The engine starts right up.

21

The terror, the thunderous hammering, and the pain are overwhelming. He feels himself being torn from his body, ripped from his own flesh and sent hurtling down a black passage at a speed too great to comprehend. Everything he's ever known, all that he was, all he might have been, is shredded away in an instant.

An ocean of searing white envelops him, burning, crushing, flaying, utterly devastating. The agony is unbearable, unending. The screams of a hundred million souls writhing in torment equal to his own reverberate through his tortured being. Every nerve, every iota of his consciousness, quivers like wires alive with a savage electric current, arcing, dancing, jerking and shaking with pain.

Through it all, he senses a presence, malignant, malevolent. Drawing him deeper into the horror. Taking pleasure in his agony. Reveling in every excruciating, rending, piercing, pounding, burning pain he suffers. A monstrous evil delighting in every little twinge of anguish vibrating through his being. A diabolical horror he will never escape, though he suffers unendurable agony throughout all eternity.

And it just goes on and on . . .

22

06-16-54/17:36:04

Roll cam.

The datajacked Sony CB-5000 in the steady-mount atop his helmet comes on-line with a minimum of fooling

around. His Seretech Evening Shade cybereyes with
FlareGuard and thermographic enhancement seem to be
working okay, for once, damn frag it, interfacing with
the Eyecrafter opticam implanted inside his skull. It's
another monkey-drek sumfabulous miracle. He keys the
tridlink controller on his right forearm to overlay his
direct-view vision with a full data readout, just to be
sure.

"Skeeter . . . ?"

J. B. looks back and forth like she can't see him. Skeeter's standing there on the sidewalk in a cloud of the
Asian biff's own elf-mage golden fairy dust, so of course
now the fraggin' biff can't see him. The stump-skanking
dust works so well he's invisible even to her! That's great,
just great. Real pro news, J. B. turns her back to him,
still quietly calling his name, sounding as muck-drekking
impatient as usual, Ms. High and Mighty Trid-o-Genic
News snoop Poop!

"Skeeter! *Where*—!"

Skeeter snaps his fingers.

"Oh!" she says, then turns around, peering toward
him. "Are you there?"

Skeeter clears his throat, snaps his fingers some more.
"Am I on?"

What in fragging drek does she think?

"Well . . . Here we go." J. B. flips at the long black
wave of hair curling down over her forehead. Skeeter
shifts his feet to get a straight-on view of her face. She
shifts the other way, damn dumb drekking dithead.

"This is Joi Bang for WHAM! Independent News,"
she says in a hushed voice, "and we're here on Twenty-
ninth Street in North Central Philly to take you inside
the international headquarters of the Humanis Policlub,
reputed arm of the Alamos 20,000 terrorist group and
alleged to be responsible for the murders and assassinations of metahumans, meta-posers, and meta-
sympathizers worldwide."

Damn frag it all anyway.

"Naturally we'll be using a hidden camera."

No dingle-dockle kidding, dork.

* * *

06-02-54/17:49:53

Establishing shot: Humanis Policlub HQ, slow pan across brick façade, entranceway framed by white columns, guarded by two big slags in stretch tees. A faint gold cloud glinting with motes of light wafts slowly about the faces of the muscleboys.

J. B. smiles. "Isn't it true," she says, "that the Humanis Policlub is a faction of Alamos Twenty-thousand?"

One of the muscleboys grins. "Who?"

"Never heard of 'em," says the other.

"Then, as members of the Humanis Policlub, you disclaim any involvement in the murders of hundreds if not thousands or millions of metapersons throughout the world?"

"We never killed anybody."

"We just trash 'em."

"*Beat* 'em to hell!"

"But we don't *kill* 'em."

"That wouldn't be moral."

"We're very moral people."

"We only give 'em what they deserve."

"Make 'em pay."

"For what they did."

"What they did to the world."

"And everything else."

"Yeah. Exactly."

06-02-54/18:03:21

Close-focus: a blonde biff with flawless features and *huge* jutting milkies smiles from behind her high desk in the lobby.

"No," she says. "In fact, as far as I'm aware, none of the members of the Humanis Policlub has any sort of criminal record whatsoever. The screening committee of the membership council would never accept such undesirables into the organization."

J. B. turns, peers off to Skeeter's right, and mouths the words, *"Are you getting this?"*

Of course he's getting it.

Fragging dithead brainless twit.

* * *

06-02-54/18:27:33

Slow pan, zoom in, close-focus: main hall, Policlub HQ. Doors closed and locked, guarded by muscleboys in tees. An easy five hundred fraggin' pixelhead citizens, pure humans supposedly, fill the folding chairs that flank the center aisle running straight to the head of the room.

Tonight's special guest: Armant DeCreux, imported direct from Euro headquarters. "Theees mongreel rassses challeeenge de veeraaa exeestonnnce of de puur humannns . . ."

Blinking dotbrain foreigners.

"Theees cray-churrss arre eeevilll by nat-churrr . . ."

Nithead dirtbrain crap.

"Theees eeelves espeeeciallie . . ."

Now there he might have a point.

Never trust a bulldink fraggin' elf.

Skeeter wouldn't trust a damn dandelion-eating elf even if his mudbrained sister *married* one, which she wouldn't, because she's got at least enough brains not to. Besides, he'd stomp one or both of them before they could ever pull it off.

06-02-54/19:14:06

Split image: main lens on Horace Glick, Philly chapter commander, cybereyes on J. B.

Zoom in, close-focus.

Roll cam.

"You say that the Humanis Policlub has irrefutable evidence that orks within the city of Philadelphia have banded together into outlaw groups that are committing savage acts of violence including murder-mutilations and cannibalism against the general populace?"

"It's not just the orks," Glick says. "The whole range of metatypes is involved. And this isn't just a local phenomenon."

"And you have evidence to prove that?"

"Absolutely irrefutable evidence."

"What sort of evidence?"

"Are you a news snoop or something?"

"Just a concerned citizen. What kind of evidence?"

"Vid, stills, you name it."

"Any eyewitnesses?"

"Dozens. Hundreds, in fact."

"Why haven't you presented this body of evidence to the city attorney for prosecution?"

"Oh, we have. You bet we have."

"And the city attorney has done nothing about it?"

"I think it's pretty clear where the city attorney's sympathies lie."

Sure it is.

Effin' dirtbrain poli skank.

23

When the blindfold comes off, Neona finds herself standing in some dark old decrepit hallway with black floor tiles and brown paneled walls covered with graffiti. Back the way she thinks she came, maybe ten meters off to her right, the corridor ends at a metal door. In the other direction, to her left, the hallway dissolves into black. Standing immediately around her are Hammer and his crew: Mickey and Dog Bite, the mage Dana, and Axle the rigger.

Smirking at her, Mickey now ties the black strip that had served as a blindfold around Neona's right upper arm. "Somethin' to remember me by," he says.

Sure.

Neona swallows, feeling a shiver and trying not to be too obvious about it. She's a little on edge. Mickey's chrome-silver eyes make him look inhumanly cool, and his whole sneering attitude suggests that his only interest in her is what she's got between her thighs. Dog Bite acts like he hates her, snapping and snarling, growling at her, arguing over practically anything she says. Hammer's stone-cold and treats her like she's utterly useless. Axle seems plain suspicious. Dana's the only one who behaves at all like a potential chum, willing to let her strut her

stuff. But just how much influence the mage has over the
rest of the group isn't at all clear.

Dog Bite presses a black stud in the wall. The doors
to an extra-wide elevator, maybe a freight elevator, slide
open, one rising, the other descending into the floor.
Hammer lights a Millennium Red with a click of a silver-
cased lighter and leads the group into the elevator.

Neona hesitates for the briefest moment, but there's no
point in trying to be careful now. If anybody has ideas
about acing her and hijacking her deck, they could do it
just as easily in this dingy hallway as wherever the elevator's going. She's past the point of no return. She'll
just have to play this one out, hope for the best, hope her
luck improves.

The elevator rumbles and vibrates, going up maybe
five or six stories. As the doors slide open again, Hammer lifts the smartgun that always seems to be dangling
from his hand, and rests the weapon against his shoulder.
Neona gnaws anxiously at her lower lip.

Someone, Dog Bite, nudges her from behind, pushing
her out of the elevator and directly into a room. The
room is gigantic, bigger than most apartments, any that
Neona's been in, anyway. Maybe fifteen, twenty meters
wide and almost as long. The ceiling is kind of low, but
that's standard for lofts, if this really is a loft, tucked in
above the main floors of the building. Neona sees a
kitchen area off to the left, a rolling bar and living room
furniture off to the right. Directly ahead is an open aisle
that leads to a hallway. Probably to bedrooms, Neona
guesses.

Dog Bite nudges her toward the right, and points,
"Over there! Ain't you got eyes!"

"Uh, yeah . . . yeah sure."

Set against one wall is a cushioned armchair. On the
table beside it is what looks like an industrial-grade telecom, black plastic and gleaming chrome, all the options, though the casing has apparently seen better days.
One chrome port in particular is blackened and scorched,
the black plastic around it seared.

"What happened to the telecom?" Neona grunts.

It's just a casual question, more a symptom of surprise

than anything else, but Dog Bite barks, "Never you mind! It's none of your effing business, slitch!"

Neona bites her lower lip, tries to contain her nerves. She's never met a real group of runners that didn't at least *know* a decker. A lot of groups *have* one. Probably most did. Maybe the scorch mark on the telecom is what happened to the decker they used to work with. Better just keep that thought to herself.

Hammer settles his bulk into an easy chair, crossing his legs over a hassock.

"Any time you're ready," he says.

Easy to say, but it's not that simple. Neona steels herself inwardly. If she's gonna get anything out of this at all, she can't let them think she's a total rube. They'll just take her for all she's worth and run, or worse. She turns to face Hammer squarely. "If I'm gonna do this for you guys, I want something up front. I don't work for free."

Before Hammer can respond, Dog Bite jumps on her again. "You want somethin'? I'll give you somethin'! Who the hell you think you are! You didn't tell us drek about that chip!"

"That chip was virgin."

"Sure it was!"

"There was nothing on it but that one data file! I can't pull out something that was never there!"

"You're a poser! That's what you are!"

Hammer and his crew are in the midst of getting started on a run. All Neona knows about it is that the group has to locate someone. Why they must do that or what happens when they succeed, she doesn't know, and at this point she doesn't really want to. She's got her own problems.

The chip in question contained a single data file on the person they're supposed to find. Examining that chip was the first hurdle. Ransacking the global Matrix for any data that might aid in the search, that might pinpoint the person's location, is the job before her now, and that's enough to worry about. That and what a successful run through the Matrix will do for her relations with Hammer and Company. Even if she never works with the group again, a good run might earn her a good contract through them, and that's just what she needs.

Hammer holds up a slip of paper, offers it to her. She walks over and takes it, looks at it, letters and numbers, a bank address. "There's five thousand nuyen in that account," Hammer says. "If you get what we need, it's yours. And maybe we'll have more to talk about then."

"Okay." It sounds fair, even good.

"If you don't get what we want, the money better still be there, or you're meat."

Neona nods. "You got no worries."

"I know."

"I mean, I'll get what you want."

"Just do it."

Like the man says . . .

Neona sits in the cushiony armchair beside the telecom and slides the gray macroplast case marked with the Fuchi logo out of her nylon bag. As she opens the case to bare the keyboard, she notices Axle, the rigger, peering at her intensely.

"Is that a Six?" he asks.

"Just the case."

The rigger nods, looking like he already knows the whole story. Neona figures he must know something about decks and deckers. Must be surprised to see her using a stock case. A lot of deckers would rather cut off an arm than work a deck right off the shelf. Or so they say. To hear them talk they'd much prefer some freakish collection of spare parts stuffed inside a junk case. And maybe that's what Neona would have said before she got her hands on a real Fuchi-6.

Back where she comes from, you don't tear up a perfectly good Rolls Royce just because it's "off the shelf." You scope it out to make sure it don't contain any surprises. You do what you can to improve it when you got the time and the money. The one thing you don't do is cannibalize it for parts and start building something on your own. Not unless you've got the equivalent of a Fuchi research lab and a mega-nuyen budget. A deck like a Fuchi-6 is too hard to come by. People die for a lot less.

She slots the deck's fiber-optic lead into the blackened

port on the telecom, powers up, and watches the deck's display as her start-up utility runs a quick diagnostic. Software is where she really takes pride in herself. She wrote her own start-up utility out of whole cloth in just a few hours. She also wrote or modified every other prog in the Fuchi's memory.

The deck checks out, like she knew it would. The telecom seems okay, too. She'll leave the deck's display on in case Hammer or someone else decides to watch over her shoulder. That might encourage them to trust her. Nothing she needs to keep secret will show on the screen anyway.

She slips a fiber-optic lead into the datajack in her head and slithers down a quick blackness.

Into the neon room . . .

It's a virtual workspace inside the deck, useful for programming and for aligning her head before she dives down a dataline and into the Matrix.

Tonight, she dives straight through . . .

Down the line . . .

And suddenly she isn't plain old Neona Jaxx anymore. Her infamous streaks of bad luck don't mean nothing. Her uncertainties fade to zero. She navigates the data stream like a born-to-fly electron angel, a ramjammer in pulsing gold neon, with a halo and wings and a keyboard guitar, and now she's skating ahead and into the glowing face of a pyramidal node. Her fingers rush over the keys of her keyboard guitar and a swirling stream of alphanumerics sluices from the integral speaker, spirals into the node and disappears. An instant later, the node's open and she's streaming ahead, into the Northeast Philly local telecommunications grid.

She makes a telecom call of herself and heads straight to Directory Assistance, then fires herself through a succession of nodes till she hits the Delaware County LTG and the Sanwa Bank's W.C.C.A.N., Worldwide Customer Computer-Access Net. Like any legitimate customer, she takes the front door, checks on the account Hammer described, and uses the secret passcode to stash five thousand nuyen in an account of her own.

Somewhere back along a few hundred klicks of fiber-

optic cable, her meat fingers race across the keys of her
Fuchi-6, and her meat-body voice says, "Okay . . . The
nuyen checks. Here I go . . ."

A discontented male voice barks something nasty, but
she doesn't hear it, just the tone, and right now that
doesn't mean anything to her.

Next stop: Austin LTG.

She loads and executes the Chinese Flyer. She got this
along with the Fuchi deck in that run back in Miami, the
run that killed her chums. In its original form, the Flyer
had a traitorous subroutine that launched an independent
prog the moment they started their run. That prog informed their intended target that she was coming, and
what her chums would be doing while she rode Matrix
overwatch. That's how her chums got killed. She almost
got fried herself. Since then Neona has written the secret
subroutine out of the program code. The Flyer was more
than worth the effort.

The Chinese Flyer isn't subtle, and she has to rewrite
the code after every run, but she's never found anything
faster—and right now fast is what she needs.

Fast is what she gets.

The Flyer kicks in and suddenly she's a U.C.A.S. military red alert screaming into and through the Philly Regional Telecommunications Grid with all the authority of
a Federated-Boeing Black Eagle pitching full-bore into
an attack run. System access nodes slam open ahead of
her. Subprocessing units snap to and shunt other bitstream traffic the hell out of her way. She hits an ITT-Rand
code-orange satellite uplink under the guise of a crash-
priority override, and in just milliseconds she's through
the link and blasting down into the regional grid for Austin, Texas.

Every kind of alarm goes off in her wake, but now
she's an ordinary telecom utility merely going through
the motions per her imbedded autoexec commands. The
Rand deckers who come screaming after her ass whip
right on by without giving her a second look.

That's about as subtle as the Flyer gets.

In the real world, meat fingers play over keys. In the

virtual reality of the Matrix, her angel icon dives through a node into the Austin LTG.

She streams past the octagonal MCC cluster and the Sematech pyramid, then through a node with whirling revolving doors. That puts her into Doogie's Palace, a virtual Voodoo Chili stand in snowy black and white, with a bell on the counter and a sign in pulsing red neon that reads Press for Service.

Her master persona control program is already on-line. The gold ramjammer Angel plays her keyboard guitar. A swirling stream of alphanumerics streaks from the keyboard speaker, arcing up and spiraling down to tap the bell on the counter.

The bell blats like an air horn.

Doogie flashes into existence, or rather his icon does. There's a burst of spectroscopic color and then suddenly there he is, looking like an oversized lap dog, a mutt or a mongrel as big as a man, and fat, with long, floppy ears and neon shades. He sits on a tall stool behind the service counter.

"What's up, Angel?" Doogie says.

"Where's the Bazaar?"

"Three guesses."

Neona doesn't hesitate. To find the Bazaar, you have to know Doogie or someone else who keeps track, and to get what you need out of Doogie you have to play his guessing game, and play it like you mean it. Ordinary meat people might think it strange. Neona knows better. "Okay," she says. "Zürich!"

"Nope."

"Hong Kong!"

"Nope."

"Managua!"

"Nope."

"Well, I give up!"

Bells, whistles, sirens, flashing, flaring lights, and even a foghorn all go off. "Rabat!" Doogie shouts. *"Ha!"*

"Thanks, Doogie."

"Sure, babe. See ya 'round the trons."

The golden angel blasts into the regional grid, through a series of uplinks and downlinks, then down into the

Rabat LTG. Neona's meat fingers never stop moving.
There's always new code to be written, ice and deckers
coming after her, and nodes coming up ahead. The Chinese Flyer is her ramjammer engine, but she's the captain
and her fingers are the helm. Think fast or die, write that
code or crash. If she isn't fast, she's going nowhere and
maybe something big and nasty's coming up from behind.

Down at the far end of the local grid, she skates
through the pulsing neon tent flaps of a node, down the
curving kaleidoscope of a sculptured dataline, through
another set of tent flaps, then comes abruptly to a halt in
front of Hassan's Arch.

The Arch is huge, like the front face of a castle, but
with a giant keyhole archway bored right through the
middle. The huge keyhole opening blazes with blue electric. A pair of enormous, shiny chrome trolls with massive war axes stand guard in front of the keyhole. An
army of paranormal animals flank the trolls: aardwolves
and bogies, boobrie birds, deathrattlers and devil jack
diamonds, firedrakes, gila demons, greater wolverines.
Hell hounds and more. The ledges above the keyhole are
lined with harpies and troglodytes, black annis apes like
huge orangutans with vicious fangs. Up on the battle-
ments squats a wyvern.

How much of this is just animation? How much is real
IC? Neona doesn't know and isn't real interested in finding out.

A radiant red window appears and then disappears
right in front of her. From it comes a neon eyeball the
size of a basketball, but sporting a little red beanie and
a pair of mirrorshades. It zips straight into her face, zips
all around her, back and forth, up and down. This much
is standard stuff—access ice—a Fuchi Watcher 7K, though
apparently modified. Most systems use access intrusion
countermeasures as the switch to turn on serious ice if
an illegal entry is detected. Here at Hassan's Arch every
entry is illegal till proven otherwise. Neona's fingers fly.
The golden angel strums her keyboard guitar. Alphanumerics stream up and around and right in through the
Watcher's shades.

The eyeball sprouts a pair of skinny arms, snaps its fingers in time with her bitstream, does a little dance, then zips away, vanishing through another window.

"Welcome to Hassan's Gate," the wyvern says.

The golden angel laughs, laughs loudly, and exclaims, "Bismillah! Balek! Balek!"

That means something like, "Goddammit, get out of the way!" in some Arab language, or so Neona understands. Whatever it means, it's a virtual code. The last part of the entry code sequence.

The blazing blue electric filling the keyhole archway vanishes. A dozen different massive doors, gates, grills, and iris-openings slam open in rapid sequence, thundering.

The trolls step aside.

The golden angel janders through.

Beyond the arch comes the Bazaar, a labyrinth of booths and stalls, wandering alleys populated by clowns and acrobats, fire-eaters and jugglers, fortunetellers and a never-ending variety of merchants. You can find almost anything you want here, from classic master persona control programs to killer utilities to secret data on the latest techno-wizardry being cooked up by Fuchi I.G. Call it a private LTG.

What Neona wants is a dusty chrome snake charmer in a flashing green and red striped turban, and she finds him standing in front of a pulsing green and red tent with his dusty chrome cobra. Swirling alphanumerics emerge from the charmer's flute. The golden angel plays a few chords of her own. The charmer raises a hand in a wave. Neona skates in through the tent entrance.

Down the rugged stone steps of a sculptured dataline.

And into the face of a node like a pair of massive metal bank vault doors. Before the doors stands a skinny little man in a white robe. He holds a big white book. He's called the Usher and he bows as Neona approaches.

"Usher," she says, "I need to see Book."

"The Book is very busy, Angel."

"Usher, it's important."

"Your membership is expired, Angel."

The angel lifts her iconic hands and shows the Usher

the treasure she holds, a pile of shimmering gold coins winking with the logo "Two thousand nuyen." Somewhere a million kilometers away to her backside her meat fingers are racing over the keys, snatching the nuyen from her account, bringing it up.

The Usher smiles and extends a broad, flat plate. Neona opens her hands. The coins sluice down into the depression of the plate and vanish. The Usher nods.

"You can go right in, Angel."

The doors slam open.

She skates through, into the claustrophobic alleys of the Exchange. Orange and red datastores like books rise on row after row of shelves till they blur into infinity. Neona skates down the aisles till she spies the familiar icon of what is supposed to be a chubby old man with wispy hair, eyeglasses, and a rumpled suit. A chubby old man, except that he is pure, gleaming chrome and his glasses and suit are electric blue.

"Book!"

Book turns toward her, peering at her over the rims of his glasses. The golden angel skates right up.

"I need some data."

"What do you have to exchange?"

That's why they call it that, the Exchange. The membership fee gets you in, but you have to tell something to learn something. It can be a high price to pay. This time, the price of her future is the best and only real secret from her past.

She tells about the run back in Miami, the fixer who set up her and her chums, who got her friends killed and forced her to flee. One day, she'd like to get back at that fragger, but right now she's got to concentrate on making herself a new life.

When she finishes, Book smiles faintly and nods. "Interesting data. What would you like to know?"

"I need to find somebody called Striper."

Book stares at her for a moment, then says, "You'll have to give me more of a handle than that. I'm not a miracle worker, you know."

Neona smiles to herself. Book may not be a miracle

worker, but he can sort through mega-reams of data like nobody she's ever met. Nobody and no program.

"Striper's a runner. Heavy-duty. You know. A real wetworker."

"A professional killer."

"Yeah, I guess."

"Is she chipped?"

"I don't know." The data file from Hammer wasn't clear about that. "She's supposed to be strong, and really tough. There's a report that she got shot up by the cops one time, then just up and ran off. Maybe she uses magic. I don't know."

"Where's she from?"

For some reason, she had expected Book to just reach out, pull a datastore book from some shelf, and tell her everything she needed to know. Because that was the way it worked in the past. She decides to speed things up and sends her fingers flying across the keyboard of her virtual guitar. The bitstream of data spirals into Book's book. That's everything she knows, all the data from the chip Hammer made her examine: digitized photos, coded police and news reports, and so on, including a lot of what might be only rumor. It's enough to sketch out an image, but that's all. If Neona's going to find Striper, she'll need a lot more data, hard data.

"Seattle," Book says after a couple of moments. "I think we'll start with Seattle references." Book leads her around the stacks of virtual datastores. Around and around and around. It's a while before he pauses and says, "There's a good chance, say seventy-six percent, that this woman you're looking for once traveled from Macao to Seattle under the name of Mari Tan, and also from Hong Kong to Manila, Taiwan to Macao, Shanghai to Osaka . . . Hong Kong to Taiwan . . . and Osaka to San Francisco."

"So that's like . . . all over southeast Asia."

"China, Japan, the South Pacific, and the west coast of North America."

Wow.

"There's also an even better chance, say eighty-three percent, that this same woman traveled from Seattle to

Los Angeles and Seattle to Chicago under the name of Fallon Sontag.''

"How do you figure?"

"Data from the Seattle Bureau of Customs and Passport Control. The probabilities I quoted primarily reflect the degree of correspondence between the digitized images you gave me and those registered with the data base. I could tell you the algorithm I used in making the comparison, but let's just say it's better than any the government uses and leave it at that."

"What else you got?"

"Well, let's see." Book looks into his book, adjusts his glasses. "Mari Tan is listed as Han Chinese, twenty-three years of age, black hair, brown eyes, one point seven meters tall, fifty-six point five kilograms in weight, a citizen of China and resident of Hong Kong, and a dealer in antiques. Fallon Sontag is listed as twenty-five, brown hair, hazel eyes, one point seven meters tall, weighing fifty-nine kilograms, a citizen of Seattle and a freelance media snoop."

"Sounds like two different people."

"I imagine that's the idea."

Neona doesn't doubt it. The idea of a bogus ID is, after all, to let a person go around like someone other than who she really is. The trick, Neona guesses, would be to paint a picture close enough to fool the Customs inspectors, but different enough to really frag up a computer-based search for comparisons. A minor difference in vital statistics might do it. The kind of search some hokey government office might run probably wouldn't use digitized images because it would eat up too much memory and too much processing time.

And, come to think of it, Neona wouldn't be surprised if Striper the person corresponded to neither of her supposed physical descriptions, that of Mari Tan or Fallon Sontag. More likely, the real Striper was somewhere in between.

"Which identity's more recent?"

"Didn't I say that?"

"You said Sontag's twenty-five—"

"And Tan is, or was, twenty-three. The Sontag ID is more recent."

"Do you think both IDs are bogus?"

"From you, Angel, I'll take that as a legitimate question, rather than a sassy remark. Yes, I think they're both bogus. Did you ever hear of a killer having a real ID?"

"Not lately."

"Well, there you are." Book checks a few more datastores. "The Mari Tan identity originates in China, in Beijing, so you can forget about getting more on that ID. Not even the Chinese know how to penetrate the bureaucratic morass of their government data bases. As for the Fallon Sontag identity, there are some possibilities. Have a look at this code."

Book hands her a book, a pulsing red virtual datastore. The pages swirl with alphanumeric characters, but they're sweet sweet music to the golden angel. She recognizes the style of the code at once. "This is Kidd Karney's One-Oh-One-Oh!"

"I'd say that's probable."

The original Matrix mon and cyberjock—Kidd Karney—what a shock, and a good one, too. Kidd Karney was one of the first real ramjammers she ever met, and they're still friends, good friends too. Kidd Karney helped her escape from Miami. He taught her what real Matrix-running was all about. Now she finds that the very same decker almost certainly wrote the code that created Striper's bogus Fallon Sontag ID.

Her luck is definitely on the rise.

24

Neona wastes no time exiting the Exchange, pausing only to make Book blush a strobing orange and red by giving him a kiss and a hug. She's on through the Bazaar and Hassan's Arch in no time flat. Kidd Karney's node is just a flash and a half away by satellite. She hurtles down into the LTG for Reno, Nevada, and starts hunting through the constructs blazing to the horizon with garish lights. Along one narrow alley she finds a neon carnival tent bedecked with a dozen flashing signs advertising the "meanest decker in the Matrix." A construct like that is easy to miss in the Reno LTG, all the more so because half the deckers on the local grid imitate Kidd Karney's style.

A squeeze of the big fat red nose of the animated clown standing in front of the tent puts her through the door.

And into a cage . . .

The bars of the cage are black and sizzling with coded-red security IC. Sizzling too are the chains and manacles that seize the golden angel's wrists and ankles and tug her spread-eagled up off the floor. The whole node takes on a reddish hue as the color encompasses her icon. It feels like a swarm of little bugs with creepy-crawler legs are skittering all over her meat body somewhere a billion klicks away to her rear. The feeling makes her squirm. The virtual effects may be red but the ice is pure black, the blackest. It's a virtual trap with electron teeth. Kidd Karney has been known to brain-fry the occasional corporate decker who finds the datapath to his tent. There's nothing to do now but wait, wait and twitch.

"Dammit, Kidd!"

And exclaim.

Momentarily, a bullet-shaped roller coaster car with a leering demon mask of a front-end comes roaring out of one of the two black sculptured datalines at the rear of the tent, screaming to a halt in front of the sizzling cage. Kidd Karney likes dramatic entrances. Tonight, he's in his sheik get-up, wearing a hat like a golden pillow with tassels, a flowing robe, all kinds of sparkling jewelry and funny shoes with curling toes. With him in the rear of the roller coaster car is a bevy of absurdly voluptuous bimbos garbed in bellydancer outfits and fawning over him like slaves.

"Hoi, Angel!"

"Hoi yourself!"

Kidd Karney points a remote. The sizzling stops, the manacles release, and the front of the cage swings open.

Neona skates over to the roller coaster car. Kidd Karney
waves her into the rear-facing seat, which she hates, but
there's no room to spare on the front-facing seat, even
though it's as big as a bed, because of all the bimbos.
Neona barely has time to sit down before Kidd Karney
shouts, "Here we *goooooooooo!*"

The car hurtles ahead into blackness, looping upside-
down and around, whipping through curves with a demon's fury, turning backward, spinning like a top. It's
heart-attack city. Neona screams. Kidd Karney screams
louder. The bimbos scream even louder. The car hurtles
around a curve and suddenly they're all flying right out
of the car, landing on massive pillows in a room like a
desert sheik's tent. Neona takes a moment collecting herself. Kidd Karney and the bimbos of course land in a
luxurious sprawl. The bimbos shift from screaming to
fawning without missing a beat.

"Glad to see you're still in the trons, Angel."

"Yeah, thanks," Neona replies, just a bit breathlessly.
"I need your help with something."

"Heavies still coming on?"

From Miami? "No, this is new. I'm on a run."

"Spreading some nuyen around?"

"Yeah, I got a little to play with."

"Zero sheen, muchacha. I just slotted mucho dinero
with my Johnson. Took a run down Yucatan way. Got
coin to spare. What kinda goose you lookin' t'douche?"

Kidd Karney had a way of phrasing things sometimes,
ranging from the genuinely weird to the monumentally
disgusting. Sometimes, it was cute. Other times, it was
just odd or disgusting. "I need some data, jammer to
jammer, you know? You wrote some code, made this
Striper babe a bogus ID?"

"I did?"

"No question." She runs her fingers across her keyboard guitar, cuts a few quick riffs. Kidd Karney lifts his
head like he's taking in pure ruby tunes from the alphanumerics that spiral down to encircle him.

"Nova code," he says finally. "But it ain't my One-
Oh, Angel."

"You gotta be yakking."

"Uh-uh," Kidd Karney replies. "I never even heard of X. Striper? Whoever. But I'll tell ya who did write the code."

"Who?"

"The ebon boy."

"Who?"

"Jammer called the Dodger."

"Yeah?"

"Ain't you heard the handle?"

"Should I?"

"Well, he's only a silicon god, a ram-jam-thank-you-ma'am coded-to-the-max cyber hero, coming on with lightning fingers and killer chips from hell! Are you a Mona Lisa or what? You never heard of *the Dodger*? Where you been living, lady?"

"Well, how would I find him?"

"Find the Ghost in the Grid? You don't find him, babe. You post bulletins. Dear Dodger, I'm a teeny-weeny decker doobie. Please write home. End of message."

"He must be slick."

"If you gotta ask, don't ask."

"Where do I post?"

"Try Seattle."

That again. It's beginning to look to Neona like Seattle might be the key to this crazy puzzle of tracking down Striper. By the end of another frenetic roller coaster ride, she's more or less convinced of that.

Satellite links to Seattle RTG.

She takes a wide sweep of the local grids. Kidd Karney clued her in about the most likely virtual hangouts, networks, and bulletin boards to try. She leaves messages for the Dodger.

Nothing much happens.

She runs down a few leads on her own. What little she uncovers merely confirms that Striper's Fallon Sontag identity originated in Seattle about two years ago. Sontag comes complete with SIN, address, telecom number, social security, med plan, etcetera, etcetera.

Time keeps slipping by.

What she really should do, Neona decides, is check out the Philly LTGs for references to Sontag. It's the best

lead she's got for the moment. She blasts through the
links, up and down, and hurtles down into the Central
Philly grid. As she streams past the mammoth, pulsing
disk of the SmithKliner system construct, she spies an
unusual figure, a little black boy in a sparkling cloak of
silver, standing right there on the datalines in front of
SmithKliner. Isn't that supposed to be the Dodger's icon?

The ebon boy?

It's too much of a shock for her to react in time. She
streaks on down the lines, then doubles back. As she
rounds the curving façade of the SmithKliner disk, a voice
speaks to her from behind, from right behind her shoulders.

"Thy voice is loud, yet sweet in my ears, Angel with
an axe. Yea, dear lady, I have come to hear thy song."

She stops, turns around.

Nothing's there.

"What . . . ?"

Suddenly, the voice is coming from right behind her
again. "Fair lady, have thee no music to play for me?"

"Where are you?"

She turns again, and again there's nothing to be seen,
no icon, no clue as to who or what she's talking to. The
voice again comes from her rear. "Prithee, play for me,
Angel. Play and explain thy summons."

This is incredible, unnerving. "What are you doing?
Stop it! *Stop it!*"

She turns and suddenly he's there, right in front of her,
facing her, the ebon boy in his silver cloak. He bows
with a flourish of his arm. "Forgive me, dear lady."

"What?" That's all she can think of to say. She blurts
it. She's too busy wondering how this small iconic figure
came to be in the Central Philly LTG. That's the impossible part. The messages she left for Dodger requested a
meet in Kansas City. How could he have traced her to
Philly? through satellite links and everything? That was
more than just wiz decking. More like magic.

"How . . . how did you find me?"

"Modesty forbids the necessarily complex explanations."

"You're . . . you're the Dodger, right?"

With another bow the ebon boy replies, "At your service."

Neona opens her mouth to reply, but then a thought occurs. She doesn't want to play this like she played with Book and Kidd Karney. Dodger's not a chummer of hers. He's an unknown quantity. Who knows what connections or secret agendas he might have? She should play it careful, maybe just a bit cagey. Just in case.

"Ummm," she says. "I guess you don't know me . . ."

"A lady of such dazzling electron beauty could not long escape the notice of any true gallant of the Matrix."

"Yeah?" What a concept. She wonders where the slag learned his lingua. It's like nothing she ever heard before. "Well, I'm a chum of Kidd Karney."

"Verily."

"Yeah. Yeah, *right*! And Kidd Karney said, he thought . . . well, maybe you can help me out. I'm trying to contact this wiz runner called Striper. I'm working go-between for somebody . . . who wants to hire Striper."

"Why come to me, lady Angel?"

"Well, I heard Striper's based in Seattle. And so are you. And, I mean, you're *the Dodger,* right?"

A little bare-faced admiration never hurts. From what Kidd Karney said, and what she's seen for herself, Neona figures that the Dodger could find just about anyone he might want to.

A few moments tick past.

The ebon boy just gazes at her. There's nothing about the icon to suggest what the Dodger might be thinking. "At last," he says.

"Huh?"

"Fair lady, allow me to guide your search."

"Oh . . . well, great!"

"Pray, take my hand."

She hesitates over that, but what choice does she have? Search the Philly LTGs for a connection she may never find? Better to take the ebon hand of chance in hopes that the Dodger will lead her right to the source, directly to Striper.

One touch and it's like they're welded together.

For a moment, it's panic time. She realizes she couldn't pull free even if she tried. She feels a tug and suddenly the grid's hurtling past, becoming a blur that resolves into blackness. She has no idea where they're going, but it's faster than she's ever gone before. She's helpless and squirming. She feels like a billion creepy-crawlers are running all over her body, only this time they're on the inside, all throughout her insides, even inside her head, behind her eyes, and she can't stand it. She's twitching convulsing, crying out . . .

And suddenly she's in a node, a sculptured node. It looks like a small square room with bare plastiwood walls and a matching floor. A bare bulb hanging down out of the darkness casts a stark white sheen over the pulsing brownish hues of the virtual room. A tall iconic man with black hair and heavy brows and wearing a casual black suit comes in through the only door, closes it, then pauses facing her, hands at his sides.

"You want Striper?" he says.

His voice is like a low, raspy whisper, like a voice gone too raw for speech. It makes Neona nervous. This whole biz is making her nervous, more than nervous. She can feel the sweat streaming down her meat body. She better be really careful. "Uhh, yeah . . . I, I got a job for Striper. I'm contacting for a Johnson. You know?"

"What's the job?"

"I don't know that. I just know it's hot. And the pay's wiz. I'm supposed to set up a meet."

"I can smell lies."

"What?"

"Your lies."

"Hey, it's no lie!" She turns to look to her rear, for some way out of this node, but there's nothing back there but another blank plastiwood wall. She sends her fingers flying over the keys of her guitar, but before she can initiate even a single prog, two more iconic men appear, like they're coming right out of the walls. Neona catches a blur of movement from the corners of her eyes and suddenly the two iconic men are right there, on either side of her. They seize her arms, tug her hands from her keyboard guitar, hold her like they're welded to her, becoming a part of her program.

And now she can't get her hands to her keyboard.

A whimper escapes from her lips.

"Please . . ."

The man in front of the door steps toward her, and now his face is changing, darkening, turning black, like he's growing fur, and swelling, growing huge with eyes that burn like fire and fangs that flash like ice, and his massive snarling maw comes closer and closer, then swallows her whole.

Switch off, lights out.

She's gone.

25

The main entrance of the Wanamaker Mall just off Market Street soars atrium-style to seven stories, and echoes with the voices of the hundreds passing across the main floor. Tikki joins the crowds taking the escalators to the sublevel concourse. A broad passage leading off the northern end of the concourse connects directly with the Thirteenth Street subway station. Telecoms line the walls. Tikki makes calls from places like this, at the heart of the metroplex, to minimize the chance of police or other security agencies picking up her conversations in random scans of telecom lines. She picks a stand, puts a wad of chewing gum over the visual pickup, then checks her wrist chronograph. When the time hits 20:05:00, she starts dialing.

The telecom's display goes black.

"Who's this?" a male voice says in Japanese.

"Two guesses."

In another moment or two, Black Mist comes on the line. "Yes?"

"Anything?"

"One interesting inquiry."

Interesting means trouble. It could be as simple a thing as trouble in the telecom lines or trouble of a more profound variety. Protocol guides her response. She hangs up, folds another piece of chewing gum into her mouth, then joins the crowds moving into the subway station. The next arriving train fires her two blocks down the line to the Market East station. She picks another telecom, gums the visual pickup, and dials.

Black Mist answers. "Yes?"

"What's interesting?"

"Contact Steel."

That *is* interesting. Steel is a special name for a special person. It demands her immediate attention. "What else?"

"Nothing."

She hangs up, turns. Stepping up from her rear is a Flash Point Enforcement trooper carrying a compact H & K MP-5 TX submachine gun and wearing a full array of semi-flexible body armor, including helmet with polarized faceplate and heavy insulated boots. Tikki is not surprised. She not only heard him coming, she smelled him coming. She wonders just in passing if he noticed an errant bulge in her jacket created by the Kang automatic holstered at the small of her back.

"What's that?" asks a metallic remodulated voice.

The trooper points toward the telecom. Tikki keeps her eyes on the trooper, gives him a puzzled expression and a noise of inquiry. "Uuh?"

"I'd call that defacing private property."

She replies with a quick burst of Russian, a few stock phrases. She also gives him a look like she doesn't know what he's trying to tell her. The trooper shifts toward the telecom, pointing, jammering ever more vehemently. When he's near enough to touch the unit, Tikki reaches over, pries the gum from the lens of the telecom's visual pickup, and pops it into her mouth. The gum is what this is all about.

The trooper stares at her for a couple of moments.

"Get the hell out," he says.

Tikki turns and goes.

* * *

She dumps the stolen Suzuki Aurora in an alley leading
off Delaware Avenue, not far from the river, then crosses
another alley about as broad as a football field and strewn
with garbage, piles of debris, broken chunks of concrete,
twisted metal struts, burnt-out rusted cars, and old junk.
At the rear of a deteriorating three-story brick building
stand a trio in worn black synthleather jackets: two males,
one female. They're dressed like gangers, but that's deceiving. They are sentries, Tikki knows, and they see her
approaching despite the dark. In all likelihood, they
smelled her before she ever stepped into view. Tikki
knows that because she knows what they are. Their smell
makes it clear. Like her, they may look human, but are
in fact a very different kind of animal. In some ways,
they have more in common with her than any human.

The three standing sentry duty wait with weapons at
the ready. One male holds a Colt Manhunter, the other
a Mossberg CMDT combat shotgun. The female holds a
Scorpion machine pistol with a curving thirty-five-round
clip.

As Tikki draws near, the darkness to her left and right
flickers with movement, dark shapes barely glimpsed out
the corners of her eyes. She knows what's moving in on
her flanks without having to look. Without needing to
hear the quiet growl that arises briefly a few meters away
to her right. Wolven Weres in their natural form—two
males, two females. The pack is taking no chances tonight. They know a serious predator when they see one.
And when they smell one.

Tikki pauses, facing the two-legs at the rear of the
building. The male with the big Colt automatic steps out
a little ahead of the other two. He smells wary, uncertain,
even a little confused.

"If you want to live, go away," he growls.

Faintly, Tikki shakes her head. She isn't worried. Not
even about the pair of four-legs creeping around to her
rear, boxing her in. Doubtless, that's part of the reason
why the male in front of her is being so cautious. She's
very calm. That means she smells calm, too. Calm and
in control.

"Need to contact Steel," she says.

"Don't know the name."

"Don't yak me, *boy*."

Tikki summons a quick surge of anger, feels the heat flash up the back of her neck. That breeds an unmistakable change in the air, and wolven Weres never miss a scent. Even in human form their sense of smell makes a human's insignificant, irrelevant, by comparison. The male shifts his stance. His whole attitude changes, as though he's not sure whether to attack or back off. He glances at the other two-legs, then looks back at Tikki. "Who are you?"

This is a first contact here in Philly. Tikki doesn't plan to give anything away unless she has to. "I know Steel. Steel knows me. Steel's waiting for me to call."

The two-legs exchange more glances. Do they know one another's thoughts by means of scent alone? That's Tikki's guess. None of the three speak or make any obvious gesture. They simply look at each other, then the female turns to descend the concrete steps leading to a basement-level door. The pair of males look back at Tikki. They all wait.

In a few moments, the female returns.

"Follow me," she says.

Tikki follows, down the steps, through a door, through a dark section of corridor maybe three meters long, then through another door. One door is closed before the other opens, so the light from inside the second door never shows outside. The second door lets into a small, bare room lit by a single bulb hanging down from the ceiling. The only furniture is a worn wooden table with a single chair. The male who sits in the chair is big and brawny, trim but heavily muscled. His hair is black. His eyebrows all but meet above the bridge of his nose. His arms, too, are covered with black hair. More hair shows from his palms. He wears a black synthleather vest, shatjeans, and big black boots. His right arm lies casually on the table. Embedded into the table top is a long knife standing upright next to his hand.

He gazes intently at Tikki for almost a minute, then says in a low voice, "What are you?"

Tikki ignores the question. The male probably knows

she's Were just by her smell. He's probably never encountered one like her before. Her particular breed is
very rare. Let him wonder what she is. "I'm supposed
to contact Steel."

"You're not a sister."

Not one of the pack, is what he means. Tikki's heard
the style of talk before. She is anything but one of the
pack, this male's pack, any pack. She shakes her head.
"The handle is Striper."

"How do you know Steel?"

"Not your problem."

The male watches her a few moments more, then rises,
pulling the knife from the table top and slipping it into
the sheath hanging from his belt. "Wait here."

Tikki nods, very faintly.

The male goes through the door opposite where Tikki
entered. She waits, standing still, arms at her sides. She
doesn't need to look to know that the female who led her
in here is waiting by the door at her back, and that a pair
of the four-legs are waiting there also. Their smell is
plain. If she looked, she would see a pair of massive
wolven Weres in their true form, ears laid back against
their furry skulls.

The big male soon returns. He looks at Tikki, then
very deliberately reaches across to her side of the table
and plants the knife firmly into the table top. This is not
an invitation to participate in some obscure ritual of the
pack. Rather, it's a challenge to prove herself, a special
protocol, previously arranged with Steel.

Tikki tugs the knife free, wraps her left hand around
the blade, checks to make sure the male is watching, then
squeezes and tugs the knife free. The feel of the blade
slicing through her palm tugs at her lips, forming a ruthless sneer. She lifts her hand, palm out, so the male can
see the cut. Blood forms into rivulets trickling down over
her palm. Then it stops. She licks the blood away and
shows her palm again. There is nothing to be seen now
but the palm of her hand and a faint reddish smear. The
cut is healed.

The smell of the blood and her physical reaction to
pain and injury wash through the air. One of the four-

legs outside briefly howls. One of the Weres behind her growls, deep and low, as if responding to menace. The big male before her watches with eyes that grow wide, then narrow.

Tikki buries the point of the knife in the table top. The male reaches over and jerks it free, then returns the knife to his sheath. "This way."

Tikki nods.

The male leads her down another short hall, past several doors, all closed. The air in the corridor reeks of female smells, like someone has just given birth. That probably explains the number of sentries outside, and the numbers keeping watching in their natural form. When the alpha female goes into labor, the entire pack goes on the defensive. Wolven Weres are very protective of their young. Tikki has learned that from experience.

The male opens a door near the end of the corridor, motions Tikki inside, and closes the door behind her.

The room is small and almost bare. On the table along the left wall is a standard Mitsuhama personal telecom with a micro screen and visual pickup and a molded plastic handset for privacy. Beside that is a gadget the average citizen probably never sees.

Tikki spends a moment looking it over. She's seen models like it before. It comes in a hard-shell case a bit bigger and thicker than an ordinary briefcase. The lid, standing open, bares a black macroplast faceplate fitted with a display screen, a small keyboard, some switches, and graphic indicators. The fiber-optic line from the telecom plugs into a port beside the keyboard. Another line, plugged into the adjoining port, rises up to vanish through a small hole in the ceiling. That probably connects to a satellite dish on the roof of a nearby building. What the dish is linked to is anyone's guess, but Tikki is confident that any call made through the setup will be virtually untraceable.

She takes up the handset from the telecom, lifts it to the side of her head.

The voice she hears is inhumanly hoarse, a rasp, a coarse, breathy whisper. It belongs to Castellano, also known as Steel. He is one of a handful of people whom

Tikki regards with a special degree of respect. He would make a dangerous enemy. More than that, he understands what it is to be loyal.

"Problem," Castellano says.

"Yes?" Tikki replies. To anyone else, she might have said, "Whose problem? Yours or mine?" With Castellano, things are not that simple. His problem might well be hers, too.

"Decker came to my node."

"Your what?"

"My computer."

Tikki exhales deeply, rolls her eyes. Decker lingo often seems designed to be as irritating as it is incomprehensible. She prefers plain, ordinary words. "So?"

"The decker wanted Striper."

"Why?"

"Unknown." A few moments pass. Castellano is not a big talker. His words come slowly. He uses them sparingly. "Claimed to be fronting for a Johnson."

"Yeah?"

"Big job. Big pay. All lies."

This is not a good thing. Tikki has had enough experience to realize that there are only two reasons why someone should try to contact her: either to hire her or to kill her. The implication here is plain. A legitimate inquiry for her services would not rouse Castellano to suspicion.

As far as Tikki is concerned, the truth of what Castellano says goes without question. He's proven himself too many times. There are no lies in Castellano's world. There may be half-truths and shades of gray, but he can smell a lie even as it is born, and he cannot tolerate the stink. He has the instincts of a hunter. He has the senses of a wolven Were.

If he says a thing is a thing, it's a fact.

"Traced the line," Castellano goes on to say. "Originated your area. Thought you should know."

"Right."

Castellano gives her the specifics, which are few and swiftly conveyed. "I'm expanding," he adds. "Work in your area. You available?"

"Not now."

"Later."

"No question." For tonight's favor, and others, she would make herself available. First, though, she has a problem to deal with. Before that even, she has to meet Adama.

"Call when you're free."

"Soon."

"Good."

The music throbs and pounds through the spectral dark like a thing alive, vibrant with power and thundering with menace. The round central dance floor flickers and flashes with blasts of orange, red, and yellow laser fire. Tables outlined in neon of an infernal hue line the curving walls. Between the grotesquely writhing bodies and parts of bodies on the dance floor and the infernally burning tables runs a broad, curving aisle broken into segments by four rampways leading down.

This is the uppermost floor of a place called the Seven Circles Club, where each level was named for a division of a place called Hell. Tikki is familiar with the concept. The Buddhists, for instance, named 136 places reserved for the torment and punishment of the dead, and Buddhism is something Tikki has heard a little about from time to time.

She takes the ramps down toward the lowest level.

Whores of both genders in Minimalist thongs and halters line the rampways, displaying massive pecs and perfect breasts, and offering to play any game, sate any desire, for fees and even for free. Most are obviously male or female. Others smell like one but resemble the other. Some even resemble different races, those not strictly human, such as elves. Patrons of the club come in practically every imaginable form, from poser elves to make-believe cats and sharks, phony samurai and pretend-Romans. Most wear Minimalist fashion: halters and thongs, shredded body stockings, straps and cultured chains. The elite among the decadent crowds adorn themselves with shifts and robes and electro-bodypaint that flashes with ever-changing patterns of color and graphic sexual imagery.

Down on the fourth level, someone jostles Tikki's shoulder and curses her. Tikki bares her teeth with irritation and swings her right forearm like a club, the studded guard on her arm adding impact to the blow. Staggering away from her, a man falls, spraying blood. Anywhere else that would cause a commotion. Here, though, it's just another part of the night's entertainment. The Seven Circles Club is no ordinary nightclub. This is where the suits and salarymen and exec secs come to mingle with the wannabe razor-crowd, the chippies, and the freaks to partake of the most decadent pleasures and experience life on the edge.

The man sprawls, bleeding. People cheer and shout and applaud. A female in little more than studded black straps lets out a shriek and comes at Tikki like a cat, talons uplifted as if to strike. Tikki swings her foot, knocking the female's legs out from under her. Gravity and the hard floor do the rest.

Prey should respect the hunter or be prepared to suffer the consequences. That is Nature's way.

The cheers get louder.

Tikki continues down the ramps.

The Abyss glows with a fiery haze. Adama sits at a table in his black suit, smiling and fingering his walking stick. No fewer than seven women are keeping him company, fawning over him, kissing him, laughing and smiling, whispering in his ears. Any one of the seven could have stepped out of a body shop advert. In the fiery haze of the Abyss, all appear to be redheads. As Tikki approaches, Adama briefly gestures. The seven females coo and smile, lean in to hug and kiss him about the head and neck, then turn to leave.

"Don't be long," Adama says.

The seven all turn back to assure him they won't, then smile and wave and walk off. Tikki wonders how they could even hear him against the background of thundering music.

Adama gives Tikki a smile. With a brief motion of his hand he directs her gaze to certain items on his table, a pack of Dannemann Lonja cigarros and a mug of something that smells like cider. The cigarros are no surprise. Adama's been supplying those in abundance since her first job for him. She wonders where he got the cider. Her favorite beverage is not too common. She slips the cigarros into her jacket pocket, sips the cider, then puts the mug down.

"Any problems?" Adama asks.

Problems? Tikki shakes her head. The assassination of Tomita Haruso and his yakuza comrades at the Ardmore Royal Residence Plaza went exactly as planned. No problems at all.

"Good. Very good." Adama smiles, sips his drink. "We'll have to discuss my next target."

"Now?"

"Well . . ." Adama pauses to freshen his smile. "Later, perhaps. I have other business just now. You understand."

"Sure."

"My Leandra," he adds, smiling at Tikki. Then he waves one hand as if to fan away a lingering cloud of cigarette smoke. "Or did you have something in mind?"

Tikki nods. There is one thing that should be mentioned. Considering its importance.

"Such as?"

"Competition."

"Really." Adama smiles as if pleased. "Someone's preparing to move against me?"

"It's possible."

"You mean they've targeted my principal weapon."

Tikki nods. The "weapon" he refers to is her, of course. Adama doesn't seem surprised by the news, and rightly so. He shouldn't be in the least bit surprised— Tikki isn't. She expected reprisals from the moment she first contracted to work for Adama. It's an occupational hazard. Humans never seem to grasp the essential truth of their own existence, that the majority of them are prey, and that they are born to breed and die, and little else. Even the most innocuous of humans seems to imagine that he or she possesses the rights and power of a hunter. The few predators among the human race, such as the yakuza, seem to imagine themselves indomitable, and so should be expected to turn against the hunter.

Tikki knows how to handle that. First, she'll play bodyguard so Adama can enjoy his night of fun; then, she'll hunt. Track down this stupid prey that turns to face her and do what must be done. It shouldn't be too difficult. No more than in the past.

"What will you do?" Adama asks.

Tikki gazes at him for a moment, wondering why he asks, then gives him a faint look of amusement. "Maybe I'll go on vacation," she says.

Adama smiles, then laughs out loud.

Uproariously.

26

Eighteen hours gone and he returns to the loft to find Axle and Dana just sitting around. The black girl, the so-called decker, is lying on the sofa like a lump of meat. It's enough to sour his mood. Hammer lights a Millennium Red, takes a deep drag, then walks over to the kitchen area for a bottle of Coors Extra Dry. If he or Dog Bite or Mickey don't turn up something soon, they'll be skanked. "Well?"

"We're not really sure what happened, Hammer," Dana answers quietly. "She crashed. I guess about two hours ago."

By that, of course, she means the decker biff fragged up somehow and got blown out of the Matrix. Hammer isn't too surprised. This is what he gets for skimping, for hiring unknown talent from out of town. This is what he gets for not personally supervising things. He snaps open his bottle of Coors and turns to face them, leaning back against the kitchen counter. "She dead?"

"No," Dana says, pushing back her long black hair. "I think she's just dazed. Out of it."

"Did she get anything?"

Dana looks to Axle, who's sitting with the decker's Fuchi-6 across his lap. Axle shrugs. What does a rigger know about cyberdecks? What does anyone know about anything?

"I think the deck's kind of scrambled," Axle says. "I managed to get some stuff on the screen, but that's it."

Hammer takes a drag off his Millennium Red. "What stuff?"

"Well . . ." Axle glances down at the deck, taps a key. "It looks like Striper's using the name Fallon Sontag. I don't know where Angel got that data, but there's some notes here, not much. Apparently, Striper used the name Sontag to go to L.A. and Chicago, possibly as a media snoop."

Hammer has a sip of his Coors. Knowing Striper's working alias might help. He'll have to get a decker, someone he can trust, to do a sweep of the city's data bases. A pro like Striper might use more than one alias, but at least it's a definite lead. Everything else they've turned up so far, everything he and Mickey and Dog Bite have found out, comes under the heading of maybes and maybe-nots. Striper's been seen all over the place, on both sides of the Delaware, in everything from classy yakuza hangouts to parking garages to the most scurvy dives in the city. People say she's rabid, vicious. Smart, too. She doesn't seem to make a habit of frequenting any one club or bar. She's always on the move. That makes her a more difficult target.

She also doesn't hesitate to hurt people, human or otherwise. Supposedly, she scragged some ork and then stole his cycle. That's something to keep in mind. Hammer tried his contacts in the ork underground, but they could add nothing.

It's going to be a bitch of a job.

"I don't guess either of you know if our decker friend got herself traced."

"Traced?" Dana gasps. "Traced *here*?"

Axle turns his face toward the ceiling.

Hammer downs the rest of his beer, tosses the bottle toward the sink. "Right. Let's the get the frag out."

"What?" Dana says. "Out where?"

"Do we take the deck?" Axle says.

"Wait a sec!" Dana exclaims. "What about Angel?"

Hammer pauses long enough to crush his smoke under the toe of his shoe. "Take the deck. Leave the biff."

"We can't just leave her, Hammer."

Hammer watches Dana for a moment, then heads down the hall to his room. Dana is becoming a problem. When did she get so sensitive? She won't kill anybody, she won't hurt anybody—what's next? Next, she won't do anything that isn't nice. Mage or not, if she gets any worse than she already is, she's out. Hammer's got enough trouble just trying to keep the team together, keep them all from getting smoked, to deal with any more unnecessary baggage.

There isn't much in his room that he needs. Most of his gear is downstairs in the van. He tosses what he absolutely cannot leave behind into a duffel and slings the bag from his shoulder.

The danger is that the fragging biff decker, Angel, hosed up on a run against some really major corporate data base. The megacorps are all multinational. Some have offices and/or subsidiaries right here in Philly. Those that don't have their own in-house security services have security on contract, and one thing those outfits do is hunt down deckers who violate corporate datasystems. Sometimes it takes a few hours, or even a couple of days. The point is that some of the outfits, like the Renraku Red Samurai guards or the First Force mercenaries, have been known to reconnoiter by fire, shooting first and asking questions later—if anyone's still alive to question. Hammer isn't going to hang around here till he hears the thumping of a Northrup gunship, or worse, a Hughes Stallion delivering a strike team to the roof.

As Hammer steps back into the hall, Axle hustles back into the bedroom opposite and starts banging things around, rushing to pack up and move out. Hammer returns to the main room. Dana is leaning over the decker, Angel. The mage's hands are glowing green, and Angel is moaning.

"Two minutes," he says.

"Hammer, *please!*" Dana shoots a frantic look back over her shoulder. "I can't rush this."

First aid, as Hammer is well aware, isn't Dana's strong suit. There was a time, back when she and Hammer first met, when she hardly seemed to care about people at all. Forget about first aid. Arcane knowledge was all that mattered. Manipulating power, the elements. Discovering secrets. Lately, it seems, all she does is jammer and moan. She's losing it, losing her grip, her edge. Maybe she isn't good enough to do the magic she wants. Who knows? Ultimately, it doesn't matter. She can be replaced.

"Two minutes."

Dana groans softly, and so does her patient. Hammer crosses the room and enters the freight elevator. Axle comes hurrying up the hall and into the main room carrying a pair of suitcases. At a cry from Dana, he turns. Hammer clenches his teeth and jabs at the elevator controls. The doors close. The elevator descends. One thing Hammer won't miss about this building. The elevator's too fragging slow.

The van waits by the loading dock behind the building. Hammer tugs the side door open and climbs in. He stows the duffel bag with the rest of his gear, then gets in behind the wheel.

A little more than two minutes later, the door on the loading dock swings open and out come Dana and Axle. Each is carrying one of Axle's suitcases, and, between them, the decker biff. Angel looks mostly unconscious, eyes like slits, head lolling. She stumbles and the three of them almost fall right off the loading dock. Hammer curses. It's another thirty seconds before the three are finally into the van and sliding the side door closed. Hammer keys the engine and drives around the side of the building to the alley leading to the street.

Coming up the middle of the alley is some partygirl or street ho Hammer hasn't seen around before.

One thing about her, the biff, ho, whatever she is— she's got big hair, a huge curly mass of black. Hammer likes that. She's wearing black visorshades, a black fringed jacket with gold flash, and some wispy kind of black blouse that covers her chest, some of it. Her skirt is barely long enough to cover her crotch, and she's riding ten-story heels. Overall, not half-bad.

The alley's narrow. Run the biff down or stop, that's the choice. Hammer's tempted, but then the biff waves at him like an old chummer and comes toward his side of the van.

Hammer puts the smartgun to the sill of the open window.

"Oooh, baby," the biff says, husky-voiced, smiling, and waving a hand very casually at the smartgun's muzzle. "Keep the piece to yourself. You know someone name 'a Hammer?"

Hammer frowns. "What?"

"Hammer," the biff says. "Got a doss around here?"

"What if he does?"

The biff takes a moment answering that, looking at him like maybe she already knows who he is. "I got some stuff to sell. Paydata. Very hot."

Sure. "What about it?" Hammer growls.

"Well, do you know the slag or what?"

"Talk to me."

"I'll talk to Hammer, thanks."

"That's me."

"Oh, yeah?" The biff smiles wryly. "I hear you're looking for some mainliner called Striper."

"Don't waste my time."

"You want Striper? I'll take you to her."

How does the biff know where Striper is? Anyone's guess. How does she know what Hammer wants? That much is obvious. Word travels. When it's worth money, word travels fast. Hammer steals a glance toward the rooftops, attentive to anything that sounds like approaching rotorcraft, then he looks back at the biff. "What's it gonna cost?"

"Two fine."

Hammer grunts. Two thousand nuyen? A lot of coin to spend on some raunchy slot who might be stroking his chain. "Maybe I'll just beat it out of you."

The biff smiles. "I don't think so, lover."

"No?"

The biff puts two fingers into her mouth, and blows, whistling like Hammer has rarely heard. The sound is loud and shrill and slices through the alley, faintly echoing. A sputtery rumbling arises. Out beyond the end of the alley, over on the other side of the street, five cycles glide into view, coming to an easy halt. The riders wear black synthleather and at least one of them has a submachine gun slung from the shoulder.

Hammer tenses, but hesitates to pull the trigger. The biff smiles and says, "Don't get excited, hon. They're just friends, you *ka*? Just watching out for a girl."

"I don't like surprises," Hammer growls.

"Me neither. That's why I come with my friends. You interested in transacting, baby?"

"One fine."

The biff laughs, leans toward him just like a ho, showing off her cleavage. "One point five," she coos.

"I said one."

They settle on twelve hundred nuyen.

Of course, the slitch will regret it if it turns out she's playing skanky games.

Hammer will make very sure of that.

27

The room is dark. Twenty trideo screens gleam from the right-hand wall. Adama sits opposite the screens in his ornate wooden chair. Beside him rises the gleaming black marble stand supporting a huge gemstone, like a diamond, about the size of a man's fist. Tikki waits in her natural form, lying on the floor nearby.

A red-haired female hangs splayed, spread-eagled, from the metal rack in the center of the room. Her body glows with the orange and red-tinted light of the trid screens. Each time she screams, her voice becomes a chorus of shrill echoes that bounce around the room. With each new scream, Adama grins, and the radiance of that grin seems to set the giant white gemstone to sparkling brilliantly.

None of that has anything to do with magic, Tikki knows. Adama dislikes magic just as much as she does.

The torture goes on long. Adama gives precise instructions. The instrument of his will, a black-clad elf named Sticks, seems well-suited for the harrowing of prey. The elf turns again and again to the shiny stainless-steel instruments laid out on a nearby table, selects an instrument with care, and applies it to Adama's chosen one.

His *Leandra*.

Blood pools on the gleaming onyx floor. The flesh of the chosen one comes to resemble the torn and bloody carrion of an animal freshly taken. Tikki's mouth begins to water. As the moment of death approaches, the prey gasps and shudders and moans.

"*Yes!*" Adama exclaims.

His eyes gleam.

The stink of death wafts into the air. With it comes the potent aroma of Adama's pleasure, swelling to dominate the air. It is a pleasure beyond the ordinary. There is nothing sexual about it, yet it smells like ecstasy, an ecstasy combining elation, exhilaration, and exultation all into one. To Tikki, it is as if Adama finds some special significance in the moment of his chosen one's death, as if it is a defining moment. This is a thing she understands well. The day she made her first kill, full in her mother's eyes, she felt a kind of ecstasy, too. Every kill since that first reminds her of who and what she is, and the role that is hers to play. She finds it curious that Adama should kill without ever touching his prey, but she well understands his pleasure. That is why she feels such an affinity for him. Perhaps that alone makes him seem more familiar than most other humans.

Sticks turns away from the body, looking toward Adama. The elf's only interest here is money. He was offered a certain sum to harrow the prey. There is something amusing in that. When prey turns against prey it has no eyes for the hunter. A human might call it denial, or acute myopia. Tikki considers it stupid.

Very stupid.

"She's dead," Stick says, unnecessarily. "That it?"

Smiling broadly, Adama nods, just slightly, and says, "Yes. That is it. That is everything."

"Then I'll take my pay."

"Will you?"

"My money. Remember?"

"Oh, yes," Adama says. "I remember. Money. You expect me to pay you now."

"Look, chummer, don't frag with me."

"Frag with you? Would I do that?"

"I *want* my money!"

Tikki grumbles. The sound rises from far back in her throat, deep and resonant, carrying throughout the room. Her fangs glisten, briefly bared. She gazes steadily at the elf. Sticks suddenly seems to become aware that she is something more than a fixture in black and red fur. She is three hundred fifty kilos of prime, meat-eating predator and could easily crush the head of a man, or an elf, between her jaws.

Sticks shifts back a step, eyes widening. His scent fills with a mix of fearful emotions, uncertainty, anxiety, a subtle sort of panic.

Adama chuckles. "Yes, your money. How would you like it? In gold? Or perhaps in chips or drugs. Or weapons. Automatic weapons. Machine guns."

The elf blurts angrily, "Just credsticks, dammit!"

Tikki grumbles again, but this time the sound is more like a rumbling growl: menacing, foreboding. Sticks takes another step backward, looking at her, looking at Adama. The smell of fear rises stronger into the air. Adama smiles broadly. "Credsticks. Yes. I have many of those."

"Enough of the skanky games already!"

"You must do something before I pay you."

"Dammit! *What?*"

"The tigress feels left out." With a brief gesture, Adama indicates Tikki. "She is a passionate creature. Hot-blooded. Strong. You must play a little game with her."

"Are you *whacked*!"

"Whacked? Indeed, no." Adama smiles quite contentedly. "You must let the tigress kiss you."

"What!"

Tikki rises to all fours, and the elf's smell swells with fear. "She wants to kiss you," Adama says.

"Keep it away from me!" Sticks shouts.

It . . . ? Tikki grumbles disconsolately and steps toward the center of the room. Sticks snatches up one of the gleaming stainless-steel knives from the table beside him and hurls it at Tikki's face. She swats the knife out of the air. The blade scratches her paw, but the minor discomfort is there and gone in an instant. She bares her fangs and *roars*.

Sticks' eyes go wide, his smell turns acid with fear.

"You shouldn't have done that," Adama says, laughing. "That's bad. Very bad. The tigress doesn't like that."

Prey should never turn on the hunter.

It is wrong.

Tikki advances. The elf shouts at Adama and darts around to the distant side of the table, snatching up another knife, two or three, a handful of knives. Tikki doesn't care about that. She puts her head to the edge of the table. With a quick snap of her head, the table flips onto its side. The gleaming instruments crash to the floor. The elf jumps back. Tikki swats at the table with a paw and sends it skidding across the floor to crash against the wall. The elf shouts, smelling like panic, and frantically throws the knives. Tikki waits for him to finish, then advances. What little injuries the knives inflict scab over, heal and vanish even as the last knife clangs to the floor.

She backs the elf into a corner.

"NO!" the elf shrieks. "YOU FRAGGER!"

Adama chuckles. "Don't take it personally," he says. "It's just business. I cannot risk allowing you to compromise my security. The tigress I can trust. We have an arrangement, you might say. But you?" Adama chuckles. "I'm sure you understand my position."

Terror floods the air anew.

Tikki bounds up onto her hind legs, just briefly, and drives her forelegs against the elf's chest. It's like swatting flies or monkeys. She need hardly exert herself at all, yet the force of the blow drives the elf back off his feet, slams him into the wall, and drops him to the floor. She has several times his mass and strength, and a speed and agility to equal any human, or any elf. She lets him stagger to his feet. She has time, time to do this right. Prey is best when taken on the run, possessed with terror for the hunter, heart pounding, blood thundering hot and rich through its veins. That is when the kill is truly a kill. That is when the meat tastes sweetest.

Adama begins to laugh softly.

The hunter in him understands.

28

The creature rises out of the darkness with eyes like fire and huge gnashing fangs and slashing claws, roaring like all the demons of hell combined into one malevolent form. There is no escaping it. The monster is filled with anger and hate and a primitive ruthlessness that exceeds all human comprehension. It comes roaring through the darkness, closer and closer, growing larger, growing huge, possessed by the will to maim and kill and destroy.

Ohara screams and becomes suddenly aware of the subdued red glow of his bedroom, of lying in his bed, gripping the sheets, drenched in rank sweat, his hands shaking, his heart pounding wildly. He's been dreaming again. He knows too well the exegesis of the monster, the embodiment of the horror that haunts him still, not only when he sleeps. He's been living with it since Seattle, going on three years. Will it never end?

As he struggles to catch his breath, he notices the biffs, Christie and Crystal, sprawled beside him on the bed. Christie moans and shifts, then lies still. The other one doesn't even stir. They're laxed out on dorphs. Ohara tried candy like that once. It sent him into what doctors described as a schizo-paranoid episode that lasted for most of three days.

Ohara reaches over to the shelf sweeping away from the head of the bed, and fumbles for his bottle of Dalium tranx. Dry-swallows a pair of capsules, the dosage his doctor prescribed.

The pills help slow his pounding heart, but leave him wide-awake and anxious. He takes a shower, then wraps himself in a satin and cashmere robe and steps into his study. Reddish panels in the ceiling cast a subdued light. Heavy black drapes cover the windows. He sits behind his curving, semi-circular desk and slots *The Power Master* into the datajack behind his right ear. A little track-loop BTL helps him regain his composure. Provides a very minor emotive boost. Once his hands cease quivering, he switches on his desktop comp, brings up his planning portfolio, and reviews the files there for the nth time.

Making a success of Exotech is just a starting point. Gaining control of the board of Exotech's parent, Kono-Furata-Ko, is only a first step. He has plans, long-range plans, strategic objectives, secret objectives shared with no one. He has his eyes on the real power blocs, the titanic multinationals controlling automated orbital factories and other stations. That's where the future lies. That's where the real power will arise, power enough to manipulate the entire global infrastructure, the whole of the human race.

The possibilities are endless. A railgun equipped to launch bits of spaceborne debris like asteroids could subjugate the entire planet. He's studied the data carefully. A sufficiently large rock fired at the Earth could strike with the impact of a nuclear weapon. That's one possibility. The massive orbital production of designer chemicals such as his two biffs constantly abuse could just as easily turn humanity into a race of slaves.

The telecom bleeps.

Ohara touches the pickup key, audio only, so he will be heard but not seen. The small screen on the desktop displays the number of the calling telecom, then adds a chest-up view of Ohara's chief of staff, Enoshi Ken.

"What now?" Ohara snaps impatiently.

"Please excuse this interruption, sir," says Enoshi. "I know the hour is very late. But I thought you should know. There has been a terrible incident."

"A *what*?"

"Mister Thomas Harris is dead."

"*What!*"

Enoshi briefly bows his head. "Mister Harris was killed along with his wife and a number of personal friends—"

"Impossible!" Ohara interrupts.

"Please excuse me, sir, but this information has been confirmed. Lieutenant Kirkland of the police has only just left my residence. He brought the information personally."

"What . . . ? *What did you tell him!*"

"Naturally, sir, I thanked him for his diligence, and assured him that the corporation would cooperate fully with the ongoing investigation."

"That's all? *That's all you said?*"

"Sir, there was nothing that I *could* tell him."

And there's nothing that he can say now, over a telecom line. The police might be listening in. Ohara realizes that he'll have to cut this short, before Enoshi gives something away. Before anything else goes wrong.

"See me in my office first thing tomorrow. I . . . I want a full report. We have things to talk about."

"Yes, sir. I understand, sir."

"Good."

Ohara jabs at the telecom, switches off, then tugs at a desk drawer. *The Power Master* just isn't doing it for him tonight. What he needs is something heavy, a personalized track-loop called *Omnipower*. That's his salvation.

The call from Enoshi only reminds him of the one real threat to his strategic plans, his accession to ultimate power, the fulfillment of all his goals. The police investigation into the deaths of Thomas Harris, Jorge, and Neiman are practically irrelevant compared to the monstrous evil that turns his sleep into a series of recurring, captivating nightmares, psycho-traumatic recollections of the horror that nearly killed him back in Seattle.

The demonic creature masquerading as a woman called Striper *must be destroyed*!

He stabs at the telecom, gets Enoshi back on the line.

"Your top priority job, the special biz. You know what I mean. I want a report on that, too."

"Of course, sir. I'll do my best, sir."

"See that you do!"

Ohara breaks the connection, scans the study for some clue as to where he might have left the *Omnipower* BTL chip. He can feel himself growing just a bit frantic trying to remember where he left it. There's an excellent reason for that. Neiman, Jorge, now Harris—a progression pointing straight at Ohara himself. Those three men were nothing until Ohara took over Exotech, exploiting their abilities to the max. Doubtless, the demon knows that. Killing Neiman, Jorge, and now Harris is just her way of preparing him for the death she yearns to give him. She wants him to suffer, to squirm, to writhe in unholy agony until the moment when she comes for him.

Ohara won't give her the satisfaction. He finally finds the *Omnipower* chip in his private bathroom, slots it into the datajack behind his right ear. He realizes then that he's in absolute control, not only of his emotions, but of his entire situation. He knows what must be done. He returns to the study and calmly punches up the number of Birnoth Security Associates, the emergency line.

The woman who answers promises to have a high-threat response team at his door within twenty minutes.

The time passes swiftly.

29

Seated in his small but comfortable den, still in shirt and tie, Enoshi removes his glasses to rub briefly at his eyes. The tension headache that has been plaguing him all evening shows no sign of abating, and little wonder. His briefcase sits open on the coffee table. The cursor of his portacomp winks relentlessly at him from the display. An abundance of hard copy lies scattered around him on the table and the sofa. The air is full of the smoke from the spent cigarettes now overflowing the ashtray. He's poisoning himself with carbon monoxide, or whatever it is that cigarettes produce, and he's probably overdue for an eye examination. And he's out of coffee again.

A rustling of slipper-clad feet draws his eyes to the doorway from the kitchen. Without his glasses, he sees only a colorful blur, but that's enough. His wife is wearing her favorite robe, which is a soft pink decorated with white chrysanthemums.

"It's after two," she says softly.

Enoshi nods. "Yes . . . yes, I know."

Setsuko is a very different sort of woman from Enoshi's mistress, neither exotic nor the least bit foreign. She is, rather, as familiar and as comfortable as one person could possibly be for another. She is quiet and persevering, his wife and the mother of his children, a trusted and devoted partner whom he would not forsake for anyone or anything. His love for her is more than love, physical love, more than infatuation. It is the sort of love that will certainly hold the two of them together for the rest of their lives.

Enoshi slips his glasses on. "I won't be long."

"Something must be wrong."

"I wish I were free to say."

"It's that *gaijin*, isn't it?"

"Ohara-*san* is my superior."

And for that reason, if no other, Setsuko should not speak of the man as if he were some kind of barbarian. They've had this discussion before. Ohara-*san's* position demands respect.

"Yes, I know that," Setsuko replies. "Please excuse me. But it *is* him, isn't it?"

Enoshi nods. "I must make another call."

"I'll wait for you in bed."

Setsuko bows slightly, to which Enoshi responds with a slight bow of his head. As she turns to leave, Enoshi keys the telecom, tapping in a number he knows by rote, one he could never forget. It is too important.

The other end bleeps twice, then the grave features of Torakido Buntaro appear on the screen. Some of his North American associates refer to the man as Ben, but he is always Torakido-*sama* to Enoshi, even in his thoughts. Enoshi bows his head fully, and says, "*Moshimoshi*, Torakido-*sama*."

"*Yosh* . . . ," Torakido-*sama* says softly, more a grunt than a word. "What have you to report?"

Enoshi gives a succinct recap of his conversation with Bernard Ohara, first the facts, then his impressions of Ohara's response.

"Did he seem unbalanced?" Torakido-*sama* asks.

"No, Torakido-*sama*," Enoshi replies. "He sounded greatly disturbed, but apparently sane."

This time Torakido-*sama* actually does grunt, a sound Enoshi perceives as one of thought and evaluation. As he has come to realize, the vice-chairman of the board of KFK International does nothing without at least a moment of thought. He is decisive, but not given to impulse. Unlike other executives Enoshi knows, Torakido-*sama* gives the impression of being fully in command, the master of his own fate, without ever appearing to seek to give that impression.

Enoshi waits for his next question or remark.

"Have you any more information on the matter we discussed?"

The matter previously discussed is Bernard Ohara's hiring, through Enoshi, of those persons necessary to ensure the elimination of the underworld assassin known as Striper. As Torakido-*sama* himself previously explained, this action is both good and bad. It is good, In Torakido-*sama*'s view, that an executive of the corporation should take whatever measures are necessary to eliminate a threat to his own person, and, hence, the corporation. However, it is also bad for an executive and therefore the corporation to become involved with shadowrunners and other criminals. Any action that might compromise the welfare of the corporation must be considered very dangerous. It is especially dangerous coming on the heels of the highly illegal and morally despicable Operation Clean Sweep.

Each new operation adds to the risk of discovery, exposure. Torakido-*sama* is deeply concerned.

Unfortunately, Enoshi has no further information to convey.

"You must watch this matter very closely, Enoshi-*kun*," Torakido-*sama* goes on to say, using the familiar, almost paternal form of address. "The image of our corporation could be severely damaged if the worst comes to pass."

That Torakido-*sama* would bother to say this only emphasizes to Enoshi the depth of Torakido-*sama*'s concern. Enoshi bows. "I understand, Torakido-*sama*. Please be assured that this matter is utmost in my mind, day and night."

"As it should be. As it indeed it must be. We are *daikazoku, neh*? One great family? The shame of one is the shame of all."

Enoshi replies immediately, and gravely, "Yes, most definitely, Torakido-*sama*. *Daikazoku*."

In Enoshi's view, Torakido-*sama* is every bit as ambitious as Bernard Ohara, but with one critical exception. Torakido-*sama*'s loyalty to the corporation of Kono-Furata-Ko and all its subsidiary units and all its employees is beyond question. The course of his career is guided by the needs of the corporation. If Torakido-*sama* has trod on any backs in his rise up the corporate ladder, those backs belonged to his immediate rivals, men who lacked the vision or loyalty to serve the corporation properly.

Enoshi believes that Torakido-*sama*'s karma is great and that he is destined to one day take full control of KFK. It is Enoshi's hope that when that day comes Torakido-*sama* will remember the loyal service and devotion to duty of those who rank below him.

Even now, at this late hour, in this uncertain situation, Torakido-*sama* is magnanimous. He smiles. He addresses Enoshi in a warm tone, as if speaking to a close friend. "Of course, you will do your best. You have always done so, and I know you will continue to do so. I have great confidence in your ability, Ken."

Enoshi smiles with pride and pleasure and briefly bows his head. "Thank you, Torakido-*sama*."

"Your oldest son? He will be preparing for college soon, *neh*?"

Enoshi again bows his head. "Yes, Torakido-*sama*. In a few more months."

Torakido-*sama*'s expression turns sober. "College is an important step in a young man's life. The entrance examinations can be very challenging. I'm sure that you and your wife are aware that the right tutors can provide a distinct advantage."

"Yes, Torakido-*sama*. That is certainly true."

Torakido-*sama* gazes at Enoshi for a moment, then shows the faintest of smiles. "Of course, the best tutors are difficult to engage. They are in great demand, *neh*? I will give you a few names. Certain highly recommended tutors have available slots in their schedules. You should call them immediately."

The tutors Torakido-*sama* names serve the corporate elite. Merely to seek an appointment requires that one have the proper referral. Enoshi had previously considered such tutors far beyond his reach. He bows deeply, overwhelmed, barely able to contain his gratitude. "Thank you, Torakido-*sama*. You are most generous."

"It is my duty," Torakido-*sama* says simply. "But enough. You have served our firm well tonight, and it's very late. Go to bed, Ken. Men of our age need their rest."

"Yes, Torakido-*sama*. Thank you. And good night."

30

The warehouse is six stories of grimy brick, squat and square, and very wide across. It stands north of Franklin Bridge and just east of the interstate, amid the congested confusion of streets and buildings crammed between the

highway and the waterfront. The garish neon sign rising
from the warehouse roof proclaims:

DELGATO MOVING AND STORAGE
PHILADELPHIA'S PRIMO MOVERS

Axle hangs almost motionless in the night some five
hundred meters above the rooftop sign. In reality, he's
sitting in a van on the ground, but that is a trivial detail.
He's jacked into his heavily modified Mitsuhama control
deck and flying his Aerodesign Condor LDSD-23 surveillance drone. It's like hanging from a balloon, dangling in empty air. Hydrogen gas cells provide lift.
Turboprop rotors keep him on station. His eyes are Ver-
satek zooms, thermographically enhanced, with a heads-
up display in targeting mode feeding him data from his
ground-seeking radar. He can see practically the whole
world beneath him, every direction at once, kind of like
looking through a super wide-angle lens, but without the
distortion. Targeting sights direct his attention to everything that moves in the vicinity of the warehouse.

Rats, a flight of birds, an alley cat—another hour of
this and he'll succumb to terminal boredom.

"Anything?" Hammer asks.

The voice jogs his brain in odd ways. For just an instant, he loses touch with the jacked-in analog of his
drone senses and he's back in the van, behind the steering
wheel. He *must* be bored. A quick image, more a memory than anything else, flashes through his mind. He sees
the inside of the van, Hammer in the passenger-side front
seat, Mickey and Dog Bite and Dana sitting in the rear.
They dumped Angel, the decker, at Dana's old place a
few hours ago.

"Axle!" Hammer growls.

But for the lights of the glaring sign on the roof and a
few spotlights illuminating doors and the loading dock
in the rear, the warehouse is dark. Deserted, too. "Nothing's moving."

Hammer grunts.

Axle won't be surprised if tonight's surveillance turns
out to be a waste of time. The biker biff that led them

here claimed that Striper had a doss on the upper floor
of the warehouse. There's an apartment there all right,
but no Striper. Dana's inspected the whole building as-
trally, not once but twice already. All she found was an
empty apartment and a lot of packing crates and cartons.
The only unusual thing she reported was an "ambiance
of violence." What that means is anyone's guess. Axle
supposes that the warehouse may have once been the
scene of violence in the past, but how that applies to their
situation now, if it applies at all, he hasn't got a clue.
Neither does Dana, apparently.

Abruptly, a warning bleep sounds in his ears. A targeting sight zips across his field of vision. He zooms in
automatically. Way down below, in the deep shadows between the buildings, something's moving toward the
warehouse.

"Contact," he says tersely.

Hammer demands more data, but for the moment Axle
ignores that. His thermographic enhancement is showing
him the reddish silhouette of a bipedal figure, slim
enough to be a woman, climbing onto the lid of a garbage
dumpster and then vaulting over the top of a chain-link
fence. In another moment, he's got a radar lock-on and
brings his light-intensifying lens to bear. That makes the
alley look dusty and gray, like in the early evening, and
the silhouette becomes a woman, tall and slim, in red-
and black-striped facepaint and synthleather to match.
She yanks on a door at the rear of the warehouse and
disappears inside.

"It's her," Axle says. "Striper. She's here."

Dana feels a churning in her stomach even as Axle
makes his announcement. Their target has arrived. Just
went in the back door. What they're supposed to do now
is go into the warehouse, find Striper, and kill her.

Just *dust* 'er.

"Okay," Hammer says. "Slot and run."

"No. No way." Dana closes her eyes, shakes her head.
It's hard for her to believe that she's actually said it, but
she can't hold back anymore. Running the shadows didn't
used to be like this. Somewhere things got skewed. In

Hammer's quest to make a name for himself and the group, he's gone over the edge. She's believed for a good while that he's been pushing the limits, but she can no longer avoid seeing that Hammer's making them as bad as the people they're supposed to be fighting.

The kind of jobs they used to run . . . People got hurt and sometimes even killed, but it was always in a good cause. Stealing back data that some corp had hijacked, busting some salaryman out of a corporate contract that was the moral equivalent of a prison sentence—things like that. The kind of runs where no matter what kind of laws they might be breaking, any rational person could see that they were really just putting things right.

She opens her eyes, finds the rest of the team staring at her. "I'm out. Outta this."

They go off on her at once, Mickey and Dog Bite. "Dammit, you!" Dog Bite growls. "This is the run that'll make our reps!" Meanwhile Mickey is laughing. "You gotta be fragged! Are you fraggin' kidding!"

Hammer snarls, "You want your *share*?"

"Keep it." Dana doesn't care, doesn't care about the money. Now that the decision's finally made, she doesn't care about anything but getting out. She struggles with the latch on the van's side door, yanks her arm free of the hand that snares her elbow, shoves her way out, out through the door and into the alley, then walks rapidly into the dark, heading for the next street.

She wouldn't be surprised if Mickey or Dog Bite came after her and grabbed her by the arm again and started arguing with her, but that wouldn't change anything. She's had too much of killing. That last run taking out the BTL lab was what did it. Dana has regretted it every day and night since. The guilt she feels is almost overwhelming, the thought that she's become a killer is unbearable. She isn't going to be a party to murder ever again.

Maybe she'll give herself up to the cops. She hasn't thought that far ahead. For the moment, it's enough just to be getting out. She'll deal with tomorrow when tomorrow comes.

* * *

Mickey suppresses a grin long enough to light a smoke. Watching Hammer and Dana go at it, however briefly, makes him want to laugh. Hammer's ex-corporate mercenary approach just doesn't work in the streets. Down in the streets, you gotta chill, stroke people's egos. Trying to hammer people into line only gets their backsides into a huff and drives them out. And when the person you're hammering is not only your bedmate but a mage besides, you're just jerking your own chain. The mages Mickey has met up till now have all been twisted fraggers and Dana's no exception. She's so hosed up over spit she can't tell her money from her mouth.

Mickey isn't the least bit surprised to see her get out of the van and hike away. He's been expecting it for weeks.

"What now, commander?" he says with a grin.

Hammer glares at him over that one, but only for a moment. Dog Bite is cursing Dana, cursing her for the *biff she is*, till Mickey can't help laughing out loud. Hammer, of course, gets bent. Hammer's biggest problem, in Mickey's view, is having no sense of humor. None whatsoever. "Shut your effin' mouth," Hammer growls at Dog Bite. "We got a problem."

"You noticed," Mickey agrees, smiling.

"So what we gonna *do* about it?" Dog Bite snaps.

Hammer puffs his smoke for a moment, then slaps at Axle's shoulder. "Bring the drone down. We need another gunner on the inside. You're it."

Mickey laughs out loud again.

Hammer glares at him. "You got a better idea?"

"You're strokin' us, right?" Mickey can't help grinning, chuckling some more. Tapping a rigger like Axle for extra muscle on a job like this is enough of a bad idea to be just plain stupid. Coordinated movement and fire could make all the difference in deciding who walks out of the warehouse alive, especially going up against first-rate talent like Striper. Axle just doesn't know the moves.

Mickey is saved the trouble of answering Hammer when Axle says, "I'm just the delivery boy, chummer."

Hammer glares some more. "You want your share?"

"Get me a gunship or a robo-drone. I'll play fire support, no problemo. But I ain't going in mano-a-mano."

"Our fraggin' fire support just walked out, dammit!"

"I ain't no muscleguy, Hammer."

"Then you're out!"

"Fine. I'm out."

And they're better off that way, as far as Mickey's concerned. Nobody to get in their way. Mickey pulls on his Nightfighter goggles and headset, loops the strap of his AK-97 over his shoulder. "If we're gonna do it, let's do it."

Hammer grunts agreement.

They leave Axle to recover his airborne surveillance drone and head across the street to the alley running up the east side of the warehouse. Hammer and Dog Bite don their goggles and headsets. The goggles turn even the darkest shadows into shades of gray. The moon is high up in the sky and almost a perfect orb, making for plenty of ambient light.

Halfway up the alley, Hammer says, "How does a one-third share of forty-kay sound?"

Forty thousand nuyen is the price of hunting down Striper and taking her out. Until tonight, Mickey could look forward to only a one-fifth share of that. Eight fine is good pay for a few days work, but thirteen is better, no question about it. He pauses to look at Hammer, whose faint smile is just visible.

"You skanky bastard," Mickey says, laughing softly. "You pushed 'em out of the game."

"Yeah?" Hammer says.

Dog Bite grins, catching on.

Hammer conned Dana and Axle into quitting before show time. Exactly how he conned Dana, Mickey can only guess. Hammer must've been working on her in private. Mickey chuckles again. This isn't the first time Hammer's rewritten the game. He's so short on humor, so deadly serious all the time, that people make the mistake of thinking he's a straight suit in urban camo. The only reason Mickey still trusts him, after seeing all the skag he's pulled, is that Hammer always takes care of his original partners. Mickey and Dog Bite have been with

Hammer a long time. The three of them are the real team in any situation, regardless of who's in or out of the game.

"Rock 'n' roll," Hammer says.

Dog Bite growls agreement.

Going around the rear of the warehouse, they find the loading dock and the door where Striper entered. Dog Bite stays on ground level to train his AK over the front edge of the loading dock and dead-on at the door. Mickey and Hammer flank the door. Hammer grabs the handle and tugs the door wide open.

"Clear," Dog Bite grunts.

Mickey darts inside. Hammer and Dog Bite follow.

The interior of the warehouse is huge. The ground floor is two stories tall and piled to the ceiling with boxes, cardboard cartons, plastic containers, and wooden crates. Fire exit lights add a reddish tint to the ambient light gathered by Mickey's Nightfighter goggles. A red and white sign leads him to a stairwell. He waits for Hammer to pull the door and Dog Bite to signal clear before slipping inside.

They head up the stairs in bounding over-watch style, Mickey and Hammer taking turns covering each other while Dog Bite handles rear guard. Reaching the top floor, six stories up, they come to two doors at the top of the stairs. One is marked Warehouse, the other Private. The Private door leads into a narrow corridor about ten meters long—a fact Dana neglected to mention in describing the warehouse interior.

The corridor would make a great place for killing, Mickey sees at a glance. There's absolutely no cover. Naturally, there's no other way into the apartment.

That they should find the Private door unlocked, even a little ajar, only adds certain titillating spice to the moment, as far as Mickey's concerned. If he had any fears about his own mortality he wouldn't be running the shadows. He'd be sucking up to his mother, wearing suits, diddling desktop keyboards. He'd rather live like a suicide, die young, than face a life in the steel and glass coffins downtown. Now, he advances into the corridor, crouching, putting his back to the wall and pointing his AK at the wide-open doorway at the end of the corridor.

No need to check his pulse to make sure he's still alive. He can feel it pounding. The feeling brings a grin to his lips.

Somewhere beyond the end of the corridor, a trid is roaring with the laugh track of a sitcom that Mickey's seen before. It sounds like OTQ's "Sans Reproche," a funny show about a real bone of a loser who never figures out what's going on. The noise should help conceal any sounds Mickey might make while moving down the corridor. He feels his grin widen. This is gonna be easy.

The doorway at the end of the hall leads into a smallish room with no windows. A mattress lies on the floor beside one wall. A trideo faces it. A lamp sits within an arm's length of the mattress. The lamp and the trid are both on. Mickey moves across the room into a hallway that leads past a claustrophobic kitchenette, a closet, a bathroom, and then ends at another room with another mattress and a pair of lamps. Both lamps are on. The glaring neon of some advert on an adjacent building shines in through a window at the end of the room.

Mickey glances around and sneers. The good news is that he's gotten this far and is still alive, as are Hammer and Dog Bite. The bad news is that Striper isn't where they expected, anywhere in this apartment, and it's beginning to look like either the biff knows they're here or knew they were coming.

"Double back," Hammer says from the doorway. "Back to ground."

"Right."

Mickey turns toward the door, but before he can take another step his headset fills with a loud, piercing scream that rises suddenly, and just as abruptly ends.

For an instant, he and Hammer just stare at each other. Then they break toward the front room of the apartment.

Hammer stops on the threshold, sweeping the front room with his smartgun, the red triangle of an optical targeting sight flying across the room even as he looks down. Dog Bite lays sprawled face-down on the floor. What's left of the back of his studded synthleather jacket is in tatters, shredded. There's almost nothing left of his back. Four vicious gouges descend from the base of his neck to just below the shoulder blades, melding there into a single gory wound that reaches to the base of his spine. Blood and gore from the wounds are still oozing down his sides, spreading across the floor.

It reminds Hammer of what a grappling hook can do when used as a weapon. Only this is worse. Much worse.

Mickey curses, standing at Hammer's left shoulder. For once, Mickey's lost his sarcastic smirk. "What the frag happened?"

Hammer shakes his head.

"You didn't see anything?"

"Slot it!" The question brings Hammer a sudden rush of anger. Of course he didn't see what happened. He'd been doing his job as part of the fire team, backing up Mickey, supporting the advance into presumably hostile territory. If Dog Bite had been doing what he was *supposed to be doing*, which was watching their rear, he'd probably still be alive. Obviously, he turned his back to the corridor leading in from the stairs. Either that . . . Either that or whatever killed him materialized out of thin air.

"What kinda sword could do damage like that?"

"Don't ask stupid questions." No *sword* could've gouged Dog Bite's back like that. The wounds look more like something an animal might inflict, something big and powerful and equipped with massive claws. Hammer adjusts the settings on his Nightfighter goggles and finds a tide of orangey-red flowing up and out from around the center of the room, slowly fading into the ambient temperatures. As he steps across the room, he sees that the heat trace leads right up the corridor to the stairs. He also spots bloody patches on the floor, leading toward the stairs. Something big, bigger than man-sized, passed through the room and the corridor within just the last few instants. It couldn't have been a troll because a troll would be lucky to fit into the corridor, never mind get through it at speed. Trolls also come on two legs and whatever went up the hall left smears, tracks, paw prints, like something on four legs.

"Some kinda animal," Hammer mutters.

Mickey chuckles, but it's not his usual chuckle. It sounds nervous. "Don't frag with my brain, Hammer."

"Look at those tracks."

"You're saying an animal did this?"

"Maybe a talis cat."

"Oh, *crap*! Come *on*!"

"You got any better ideas?"

It would fit, and fit real good in Hammer's view. The data they got on Striper says she uses magic, that she does vicious damage. Maybe she's really a mage, a mage with a vicious pet. A mage could probably teleport her pet talis cat wherever she wants, behind someone's back, make it kill and then run. A talis cat could do that, tear open Dog Bite's back, then dash up the corridor and out of sight. What noise it made would have been covered by the blaring trid.

If Hammer's memory serves correctly, talis cats stand just under a meter at the shoulder, making them about as big as the average tiger. Big and powerful enough to tear a man wide open.

"This is crazy." A nervous laugh bubbles out of Mickey's mouth. "Fraggin' slot. Now what?"

"We do what we came to do."

Mage or not, it's killing time. They owe it to Dog Bite and to themselves, if they're gonna earn the rest of their pay. Striper obviously knows they're here. They'll just have to be careful. Hammer motions Mickey toward the hall, and follows, a step at a time, up the hall to the stairs. The infrared trace is gone, faded into the air, but the reddish blotches on the floor show that the cat, or whatever it was, went through the door marked Warehouse, which now stands wide open. Mickey crosses to the far side of the doorway. Hammer sets himself to provide covering fire, then motions Mickey inside.

The third floor of the warehouse is like each of the floors below, two stories tall and piled high with crates and shipping containers, arranged into aisles. The bloody paw prints, growing faint now, lead off to the right. Hammer decides to ignore them, to play the game by the book. He and Mickey will do a methodical sweep, take no more chances. Run the witch and her cat to earth.

They're halfway through the grid of aisles when they hear a bang somewhere off to one end of the warehouse. A deep-pitched humming arises. Hammer recognizes the sound.

"Freight elevator."

Mickey curses. "Frag! She must be heading down! The slot's getting away!"

Not this time. "Head for ground."

They double back to the door and hustle onto the stairs. They've gotta move fast if they're gonna reach the ground floor in time to make their target. The third floor is six stories up and that means six flights of stairs to get down.

They're down three flights when a loud bang echoes through the stairwell. Hammer catches himself abruptly before the top of the next flight down. The bang came from above and sounded suspiciously like the bang of a door slamming shut. Mickey stops and looks up at him from the landing below.

The slitch is playing games with them.

Hammer clenches his teeth.

The freight elevator must have been a ruse, sent down just to confuse them, run them around. Maybe Striper sent her animal to the ground floor, but it's irrelevant. The key point is that animals don't operate freight elevators and they don't slam doors shut, not like this, not in a way that's sure to attract attention. Striper must be above them, regardless of where her animal went. Hammer's going to enjoy killing the slot. If only because she's dragging things out so much. Really getting him bent.

He motions at Mickey.

Up one flight, they flank the door to the second floor. Hammer's sure that the bang came from higher up, but he's going to be methodical and check things out. Mickey sets himself and nods. Hammer yanks the door open. Mickey darts inside and Hammer follows. There's no sign that anyone's been there, so they head on up the stairs to flank the door to the third floor. Mickey sets himself and nods. Hammer reaches across for the door handle and suddenly the door is swinging open, ramming into him like a freight train and slamming him back off his feet.

As he falls, he hears someone shouting and the rapid-fire stammering of an AK on full automatic.

Then suddenly it's very quiet.

Hammer struggles up onto one knee, then has to wait a moment, breathe, clear his head. He's getting pain from his head and wrist, from practically every part of his body, but that's just incidental. Pain he can handle. The real problem is his brain, and his balance. He feels rattled upstairs, like the floor is tilting slowly back and forth beneath him. He puts one hand to the wall in getting to his feet. It's a few more moments before he trusts himself enough to look around.

The door's standing straight out from the doorway, blocking his view. He pulls it fully open, flat to the wall. Mickey's lying there in the doorway. What's left of his head is a bloody ruin, like something took off the front half of his skull and let the gory remains pour out. His right arm looks eviscerated, pared practically to the bone. His chest is one big bloody wound oozing onto the floor.

Hammer grits his teeth, and realizes he's sweating and shaking. That's pure adrenaline, not fear—anything but fear. The sight on the floor incites him to rage. He lifts the smartgun and fires a burst into the ceiling, then screams, "You Fraggin' BITCH! You're DEAD! I'LL KILL YOU!"

There's no way out for Striper except in a body bag.

She's dead meat.

Tikki pauses amid the aisles of stacked packing crates to listen. She isn't impressed by Hammer's expression of anger or his foolish waste of ammunition. She suppresses the urge to reply in kind, with a ferocity all her own, and merely thinks, *Come and get me, little man. . . .*

See what happens.

She wouldn't be here tonight if she didn't believe herself fully capable of meeting any threat Hammer or his cohorts might present. No matter whether she follows her wildest urges or adheres to the dictums of a rational mind, whether she runs on two legs or four, Tikki isn't stupid, nor suicidal. This is personal, so she hunts in her natural form. She uses the tactics of deception, just like her

mother taught her. She takes as prey these hunters who
hunt the hunter, just as Nature would command.

At about the middle of the warehouse floor, she lowers
her head and butts a tall stack of packing cartons—once,
then again. The stack sways and then topples. As cartons
crash down to the floor, she lopes away, up a side aisle,
around a corner, then down a main aisle toward one end
of the warehouse.

She moves effortlessly, supple and flowing, a phantom
in red and black. Her claws provide an unfailing grip
against the concrete floor. Her heavy padded paws are
virtually silent.

It wasn't hard for her to find out who was hunting her.
Word was all over the street. The hunters had offered
nuyen to anyone with information. Offers like that travel
fast.

Leading the hunters here to this warehouse on the waterfront proved to be childishly easy. Steel's friends handled that.

Now, off a ways to her left, Hammer shouts again and
fires another burst from his weapon. He's moving toward
the fallen cartons. Tikki knows that without even needing
to hear all his noise. She knows it simply by breathing
the air around her. A thousand traces of scent flood her
nose with every breath. Some of those scents are irrelevant, the smells of plastic and cardboard cartons, the
dusty smells of concrete. Hammer's smells stand out in
sharp relief, like a beacon, drawing an ever-changing map
in her mind.

"You're DEAD! DEAD MEAT!" Hammer bawls.

The smartgun stammers.

Tikki pauses. Hammer turns a corner and she's right
there, facing him from less than half a meter away. The
man reacts as instinct commands—he jerks back. The
scents of surprise and fear flood the air. Hammer raises
the smartgun toward her face, but she's already bounding
onto her hind legs and lashing out with one paw. She
smacks the gun aside even as it erupts, stammering loud
as thunder and assaulting her ears.

The gun goes flying. Hammer screams and staggers
away, stumbling, turning a full circle, exclaiming,

clutching at his bloody hand. Her claws raked his flesh
even as the weight of her paw drove the gun from his
grip. Now she advances, bounding up again and again,
slamming at him with her forepaws, slashing with her
claws. Hammer pulls another gun. She slaps it away. He
pulls a knife. She smashes it from his hand and claws his
arm from shoulder to wrist. He screams and falls over
backward, tumbles over the floor, scrambles up and starts
running, but she's already there, slapping him down,
down and down and down, till he rolls screaming onto
his back.

"LEMME GO! LEMME GO!"

She straddles his body, bares her fangs, and then roars.
The air fills with the rank stink of his terror. That is the
proof she demands, the surest measure of her power.
Any hunters who come this way will smell the terror she
has inspired and take warning.

She flicks an ear with satisfaction, then rips out his
throat. That is the price to be paid for turning on the
hunter.

The price Nature demands.

It makes things right.

07-14-54/04:46:51

Roll cam.

The datajacked Sony CB-5000 in the steady-mount
atop his helmet comes on-line with a shower of electronic
snow and a quick burst of static. Skeeter keys the Bion-
one tridlink controller on his right forearm to overlay the
view through his Seretech Evening Shade cybereyes with
a complete technical readout. No point in risking his
fraggin' skin if the blinking dingo equipment isn't going
to record every gore-drenched bit of action.

"Skeeter!" J.B. says impatiently. "Am I—?"

Skeeter thrusts a finger at the dink-fragging biff. *You're
on already*! Start babbling, dithead! J.B. lifts her mike.
"This is Joi Bang for WHAM! Independent News and
I'm here on the Philadelphia waterfront where only moments ago a broadcast on police comm frequencies reported that a small war has begun complete with
automatic weapons fire."

Skeeter lifts his right arm out to his right, then across his chest to his left to get some extra images of the street with the AZT Micro25 strapped to his wrist. The skank blasted street is deserted, of course. Nobody but a dit-brained newshead like the so-very-trid-o-genic Asian-faced J.B. would come into this part of town any time before dawn.

Abruptly, an engine roars and tires scream. Skeeter jerks around to train his helmet-mounted cam on the street. A black van peels out of an alley across the street and goes racing up the block, smoke pouring from its tires. On the van's roof is something that looks like a half-inflated black balloon.

"Police have apparently not yet arrived on the scene," J.B. remarks, so very muck-headed astutely, and then she's off, running up the sidewalk and right into the alley at the side of the warehouse. "Skeeter! *Skeeter, come on*!"

Un-be-fragging incredible.

07-14-54/04:49:12

"Skeeter! Skeeter, look!"

The damn fraggin' biff is up on a loading dock at the rear of the warehouse. Skeeter marches up the steps and onto the dock. J.B. pulls on an open door and turns to face him, lifting her mike.

"Am I—?"

You're on, dag-fram it!

"As you can see, the door is open," J.B. says into her mike. "Any possible perpetrators may still be inside."

Right.

"This could be very dangerous."

No frinkin' kiddin' ding-brain.

"We'll take a look."

Damn ditheaded biff.

07-14-54/04:56:30

Main lens, close focus. Three floors and six flights of stairs up, they find a freakin' ripped-up mutilated mess of a corpse sprawled on the stairway landing. Skeeter's thermographically enhanced view through his Seretech

cybereyes show that the corpse is still hot, not quite at
normal human body temperature, but close. J.B. immediately starts babbling. The effin' scrod-headed newscoop
is naturally just *delighted* over the find.

"Here we have further evidence of the string of cannibalistic mutilation killings that have been terrorizing
northeast Philadelphia!" J.B. gushes in an undertone.
"What other monstrous mutilations have been committed here? Only—"

The bimble-brained biff abruptly hesitates. From beyond the open doorway where the corpse lies comes a
low, rumbling growl. The only thing Skeeter's heard to
compare with it is the animal growl of a troll, one who
is very unhappy.

Mouth open, yet damn-fragging miraculously silent,
J.B. turns from the lens of Skeeter's helmet-mounted
Sony to face the doorway. That's when something steps
into the doorway. Something big. Very big. Its eyes glint
blood-red with a phantom ray of light. Its face is a ferocious alien mask of bloody red and stripes of black. It
bares enormous gleaming fangs. Its mouth, stretching
open wide, seems easily big enough to swallow the very
trid-o-genic head of J.B. in one gulp.

"*Oh my god oh my god oh my god!*" J.B. babbles.

Skeeter presses the PANICBUTTON button on his Toshiba portable wristfone. The monster in the doorway
roars, and the roar is thunderous, reverberating through
the stairwell. J.B. screams, turns and runs, ramming right
into Skeeter.

"*OH MY GOD OH MY GOD OH MY GOD!*" the
muddle-headed dithead screams, racing down the stairs.

Skeeter scrambles back onto his feet and charges down
the stairs right on the damn fraggin' dithead's heels. The
monster roars again. J.B. screams. Skeeter concentrates
on running like he's never run before, down six flights
of stairs, through the ground-floor warehouse, off the
loading dock in the rear and up the alley to the street.
Even then, his dimble-headed muck-brain news snoop is
still gasping. "*Oh my god! Oh my god!*"

Yet another damn-skanking night on the town!

Obviously, J.B.'s theories about cannibalistic orks is

down the toilet. Obviously, some paranatural animal like
a tiger got out of the zoo, the Philly zoo or some other
zoo, and has been prowling the city, killing anything that
moves. The one good thing about it all is that he got
some fantastic footage of J.B. running away like her
shorts were on fire and her behind was catching.

That much is worth a chuckle.

A short one.

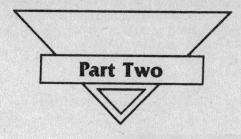

Part Two

Were

31

The waterfront slums begin just north of the port. The streets are lined by three- and four-story tenements that go on for kilometers, on and on, flanking the Delaware halfway to Trenton. Tikki stops just short of the House of Corrections in northeast Philly. The district around the prison tends to be quiet except for a lot of police vehicles coming and going. Many are indistinguishable from the area's regular sector cars and so, to some, the district seems heavily patrolled.

The building where Tikki stops is just a little taller than the others on the block, five stories of grime-blackened brick and dark, smog-smeared windows. She turns off the sidewalk, pushes through a recessed door, and steps into the face of a Konoco Combat Master shotgun, pointed right at her.

The slag holding the gun is dressed like a ganger and has bright orange hair and teeth filed to points. He sits on the stairs. He sits there because that's his job, to keep everyone but tenants out of the building.

He immediately lowers the gun and nods.

"You know me?" Tikki says.

The guy shakes his head. "Never seen you before. In fact, I ain't even seeing you *now*."

Good boy.

Tikki takes the stairs to the fifth floor, which has three small apartments. All three belong to her. Tonight, she decides to use the one on the left. She opens the door lock with a simple four-digit combination. There's no other mundane way through the door except by brute force or major mechanic surgery, either of which would leave observable traces.

The apartment is two rooms, main room and bathroom. The main room has a counter at one end that conceals a micro-kitchenette with a small refrigerator and a sink. There's a low Japanese table and pillows and a mattress for sitting and sleeping and a portable trid for entertainment. The bathroom is micro-sized, too. Shower, toilet, sink. Both rooms have lighting fixtures on the ceilings, but Tikki never uses them. The windows provide adequate lighting, day or night, and if for some reason she needs more she's got the trid.

Standard lighting makes a target of people. So do windows. That's why the first thing she does upon entering her doss is to draw the Kang and look out the windows of the main room across to the roof of the building adjacent. Tonight no one is about. Admittedly, windows like these pose something of a security risk; but they also provide a means of escape if someone should come smashing in through her front door. Given the choice, she'll accept the added risk in exchange for the avenue of escape.

The night is almost over, but what remains of it is not for wearing clothes. She strips naked, dumps everything, clothes and weapons included, onto the mattress, then turns on the trid. News Now 38 has a story about some suit called Neiman who got hosed in a parking garage. Nothing new about that. Like they say in the adverts for adventure trids, the modern metroplex is a dark and dangerous place. Somebody's always getting sliced or diced or chopped to ribbons. What surprises her, though only briefly, is the absence of any mention of all the yakuza she's been scragging for Adama. The cops or the corps must have the gag on. It wouldn't be the first time.

She goes into the bathroom to use the toilet, then checks herself in the mirror. The faint rash around the base of her neck has been annoying her for weeks. The redness is still visible. That puzzles Tikki because she doesn't usually suffer from such problems, from any sort of physical complaint. Evidently she came into contact with some toxin that her body has not been able to cast out with its usual ease.

Probably silver—the stuff is like poison for her.

She rubs at the redness, but that's a mistake. The more she rubs, the redder the skin gets and the more it complains. That ticks her off, and her sudden rise of anger speaks to her instincts. The change begins before she can stop it, before she's entirely aware of having started; and once started she finds she hasn't the will to stop. Somehow, it seems written into the fabric of the night. Fur rushes over her skin. Her body lengthens and swells. Her breathing becomes a rough, husky rumble too deep and resonant for anything even remotely human. She drops to all fours, and walks back into the center of the main room.

Moonlight flowing in through the windows sets her back to bristling. She flicks her ears, feeling a sudden urge to grumble, to growl or roar, announce herself to the night, declare her dominion over the city, but she resists, keeping her silence. That's the smart thing to do. Discontented, Tikki stretches and yawns and drops belly-first onto the mattress. On a night like tonight, when the moon fills the night and her predator's soul yearns to run wild and free, she should be out in the wild somewhere, in the dark reaches of some primitive land, like the woodlands near Seattle, or the forests and river valleys of Manchuria and southeast Siberia. . . . Stalking. . . . Hunting. . . . rising out of the brush around some waterhole . . . striking like lightning. . . . Silent and swift. . . . Bringing down prey . . .

Life in the wild is so simple. She was born to it. She understands it. She knows it well enough to act, and act correctly, without even pausing to think. By comparison, her life within the human domain often seems . . .

Complicated . . .

Hard just to think about.

She lowers her head onto the cradle of her crossed

forelegs, then rolls onto her side, looking up at the windows.

Tonight, she took three humans as prey, and let two others escape. The three she killed, the one named Hammer and his cohorts, deserved what they got. The threat of death must be answered with death. Her every instinct commands it. If she had not killed those three men, they would be hunting her now, and they would keep hunting till they found and killed her.

The contest between predators is as much a part of the world as life and death, and so it must be. The hunter who shares her land with other predators soon grows weak and dies for lack of prey. That does not mean that all killing is right or even justified, even to her. It means that it is better to kill than be killed, better to dominate than submit. Were Tikki meant to simply bare her throat and let herself be murdered by any animal, two-legged or four, Nature would not have given her the soul of a hunter or the weapons with which to hunt.

What then of her human guise? What is the point of it? Is it merely a deceitful mask? She finds that hard to accept. Tikki has come to believe that Nature would not have equipped her to pass for human if Nature did not intend her to play some significant role in the human domain. Her problem is that defining the role, her proper role among humans, has proven as difficult for her as it was for her mother.

Her mother often said that Tikki must find her own way. She has been doing that most of her life, from her earliest days in Seoul and Shanghai, to her recent experiences in Seattle, and now to the present moment, here in Philadelphia. She came here in search of a man who used her. That man, in order to further his own plans, sought to have her killed. She wonders now if she will ever find him, and what she will do if she does.

However, for now that is not the real issue.

Tonight . . .

Things are not going as they should. That is why she came to this doss in northeast Philly rather than going to one of her usual lays, and why she hasn't checked in with Adama yet.

She doesn't understand why she didn't save Hammer for interrogation. She should have done that, if only to make him reveal the identity of those who hired him. Sure, she already suspects that Adama's competitors hired him, but it would be good to have confirmation. She could just as easily have killed Hammer after the interrogation, and she's somewhat surprised that Adama didn't suggest it. Most Triad leaders she's known, especially Red Poles, those in charge of enforcement, have been big on symbolism. Few things are more symbolically endowed than leaving the torture-mutilated body of an enemy's assassin on the enemy's doorstep. In some parts of the world, that's standard practice. Doing anything less would entail a serious loss of respect.

But that is not all that doesn't seem right. What really bothers Tikki is the realization that she went to the waterfront warehouse intent on killing, slaughtering, totally annihilating the animals hunting her. That was very stupid. She knows better than to think in such limited terms, she's known better since she was a child. Maybe she can afford to think that way in the wild, but in the city, she must be smarter, more scrupulous in evaluating the possible effects of her actions.

There's also the question of identity. In certain circles, a great many people believe Tikki to be a killer, and even more accept without question that she hires out as muscle. In recent years, however, she has taken steps to conceal her identity while taking two-legs as prey. The question then is how Adama's competitors, the Honjowara-gumi yakuza, could have known that she is the one who has been dusting their mid-rank executives? How did they know to send Hammer after her? Just a guess? Did she commit some error? Could there be a spy or informant in Adama's organization? Could Adama himself have betrayed her?

Disturbing questions, for which she must find answers, but none are quite as disturbing as something else that happened tonight.

Back at the warehouse, she let the elf media-girl and dwarf camera-guy escape, but she had briefly considered slaughtering them both just because they were there. In-

stinct seemed to demand it, telling her to kill them, tear
them apart, sate herself on their meat. She felt the moon
burning into her, reaching down into her predator's soul.
She resisted because she did not like that, did not like
what she felt, did not like it at all.

Now, she likes it even less.

The elf girl reeked in ways that only mages ever do.
The dwarf stank of cybernetics. Tikki would be hard-
pressed to decide which is more revolting, the flesh of a
metahuman or the metal-infected meat of the cyberneti-
cally enhanced.

But that was beside the point.

The point was this: *Tikki* decides what she will do,
where and when she will kill, *if* she will kill. No one
else makes that decision. No one. That is her absolute
rule, her law. All must obey. Even she. Even instinct.
Ruthlessly enforcing that law is how she has managed to
survive for so long. If she had killed every time the desire arose, she would have been like a creature run
amuck, and humanity would have banded together long
before now to hunt her down and destroy her.

Admittedly, her eternal argument with the darkest
urgings of her instincts sometimes goes against her. She
has done things even in the recent past that she now re-
grets. She does not moan and cry about it because that
would accomplish nothing. Rather, she strives to learn
from her mistakes so that the next time she will not re-
peat the error. So that one day soon she will know her
place in the human world as well as she knows her place
in the wild.

She might take humans and metahumans and other
species as prey, but they are not her *natural* prey. She
would never hunt them for their meat. No more than she
would hunt another tiger or Weretiger, or any Were at
all.

That is why taking the elf and the dwarf would have
been wrong. What the humans call murder. What she has
always thought of as simply unnatural. A crime against
Nature. The two metahumans were neither predators nor
prey. She could have no justification for killing them.
They were just bystanders, as innocuous as they were

irrelevant. She had every reason to let them go un-
harmed, and that should have been apparent to her from
the moment she first saw them.

What's wrong with her?

She shakes her head and grumbles.

32

The raid gets under way at about 05:45.

Kirkland waits and watches from behind the wheel of
his unmarked car. At first, nothing too dramatic happens. The sky is overcast. What little sunlight that gets
through the clouds and the haze is barely enough to tickle
the photocells of streetlights and security floodlights. Everything looks gray and damp.

A van and a Ford sedan appear at opposite ends of the
block. Five men in casual clothes emerge from the van;
another four get out of the sedan and begin walking toward the middle of the block. The men are wearing neo-
Kevlar insulated clothing and are armed with everything
from heavy automatics to submachine guns, but at a
glance the average citizen would never guess.

Directly across from where Kirkland waits at about
mid-block is a big, three-story building of chrome, steel,
and glass. Most of the chrome shows signs of fire damage, and most of the glass is either smashed or covered
with plastic sheeting. The asphalt lot surrounding the
place is littered with trash and there are even a couple of
abandoned, smashed up, stripped-down autos. A chain-
link fence with twin gates crosses the front of the property. A large sign standing just inside the fence announces
that the place is available for sale or lease, et cetera,
et cetera.

All seems quiet.

Kirkland keys the comm mike lying in his lap and says
in a calm, casual voice, "Traffic Five-David, ten seventy-
two."

Traffic Five-David is the comm call-code of a chummer of Kirkland's who happens to be on vacation this week. A 10-72 is a request for a time check. The computer-synthesized female voice of Central Dispatch replies with the time. The plainclothes cops across the street take the time-check request as their signal.

One member of each of the teams makes a cradle of his hands and gives his partners a boost up onto and over the chain-link fence. It isn't a very tall fence. Within mere seconds both teams are over the fence and heading into the building.

Kirkland checks his watch. The raid is occurring at his request, but he has no problem sitting back and watching the action with a coffee in one hand, a Pyramid Gold cigarette in the other. He's done his time on the front lines. Breaking down doors and rousting suspects is, by and large, a job for people with a few less years and a bit less weight than he's carrying around. His ex-wife has been telling him that for years. Lately, he's begun to wonder if she might be right. The more Kirkland hears about the hot-blooded warriors of Flash Point Enforcement, the more he's convinced that he should stick to interviewing homicidal maniacs and serial killers and leave the heroic bulldrek to others.

For the sake of good form, he's carrying a Predator II under his jacket today instead of his usual automatic, but he's not planning to get out of his car—not now, anyway—not unless things get really out of hand. And if something really does go wrong, he's got a fully loaded MP-5 submachine gun stashed under his seat. Whether he reaches for that or just throws himself across the front seat in hopes of not getting shot depends on what happens.

About four minutes go by.

The comm under the dash gasps briefly, and somebody says, cheerfully, "Tac-Seven . . . join the party."

Kirkland takes a drag off his Pyramid Gold.

A big Chrysler-Nissan cruiser comes roaring up the block, streams right on by, then comes to a screaming halt just past the building, turning sideways to block off the road. Right behind it is a pair of heavy security vans.

The first cuts sharply over the sidewalk, smashes through the gateway of the cyclone fence, and screeches to a halt in front of the building. The second van stops beside the first. A pair of cruisers stop at curbside, flanking the entrance, while a patrol wagon cuts sideways to block off the other end of the road.

All the vehicles bear the Flash Point Enforcement logo. So do the heavily armored troopers who jump out of the vans and heavy cruisers to train a variety of semi- and fully automatic weapons on the building: shotguns, assault and sniper rifles, even a pair of medium machine guns. This is one of Flash Point's Tactical Response Teams. They're known to move fast, hit hard, arrest first, and ask questions later. Sometimes, that's a good thing.

The double doors at the front of the building swing open. One plainclothes cop emerges, grinning broadly and holding up a bag filled with some white substance. Kirkland supposes they got lucky. The rest of the plainclothes cops bring out a line of prisoners, twelve of them, a mixed bag of humans, orks, and elves. Most are in their underwear. One of the three females is wrapped in a blanket.

The armored troopers take over, applying prisoner restraints. Kirkland checks that he's got his Minuteman shield hanging securely from the breast pocket of his jacket and stands up outside his car. Sal Maroni, the Tac Team C.O., walks over.

"Got some felony narcotics," Sal says.

"Nice," Kirkland says. "Nice work."

"Where's your boy?"

"I think that's him now."

Carefully creeping around the patrol wagon blocking off the east end of the street is a dark blue Mitsubishi sedan with a Minuteman Security placard on the driver's sun visor and winking red and blue emergency lights discreetly planted in the front end. The sedan stops in the middle of the street, just a few steps away from Kirkland. The man who gets out from the back wears a black fedora and a dark blue suit. The brim of the hat casts a shadow that hides the man's face above the level of his mouth.

His name is Moshe Feinberg, but he isn't Kirkland's

"boy," never mind what Maroni says. For all matters involving magic, Feinberg is the number one man on the Minute Man force. He holds the rank of Inspector, which puts him just one step below Deputy Chief.

Sal Maroni flashes a big grin, then rejoins his troops across the street. Kirkland waits for Feinberg to finish looking around, then walks over to meet him.

"Good morning, Kirkland."

"Morning, Inspector. Sorry to get you up early."

"Perhaps you will explain why I'm here."

The reason that Feinberg, rather than one of his flunkies, is here is because the Chief of Detectives has quietly passed the word on behalf of the Commissioner that what Kirkland wants, Kirkland gets. A little matter involving mass murders, execution-style mass murders, including as victims a number of execs and secs employed by a local firm called Exotech. That's what Kirkland's case is about and why he's here in Germantown this morning. In answer to Feinberg's question, he directs the inspector's attention across the street to the line of perps kneeling by the security vans. "I'd like you give them a quick scan, find out what you can, then have a look at the building."

Feinberg looks toward the perps. "Are you asking me to read them or probe them?"

"There's a difference?"

Feinberg briefly compresses his lips, as if mildly irked by the question. As a general rule, Inspector Feinberg seems mildly irked by most questions related to magic coming from non-magical persons, including cops.

"I'll put it to you this way," Feinberg says. "I can read auras all day. To actually probe an individual's psyche requires time and energy."

"Ahh . . . just read them. Maybe do a quick probe on the leader."

"Right," Feinberg says quietly, maybe a bit sarcastically. "I trust that you recall our discussion concerning the legality of hermetically obtained information."

"Sure, that's no problem," Kirkland says with a nod. As far as the courts are concerned, information magically extracted from a suspect's mind rates just slightly better than data obtained through torture. Little problem there involving civil liberties. But not a problem here this morning because Kirkland is fairly confident that the twelve prisoners have nothing to do with his case. They're gangers who just happen to have taken up residence in the former site of Exotech Entertainment's Special Projects Section.

"I just want to cover the angles," he says. "The building's my main interest."

Feinberg spends a moment gazing across at the building, then nods. "Let's begin."

By now, the prisoners are lined up on their knees facing the security vans. Standing in a semicircle facing them are eight troopers sporting assault rifles and SMGs. Feinberg steps among them, looks the prisoners over, then stands back, facing them.

"Give me some room."

Kirkland motions to the troopers, who all move back a few steps.

Feinberg draws a small book with a deep red cover from his coat pocket. As he opens the book, something appears on the ground beside him that wasn't there a moment before. It sits on its haunches like a dog, and is about the size of a Doberman, but that's all it has in common with any dog Kirkland's ever seen. The creature has a head like a hawk's and golden-feathered wings. Its forelegs end in claws, bird claws. The rest of its body resembles a lion's. The sum effect suggests a griffin. Kirkland once looked it up in an encyclopedia.

The general consensus is that the beast is Feinberg's familiar, but Kirkland knows no one who's ever had the balls to ask.

Feinberg speaks, as if reading from the book.

"In gremio legis . . . in hoc salus. Ex facto ius oritus. Hypotheses non fingo."

The griffin briefly flaps its wings.

A bluish aura comes into view, surrounding the female prisoner wrapped in a blanket. The girl abruptly stiffens and lifts her face to the sky. When the aura fades, maybe a minute later, she slackens, then begins cursing viciously.

Feinberg closes his book. The griffin vanishes. One of the tac troopers gives Kirkland a look of uncertainty. Feinberg turns his back to the prisoners, then steps over to Kirkland. Together, they move a short distance away.

"They're all members of one gang," Feinberg says.

"The Walking Wounded."

"Yes."

The Walking Wounded is headquartered in London, with a few chapters in Europe and here in North America. Kirkland suspects that if the founding members could see the motley bunch in their Philly division they'd zook all over themselves, by which he means, they would vomit.

Feinberg pauses a moment, drawing a pack of Dunhill Platinum cigarettes from his jacket. Kirkland offers a light. Feinberg accepts it, then takes a drag, holding the cig between his fingertips. "The female in the blanket fancies herself a shaman. She is unskilled, poorly trained, but very strong-willed. She brought the group here. In her view, the building is colored darkly . . . her words not mine."

"What does that mean? Colored darkly."

"It means that there is something bad about the place. There is much negative energy here. I sensed it when I first arrived."

"And that's what attracted the gang."

"It attracted the shaman, who brought the gang."

Right. "She got a totem?"

"*G. saxi sexus*. Gargoyles. She subscribes to the myth that gargoyles are an ancient race of intelligent beings with the ultimate aim of dominion over the Earth."

"Oh, yeah?" Kirkland doesn't know about gargoyle totems, but he imagines that the anti-terrorist squad would be interested in hearing more about plans to take over the Earth. "We talking enslavement or eradication?"

"In what regard?"

"You wanna take over the planet, first there's a lot of humans you gotta do something about."

Feinberg takes another drag off his cig. "She has thus far been unable to contact her totem of choice. Making that contact is as far as her plans extend, in so far as I could determine.''

''So the human race is safe for the moment.''

''The threat seems negligible.''

Kirkland can go along with that. But it doesn't mean the data isn't worth submitting, if not to the terrorist squad then to the criminal intelligence division. Big ideas usually start small, small and apparently innocuous. Hitler started as an effing corporal in the Austrian Army, for chris'sake. Napoleon was a runt. New York's Forty-four-Caliber Killer worked for the post office. Serial murderers are usually considered the nicest guys on the block till the truth comes out.

''Shall we look at the building now?'' Feinberg says.

''Sure thing.''

Sal Maroni declares the building clear, which makes leading a guy like Inspector Feinberg—who isn't without connections—a whole lot safer for a guy in Kirkland's position, which right now is somewhere between the Chief Executive Officer of Minuteman Security and the board of directors of the city corporation.

He pulls out his Predator II and pushes through the left of the front double doors. The lobby is wrecked: furniture smashed, graffiti on the walls, busted glass and ceiling panels scattered around. He shoves some of the crap aside with his foot, clearing a path. Feinberg pauses in the center of the room.

''Very intense psychic interference,'' he says after a moment. ''We'll have to go upstairs.''

''What's upstairs?''

''I'll let you know.''

Great. Kirkland finds the door to the stairs. A stench assaults his nose as he presses the door open. It isn't as bad as a two-week-old corpse shut up in a closed apartment, for example, but it's close. Somebody's been using the stairwell as a lavatory. What Kirkland can see of Feinberg's face beneath the fedora, just the lower half, shows no reaction.

At the second-floor landing, Feinberg says, ''Down the hall, third door on the right.''

''You been here before, Inspector?''

"I scouted ahead from the lobby."

"You what?"

"The focus of the disturbance is like a lighthouse on a moonless night. Unmistakable."

"You're talking about that negative energy."

"Correct."

The smell in the air doesn't get any better in the second-floor hallway. It gets worse. Kirkland feels a faint zephyr of a breeze against his cheek and suddenly his hackles are standing on end. A subtle film of sweat slips down from under his arms. He's clenching the grip of his Predator II without really knowing why. The place is making him antsy.

He pauses a moment, listens, glances back at Feinberg. "Hear anything?"

"There's nothing here to threaten us," Feinberg says.

"You sure about that?"

"Are you magically active, Kirkland?"

"How the hell should I know?"

"Many people are, to a limited extent. You're probably picking up the vibrations running through this place. They're very intense. I assure you, there's no danger. We're quite alone."

Kirkland takes the man's word, but only as far as it goes. Right this instant, they're alone. His gut is telling him to watch it. The nervous tension running through him probably has his blood pressure up to two hundred and ten. He takes it real slow moving up the hall. It's a long walk to the third door on the right, and every step of the way he expects someone or something to jump out at them.

The door in question is marked Lab 3. The door is ajar. Kirkland opens it and goes through it like maybe there's a squad of terrorists waiting inside.

Dropping into a combat crouch, he sweeps the lab with the barrel of the Predator. The "lab" looks like a battlefield: everything smashed and scorched by fire. Lots of technical equipment, recalling to Kirkland's mind police reports on the fire that swept through the place. Nothing moves. Nobody's here. The floor is midnight-black and it crunches under his feet as he carefully walks around, checking the place out. The stench is incredible, worse than week-old corpses, and the air feels cool, almost chilly. Kirkland pulls out his handkerchief and holds it over his nose and mouth. There's a big cutout in one wall, like for a window, about half the length of the lab. The room beyond is just as blasted as the main room. More technical gear, smashed, shredded, scorched.

When he turns around, Feinberg is standing in the center of the floor with his book open and the griffin sitting at his left. He gives another little spiel as he did outside, in some language Kirkland's never heard before. The griffin flaps its wings, then sits still. An hour passes. Neither Feinberg nor the griffin move. Kirkland leans back against a wall and reflects. This lab, Lab Three, is where Exotech's Special Projects Section conjured up the wet record for their hit simsense chip *The Summoning of Abbirleth* and others. If Kirkland's guesses are correct, the creation of that wet record is intimately related to the recent slayings of Exotech executives.

If that fragger Ohara would just get him the records he wants. . . .

Abruptly, Kirkland realizes that the air in the lab is getting cold, more than just chilly. The stench becomes so powerful his eyes start to burn and he comes close to gagging. Voices arise, echoing, babbling, laughing madly, exclaiming, even shrieking. The cold and the stench and the maniac screams and laughs become overpowering. Kirkland staggers toward the door, coughing, almost choking on his own bile, eyes watering, ears ringing. Along the way he grabs Feinberg's elbow, intending to pull him from this noxious, infernal atmosphere. He pulls but Feinberg doesn't move. It's like he's cast in stone.

"Feinberg! . . . *FEINBERG*!"

Abruptly, the room is silent and cool again. The stink is tolerable, putrid but tolerable. The griffin screeches and vanishes. Feinberg slumps to the floor. Kirkland manages to grab enough of the guy to slow the descent. Before he can check for a pulse, Feinberg is awake, lifting his head, slowly sitting up. The fedora never left his head, the book never left his hand.

"You okay?" Kirkland asks.

"Physically." Feinberg sits up, rubs a hand around to the rear of his neck, then slowly stands up. Kirkland holds the man's upper arm until he's sure he's going to make it. Feinberg takes out a pack of cigarettes, his fingers shaking as Kirkland provides a light.

"There is something new to this world, Horatio," Feinberg says quietly. "Something undreamt of in your philosophy, and which you cannot arrest."

Kirkland pockets his lighter, wondering if Feinberg is delirious. "Come again?"

"A war was fought here, Lieutenant. A small, vicious little war. Do you know what a shadow spirit is?"

Whatever it is, Kirkland doesn't like the sound of it. He pulls at his necktie and considers lighting a cigarette of his own. For the moment, he prefers the feel of the Predator in his hand. "Better fill me in."

"Shadows are a form of free spirit. Darker, more menacing than the average spirit. Most are elementals or former allies, but there are other kinds. Some can be described as demonic. They revel in bloodletting and can be difficult to control. Some authorities believe that shadow spirits may be addicted to the psychic energy of humans suffering great physical or emotional torment. They have been known to ally themselves with or to enlist the aid of criminals or the insane."

"You're saying that one of these shadow spirits was here?"

"I'm saying a shadow was born here. It was summoned, but could not be controlled. I'm not sure why that is. The interference is too intense. There may have been a flaw in the magic. The shadow won the battle for control. Likely, it killed whoever summoned it. Perhaps it even possessed him. I can't be sure. That's all I can tell you."

"You think this shadow-thing is still around?"

"Did Satan willingly give up paradise?" Feinberg shakes his head. "The entity is too powerful to simply disappear."

"How powerful?"

Feinberg takes a drag on his cig, then says, "Would you say the sun is powerful, Lieutenant?"

"It's as powerful as God, in other words."

Feinberg pauses a moment, then says, "God? I don't think so. But something *like* God, perhaps."

33

The final cars of the freight train clatter past. The clanging bells of the grade crossing fall silent, the flashing red warning lights go dead. As the red- and white-striped barricades rise, Raman twists the throttle and rides the Harley chopper over the grade crossing, up the road and between the rusted chain-link gates of the abandoned naval base. Another short road brings him to the stocky buildings standing along the waterfront.

The boat is already waiting, idling beside the concrete bulkhead where land meets water. He can hear the low rumbling murmur of the engines. The craft is not clearly visible in the murky dark, but he knows well enough what it looks like.

It's a GMC Riverine, sleek and black, a model they don't list in the catalogs. More than twelve meters long and fitted with concealed weapon mounts, computer-controlled miniguns, rocket launchers, and other special hardware like a satellite uplink. As Raman approaches, an elf in a black duster steps from the boat carrying a submachine gun under one arm. Raman pauses before him.

Weapons check.

"*Está bien.*" The elf nods toward the boat.

Raman steps aboard, the elf following close behind. The boat eases away from the bulkhead and begins to rumble out toward the center of the river, cutting smoothly through the water, heading south, away from the city.

Raman leads the elf down a short flight of steps into

the luxuriously appointed rear cabin. It is furnished in black and gold, and has a bar standing to one side and a plush sofa sweeping around two walls. Alongside the bar is an elaborate console that appears to integrate a desktop computer with various communications equipment, including a telecom. A big Asian male stands to the left, a large ork male to the right. A woman in black mirrorshades and a gleaming gold body suit that clings to her like a second skin sits on the curving sofa, more or less in the middle. Her name is Sarabande. Raman has dealt with her before.

She finishes sipping from a glass, then holds it out to a skinny male in a white servant's jacket, who takes the glass, puts it behind the bar, and then leaves. *"Buenas noches,"* Sarabande says. "Would you care for a drink?"

Raman shakes his head. He does not like distractions while engaged in biz. Any biz. He ate and drank fully before coming.

"You're prompt as usual, amigo." Sarabande pauses and leans her head to the side. Raman gets the distinct impression that she is scrutinizing him closely from behind her mirrorshades. It's the way she always behaves around him, careful, attentive to detail. "So, what are you calling yourself this week?"

"Ripsaw."

"It suits your costume. Is that an Amerind jacket?"

"It was."

"Now it's yours."

"Yes."

"I understand. *Sientese.*" She gestures casually toward the portion of the sofa sweeping along the right-hand wall. Raman takes a seat, and Sarabande crosses her long, gold-clad legs. The movement is nothing if not elegant. Perhaps she planned it that way. "I have someone new for you to meet. I think you'll like her. She's just arrived from Sâo Paulo."

Within moments Raman sees the long, firmly contoured legs of a woman descending the stairs on heels like stilettos. Then the body comes into view, lusciously curved and clad in a filmy black body stocking. The woman moves like a cat, slowly and sensually. Her hair

is a heavy mane of onyx silk. Her eyes glare even as her
mouth puckers. She strolls past him, gazing down at him
over her shoulder. She pauses before Sarabande, then
turns to stroll back the other way.

Her eyes never leave him, except when she turns,
changing direction with an arrogant toss of her hair.

"She's called Dominique."

Raman feels a stirring of interest, of suppressed excitement. He has of late come to appreciate Latin women,
particularly the ones with fire, who challenge him with
all the brazen defiance of a hot-blooded *she* to prove his
maleness, to take her, overwhelm her, and bring them
both to bliss. He has a feeling that he would enjoy prov-
ing himself to this she. No less than he has enjoyed doing
to all the others he has taken in his life.

Dominique pauses before the stairs, gazing at him
steadily.

Raman looks back at Sarabande, careful to conceal his
interest. Willing females are never difficult to obtain.
They appear to him along the shoulders of rural high-
ways. They approach him in bars. They are offered to
him as incentives. He could probably have a different one
every night, maybe two or three, if he felt so inclined.
He has even gotten the impression from time to time that
Sarabande herself might surrender to him were he to show
a definite interest. But perhaps that is only her witchi-
ness, mere trickery; perhaps not. With a female like Sarabande it is hard to be sure. Sometimes her mouth speaks
one way while her body speaks another.

"What is the job?" he asks.

Sarabande gestures; Dominique goes up the stairs. The
carrot has been offered—now for the work. "It's yours,
if you want it," Sarabande begins, slowly recrossing her
legs. "It is an elimination."

"The target?"

"A technician called Striper."

"The back-up?"

"Naturally, that is confidential."

A strange thought comes to mind, perhaps suggested
by something in Sarabande's manner. If so, the clues are

very subtle, too subtle for him to be certain. "Perhaps I am the back-up."

Sarabande says nothing.

"Perhaps a first attempt has failed."

Sarabande gives no indication of even hearing his remark. "The target is not fortified, but the threat-level is high. I am prepared to offer one hundred thousand nuyen."

Raman grunts. He does not mind eliminations except that they are troublesome. Work of this nature often requires extensive planning, both in terms of execution and to ensure his own escape. He is often placed in an antagonistic position relative to police, something he prefers to avoid. The work he likes best involves threats or thefts. Those jobs are the easiest. He lets Sarabande wait a few moments, then says, "I have heard of Striper. In Hong Kong. She uses magic."

"That should be of no concern to you."

Indeed, he has no hesitation concerning magic. Where appropriate, he has even hired mages to further his work. Magic sometimes simplifies matters. "Technicians can be difficult targets. A user of magic makes for an even more difficult target."

"Hence, the price I am quoting, and certain fringe benefits."

Raman pauses as if considering this, then says, "Two hundred kay."

"I'm offering one."

Raman shrugs. "I have expenses."

"I have other available technicians."

"None as good as me."

"Perhaps, perhaps not. We have had a long and lucrative relationship. That is why I say the job is yours if you want it. If not, I will take it elsewhere."

Raman smiles. "No one worth one hundred kay would take this job for a hundred key. And you know it."

They pass several moments in silence. Sarabande recrosses her legs. "Naturally, I'm also prepared to pay expenses. Shall we say fifty thousand? And, if you wish, you may use Dominique until the job is complete."

Offering Dominique is so blatant a ploy that Raman

almost smiles. The last thing he wants is one of the fixer's own *shes* watching over his shoulder while he's working. That Sarabande would even suggest such a thing
amuses him. This she has fire, too.

The extra fifty thousand make the total acceptable. Not
great, not bad. Likely, he will use only five or ten thousand for any equipment he may need. That leaves him
with most of a hundred and fifty thousand nuyen to do
with as he wishes.

"Very well," Raman says. "One hundred and fifty
thousand. I will have two-thirds in advance."

"The entire sum will be placed in advance in a Carib
guarantee account."

That, too, is acceptable. "Where is the target now?"

"In Philadelphia."

That is good. He hates having to commute to work.

"I have a datachip you'll want to review."

"Later."

"Of course."

Dominique awaits him in the forward cabin. For her
Raman has a treat she will not soon forget.

34

Cop Central is on Race Street, between Seventh and
Eighth. The thirty-story complex that stands there now
replaced the old police headquarters building about four-
teen years ago, after the old one burned to the ground.
Right about the time that Minuteman Security took over
the city's police contract. Kirkland had no problem with
the change in corporate leadership. He'd been a card-
carrying member of the Philly P.B.A. almost ten years
before Minuteman came into town. He knows where he'll
stand the next time contract talks come up. So does every
other cop.

He catches an elevator to the fourteenth floor and gets

off in front of a pair of smoky, plasti-paneled doors. The lettering on the smoky panes reads:

Homicide Bureau
Central Division

He pushes through the double doors and cuts an immediate left, avoiding the aisle through a rabbit warren of cubies leading up the center of the room. The aisle along the left-hand wall goes past the doors and windows of holding cells dressed up as "interview rooms." Kirkland is barely halfway up the aisle when one of his men, Detective-Sergeant Murphy, steps out through the door of Interview Room 3.

"Hey, boss—"

"Not now, Murphy."

"You really gotta see this."

Yeah, right. Kirkland stops, looks at Murphy, looks through the window to IR 3. The girl sitting at the macroplast table looks to be in her early twenties. She wears a broad-brimmed black hat and matching pullover. Her hair is black, too, and long, tumbling over her shoulders. Kirkland can see clearly that her eyes are beet-red and her face looks clammy. Kirkland returns his gaze to Murphy. "So?"

Murphy smiles like something hurts. "She walked in about an hour ago. You know those DOAs on Bridge by the waterfront?"

Kirkland exhales heavily, takes out a cig, lights it. Just another day on the job, a few more killings he hasn't heard about. Yet. "Gimme the short form."

Murphy nods. "Three guys turned up dead at the Delgato Moving and Storage warehouse. News snoop found 'em. They were ripped up pretty bad. Ever hear of a slag named Hammer?"

"Maybe three million. What's your point?"

"Well, one of the DOAs was called Hammer. A local kick-artist. Been moving into the big time. Wetwork. Anyway, this girl here walks in downstairs and tells the desk she was part of Hammer's team till their last job came along."

"What job?"

"Ace Striper."

That's real interesting. Anything that involves a name like Striper is real interesting as far as Kirkland's concerned. The question is whether the girl in the interview room is a psycho manic-depressive with masochistic guilt-delusions, or does she really know something?

"What's her name?"

"Dana Giachetti. She's a mage."

Kirkland wishes he had a cig for every hosed-up hustler he's heard claim that. He could open a smoke shop. The name doesn't ring any bells. Kirkland decides that this is a problem Murphy can wrestle. "Delgato's is a mob joint, right?"

"Yeah."

"Find out if there's a connection. If the mob's bringing in hired talent like Striper we may be in for another war. Cross-ref with Organized Crime and D.E.A. Get somebody on it. Pump the girl for everything she knows and then get an A.D.A. in here and pump some more. If she decides to walk, make her an accessory and book her."

"Boss, this ain't my first day on the job."

"Tell me about it. *Some other time,* Murphy!"

Kirkland's already moving on, heading up the aisle. Murphy closes his mouth, smiles, nods and waves a hand as if to signal okay. Murphy's a good detective, he just takes too damn long to explain things. Kirkland's got about five thousand items on his mind at any one moment and another ten thousand demanding his immediate attention just going to the goddamned john.

Did Striper hose Robert Neiman and the other Exotech execs? Did Exotech hire some kick-artist named Hammer to ace Striper in revenge? Are any of those individuals or organizations into something that Kirkland hasn't even heard of yet?

Kirkland grunts.

The only thing he hates more than unanswered questions is the prospect of unanswered questions leading to still more questions. He should've become an auto mechanic like his father.

The aisle crossing the rear of the room is flanked by a carpeted space where sit the bureau's five civilian data aides. Passing quickly through them, Kirkland is through the door of his office before any of them can even look up at him. He flips on the kaf maker, sits down at his desk, snuffs his cig, and immediately lights a new one. Taking a deep drag, he flips on the telecom. The unit has a monitor screen, integral computer, and the city phone directory in its memory.

He presses a few sensor keys. The Unit Calling screen of the local telecommunications grid appears on the monitor. Two bleeps and an attractive blonde appears. "Good afternoon, KFK Plaza, my name is Melissa," she says melodically. "May I help you, sir?"

"Mister Torakido, please."

"Who may I say is calling?"

Kirkland holds his shield case up to the telecom's visual pickup, showing his badge and ID card. "Lieutenant Kirkland, Homicide."

"One moment sir. I'll connect you."

The blonde is replaced on the screen by an aerial view of the KFK headquarters building, situated on an expansive, rolling patch of green-turfed land that the voice-over informs him is located somewhere just outside Tokyo. The vid, accompanied by orchestral music, goes on to tell about the humanitarian philosophy of KFK International. The vid doesn't run long enough for Kirkland to hear about the organization's many contributions to improving the quality of life of all humanity, which is what usually comes next in promos like this.

Instead the screen blanks. The brunette who next appears is attractive enough to have been the recipient of a small fortune's worth of cosmetic surgery. Kirkland looks very closely but doesn't spot even the tiniest flaw in her deep blue eyes and tawny complexion.

"Good afternoon, Lieutenant," she says in a dulcet, British-accented voice. "I'm Theona MacFarlane, Mister Torakido's confidential assistant. How may I help you?"

"I'd like to talk to your boss," Kirkland says.

"Mister Torakido is out of his office at present. Perhaps I can be of assistance."

The words and tone of voice give nothing away, but the woman's expression is pointedly interested, like she's been sitting around all day waiting for him to call. Kirkland wonders what's going on. Corporations are usually big on talk and short on action where police investigations are concerned.

"Okay, it goes like this," he says, deciding to take the offer of help where he finds it. "I'm investigating the deaths of Robert Neiman—"

And that's as far as he gets. Before Kirkland can get another word out of his mouth, MacFarlane says, "Yes, Lieutenant. I know."

She's clued in. Kirkland isn't sure whether that implies that MacFarlane is anything other than well-informed. He wonders about it, though. "Then maybe you're aware that I've requested certain info from the president of Exotech, a Mister Bernard Ohara. Things like employment files, data on the Special Projects Section, information that could be critical to my investigation." Without waiting for MacFarlane to respond, he adds, "So far I'm not getting much cooperation."

MacFarlane's expression becomes one of subdued surprise. "You made these requests to Mister Ohara personally?"

"Yeah. Face-to-face."

Another very subdued look of surprise; then, again, the pointed look of interest. "Tell me exactly what information you would like, Lieutenant."

The look and the request together convince Kirkland that something is definitely going on behind the scenes at KFK International. What it is, he can only guess. His primary interest is the Special Projects Section: who worked there? when? what were they doing? He also wants personnel files on all the dead executives and their associates, living and deceased. He runs down the list.

MacFarlane says, "I must tell you, Lieutenant, that Kono-Furata-Ko prides itself on being a responsible corporate citizen, and that it has always been the policy of the corporation to cooperate with the official investigations of any legitimate public authority, such as the police."

Kirkland nods, he's heard speeches like this before.

"Give me one hour," MacFarlane says.

Kirkland is surprised enough about the time frame that he hesitates, and then it's too late to respond. She disconnects. The screen blanks. He takes a long, slow drag on his cig. Then the door to his office swings open and in walks Captain Henriquez, Commanding Officer, Homicide Bureau, Central Division. Henriquez' office is two doors over. Kirkland lights a cig on the embers of the last one and sits back in his chair.

"How'd it go in Germantown?" Henriquez says.

"It looks like things'll get worse before they get better."

"Better? You and I'll be back in Traffic Division before that ever happens." Henriquez drops into one of the two plastic-molded chairs facing Kirkland's desk. "Where do we stand?"

Kirkland suppresses the first reply that comes to mind, and says, simply, "I'm just about to call the troops in for a meet."

"Oh, yeah? In that case, I'll catch up with you later."

"Right."

Five minutes later, Kirkland's little cube of an office is packed wall-to-wall and halfway around both sides of his desk with half the homicide specialist-detectives of the Central Division. About thirty-eight people in all. It doesn't seem like much against a metroplex of some three million, and that's just the official population.

"Who's got what?" Kirkland says.

Three or four start talking at once, then settle down to taking turns like good boys and girls. They've been running down the myriad leads and possibilities and tenuous ghosts of clues that might resolve the string of Exotech exec murders. So far, they've managed to eliminate as suspects most of the freelance kick-artists based in Philadelphia, along with most of the known yakuza, mafia, and Seoulpa gang assassins. They've also eliminated most of the blood relations, friends, and associates of the victims. That's a good start, but not the kind of thing Captain Henriquez or anyone else can shoot at the mayor for a pat on the back.

Detective-Sergeant Lisa Wu runs down the current data on out-of-town killers. Striper's name comes up, but that's no coincidence. The name is on the list.

"We've got nothing much on her activities so far," Wu reports. "A.T.F. spotted her in Chinatown about six weeks ago. A few squeals have seen her around since then, but she's not making any waves. Not that we know of. That's kinda weird in itself. Heavy muscle doesn't usually sit idle. We've got at least one informant who says she's playing bodyguard for some slag . . ."

"What slag?"

Detective Wu shrugs.

"Nice answer. You're fired."

"Sorry, boss."

Sarcasm isn't enough to vent his irritation. Kirkland sits back in his chair, stares briefly at the ceiling. "This is somebody who gets, what? Ten-kay to muss somebody's hair? Twice that to bust an arm? She don't bodyguard *some slag*. Some slag she met in a bar? Christ Almighty! *Get real*, people!"

Wu briefly lifts a hand to her brow, looking mildly over-awed. Others look at the floor. The air starts getting a little muggy with sweat. That's okay, though. Kirkland's got half of Central Command coming down on his ass over this Exotech mess. If he has to pressure people to get paydata out of them, he will. He lights another cig, then notices the one already burning in his ashtray. He ignores it. If anyone else notices, they ignore it too.

"What else we got?"

Ramirez rattles his hardcopy.

"*Talk*! dammit," Kirkland growls.

"We got a tentative match through the F.B.I. on hair found in the elevator where Neiman bought it."

Robert Neiman was the first Exotech exec to bite it. It happened in a parking garage. The killer was the only one in the elevator, firing into the parking garage with a fragging Vindicator minigun. Kirkland doesn't quibble over the point. "What hairs, matching what, and how tentative?"

Ramirez nods, swallows. "The hairs found in the elevator match hairs the Seoul P.D. found at a crime scene of a killing tentatively ascribed to Striper a couple years back.''

"F.B.I. is sharing data with Seoul? When the hell did that happen?''

"Well, actually the rumor is that some Company hacker—''

Kirkland waves a hand. "Forget I asked. How tentative is this match?''

"Almost exact. The problem is that nobody knows whose hair it is. Or what kinda hair it is. The F.B.I. ran some tests but didn't pursue it. It's not human or meta-human hair, not any known species.''

"So . . . what? It's animal hair?''

"We don't know.''

"What else is there?''

"Nobody knows.''

"The F.B.I. *doesn't know*?''

"They said try a zoologist. Preferably one with a background in paranormal species.''

On another day, Kirkland might have smiled, if just briefly, to hear that God's gift to humanity, the all-knowing F.B.I., didn't have all the answers. It reaffirms his sometimes shaky confidence in mere police departments. As for zoologists he's heard of lately, he waves his cig around, but that doesn't help jog his memory. Too many names, too many datum.

"Who's the woman working on the ghoul thing? The one from the Science Center.''

Detective Kyowa speaks up. "Liss. Doctor Marion Liss. I think she's a parazoologist.''

"Make the call, Ramirez.''

"Right, boss.''

"What else? Shackleford.''

Detective Chris Shackleford is by far the shortest member of the unit, barely more than a meter tall. Min-uteman Security doesn't hold that against her, that or being dwarf, and neither does Kirkland. Shackleford's got strong skills in computers and statistics, and, more important, what seems like an agile brain. She's always coming up with ideas. Now, though, she shakes her head. "It isn't Striper.''

Kirkland exhales heavily and looks at the ceiling.

"Striper's target profile runs to drug lords and crime kings. She'll muscle anybody, but she doesn't ace corporates unless they're pushing into the underground."

"Is that your psych evaluation, Shackleford?"

Detective Shackleford clenches her lips, briefly looking as irritated as Kirkland feels. The only psych profile they've got on Striper is too half-assed to be worth anything. That means Shackleford's speculations fall into the realm of guesswork.

"There's nothing wrong with profiling from target-type and method," Shackleford says emphatically. "There was a time when that was the only kind of profiling we had!"

Nothing's carved in stone, as far as Kirkland's concerned. Admittedly, what Shackleford says is true. It's also true that things change. So do people. Kirkland has known pro killers and kick-artists to suddenly change style with the specific goal of screwing up their police profiles. "So you want Striper off the list."

"We've got people in town who aren't even on the list who'd hose their own mother for taxi fare."

"So what are you saying?"

Shackleford doesn't get a chance to answer. The office door swings open, the crowd of detectives parts, and Deputy Chief of Detectives Nanette Lemaire steps into the void, looking quickly around, then at Kirkland, then saying, "What's the latest on the Exotech suit killings?"

God curse all brass.

35

Sunlight dwindles.

Shadows grow long. . . . The time is come when her red and black-striped fur blends to perfection with twilight patches of sunlight and shadowy dark. The time is come for hunting.

Tikki rises from her leafy hiding place, a grassy ridge in the rocky face of a hill whose trees and bushes have sheltered her from the sun and the worst of the day's heat. She steps under one of the cascades rushing down over the rocky outcrops and briefly glories in the shower of cool water gushing through her fur. It leaves her feeling fully awake, invigorated, alert.

She lifts her nose to the air.

She knows, by the strength of their smell, that sambar deer are nearby, well within her range. She has listened to their cries throughout most of the day. The season of their mating has arrived. Their husky barks and calls carry far through the still air of the forest. Their smells come to her like an invitation. If they have noticed her or her smell, they give no sign.

Tikki flicks her ears, shakes herself off, briefly paws at her neck, which is unaccountably itchy, then makes her way down to the forest floor. She does not hasten to the hunt. A cub might make that mistake, not her. She moves with a slow, deliberate stride that carries her quietly over fallen leaves and through the green branches of shrubs and trees. High up in the trees birds exclaim, but none cries out in alarm. Perhaps none has noticed her yet.

A sudden squalling erupts, sharp with tones of fear and anger. Tikki pauses to look up. The trees are alive with monkeys. Branches quiver and shake, leaves rustle. The monkeys screech and shriek, warning her to stay away, warning all within range of their sharp, annoying voices that danger has come.

For just a moment, she considers climbing up a tree to silence these exasperating creatures, but there is no point. She has tried that before. Her mother tried it once and nearly fell out of the tree while trying to get back to solid ground. Trees do not easily accommodate a creature of Tikki's size and weight.

She continues on, following the smells in the air.

Before long, the sambar resume their mating calls. They are off to her left and farther away than before. She adjusts her course. Fresher scents greet her nose from the tree trunks and the ground as well as the air. She has reached the spot where the sambar were when she first moved to the forest floor.

Soon she has them in sight, a small group, several males and females ranging around a small clearing. Tikki moves very carefully now, hunching low to the ground, using every snatch of cover. Abruptly, the sambar pause, heads held erect. She freezes, half-concealed by a jumble of rocks only a stride away from the clearing's edge. Have they seen her? Have they smelled her? She advances another stealthy step, then another, then suddenly some bird high up in the trees begins to scream. As one the sambar break, turning in flight.

By then, Tikki has launched herself from the brush and is hurtling across the clearing, paws tearing at the earth.

Now a million birds begin to scream as the sambar scatter in every direction. The first shriek of warning made them panic, rushing straight at her. Before they realize their mistake, she is among them, snaring one's rear with her claws, dragging it down, seizing its throat between her jaws.

That is her death grip. The kill is a certainty now. Her weight alone is enough to pin the animal to the ground, no matter how desperately it struggles. Tikki would not be surprised if the creature died of fear alone. It's happened before. Some prey seem to realize that once she has them in her grip there can be no escape. She has only to squeeze with her powerful jaws and perhaps twist her head to the side for the creature to strangle or for the bones of its neck to split and break.

That is what should be happening now, but something strange occurs instead. The sambar continues to struggle. The desperate gleam in its left eye becomes a spectral glow that spreads across its body. Tikki snaps its neck and still it struggles. She claws at its flesh and still it struggles. She rips at its body till its blood gushes over the ground and its organs split and burst around her claws and still it struggles to escape.

She tears its body into ruins, and then . . .

Abruptly, Tikki wakes. She is lying on the floor of her doss in northeast Philly, hearing her mother's words about what to do when things go wrong: cut your losses, get out. Get clear and never look back. Never mind about money or what it might cost your rep. Survival is paramount. There's always another sprawling metroplex with any number of hungry predators willing to pay for her kind of talent, and most of them care only about what she can deliver.

She lifts her head and looks around. Late afternoon sunlight fills the room. The mattress beneath her is in tatters. Bits of foam and white bedding cling to her claws.

The building around her is quiet.

She seems to be alone.

Time then to change. She forces herself back into human guise. It's easier in the light of the sun, but this soon after the full moon it's never easy. Tikki feels like she's changing from a creature of near-indomitable strength into a little pip-squeak of a two-legged weakling. It's like surrendering a kill to a more powerful predator. She knows that she must, but it so fills her with anger and frustration that a very human-sounding growl comes from her throat. The change leaves her lying on the mattress and staring up at the ceiling, wondering what she's going to do now. What should she do? So much seems wrong. The feeling that her situation has somehow gotten out of hand gnaws at her relentlessly.

She feels . . . confused.

For some reason beyond her ken, Tikki recalls the last man she killed for Adama—Tomita Haruso—how he continued to move even after he should have been dead. Had she not known better, she might have supposed that the man was not really a man, but some paranatural creature, perhaps even a Were such as herself. She might have suspected that magic was somehow involved. The only reason she did not suspect any of that was because everything smelled so right at the time. The humans smelled human. The air smelled of blood and terror and death. Only the evidence of her eyes indicated that something peculiar was occurring, and Tikki still does not know what to make of it.

One thing is certain: she won't resolve any of her uncertainties lying around naked in this doss. She applies her red and black paint and dons her red and black synthleather, assuming her Striper guise. She spends a moment checking the Kang—one shell in the chamber, a full clip securely installed—then slips it into the holster at the small of her back.

Late afternoon is slipping into evening as she steps onto the street. A blue and white Minuteman Security bus grinds up the block, heading toward the House of Correction. The blare of air horns and a low rumbling signal the passage of a train along the tracks off to the west. She walks that way, west. A few blocks and she's at the Hunan Mayfair, a little storefront restaurant mashed between a German deli and a pizzeria. The display in the window flashes the words "Kung Po Beef! Hot! Stir fried with water chestnuts, bamboo shoots, and peanuts in hot & spicy pepper sauce!" She steps inside, takes a seat at one of the plastic booths, and orders a plate of the Kung Po.

"Make it hot," Tikki tells the old man who takes her order.

"Ehh?" he says, frowning.

She removes her shades and meets his eyes. An Anglo would probably see only the red and black-striped mask painted onto her face and hair. Perhaps the old man sees more. A quick flash of surprise shows clearly in his eyes. Tikki guesses that he has noticed the subtle Asian cast to her eyes. For a man who is obviously Chinese, it would make a difference.

"I want it hot," she says in Mandarin.

"Very hot," the old man replies in the same tongue, flashing a smile. "Hot as you like. You'll see."

She nods, and the old man bows and withdraws.

A combat biker match between the Texas Rattlers and the L.A. Sabers is playing on the tiny pyramidal trid set into the center of her table. She switches to News Now 38, and listens to a replay of the story about that Neiman suit who got hosed in a parking garage. They still aren't saying anything about the yakuza getting smoked. Why does that bother her so much? Perhaps because the story about Neiman includes many details that recall her assassination of Ryokai Naoshi in a parking garage, and she has known the media to spill stories despite court-ordered blackouts and the efforts of the cops or the corps to keep certain incidents quiet.

She wonders if Adama could have been lying to her about the identities of those she has taken as prey. Could she have been tricked into murdering ordinary citizens? It seems unlikely. Tikki always verifies the information given her. To deceive her, Adama would have had to use magic on her, and Adama is no mage.

The meat arrives, Kung Po beef, hot enough to burn. The food helps settle her mood, making it easier to think. She considers ordering a second plate, but this is no time for gorging herself. She needs to think. Think clearly. Think smart.

Someone has marked her, put a price on her head. Never mind how they figured out that she's the principal weapon in Adama's ambitious rush toward dominance over the Philly underworld. What should she do about it? That's the point.

Be prepared for the worst.

Pick up her money.

Tikki doesn't like the idea of running, but if necessary, she will. And if and when the crunch comes, she may not have time for a trip to the bank.

The ''bank'' in this case is located beneath the ruins of the Northeast Mall, a quick taxi ride from the restaurant to a district called Holmesburg. The parking fields are littered with trash, junk, and burnt-out autos. Fires burn in metal drums. Five Minuteman patrol cars with flaring turret lights sit before the main entrance. A dozen gangers with cycles are holding a party on the west side. Around the north side of the mall, Tikki finds an open fire door that gives her access to a stairway down to the sublevel concourse.

It's dark down here, dark as night. The air smells of kerosene and petrochem. Laser light flares, flashlights gleam. Music roars, half a dozen discordant melodies, conflicting rhythms, throbbing, pounding. A racing bike whines, hurtling up the center of the concourse. Humans and metahumans, a few elves, orks, even some trolls, gather in groups or wander around, talking, laughing shouting, crying out. Some drink, others doze. A pair in black synthleather writhe and rut on one of the marble-ized benches along one side. Garbage and other debris make the footing treacherous in places. Vomit and other droppings mingle with the garbage and add to the rank smells fouling the air.

The shops lining both sides of the place have been converted to various purposes. One offers pirate sim-sense chips and tapes—all *Better Than Life*. Guaranteed. Another specializes in mind-altering chemicals. Several have a great variety of merchandise on display, all un-doubtedly stolen. Most places are guarded by artists with guns, mostly automatic weapons, including machine guns.

Toward the middle of the concourse is the store now used as the headquarters of the Death Angels, one of the city's most powerful biker gangs. Many members are cheap muscle, low-rent kick-artists, and killers. Minor talent as far as Tikki is concerned, but worth treating with a measure of respect, worth watching if only out of the corners of her eyes.

One of the gangers hanging around the headquarters entrance lifts a bottle of liquor toward her and calls, "Hoi, Striper!"

"Yo, *suit*!" she growls.

The ganger cackles with laughter, then makes a fist and pumps it back and forth from the hip, growling, "El numero uno!"

Respect goes both ways.

Necessarily so.

When it doesn't, life gets dangerous. The Death Angels know that. They wouldn't survive in northeast Philly if they got heavy with everyone they met. They also seem to know that Tikki is a predator worth treating right. She isn't exactly sure how they figured that out, but she hasn't had any problems with them since the day she arrived.

The bank is next door to the Angels' headquarters. The front is guarded by a wall of metal, broken only by a single narrow door. Tikki pounds on the door. The nar-row slit in the door flips open. One large eye looks out. A moment later, the door swings open and Tikki steps into the bank's outer room. Facing her is a wall of metal that shows the outlines of another door. To her left is a plastic table. To her right is a troll, and a big one. Known as Duke, he has such heavy bone deposits under his skin that it looks more like lumpy leather hide with rocks sewn into the fabric. The lumpy bits rise into short, stubby spikes that climb over the top of his head.

Duke isn't quite tall enough to be twice Tikki's height, but he's close. At least so it seems, standing there in front of him. Looking up into his face is like looking at the ceiling. He's easily tall enough to have to bend down low to pass through a standard doorway. And if he could wedge himself into the average automobile, there wouldn't be room for much else. Duke may not weigh as much as an automobile, but he looks it. Well over a hundred kilos. Also contributing to the impression of massive size and imposing power are his Ares body armor, studded and spiked arm bands, and the Stoner-Ares M107 heavy machine gun slung from his shoulder.

"You want trouble," he says in a voice deep and guttural. "I'll give you all you want."

Tikki believes him, and merely shakes her head. She's impressed. Not impressed enough to be scared, but enough to realize that if she did decide to make trouble she'd have to be very careful about this slag Duke. She only wonders why the troll feels a need to talk big. She isn't in the habit of making trouble for no reason.

"No guns allowed inside."

This is standard. Tikki lays the Kang on the table, then submits to a quick frisk. Duke grunts, then jabs with a horny, lumpy knuckle at a button on the inside wall. A buzzer sounds. The slit in the inside door flips open, but several moments pass before the door swings open. Some people never get through that door. You have to know the right name. You have to be considered safe.

"Remember what I said," Duke growls.

Tikki nods, though a bit irked by the reminder.

It's unnecessary.

The room beyond is very plain. Flanking the inner doorway are a pair of razorguys, one male, one female, both holding assault rifles. Tikki can almost smell the metal in them. A rectangular table stands in the center of the room, the only light coming from the glowing screen of the terminal sitting on it. Seated behind the table is André, Fat André. He is human, black, and immensely obese. His jowls have jowls, his chins descend to his chest. A slender, fashion-conscious woman might envy him his breasts. His gigantic belly seems to begin somewhere just under his arms and disappear beneath his side of the table. Oddly, he smells like fish.

Tikki has a hard time imagining a fish-eater ever becoming so obese. She has seen the occasional fat Japanese, but only rarely. Fat André's smell, his stink, is probably an unusual combination of sweat and other naturally produced aromas.

"Hoi," Fat André says.

Tikki nods, pausing before the table. "I'll take fifty kay of my money. In five certified sticks. No SINs."

Fat André watches her briefly, just long enough to make Tikki wonder if she got her English wrong. Though many say she handles the language well—she's had plenty of practice—it's not her native tongue and she can never be absolutely sure she's using exactly the right words. That is just one of the reasons she often relies on nods and shakes of the head when dealing with English-speakers.

Her concern over language diminishes when she hears a rustle to her rear, accompanied by the shuffle of a footstep. The smell in the air changes subtly as those sounds arise. Someone, maybe the two razorguys, are feeling a little bit stirred, a little tense. Tikki isn't sure why but she's getting the impression that a pair of assault rifles are now pointing at her back.

"I ain't laughing no more," Fat André says slowly.

Tikki puzzles over this for a moment. "What?"

"You ain't got no money here, Striper."

"What?"

That comes out a little sharply, perhaps more so than is wise. Puzzlement turns to anger and swells up too swiftly for her to completely control. That one word slips out, then she knuckles down, seizes her temper and holds it rigidly in check. As she does that, the steel muzzle of an assault rifle presses lightly against the left side of her back, just beneath the shoulder blade.

Tikki holds herself motionless, gazing intently at Fat André.

"We been through this before," he says. "You ain't got no money here. You ain't never had any money here. I'd give you a loan, but I'm sick of this drek. You scan?"

Drek is the operant word as far as Tikki's concerned. That's what's coming out of Fat André's mouth, and it doesn't make any sense to her. He and his bank came highly recommended, both as a safe drop for money and as a potential employer. She did a few jobs for him after first arriving in town. They didn't pay much, but they kept her skills sharp and gave her first-hand experience at how things worked in Philly. Till this very moment, she thought she had a valuable and trustworthy contact in Fat André. Now she isn't sure what to think.

"You hear what I'm saying?" Fat André says in a demanding tone.

Tikki says quietly, "I left more than a hundred kay with you."

"More drek. I can't slot this."

"Don't frag with me."

A second steel muzzle presses into her back, the back of her head. That's enough to get her worked up regardless of the cause. It's becoming harder for her to stand stock-still. Instinct is telling her to do something about the guns pressing against her. Tikki is trying, trying very hard, to stay calm, to keep darker thoughts out of her mind.

"I want . . . my money. All of it. Now."

Fat André looks toward the ceiling, then leans forward, extending a hand to the terminal on the table. His chair creaks with the shift in weight. The terminal screen changes displays. Tikki lowers her eyes enough to look. "This is what I got on you," Fat André says. "That's it."

One line on the screen reads Striper.

The next line reads File Not Found.

Tikki closes her eyes. That's both stupid and smart. She can't fight with her eyes closed, but if she doesn't close them for just a moment she'll do something she'll regret. She clenches her teeth as well, fighting back the anger.

"I came here three times," she growls softly. "Three times with money. Forty kay each time. A hundred and twenty kay. That's what you owe me."

"You wanna see the tape? Fine. I'll show you the tape."

Fat André keys another change in the display, which now shows the view through the security camera on the wall behind Fat André's back. Tikki watches what seems like a veritable replay of the last few minutes, except that on the screen the two razorguys standing guard to her rear are both male.

"You've got eighty kay of my money," her screen image growls.

"You never left me any money!" Fat André's screen image exclaims.

What the hell is this?

Tikki doesn't believe the vid. She looks at the real Fat André and says, "This is skag. Doctored."

"Yeah? When did you make your last deposit?"

She thinks about that. "A week ago."

"You ain't been here for a month."

The point isn't important. Or is it? She can't be sure when she came here last. She's been busy. Not that busy, or was she? Working for Adama has kept her occupied. Handling that amateur Hammer and his drekheaded chums took up some of her time. Has she been so busy that she's gotten confused about dates? Is that possible? Why does she feel so confused? Like this is just one more thing that's gone completely out of control?

She can't believe that Fat André would deliberately steal her money—he comes too highly recommended— but what other explanation is there?

Has she lost her mind?

Tikki shakes her head. "I don't get it."

"And you ain't gettin' anything, either," Fat André says. "Not from me. Now I think it's time for you to leave. And do me a favor. Don't come back."

With two assault rifles pressing into her hide, Tikki

has little choice. Leave or fight. She could fight, but she'd probably end up battling the troll, which could mean getting in deeper than she'd like. She might be forced to change into her four-legged form. Tikki prefers to reveal that truth only in the most special circumstances, such as when everyone but her is going to die.

Fighting is not really an option. Killing Fat André is not the way to get her money back. Killing will explain nothing.

She turns and leaves.

Carefully.

36

The bar is near city hall. The alley behind it is rank and dark. Raman waits in a shadowed niche formed by the rear walls of surrounding buildings. Hearing the scuffing of a shoe against the gritty concrete, he draws a stiletto from the sheath concealed inside the left arm of his jacket. The stiletto is balanced for throwing and he is well-practiced in that skill.

Footsteps come slowly up the alley. Raman leans forward slightly to look around the corner. The heavily built man approaching has dark, mottled skin and the fangs of an ork. He wears a black duster, and beneath it the dark blue uniform of Omni Police Services, the Camden police department. The man calls himself Gunter. He is an O.P.S. sergeant, works at O.P.S. headquarters.

Once assured that Gunter is alone, Raman steps fully into the alley, hands empty and held at his sides. Gunter hesitates, then comes forward. "The price is five hundred," he says in a low, gravelly voice.

Raman extends one hand.

"The money first," Gunter says.

Even as the words are being spoken Raman makes his move. He seizes the ork by the throat. Razor-sharp blades snap out of the mount on his right forearm. He lays the tips against Gunter's face. Eyes bulging with fear, the ork staggers back against the alley wall.

"You know how we do biz," Raman says quietly, his tone as sharp as the tips of his claws. One of the claws presses slightly into the ork's skin, drawing a trickle of blood. Gunter quivers visibly and turns his head flat to the alley wall, baring his throat. "Show me the merchandise," Raman growls. "I pay what it's worth."

Gunter smiles, once, then again. His voice wavers with anxious fear. "Sure . . . Okay! I was just . . . just kiddin' around." Gunter shudders, inhaling. "It's in my pocket."

"Take it out."

Gunter draws a clear plastic bag from his right duster pocket. Raman lifts it to examine it. On the bag is an orange sticker marked "O.P.S." and "EVIDENCE." Inside is what looks like a broad strip of black cloth. The ends are tapered, narrower than at the middle of the strip. "What is this?"

"Crime . . . crime-scene evidence. It came from the Gingko Club. Behind the club. It's supposed to be a mask, a face mask."

"You aren't *sure*?"

Raman's tone grows threatening. Gunter smiles nervously. "Nobody's *sure*. O.S.P. don't know what's going on. The Philly cops think Striper did the job at the Gingko Club. That's what I heard. If it's true, Striper wore this mask."

"If you lie, you're meat."

"I ain't lying."

Raman decides that's probably true, as far as it goes. He thrusts the bag into his jacket pocket. He stuffs a certified credstick for two hundred nuyen into the breast pocket of Gunter's uniform shirt, pressing the stick in firmly enough for the ork to feel him thrusting, thrusting down, slightly disarranging Gunter's shirt.

"Next time, no jokes. I don't like stupid jokes. They make me angry."

"Sorry . . ." Gunter smiles fearfully. "I'll play it straight from now on."

Raman draws the snapblades back into his forearm

mount with a soft snick, then releases the ork's neck and
nods up the alley. Gunter smiles nervously one last time
and turns to go.

Raman does the same, picking up his chopper nearby.
Taking I-676, he travels through the expanse of yakuza-
controlled territory known as Camden, the entertainment
mecca of the entire region: casinos, brothels, simsense
parlors, and the like. Beyond the interchange with the
Whitman Bridge, the road's name becomes I-76. The land
changes names as well, becoming known as Gloucester
City, a mostly industrial district with only scattered res-
idential neighborhoods. Raman takes the next exit and
rides onto Crescent Boulevard.

On the other side of the divided roadway passes a pha-
lanx of gangers, riding their choppers two-abreast. Raman recognizes the colors as those of the Paradise
Slayers, who claim the east side of the Delaware as their
own. Their most dangerous fighters are tuskers. Raman
has been forced to kill or maim one or more members of
the Slayers at various times in the past. Now, he notes
several of the riders turning their heads as if looking at
him as they pass. Rather than give the Slayers any chance
to interfere in his biz tonight, Raman turns at the next
traffic light, then guns the chopper's engine.

If the Slayers want to challenge him, there will be other
nights. Tonight another matter preoccupies him.

Somewhere, he has heard of this Striper before. Possibly it was in Hong Kong, involving a run on some Chinese warlord, though he is not sure. He has heard, too,
that Striper uses magic, but the form the magic takes is
unknown. He has also heard that Striper has never been
defeated in one-on-one combat.

All this intrigues him. First-rate artists are rare, and
ones who are also female are rarer still. He wonders what
sort of female might succeed in so dangerous a trade as
his. She must be very strong and clever. Perhaps exceed-
ingly clever, to compensate for a female's lesser strength.
It almost goes without saying that she must be cybernet-
ically enhanced, and yet this would seem unlikely if the
rumors about her magic, her edge, are true.

Such a female could be very challenging, in many

ways. Too bad he and Striper have never met. Now he will never know if she would have surrendered to him, willingly, as have so many other females. Now he must find her and kill her. That must remain in the forefront of his mind. The key to accomplishing this will be taking Striper unaware, nullifying any edge she may possess. That is how he will bring about her death.

The kill will doubtless do less to enhance his rep than simply remind various persons that he is still around and in the full possession of his powers.

The money . . . that should provide him with some amusement.

Just short of Broadway, he turns down a narrow street flanked by three-story brick row houses. Various small and mid-size autos line the curbs. Streetlights take the form of antique lanterns set on poles. Most of the houses contain ground-level shops. Some also have shops one story down, with stairs descending from the sidewalk. A small crowd of people stands around on the walk in front of one place, a cafe or coffee shop. Raman catches a few notes of what sounds like a flute. Just past mid-block, he slows the chopper almost to a halt, then rolls it between a pair of parked cars, and lowers the Harley's stand.

A male ork passes by. He is carrying a guitar case, and merely glances at Raman with a nod as if in greeting.

Not unusual for this neighborhood.

His pace casual, unhurried, Raman steps over the curb and across the brick-paved sidewalk. A small sign hanging from a curling metal bracket on the house there reads R. Liddy—Herbs & Artifices. The small arrow painted on the sign points down. Raman steps around the metal railing guarding the stairs and looks down. A single flight of stairs leads to the white paneled door of the shop.

Sitting around on the narrow steps is a small group Raman has seen here before. Some kind of gang, he supposes. Tonight, there are seven. Five females and two males, all young. Adolescents. Some dress like kick-artists, others like fans, wannabes. All have had their features remade to resemble cats, alley cats, house cats. Their heads are covered with a thick, downy hair like fur. Their eyes are golden. Their ears protrude from near the tops of their heads and flick back and forth. Their bodies are slim enough to seem almost elven. The females have little more than the mere suggestion of breasts. The downy hair that covers their heads runs down their arms and over the backs of their hands. All have long fingernails resembling claws.

As Raman starts down the stairs, one of the females whips her head around to look up at him, the others immediately following suit. Raman steps around them. There is no problem. As usual, the group merely watches, saying nothing. If they consider the stairs their private territory, they give no sign. Their presence here is significant, but Raman can only guess at their purpose.

The sounds of the flute carry to him clearly through the squarish passage of the underground sidewalk, which parallels the one at street-level. Several people pass by, heading both up and down the block. They are black and white and several shades in between, and include three humans, an ork, and a pair of elves. Some are dressed like artisans or painters or musicians. Raman turns and goes through the door of the shop of R. Liddy, Herbs & Artifices.

A small bell rings as he pushes the door open.

The shop is small and cluttered. Incense drifts like a haze through the air, accompanied by the soft strains of what Raman takes to be a sitar. Roots and plants dangle in bunches from the ceiling. Stones and crystals line the shelves. Cups and flasks of powders and more exotic materials fill the transparex-lined display cases running up the sides and across the rear of the place. These cases also contain a variety of ornate knives, sticks, scepters, drums, rattles, and jewelry. A number of cats, ordinary cats, lie about the place, on the floor, the shelves, and the display cases.

The woman who comes through the beaded doorway at the rear of the shop is called Risa. She wears an extravagant abundance of jewelry and a long, flower-printed dress of some antique style. Her expression darkens as she meets Raman's eyes. She joins her hands before her, lacing her fingers, and looks at him questioningly.

"Eliana," Raman says.

Risa shakes her head. "Not here."

"You lie."

Risa's eyes widen, her lips pressing tightly together as a hot red flush rises to her cheeks. Her eyes show fear, her lips and cheeks show anger. "She won't see you," she says adamantly.

"Tell her I'm here."

"She already knows—"

"Tell her," Raman growls.

Risa turns and walks swiftly into the rear of the shop. Her attitude is unimportant. She is a servant, nothing more. Her opinion of him will not influence the person he has come to see. Risa returns a few moments later to announce haughtily, "Eliana will see you."

As Raman expected.

He steps through the doorway hung with beaded strings and into a small room lined in satin drapes. Occupying the center is a circular table, richly inlaid. The inlays form an intricate image of mystic shapes, figures, and arcane symbols. The meanings of these shapes and symbols Raman cannot guess, for he is no mage, nor shaman. He skirts the table. Opposite where he entered, he draws back the drapes and steps into a short, narrow corridor. Both ends of this passage are cloaked with drapes. In the doorway along the left stands a heavily constructed ork, naked to the waist but for the straps of a shoulder holster bearing a large automatic.

The ork nods as Raman passes along.

The drapes at the end of the passage lead into another small room, one richly furnished. A small chandelier hangs from the ceiling, which is covered with mirrors and ornamented in gold. The walls are paneled in lush red velvet. Luxurious drapes cloak all four corners. The floor is thickly carpeted. Opposite where Raman enters is a kind of sofa, possibly an antique, composed of intricately carved darkwood and plushly appointed with dark red tasseled pillows.

Here lies Eliana, sprawled languidly on her side. In form, she is a most appealing female. Her hair is a pale shade of blonde, cascading about her face and against the pillows. Her features are fair, as fair as her complexion, yet tinged with the quality of a vixen. She wears a loosely flowing robe as lustrous as gold, but otherwise appears to be naked. Her long, tapering fingernails and the nails of her toes are anointed in gold. She wears one item of jewelry.

The large medallion that dangles from a ropey chain at the base of her throat is an unusual orange-gold color. Impressed into the medallion is a strange image, a face like that of a kind of feline Raman has rarely seen. Its pupils are slitted, the face slim and alien. Raman supposes that it most closely resembles the type of feline that occupies this room, ordinary house cats.

Five such cats share the sofa with Eliana. A dozen more lie about the room. Though they come in varying shapes and colors, only one is black. Several of the cats have collars, but only the black one's is golden. The black cat sits on the floor midway between Raman and Eliana. It sits unmoving, gazing at Raman.

Raman pays it no attention.

"Eliana," he says.

The name is pronounced in a specific way: E-lee-ana. Rolled swiftly off the tongue with equal emphasis to each part of the word. *Eliana* . . . To pronounce it in any other manner is to guarantee that the she will take offense and refuse to cooperate. Eliana is haughty to the point of arrogance. She looks at him as might a queen, with one arched eyebrow, bidding him enter with a vague gesture.

Raman steps through the doorway, which is flanked on either side by more plush seats. He prefers to stand, stand and wait. To speak before she makes some inquiry would also offer offense. Raman has been here often enough to learn the ways and means, what is done and what is not.

Eliana gazes at him a few moments, looking him over, then pushes against the thick cushions of her sofa and slowly sits up. Tossing her hair back behind her shoulders, she crosses her legs and smoothes her robe. She takes a cigarette from the darkwood box on the table beside the head of the lounge, then extends her left arm fully, shaking back the sleeve of her robe. Softly, she hums. A small flame bobs into existence at the end of

her index finger, just above the top of her long, tapered fingernail. She uses the flame to light the cigarette; then, without warning, the flame rises toward the ceiling, swelling into a slowly boiling cloud of fire that fades into a haze of orange-red spreading slowly across the ceiling, deepening in color as it gradually disappears.

When Raman looks at Eliana again, she is gazing at him steadily with a smug smile and one sharply arched brow. "Why do you come here?"

"To ask your help."

"Indeed." Her smile grows very smug. She closes her eyes as she takes a puff from her cigarette. She is several moments blowing the smoke away through puckered lips. "Perhaps you offer me money?"

"Yes."

"I have all the money I desire at present."

Raman has known this she to refuse work, refuse to cooperate, on just such a basis. "Perhaps there is work you would like done."

"Perhaps there is," Eliana replies. "That is for me to know, of course." She pauses to smile at him, and now the smile turns seductive. She gazes at him from the corners of her eyes. One eyebrow rises discreetly. "What do you wish of me?"

Her tone and manner are like a sensual invitation, but Raman knows better than to respond in kind. She is just toying with him, something she delights in doing. It makes her difficult to deal with. Reminding himself of just who and what he is facing, Raman suppresses his rising impatience. "There is someone I would like to find."

"And why should I desire to help you?"

"I will help you in return."

"What makes you think I need your help?"

"Perhaps there are matters you would prefer to leave to others."

Now she smiles broadly, and tosses back her head as if to laugh, but does not do so. Rather, she leans down on one elbow. Her long, thick hair tumbles across her shoulders and over the pillows. "You know I loathe getting smudged," she says, still smiling. "That's not fair."

Doubtless, she would much prefer that he not know why she might desire his aid. They could go on talking for hours. She could continue toying with him all night.

"There are others I could persuade to do my bidding. Why should I use you?"

Raman recalls the seven youths sitting on the stairs outside. Perhaps they are her followers, her band. Eliana has hinted in the past about having many connections, and has even remarked about "her servants" a time or two, but has never explained herself fully, in this or any other context.

"What's so special about you that I should do you this favor?"

Raman simply speaks the truth. "Few have my qualifications."

Again, Eliana smiles as if to laugh, but does not. Raman has never heard her laugh. The closest she has come to it in his presence is a soft expulsion of breath. Sometimes, she hisses. Now, she hums. The black cat turns its head and looks back at her, then goes to her. She takes it into her lap and begins to gently stroke it between the ears. The cat purrs audibly, gazing at Raman through eyes like slits.

Raman waits.

Eliana looks up from the cat and across at him. "You must think I find you very appealing."

Raman says nothing. It is obvious to him that the she finds him appealing. He has sampled her talents on a number of occasions, and each time she was the initiator. This does not surprise him. Many females he has met find him dangerous and therefore seductive, and so consider him extremely desirable.

"Perhaps I *will* grant you this favor," Eliana goes on to say, smiling vaguely. "Tell me more. Tell me everything."

The she is as inquisitive as she is arrogant. "The person I want to find is called Striper," Raman explains. "She is an artist like me."

"How like you is she?"

"She is freelance muscle. She kills and intimidates.

She has eluded capture for many years. She is reputed to be a powerful fighter and very clever.''

"Does she kill with blades?"

"Usually with guns."

"How old is she?"

"I do not know."

"She is tall?"

"For a female."

"What color is her hair?"

"She paints it. Sometimes it is red and black. Other times brown. Brown with some blonde. She also paints her face. Red with black stripes."

"Is that why she is called Striper?"

Raman shrugs. It seems as likely an explanation as any other. "Perhaps."

"She is human?"

"Apparently."

"Does she have magic?"

"No one knows. Some say she has an edge. Perhaps a magical edge of some kind."

"She is a physical adept?"

"She is very adept."

Eliana's lips curve into a sneer. "I mean a *physical* adept. One who uses magic to improve only her body and physical abilities. A semi-mundane."

"That I do not know."

"Obviously."

Raman draws the plastic O.P.S. evidence bag from his jacket pocket. "I have this. Striper wore it on one of her kills."

Eliana looks at him briefly, then seems to sigh, softly and with exaggerated frustration or impatience. The bag flies from Raman's hand, tugging free, then arcing across the room. It slows in descending into Eliana's left hand.

"What is this?" she asks, examining the bag as if quite curious, tilting her head from side to side. "Some kind of mask?"

"Yes," Raman replies.

"It will do," Eliana says, abruptly rising. "Come."

Lifting the black cat to her breast, Eliana crosses the room and opens a narrow door. That door, Raman knows, leads to a narrow stairway. Raman starts to follow, then stops. Each of the two dozen cats in the room converge on the door in a headlong rush. Several more come dashing past Raman's ankles from beyond the doorway behind him. Why they hasten to follow Eliana, Raman does not know. He does know, however, that accidentally stepping on one of the creatures would make Eliana very unhappy, though she rarely shows more than a token awareness of their presence.

Of the cats, Raman can say only one thing for certain: the black one is special. It often gives the impression of possessing a degree of intelligence far greater than an ordinary cat's. It responds to Eliana's smallest gesture and is always watching.

Even as Eliana descends the stairs, the black cat appears at her shoulder, its face veiled by Eliana's long tresses, its golden eyes staring straight at Raman.

Raman waits for the creature to descend out of sight, then checks the floor around him and follows.

The stairway is steep and barely wide enough for Raman to descend without brushing his shoulders against the walls. The steps are carpeted and seem as sturdy as stone. They end at a small space barely a meter square. To his right is an opening cut from the juncture of two concrete walls, through which Raman can only fit sideways. He pushes aside a heavy black curtain as he passes through.

The room he enters is moderately large. Its walls, ceiling, and floor are black. The floor is as smooth as glass. The only light comes from the hundreds of candles climbing the wall in six tiers at the far end of the room.

As on previous occasions, Raman notes not a hint of dust or dirt anywhere. The air is cool and fresh and pure. Doubtless, the place is routinely cleaned. A small ventilator whirs softly from a recess in the ceiling.

The twenty-odd cats that followed Eliana down the stairs are scattered around the room, some seated on their haunches, others sprawled on their sides or bellies. For the moment, they seem like ordinary cats, disinterested or unaware of anything involving anything but themselves. That will change as the time progresses.

Eliana stands before the wall of candles. At its center is a small cabinet covered with a black cloth. The she calls it an altar. On the altar is a large mirror and a variety of containers, including several cups and urns, plus other items like those Raman has seen in the shop upstairs. There are more such supplies on the shelves hidden within the altar.

Abruptly, Eliana lifts her arms out from her sides and the light of the candles swells in intensity. The cats all look up, then return to washing themselves, or stretching, or napping.

This is just the beginning.

Eliana removes her lustrous robe and lets it drop to the ground. That leaves her clad in only the briefest of string bikinis, a black one. Raman surveys her form from behind. The she's body is delightful, slim and supple, enticingly curved, neither extreme nor spare in any of its proportions. Raman feels a stirring of arousal, as he always does at the sight of a female so nearly naked.

Knowing this one as he does, he would expect Eliana to turn her head and look back at him, if only to ascertain that he is indeed looking at her. It is the cat that looks, however. From its place beside Eliana's ankles, the black one turns and looks directly at Raman, then bares its teeth and hisses. This, Raman knows, is a warning of sorts. He lowers himself to the floor and sits with legs crossed, leaning back against the wall. Standing is not allowed. It is considered a great privilege to be permitted to witness the conduct of the magic. He must sit here, remaining silent and unmoving, until the magic is done.

Eliana tosses her hair, then begins to hum. She steps up to the altar and casts a small quantity of some powder into a metal crucible. A peculiar bluish flame immediately bursts into life. Eliana then turns and casts more powder toward the four corners of the room. Her humming rises into a chant.

"Spirits, I call thee . . . Spirits, I call thee . . ."

Raman becomes aware of a strange buzzing tension, one that seems to pervade the room, passing right through his own skull. The tension swells into a vibrancy that makes him dizzy, as though he would topple if he tried to stand. He comes to feel rooted to the earth, fixed in his position. Such feelings are disturbing, but he has survived them before. They are a part of the magic. A side effect, the she claims.

Eliana now sways before the altar and her voice rises into song. Every intonation is like gold, ringing forth with bell-tone clarity. Such purity of tone makes the sensual beauty of her body seem so trivial as to be irrelevant. Raman has never heard another voice quite like it. The sound is captivating.

Abruptly, the she is dancing, swaying sinuously, seductively, smoothing her hands along the luscious contours of her own body, rolling her hips. Her movements carry her slowly around the circumference of a broad circle, and rival even the beauty of her voice for sheer sensual appeal.

What magical significance any of this has Raman does not know, nor does he care. To him, as a male, the seductive dance has only one true meaning. It is an invitation, and very difficult to resist. He becomes fully aroused even as the she begins. He spends the next quarter-hour or so struggling against the urge to rise and answer the she's enticing siren song. His blood begins to rush hotly through his flesh. The heat in his groin seems almost molten. Yet, he realizes, the she is only toying with him again, intentionally or not. Were he to follow his urgings, interfere with her magic in any way, Eliana would become enraged, and that would be very dangerous indeed.

With just a movement of her hand and a whispered word, she once hurled him against the rear wall of this room with such force he was sure his spine was shattered.

Never again . . .

Abruptly, a wall of flame erupts around the circle Eliana has sketched out with her dance. The flames send a billowing cloud of smoke toward the ceiling, then vanish. As the smoke clears away from the floor, Eliana is revealed, now kneeling at the center of the circle, facing the wall of candles, the altar, and the mirror.

Her singing continues, but softly now. From time to

time, she sways, raising her arms, and the greater
strangeness begins, brought on by the magic. The room
seems to grow blurred. Raman feels his eyes growing
heavy. The desire to sleep becomes all but irresistible
. . . and then suddenly he sees Eliana on all fours, crawling before the altar.

The magic has begun in earnest. Power vibrates
through the air. The she is changed. Her face resembles
the strange feline image on her medallion. Her eyes are
black as jet, her fingernails like claws, as long as each
of her fingers. Her hands resemble paws. A lustrous
golden down seems to cover her entire body. As she
moves, turning back and forth, sometimes turning completely around, she hisses and purrs, at times baring her
teeth, revealing a pair of diminutive fangs protruding
from her upper jaw.

Every cat in the room surrounds her. They sit on their
haunches facing her as though entranced. Each time she
moves, the ones immediately before her bolt aside as if
frantic to get out of her way. The instant Eliana stops or
turns elsewhere, they immediately halt and turn back,
sitting as before, motionless as statues and staring as if
captivated.

It is as if their god has appeared before them.

Do cats have gods? Raman wonders, but then the
strangeness overcomes him again. His eyes fall shut.
When they open again, he sees an image wavering in the
mirror above the altar, as transparent as water and yet as
clearly visible as the blurry lines of heat rising from the
tiers of candles. The image is like that of Eliana's medallion, a strange and alien feline face. Eliana sits on her
heels before it, her head thrown back, her hair cascading
almost to the floor. Behind her the cats sit on their
haunches in a perfect semicircle.

Melodic voices whisper, so soft and faraway Raman
cannot quite make out what they are saying.

Another time passes. Raman abruptly realizes that
Eliana is wearing her golden robe again. She is now lying
on her side, sprawled luxuriously in the center of the
room, head propped on one arm. The cat-like manifes-
tation in the altar mirror has disappeared. The light of

the candles is once again at a normal level. Eliana looks
at him with the languid eyes of a sensual woman. The
cats walk around her, back and forth, purring, meowing,
rubbing themselves against her, as if striving for her attention.

Smiling, Eliana extends one hand, motioning Raman
closer.

Raman gets up carefully. His head has cleared. He feels
fine, vigorous and alert. He steps to the center of the
room and lowers himself to one knee. Smiling seductively, Eliana runs her fingertips over his chest and around
to the back of his neck, then lightly pulls him downward
till his face is but a breath away from hers and that of
the black cat, seated next to her cheek.

"I know exactly where Striper is," Eliana murmurs,
eyes gleaming. She pauses to smile. "And I will show
you," she adds softly. "But first you must serve me."

Naturally. "What do you want me to do?"

Eliana releases his neck and stretches her arm out
across the floor and lays her head against it. "There is a
man who must be chastised," she says softly, lightly.
"Chastised in a physical way. It should not be difficult.
Not for you."

"That is all?"

The she smiles, arching one brow.

It is never just one thing. In this case, however, the
second thing the she desires is not at all displeasing.
Raman guesses what it is by Eliana's next remark.

"Take off your clothes," she croons.

Raman willingly complies.

37

"You set?"

Kirkland looks at the woman sharing the elevator with
him. Her name is Val Pandolfini. She's Italian, but you'd
never guess it just by looking at her. Her hair is long and

thick and a rusty shade of red-brown. Her face is almost dead-white, though touched by a pinkish hue high on her cheeks. Combined with her skin tone, the dark shadowing around her eyes and the black paint on her lips and nails make her look like a fragging vampire. The black bomber jacket doesn't help. The skin-tight, short black skirt helps some, but her bare, pasty-white legs and idiotic low-heeled ankle boots detract from what little the skirt struggles to add.

Of course, that's just Kirkland's personal opinion, and they're not here on this elevator for anything other than purely professional reasons. Ms. Pandolfini, approximately twenty-seven years of age, is a three-year veteran of the Minuteman Police Intelligence Bureau. She is a police recorder, and one trained for and experienced with undercover work at that.

"Twenty-six July," she says, looking straight ahead at the elevator doors. "Nineteen fifty-three hours. Job number 23054." She looks at Kirkland. "Accompanying Kirkland, Lieutenant, Homicide, Central Division, on subject interview, Platinum Manor Estates. Everything I see and hear from this point forward will be recorded, Lieutenant."

Kirkland gives a nod. "Good."

To look at her, you'd never guess she has cybercams for eyes and a sealed recording module implant. That's the beauty of it. Once she turns on, everything she sees and hears becomes evidence admissible in any court. Her record of events is even better than that of an ordinary hidden camera because her memory module has been sealed by the court and can only be opened in the presence of a judge. Any form of tampering with the module would be overtly obvious, if only to the court's appointed technician.

Kirkland's glad to have her along, even if she does more resemble a vampire than a cop.

The elevator doors slide open. Stepping out, Kirkland glances to his right and his left, then immediately stops. Pandolfini stops, too. The corridor leading past the elevator is very short, no more than six, seven meters long. It's a kind of private entrance hall giving access to a pair of luxury condos. To the left of the elevator stand three men in dark gray, military-style body armor, complete suits, everything from helmets with reflective faceplates to semi-rigid chest protection to armored gloves and boots. Two of them hold short-barreled assault carbines. The third holds an SMG. Back the other way, to the right of the elevator, are two more in full armor carrying assault carbines.

Kirkland immediately recognizes that if this is an ambush, he and Pandolfini are dead.

"We're cops," Kirkland says at once.

That turns out to be exactly the right thing to say.

Three move in close. The one with the SMG takes center stage. His voice is flat and raspy. Computer-modulated, Kirkland assumes. "Your identification."

"They're both armed," another one says.

Somebody's got sensors, weapon detectors.

Kirkland slowly draws the left side of his jacket fully open and slowly reaches into his inside breast pocket, then slowly draws out his shield case, flips it open, and extends it out for all to see.

"Kirkland," he says. "Lieutenant Kirkland. Homicide."

"Who's the other?" says the one with the SMG.

The "other" identifies herself, displaying a brass shield and saying, "Detective-Sergeant Val Pandolfini."

"State your business, Lieutenant."

Kirkland's arm starts to get tired. He closes his shield case and returns it to his inside jacket pocket. Pandolfini follows his lead. "I'm here on official police business. Who the hell are you?"

"Agent Two-Nine-Five, in command, Birnoth Comitatus High-Threat Defense Unit."

"Fine. You wanna get the hell outta my way?"

"Contacting command," says Two-Nine-Five. "Stand by."

The tone of voice grates on Kirkland's nerves, but he forces himself to stay calm. He's encountered corporate mercenaries plenty of times before. Some of them are fraggin' psychopaths. Others are just nuts. Birnoth mercs have a pretty good rep, based on everything Kirkland's

ever heard, but that doesn't mean the average Birnoth
operative has anything like a normal psychological profile. Caution is advised.

"Right," says the Birnoth agent. "Who is your commanding officer, Lieutenant?"

"Captain Emilio Henriquez."

"That's the name. You're clear to pass."

"Thanks a lot, chummer."

Agent 295 precedes Kirkland down the hall to the door,
then keys the intercom. The door slides open. Kirkland
steps into a small room with marbleized, mirrored gold
paneling and several pieces of antique wooden furniture.
Pandolfini comes up alongside him and runs her eyes
around the room. She knows what to watch for. In a
moment, the double-pocket doors leading into the rest of
the condo slide apart and a man in a white servant's uniform enters and approaches Kirkland.

"May I help you, sir?"

"Need to see Mister Ohara."

"I'm sorry," the servant replies. "Mister Ohara is not
here at present."

"Oh, yeah?" Kirkland lifts his brows as if surprised,
then glowers. "Well, maybe you better go check with
Mister Ohara again, because a good friend of mine just
saw him and his two girlfriends come home. And if he
still isn't here, then Detective Pandolfini and I will just
wait right here until Mister Ohara decides that he *is* here.
And make sure you tell him that, chummer."

The servant frowns very briefly, then goes back through
the double doors.

About two minutes later, Kirkland steps through a sliding transparex door onto a spacious transparex-enclosed
balcony providing a panoramic view of the expansive
Platinum Manor Estates botanical gardens. There's a
badge down there somewhere, and another one in the
underground parking garage. That Kirkland's got Ohara
under surveillance shouldn't be construed as meaning he
suspects Ohara of any crime within the jurisdiction of
Philadelphia. Kirkland's just covering the angles. Officially, he's just covering angles.

Tonight, Ohara wears a long black satin robe and slippers, not to mention an excess of gold jewelry. He sits on a velvet-cushioned lounge. He smiles like the king of the world. A bottle of champagne on ice and a dish of caviar sit on the table beside him. Sharing the lounge with Ohara are a pair of blondes who look like raunchy sex just waiting to happen. The blondes are nude, and they look enough alike to be twins. Neither makes a move to get up or to cover herself.

"Good evening, Lieutenant," says Ohara. "How can I help you?"

Kirkland considers introducing Detective Pandolfini to the group, but decides against it. Ohara's question deserves an immediate response. "You could explain why you withheld information pertinent to a homicide investigation."

"Excuse me?"

"Robert Neiman, Steven Jorge, Thomas Harris. When you took over Exotech, all three were assigned to the Special Projects Section over in Germantown. You said you redesigned Exotech's corporate structure, and that's true, but that was complete in your first six months. Neiman, Jorge, and Harris weren't reassigned until six months after that, until after the big blow-up at S.P.S."

"Excuse me, Lieutenant," Ohara says, still smiling like royalty, "but your information is incorrect."

"Yeah? I don't think so."

"Those three unfortunate men you mention were all transferred to new posts well before the incident at S.P.S."

That is almost certainly a lie. Kirkland's gut tells him so, but he's got more than just his gut with which to form an opinion. He's got a hard-copy report from the office of the vice-chairman of KFK, a fellow named Torakido Buntaro. That report states that Neiman, Jorge, and Harris were transferred to their new positions after the accident at S.P.S. There's an affidavit from the director of Exotech personnel supporting that statement. Kirkland strongly suspects that Ohara boosted Neiman, Jorge, and Harris up the ladder either as a reward or to keep them quiet. The question is what did those three men, now brutally murdered, see or do at the S.P.S. facility to warrant Ohara's special consideration?

Did they threaten to blow the whistle on something? Did Ohara himself orchestrate their murders?

"Back in Seattle, you worked for an outfit called Seretech. You were in charge of overseeing a heavy-duty bioengineering project. One of the other top executives on that project died in an auto accident the Seattle P.D. classified as suspicious. Certain information critical to the project vanished. You left Seretech shortly thereafter."

"Yes, I did leave," Ohara replies, smiling brilliantly. "You will recall, Lieutenant, that I was attacked in my home. I was more than a year recuperating. I decided then to make a fresh start."

"Ever meet a man named John Brandon Conway?"

"Why do you ask?"

"I asked you first."

"I've heard of him, certainly. Everyone has."

That much is true. Conway is a fixer, one of the biggest and most elusive. He works as a middleman for multinational conglomerates, governments. His deals involve twelve- and fifteen-digit numbers.

"Yeah," Kirkland goes on, "everybody's heard of Conway, but you actually met him. In Toronto. Maybe that's where you sold him the data you stole from Seretech."

"You should mind your manners, Lieutenant," Ohara replies coolly. "Were I to take offense, I might find it necessary to sue."

"You're denying what I just said."

"Certainly."

"Then I guess you'd also deny that you used the proceeds from that sale to buy yourself a seat on the board of Kono-Furata-Ko International?"

"I did nothing of the kind."

Ohara's brilliant smile continues to gleam, but Kirkland notices a chink in the armor, a twitching at the outside corner of Ohara's left eye. It could be just a muscle spasm, maybe brought on by fatigue, but Kirkland doesn't think so. The man is acting way too confident to be real. Too confident even for a guy with serious ego problems.

Kirkland hopes Detective Pandolfini notices the twitching.

"I guess Seretech is old news. Not my jurisdiction. And how you got on the board of KFK really isn't police business. I was just curious."

"You're a very curious man, Lieutenant."

Kirkland nods. The remark probably wasn't meant as a compliment, but he'll take it that way for the moment. "Now about your dead execs. Neiman, Jorge, and Harris were all in the Special Projects Section. Their most recent posts describe a ladder leading straight to you. What do you suppose that suggests?"

"You're the detective," Ohara replies. "You tell me."

"I'm asking the questions, Mister Ohara."

"I'm not obligated to speculate."

"Really? Well, that's very interesting." Kirkland takes a folded sheet of hard copy from his jacket pocket. "I have a copy of a memo here. You probably haven't seen it yet because you left the office early today. It's from the vice-chairperson of KFK, to all members of the board and all employees of Exotech, directing them to 'assist the official police investigation into the deaths of Robert Neiman, Steven Jorge, and Thomas Harris, without exception or exclusion.' Without exception or exclusion. That's a quote."

"May I see that?"

Kirkland folds the sheet and slips it back into his jacket pocket, saying, "Well, you understand, this is my copy. I'm sure there's one waiting for you at your office."

Ohara's left upper eyelid twitches some more.

"So what do you think about the progression? Neiman, Jorge, Harris. Then you. What does that suggest?"

Ohara's smile falters, just for an instant. "I'm sure I have no idea," he says.

"Maybe you're next."

"Next? In what regard?"

"Next to be assassinated."

"That's ridiculous."

"Really? Then why do you have a Birnoth mercenary unit in heavy armor guarding your door?"

"Simply a precaution."

"Against what?"

"We live in a violent world, Lieutenant."

"Maybe Seretech wants their data back. Maybe they want revenge. Maybe whoever killed your three execs is looking for revenge. Maybe that someone is unhappy about what happened over in Germantown."

"I . . . I'm sure I don't know."

"Harris was in charge of the Germantown group. He reported directly to you. That means you had hands-on control of what the Special Projects Section did."

"I'm Exotech's chief executive officer. Ultimately, I have control over every group and section, not just Special Projects."

"So you're saying that the group that got you the smash hits of the century, the Hermetic Library chips like *The Summoning of Abbirleth,* operated pretty much on its own? You didn't give it any special attention, no more than any other part of Exotech?"

Ohara leans his head back and laughs softly. "Obviously, Lieutenant, I played a role in guiding the S.P.S.'s activities. I don't see anything sinister in that"

"No?"

Ohara's eyelid keeps twitching.

Kirkland watches that a moment, then says, "Last time we talked, maybe the time before that, you said that Robert Neiman was just a researcher before you promoted him. Is that right?"

"Certainly."

"Well, it's a funny thing, but I've just seen some personnel records that describe Neiman a little differently."

"How do you mean?"

"Neiman was a mage."

"That's not so."

"Sure, it is." Kirkland has copies of personnel records, and a few of his detectives have dug up corroborating witnesses on the point. "You had a bunch of mages up there in Germantown, a ritual team. That's where you got the wet record for your Hermetic Library series of

simsense chips. Neiman was a mage, and the accident at
S.P.S. burned him out so bad he couldn't handle magic
after that. The same happened to Jorge. He got burned.
The same for Harris. They all got burned. Now they're
dead. So out of the original group of seven mages, only
one's still alive. Three died in the accident, three just got
murdered. That leaves one, and that one's dropped out
of sight. Do you know who I'm talking about, *Mister*
Ohara?''

The twitching gets so bad Ohara actually lifts a hand
to his left eye and rubs at it. That doesn't help. "I'm
sorry," he says, the wide smile faltering again. "I . . .
I don't recall the name. It was a man.''

"Adam Malik.''

"Yes. I . . . I believe that's it.''

Kirkland drops all pretense at politeness. "The guy
survived an accident in which he saw three of his col-
leagues killed and the other three traumatized! Then he
drops completely out of sight! Didn't it occur to you that
he might hold a grudge?''

"A grudge? For what reason?''

Kirkland sneers. The lies and attempts at deception
have become more and more lame. "You know what your
problem is, chummer? You're too busy saving your own
ass to worry about who dies for your mistakes.''

Interview concluded.

Kirkland turns and leaves.

In his bedroom, Ohara struggles out of his robe and
hurls it to the floor. He feels like he's suffocating. His
hands are shaking and his fragging eyelid won't stop
twitching. All because of that skell Kirkland, all the in-
nuendoes and lies and veiled threats. Ohara isn't fooled.
If that skell Kirkland had anything on him, he'd be ar-
resting him, not harassing him. If Kirkland keeps it up,
he's going to get more trouble than he knows how to
handle. Ohara knows how to arrange for that. If not legally, then illegally. If not by persuasion, then by killing.
It wouldn't cost much to buy the assassination of some
overweight and not terribly bright police lieutenant. And

Ohara's got more than enough change to do it. More than enough.

Just thinking about lowlife skells like Kirkland has Ohara's nerves in knots. P-fix BTL chips just aren't giving him enough of a boost anymore. Direct input or no. He needs something stronger, more potent. What he needs is waiting for him, he knows, on the marble counter of his private bathroom—a gift from one of his biffs, no less.

He steps through the communicating door. The sleek, squarish box is plated in gold, the interior blue velvet. The pneumatic injector is mirrored chrome. Ohara doesn't usually like to avail himself of narcotics so early in the evening, but tonight is a special case. He pops a vial of DeeVine into the base of the injector's handle. It's just like loading an automatic pistol. Insert the vial, pull the latch, press the muzzle against his left upper arm, and pull the trigger. He feels a sudden gush against his arm like a burst of icy pins and needles, but then the flood of sweet sweet pleasure begins.

In another moment, he's euphoric, on top of the world. In another two or three more, he's as hard as steel and ready to ram it in, and in, and in, straight through the heart of the planet.

Grinning, he opens the door to the crystal- and mirror-decorated spa. Christie and Crystal are there, where they should be, in the huge marble bath, up to their magnificent, cosmetically enhanced boobies in foamy bubbles. They look at him and smile.

What he wants them for is obvious, and they're more than willing to comply.

After all, that's their whole purpose.

38

The glowing neon sign outside reads Ristorante, but the interior of the place looks more like a bar, a dark, dingy little bar hidden along a back street in South Philly. Inside are a dozen stools lined up along the plastic-paneled face of the bar, and a dozen small round tables sit draped in stained linen, each with two chairs apiece. Opera music carries out from some room in the back.

A fat woman in a dirty apron brings out a cup of some aromatic kind of soykaf romantically described as cappuccino. The old men sitting along the bar keep looking over their shoulders toward the table in the right rear corner. From behind the mirrored lenses of her black visor-style shades, Tikki notes their glances, but considers other things.

She's here because this is probably the last place in Philadelphia where anybody would think to look for her, and she needs a few minutes respite from the need to constantly watch her back. South Philly is primarily owned by the Italian mob. What little contact she's had with them in other cities has been violent and short-lived.

No one here should have any idea who she is.

She needs to think about what happened to her at the bank, for it makes no sense at all. A guy like Fat André isn't going to rip her off and then sit there and lie about it. He just wouldn't. It would be too much of a risk. Slags running banks in the shadows don't stay in business by taking that kind of risk. And Fat André didn't smell like he was lying, anyway.

The only explanation that makes sense is that someone, maybe someone with magic, got to Fat André and scrambled his head. Made him erase any records of Tikki's account, made him fabricate that vid tape of her walking in and demanding her money. Made him actually believe that she has no money at his bank. Otherwise, she'd have picked up on his lies in a second.

The question, then, is simple: Why would someone do that to Fat André?

She already knows the answer. Somebody's trying to jerk around with *her* brain. They want her so busy trying to figure what the frag's going on that she doesn't see the kill shot coming.

No such luck.

Tikki's been in this position before. Once in Hangchow, once in Osaka. People got greedy, tried to hose her up. She kept her eyes on the big picture and when things started getting dicey she got the hell out. Only an idiot stands and fights when she's got absolutely nothing—nothing but money—to lose by running. Later, when things cool down and people forget who they've used, there's always an opportunity to settle the score.

She'd much prefer to turn and charge straight into the face of an enemy, tear him apart, but this is a case where the urging of instinct is stupid.

Who wants her dead? The yakuza? Adama? Someone else? She has no real clues. The only thing that keeps coming back to her time and again is that the yakuza would not likely hire anyone like Hammer. They'd do the job themselves.

What to do now? Get out of town. She doesn't like it, but it's the only sensible answer. The safest way out is on the fastest bike she can find. There are only two significant airports and a couple of railroad stations. Those can be watched, but even the cops can't keep an eye on all the roads. She should head north or south, stay in the main-line traffic of the northeast corridor. Lose herself in the crowd. Heading south, she'd hit Baltimore, then D.C. North gets her to Newark. A very rowdy place, Newark. A person could get lost in the Newark metroplex without even trying. A person could catch a plane to almost anywhere in the world from Newark. It may very well be her kind of town. She'll give it a shot.

Coming out of the restaurant, she takes a last drag of her slim Partagas purito, then drops it into the gutter. The night is cool. The city rumbles around her. But what she hears are the words of her mother, whispered into her ear one cool, dark night in Hong Kong: *never deal with a dragon, choose your enemies carefully, find your own truth* . . .

To that, Tikki adds her own rule: stay clear of magic-users.

If her guesses are right, a fairly powerful mage must be allied with whoever wants her dead. All by itself, that's reason enough to get out. Out of Philadelphia. Maybe out of the U.C.A.S. Maybe this whole part of the world.

She catches the Broad Street subway, rides it as far as Race Street, then walks east into Chinatown. An alley off Tenth brings her up alongside a three-story brick tenement. The alley door opens onto stairs that lead down to a metal door. She taps the entry code into the lock. The door clicks. She pulls it open and steps in.

The room she enters is a concrete box, little more than two meters on a side. A single bare bulb set into a fixture on the ceiling comes on as the door swings open. Against the left-hand wall sits a black steel footlocker. Tikki's emergency kit. The footlocker's contents include a Kang, an exact mate of the pistol holstered at her back, and ten clips of ammunition. There are also a few certified credsticks and various forms of ID. Almost anything she might need to get out in a hurry is inside that box. Tikki likes to be prepared.

What she isn't prepared for is the man seated on the footlocker. She's got the Kang in her hand before she sees anything more than the man-like shape and dark clothing. The neatly trimmed beard and the sleek black suit and shoes don't really sink in till several instants later. The thing foremost in her mind is the fact that no one should be here because no one else is supposed to know about her cache. Tikki drops to one knee and puts her shoulder to the door frame as she brings the Kang to bear. That's when she realizes the man is Adama. He smiles at her indulgently, as if wholly unaware of the mankiller pointed squarely at his face.

The bare bulb on the ceiling makes his eyes seem agleam.

"Forgive the intrusion," he says quietly, gesturing vaguely, as if to brush something inconsequential aside. "You've been out of touch for a few days. I was . . . concerned."

He adds a smile.

Tikki lowers the Kang, straightens up. A dozen questions flash through her mind. How did Adama get through the door? How did he know this place even existed? How could he have guessed that she would come here now? She opens her mouth to speak, but no words come out. Tikki is so completely confounded she can't even figure out what question to put to him first.

He extends a hand toward her, palm-up. "You haven't stepped into harm's way, I see."

Tikki shakes her head. "You?"

"I'm quite well, thank you," Adama replies, idly turning his walking stick between his fingertips. Tikki rubs at the back of her neck, feeling an itch. "Your efforts seem to be intimidating the competition," Adama says. "I'm very pleased. I presume that I can count on your continued service."

One thought comes to mind. "My money."

"You'd like to renegotiate," Adama says, smiling, briefly waving a hand. "That's only natural. I'm sure we can agree on an equitable price for your next job."

Yeah, right . . .

Her next job. Adama mentioned he had another job for her. Up until this moment, Tikki hadn't really given it serious thought. Something about it bothered her, but she can't remember what. She supposes if Adama's willing to renegotiate her terms of service, she'd be stupid to tell him no. Money, after all, is a primary issue. Money is the incentive humans use to encourage her to see the human domain in their terms and to take other humans as prey. Money buys her a pleasant urban lifestyle.

"Why don't we go have a bite?"

She could use some food.

Adama gestures. Tikki reholsters the Kang and steps back through the doorway. Adama joins her at the bottom of the stairs. She makes sure the door is secure, then precedes him up the stairs, into the alley and out to Tenth

Street. Adama's gleaming black Mitsubishi Nightsky limo is waiting at curbside. Tikki didn't see it there before. It must have been parked around the corner. She follows him into the rear compartment, and the limo glides smoothly away from the curb.

Adama offers her a Dannemann cigarro. She accepts it, and a light. "I know a wonderful little place," he says. "Marvelous food. Chinese. If you'll forgive the indiscretion."

Indiscretion? Like her Asian background is some big secret? She supposes that this is just another of Adama's little jokes. Oddly, she feels inclined to smile. Really, it's such a stupid joke she feels compelled to do so.

The limo rolls over to Front Street, rides up to Kensington Avenue and heads into northeast Philly. Before long, they're rolling up in front of a restaurant called the Hunan Mayfair, a dinky little place. The vid display in the window flashes: Moo Shu Pork! Sauteed with cabbage and eggs! All fresh! All real! Wrapped in mandarin pancakes with plum sauce!

There's something about the place that bothers Tikki, but she can't decide what it is. Maybe it's just that she's never seen Adama eat Chinese before. Despite the name he goes by, Adama Ho, he's never shown a predilection for any food other than the routinely Anglo. She follows him inside. They take a corner table. Tikki checks the menu and decides on the Kung Po beef.

"Make it hot," she tells the old man who takes their order.

"Yes. Very hot." The old man bows and leaves.

Tikki looks to Adama, but he merely smiles. She's wondering why the old man answered her in Mandarin. Mirrorshades cover her eyes, concealing the most obvious physical clue to her Asian background. What the hell is going on here?

"It's all right, Adama says, smiling benignly, briefly waving a hand in dismissal.

Tikki decides not to worry about the old man.

"It's been some days since I've heard from you," Adama says, still smiling, still turning his walking stick between his fingertips. "I take it you handled the problem involving my principal weapon."

The attempt on her life? She handled it fine. She tore Hammer and his band of stupid amateurs into bloody ribbons. She slaughtered them. Literally. "They got what they needed."

Adama regards her, smiling as if amused, gesturing at her vaguely. "You sound quite ferocious this evening."

The idea makes her smile again, a vicious smile this time. She's actually feeling kind of ferocious, now that Adama mentions it. She can't imagine what she must have been thinking before. There's no need for her to leave the city. She's got nothing to fear. Nothing can stop her. She'll kill anything that tries. Kill it, tear it to shreds, devour it. Frag the yakuza. Frag them all, all humans. Skinny weaklings. Sloppy two-legged bags of meat. They're just breeders, breeders and prey. She should slaughter every last one of them. She's had enough of their stink.

Over dinner, Adama starts to fill her in on her next job. He'll give a fuller briefing later. The important thing for now is that her next target is a high-level yakuza executive who poses the most serious threat still facing Adama and his organization. This man, this next target, must be slaughtered most viciously of all.

His name is Bennari Ohashi.

39

Raman sets the stand on the chopper and looks at Eliana. For a moment the she does nothing more than work her fingers through her pale blonde hair: smoothing, fluffing, primping. That she should waste time in so trivial a way does not surprise him. She is obsessive about her appearance, her looks, her cleanliness, to a degree that makes other females seem almost slovenly by comparison. She spends whole hours merely bathing, and hours more applying makeup, arranging her hair and putting on clothes.

Tonight, she wears a clinging black blouse and matching short skirt with a broad golden belt around her waist. Supple black boots with towering spike heels climb her legs to beyond the hem of her skirt. Over that, she wears a cloak that falls almost to her ankles, black on the outside, gleaming gold within. Dozens of wire-thin bangles slither up and down her forearms; rings adorn every finger. A host of delicate chains and necklaces hang from her neck.

Abruptly, she draws the cloak around herself, concealing even her arms.

"This way," she says, pointing with her chin.

Eliana turns and heads up the alley, into the garbage-laden dark. This is what Raman finds surprising, that she would come to such a place, an alley amid all the decaying slums near the House of Corrections. He's dealt with Eliana in various ways for close to three years. How many times has she ever come out into the streets, into the dark recesses of the city? Two times? Perhaps three? This is a very rare event. Eliana, the obsessively clean and finicky she, actually exposing herself to the risk of becoming soiled or smudged. Remarkable.

They turn a corner, Eliana in the lead. A short distance away they see a group of black-clad youths, laughing and grinning. Their grins grow vicious as the youths spot the she. Eliana looks much too diminutive and daintily female to pose much of a threat. Raman puts a hand to his knife, the killing knife sheathed inside his jacket, but no need.

"Yo! Scope the biff!"

"You got urges, honey?"

One of the youths comes up to Eliana, reaching toward her hair. The she makes a sound like a grunt, then flings her hand out from under her cloak like a cat, slashing at the youth's face. The youth flips back off his feet as if struck by the hand of a giant, crashes over a metal drum, then lays still. Blood pours from the smashed wreckage of his face and throat. The other youths hesitate. Eliana thrusts one arm toward the darkness of the sky, her fingers curled like claws. The air in the back alley suddenly begins to swirl. A cyclone arises. The youths gape, then turn and run, pelted from behind by every form of garbage.

The cyclone dissolves and fades. Eliana smooths and fluffs her hair, again wraps herself in her cloak, then leads on, further down the alley, not too far. Turning to face the rear door of one of the houses on the right, she flings back her cloak and thrusts both hands at the night sky. The door bursts inward as if smashed from the frame by a giant's fist. Dust swirls and then settles. Eliana brushes at her clothing, fluffs her hair, then leads inside.

The interior of the house is a gray and dusty ruin, dimly lit by starlight and the orange-tinted glow from streetlights on the road out front. Holes in the walls, broken bits of furniture scattered around. Water softly drips somewhere. The smell of mold and decay. Eliana grunts with obvious distaste. A narrow hallway leads to the front door. An open doorway on the left leads into a modest-sized room like a living room.

In the middle of the floor sits a cat, Eliana's black cat. The she stands facing the cat for a moment, then crouches down as if to stroke the animal or perhaps pick it up, but when she straightens up the cat is gone. It is neither on the floor nor in Eliana's arms. Raman did not see where it went. Apparently, Eliana sent it somewhere else with her magic. It would not be the first time she has done this or something like it in his presence.

There is something about the cat and its relationship to Eliana that goes beyond the purely mundane. Raman suspects that the cat may itself be a worker of magic. It surely is no ordinary feline. Of that he has no doubt.

Eliana of course explains only when she must and when she feels so inclined. Most often, she prefers to leave others guessing.

Now, the she shakes out her cloak, then her hair, and turns to the large front window. The window pane is veiny with cracks, as if it had been struck by a brick but not broken. Eliana points to a row house almost directly across the street. ''That is where you will find her,'' she says quietly. ''In one of the rooms on the fifth floor.

Striper is not there now, but she will be soon. This is her special place. Her safe place."

Eliana turns and looks at Raman. The faint light from the street glints in her eyes. The spike heels of her boots so add to her height that she need barely lift her chin at all to meet Raman's gaze. Faintly, she smiles.

"Be careful."

"Why?"

Eliana inclines one eyebrow and again looks across the street. "This Striper is most unusual. I saw it in her aura. She is very strong. Very dangerous."

"What makes her so dangerous?"

Eliana turns her head slightly, looks at him from the corners of her eyes, but says nothing.

It is typical.

40

Tikki turns in off the street, goes through the door of the row house in northeast Philly, and briefly pauses in the foyer. On the stairs the slag with bright orange hair and teeth filed to points looks at her a moment, then lowers the muzzle of his shotgun toward the floor. Tikki stares at him an instant longer, then heads up the stairs. She doesn't like people pointing guns at her, even if it is their job.

Otherwise, the evening has gone well. Adama laid out his plan for her upcoming assassination of Bennari Ohashi, yakuza executive. It's a good plan. Tikki doubts she'll have any problems. Whatever doubts she may have entertained about Adama must have been the product of her own paranoia. The man is too much a predator to betray her. He takes too great a pleasure in the kill to ever turn against her. What could possibly have been wrong with her head that she might have suspected him of treachery? She ponders that at some length, but comes up with nothing. She must have been crazy.

Out of her head.

She reaches the top of the stairs, tugs the door open and steps into the fifth floor hallway. A strange smell stops her cold. Before she can identify it, something hits her hard from above and behind, driving her flat to the floor.

What's going on? She's being attacked, ambushed. Tikki realizes that even as she feels the impact against the back of her head and shoulders as some incredible weight thrusts her down onto her belly, banging the breath from her lungs.

Before she can even start to fight, she feels a cold hard pain starting somewhere around her right kidney, then rising, tearing up through her back, and then it's too much. Over before it began. Weakness assails her. The pain smothers her mind.

She hears her heart pounding.

Fading into silence . . .

Raman retracts the claws of his snapblades into his forearm mount and gets up onto his feet. There can be little doubt that the blood-drenched form on the floor is Striper. She wears her signature red and black paint and synthleather clothing. The gory wound stretching from near-hip to shoulder makes her condition clear. Raman has seen many such wounds. A DocWagon emergency response team would not be able to revive Striper now. The damage his claws have inflicted is too extensive, too vicious. Striper is dead. His work is complete.

The fact only confirms his own beliefs. No one is invincible. No one is forever so cautious or clever or quick as to be immune to death. For every being that kills there is another capable of killing it. Somewhere in the world there is one who is fully capable of killing even him. Perhaps Striper herself might have killed him, had she known the way, had she been sent to kill him before he had been sent to do her.

Raman turns toward the stairs, but then stops, hearing something. A rasping breath, a rustling of synthleather. A glance back over his shoulder gives him a brief view of the impossible. Striper is up on one knee. Her hand

is lifting a heavy automatic. Even as Raman tugs the
throwing knife from beneath his left jacket sleeve, the
gun roars, and the first slugs pound into his ribs.

He staggers back, incredulous.

The roaring of the gun rises like thunder.

Her back feels like shredded rubber, the pain is intense, but she's handled worse. She's healing rapidly. Her
strength is returning. The water filling her eyes is a dis-
traction, but she can handle that too.

The Kang clicks empty.

Staggering to her feet, Tikki puts one shoulder to the
corridor wall and thumbs the Kang's magazine release.
Her free hand is ramming a fresh magazine home even
as the empty one drops to the floor. The fire burning in
her back is an imperious command—her hands know how
to respond. She snaps the slide, points and opens fire.
The deafening reports slam against the walls of the corridor and reverberate. The rising calamity of noise becomes an apocalyptic storm of thunder, a storm to end
all storms. Her big, synthleather-clad attacker staggers
back against the wall at the end of the corridor. She keeps
right on shooting. Blood splashes the wall. The killer
falls to one knee. She keeps right on shooting. A knife
or something falls from the killer's hand to skitter along
the floor. The Kang clicks empty. Tikki rams a fresh clip
home, snaps the slide, lifts the gun and again opens fire.
She's got at least two more full clips in her pockets and
she's going to make damn certain that anything, anyone
or anybody who tries to skrag her winds up dead dead
dead dead dead.

Something incredible happens then. She begins to hal-
lucinate. Nothing like this has ever happened before and
it's such a convincing lie that she feels a sudden sharp
pang of fear.

The killer is changing. Flesh and clothing ripple and
twitch. The killer's face becomes a furry, blood-splashed
mask. His eyes swell into huge orbs that glint red with
the light. His nose and jaw thrust forward. Bared teeth
become fangs. Between one deafening blast from the
Kang and the next, the killer's whole body grows and

stretches. Torn and tattered clothing falls to the floor.
Arms form into massive forelegs. A long, sinuous tail
rises into view. Tikki whips her free hand across her eyes,
but the lie remains. She's looking at herself in a mirror,
shooting at something that looks just like she does when
in her natural form.

It's impossible.

The creature is roaring and lunging forward, bounding
up as if to bowl her over, and she can't smell anything
but her own sweat and blood and the exhaust of the gun.
The roaring weapon suddenly seems so utterly impotent
it's a joke.

The Kang falls from her hand as she staggers back.
Then the creature hits, driving her right off her feet.

The pain is a madness driving him to greater madness,
compelling him to assume his other form, his animal
form, propelling him down the corridor toward the very
source of his pain.

All thoughts of biz are chased away by the pain. Primal
truths rule him now. To stop the pain, he must either run
away or put an end to the source of his pain, and he
cannot run away. To run away is to surrender, to admit
defeat. Better he should die here and now than give in to
another's power.

As he charges, the female drops her gun and staggers
back, but that is irrelevant. The she's attack must be answered. The pain must be satisfied. He bounds onto his
hind legs and drives his forepaws into her chest and slams
her down, flat to the floor. Momentum carries him right
over her and past. He tears at the floor, turning, reversing
direction. Bounding back, he drops his head to seize the
she's neck in his jaws, but what he sees then stops him
short.

Her jaws thrust forward. Red and black-striped fur
rushes over her face. Her body swells to almost twice its
original size. A single swipe of onyx claws as swift and
sharp as his own proves beyond any question the reality
of what he is seeing.

Raman bounds up and back, back toward the door to
the stairs, leaping away from this creature that suddenly

seems at least as big as him, if not bigger, and just as
deadly.

The she rolls onto her belly, then rises onto four powerfully muscled legs and turns to face him, roaring, roaring even louder than he, filling the air with fury, her ears
laid back, fangs bared and gleaming. Raman begins to
roar in answer, but then falls silent, astonished. *The she
is shaped just like him!* Their fur is colored differently,
but otherwise they might have been cast from a single
mold. Confusing thoughts, some only half-formed, rush
helter-skelter through his mind. He has been across half
the world and never encountered another creature like
himself. Where did this *she* come from?

Could they be brother and sister?

Abruptly, the she is right in his face, roaring, pounding at him, slashing with her claws. It's a brief but frenetic exchange of blow and counterblow, more
challenging than any Raman can recall. He bounds back
and away with surprise, barely aware of the new blood
streaming down from around his face, down his shoulders and forelegs. He immediately bounds up onto his
hind legs, roaring, and drops to all fours and charges.
The female meets him head-on, roaring and slashing, but
this time she is the one to withdraw, bounding up, leaping away.

Then they're facing one another from barely two meters distant, panting huskily, fangs bared, ears laid flat.
Growling, snarling. Old pains replaced by new. Blood
smearing their fur.

Abruptly, the she's ears straighten up. Raman hesitates, uncertain about this new sign. Everything is happening so fast. Barely an instant seems to have elapsed
since the she began shooting at him. Everything before
that now seems irrelevant. Everything that happened before the she changed shape suddenly seems completely
irrelevant.

Abruptly, without warning, the she bolts right past his
shoulder.

Running away . . . ?

No—Raman turns and sees a man standing in the doorway to the stairs. The man holds a gun, a shotgun. The

she bounds up in front of the man, launching herself at him. The gun roars and the she roars—roars louder than ever before—and both she and man fall out of sight, disappearing down the stairs.

Raman claws at the floor, abruptly tearing after them. He finds them on the landing one flight down.

The man is sprawled, a gore-drenched corpse. The she stands waiting, facing him, facing the stairs. She opens her mouth a bit, but makes no show of baring her teeth as Raman descends the stairs, stopping just short of the landing. The she advances, meets him nose-to-nose, sniffing, sniffing him all over, all over his face. Raman sniffs at her too. Her scent is unlike anything he's smelled before, musky and powerful, and . . . Different. Strange, exotic, incredibly and overpoweringly female. It reaches right into his groin, clenching, squeezing, gripping him with excitement. Only as several more moments pass does he notice the new blood matting the fur on the she's right shoulder and foreleg. This is evidence of the wound she took charging the man with the shotgun. Why did she do that? Raman wonders about it, in addition to everything else afflicting his brain.

Could it be that she had meant to protect him?

No one has ever done that before.

If she's dreaming, she's having the dream of a lifetime, because there's no telling truth from fantasy. She pauses at the edge of the landing, looking up, stretching her neck to meet the illusion eye-to-eye and nose-to-nose, as if she might uncover the truth, discover the flaw in the disguise, sniff him out. The male . . . what? Tiger . . . ? *Were-tiger*? He seems to have healed most of his wounds, just like her, faster than any human. She sniffs at his face, not quite incredulous, but seeking some clue, some scent, that will make rational sense of all this.

He even *smells* real, as real as she.

She can hardly believe it.

The only other male of her kind she's ever known is her brother, Gnao. A *male Weretiger* . . . The idea alone fills her with a strange excitement she can't control, much less comprehend. She just stands there breathing his scent

till other realities intrude, creeping into her awareness, shouts from downstairs, the far-off peel of a siren. The other Weretiger, the *male Weretiger,* looks at her and grumbles deep and low, far back in his throat. The sound and the smells that come with it speak of danger, alarm. Absolutely nothing about him now speaks of aggression. That makes up her mind.

She brushes past him, heading up. At the top of the flight, she stops and looks back. The male returns her gaze, otherwise unmoving. How to tell him what she wants? She imagines something like a wave of the hand, but her forelegs won't move like that. She shakes her head, trying to motion for him to follow, then realizes she's only wasting time. Already, somebody several floors below is pounding up the stairs. She changes, changes back into her human guise, and stands up buck naked.

"Slot and run."

Something totally inscrutable rumbles in the male's throat, then he changes, too. In human form, he seems only about as tall as Tikki, but much broader, far more heavily built. Husky even for a male, with lots of kinky black hair. He looks like a cross between some dark brand of Amerind and a native of Delhi, India. At a glance, he seems to have all the standard male equipment and in proportions she considers pleasing.

Tikki hustles up the hall, kicking torn and split-open clothes out of her way, once slipping on a smear of blood. She retrieves the Kang, the male collects his knives. She keys the locks to her apartment on the left and motions the male inside.

The moment the door is shut, he says something in a voice low and deep and intensely masculine, and in a language Tikki doesn't know. She lifts her hands, shakes her head, and turns and walks straight to the closet. The only clothes she's got that might fit the male come in the form of an oversized black duster. She throws it at him, then hurriedly pulls on a blouse, slacks, boots, and a jacket, then gets spare ammo for the Kang. The male speaks again, another bad choice of tongues. Whatever it is, she doesn't know it, doesn't even recognize it.

As she turns back to the male, he looks at her and says, in thickly accented English. "What . . . are you?"

For about one second, she wonders what that means; then she's out of time. Voices are carrying into the hallway. She can hear them clearly through the wall. She smells cop, scents that go with cops. That makes it past time to flee. She shoves open one of the windows and leads the male onto the roof of the building near door. From there, it's an easy run to the fire escape three rooftops over. The male follows her like a shadow.

Tikki still can't believe he's real.

41

07-29-54/05:17:30
Cam off, vid off.

If Skeeter had a choice, he wouldn't even bother putting the wear on his 'effin cybereyes. He and the so very trid-o-genic Asian-featured news snoop Joi Bang, scrod-scarfin' elf biff mage, stand waiting in the shambles of an office occupied by Gabriella Santini, muck-fraggin' bink drek News Director for WHAM! Independent News of Philadelphia. It's a short wait.

Santini lowers her sneaker-clad feet from amid the piles of hard copy, chip carriers, and vid cassettes on her desk, but only long enough to drop a chip carrier into a nearby garbage can.

"Get the message?" Santini asks wryly.

"Yes but—!" J. B. manages to interject.

Santini sneers. "We got ghouls digging bodies out of cemeteries. We got corporates dying like flies. We got a possible cover-up by city hall on a series of mass murders. Nobody cares about tigers. I don't care about tigers. If you want to report on tigers, even big red and black tigers, give your next chip to the zoological society."

"Yes but—!"

"Get the hell out of my office."

"Can I just—"!

"No. Get out."

07-29-54/05:41:21

Cam on, close focus and hold on the trid-o-genic features of J. B. standing in the hallway outside Santini's office. A major event is in progress. The damn bimble-headed biff has been silent for going on twenty seconds. Skeeter records this for posterity. J. B. looks at him as if mildly chagrined, like she might even cry. Skeeter records that for posterity, too.

"Well," she says, crestfallen, "our story got trashed."

Skeeter resists pointing any fingers. He could've told her what would happen. Man-eating tigers! Cannibal orks! Murdering policlub freaks! But would the dithead elf listen? Oh, no . . . never. J. B. always knows best. The trid-o-genic news snoop mage has a "Sixth-World sense" about these things.

Right.

"I guess we better find another story."

That's the best news Skeeter's heard in weeks. It's such good news, in fact, that he jabs a finger right at her: *You're on*!

"Maybe this cover-up thing Santini mentioned."

Skeeter jabs again: You're on!

"I wonder," J. B. goes on to say. "I wonder if the cover-up could have something to do with what Santini said about ghouls digging up corpses? Maybe it is ghouls committing all these cannibal-mutilation killings after all! I mean, that tiger, maybe that was just a fluke! Imagine if the mayor's in on it! And the police! And the policlubs too! Maybe the entire city corporation council master-minded the whole thing! Why, if we could break a story like that, we'd get a network feed for sure!"

Same story, different day.

Damn bingle dithead biff.

She never quits.

42

"I know a place. A safe place."

The male says it in English. That's something they both know. In the dark of the alley, Tikki cannot really read his features. Light and shadow play across his features in a way that makes his expression seem utterly emotionless, impassive as stone. She knows that's wrong. She can smell it. The male's worked up about something, excited. She isn't sure if that's good or bad, if he means her good or ill, but she's sure he isn't half as indifferent or calm as a mere glance might suggest.

Tikki pulls the Kang from the waistband of her trousers and presses the muzzle up under the male's jaw. He looks at the gun, but doesn't move. "Get sweet with me again and you're dead," Tikki promises softly.

"I won't," he says.

If he's lying, he gives no clue.

Tikki tucks the Kang back into her waistband. The male leads on. Ten blocks over, he pulls up a metal grating set into the concrete walk and starts down a metal stairway as steep as a ladder. She watches him a moment, then follows. Why, she doesn't know. All she can say for certain is that rational thinking has nothing to do with it.

One minute he's trying to kill her. Barely twenty minutes later, she's following him into a hole in the ground without so much as a thought for her own survival. Definitely not rational.

Adama would say she's gone muzzy. She doesn't give a damn. This has nothing to do with anyone or anything but her and the male. It's nobody's business but hers and his.

Nobody's.

Is he really a male of her breed?

Could he be anything else . . . ?

The metal stairs lead to a floor of concrete. Two steps to the left, a flight of concrete stairs leads down further into the gloom. The male leads, Tikki follows. The stairs turn right, lead down another long flight. The air gets stale, dry and dusty. The stairway ends at a subway tunnel, leading directly onto a narrow platform that runs like a catwalk along the side of the tunnel.

"I smell orks," Tikki says quietly.

The male pauses to look at her, then points at the concrete beneath them, and says, "Deeper."

Tikki nods.

They go along the narrow platform for about a hundred meters before coming to a metal door in the tunnel wall. The male opens the door, leading into a concrete shaft with metal rungs set into one wall. They climb. About four meters up, they step through an opening in the wall. The corridor there takes them into a room.

A strange room. Pipes running along the ceiling and walls suggest it once had something to do with the subway tunnel below. Maybe it still does. Who knows? Tikki concentrates on what's in front of her eyes. The room is like a den, a lounge, and a bedroom all in one. The combination of functions doesn't surprise her, but rather the way it's done. The look of the place. Like a forest at night. Black walls, painted with trees and dense underbrush, rise toward stars and a huge white orb on the ceiling that must be the moon. The bed sits on a low platform almost completely obscured by potted plants, plastic plants, some as big as small trees and treated with chemicals mimicking the smells of real vegetation of the wild.

"You live here?"

"I've been . . . coming here a long time."

The place smells like him. Tikki scopes the place out, but keeps one eye on the male. She sees all kinds of junk scattered among the plastic plants and odds and ends of furniture: piles of newsprint and hard-copy magazines, a car tire, a headlight, an old keyboard-style deck, a tailor's form, and other items even more obscure. She stops and looks back at the male.

"Drink?" he says.

Tikki nods.

"Water?"

Tikki nods.

"Good." The male says that definitely, as if he approves her choice of beverage. Maybe he expected it. Maybe he's got nothing but water to drink. He brings a plastic jug from the far end of the room and hands it to her.

"You first," Tikki says.

The male looks at her a moment, then takes a swig. He doesn't fall over dead, so Tikki has a swig herself.

"What's your name?"

"Raa," he says. "Raman."

"Raa Raman."

"Just Raman." He watches as Tikki recaps the jug and sets it down. He stares until her eyes meet his. He seems puzzled. "Back there . . . in that tenement. You . . . defended me. Why?"

Why? Because she got stupid. Because she knew the man on the stairs would shoot. Because, in the moment she had to think about it, Tikki didn't know if this male, Raman, could survive yet another blast from a gun. Because the idea that she had encountered a male of her own kind filled her with such urgency that she simply could not help herself. How does she explain all that? Answer: she doesn't. "You tried to kill me. Why?"

Raman gazes at her for some moments, then says, "Before. Before I realized."

"Answer the question."

"Money. A wetwork contract."

Why doesn't that surprise her? If she ever gets over the shock of what he is, she may never be surprised again. "You're an artist."

"I prefer . . . kick-work to killing. But, yes. You're right, I am an artist. A *technician*. You scan?"

Tikki supposes that the way he ambushed her could be described as fairly artful. She's still not sure how he managed to take her from above. The male doesn't look like the sort to master anything as specialized as ceiling-walking technique. A sarcastic smile tugs at one corner of her mouth. "So why am I still alive?"

Now his expression turns confused. "I . . . do not know . . . what you are. I'm still . . . not certain. We seem alike. What are you?"

"You saw what I am."

"What do you . . . call yourself?"

"You tell me."

"I don't know." He lifts both hands to his temples and slowly pushes back his hair. "I was . . . an orphan. I was raised by humans. For a long time . . . I thought I was human. Then, when I was young, I changed. One night the moon seemed to burn into me like . . . like the sun at noon. Like fire. That was when I changed. For the first time. I heard once that . . . that creatures like us are called Weres. Is that true?"

Tikki nods.

"But we aren't wolves. Werewolves. We're tigers."

"Weretigers."

"Were . . . *tigers*." He says it like he's thinking about it, unsure of it, then he looks at her. "You're the first I've ever met."

Tikki puzzles over all he is saying. If what Raman says is true, his confusion is perfectly justified. What bothers her goes beyond that, involves her own personal conceptions. She must have thought about this before—what she is, what she isn't—but it's hard to recall what conclusions, if any, she came to.

For a long time, Tikki believed she was a tigress, one that could assume human form. In recent years, she's wondered if that could be right. She isn't just a tiger with paranormal abilities. Neither is she human. She's Were, a Weretiger, and that's special, but what does it mean? What should it mean?

Sometimes, her bestial side grows so strong she can hardly think at all. It's been like that a lot lately. She wonders why.

Raman steps closer, so close their faces are almost touching. "I don't care . . . what humans paid me to do," he says, quietly. "This is more important."

"What?"

"This," he says. "Us."

"Meaning what?"

"I . . . want you."

Tikki can see that. She can smell it, taste it. The fact of it fills the air and sends a quick tremor up her back. It's madness. She knows it but she doesn't care. Her insides are getting warm, really warm, warm and wet, faster than ever before, more than ever before in her life. Like her body has already decided something that her mind had barely begun to consider. She doesn't like that. It makes her angry.

She puts her hands to his chest and shoves. Raman staggers back a couple of steps. Nothing changes. He's still there, looking at her, smelling like he does, and the heat inside her keeps growing. Tikki steps up to him and gives another shove. Again he stumbles back a few more steps. She shoves twice more. He stumbles over the steps leading onto the platform of the bed and abruptly sits, as if about to fall anyway. Tikki stands facing him for a few moments, then straddles his legs and sits on his thighs.

"We do this my way," she says in a voice like a soft, low snarl.

"Yes," Raman says. "Your way."

It's the only way.

43

The telecom bleeps. Kirkland hits the key to answer, but doesn't look up from the hard copy on his desk till he hears the quiet, familiar voice, "Hoi, Brad!"

"Hoi, old man."

The face on the monitor could be that of a forty-year-old, but the curly white hair and dark-ringed eyes more suggest the truth. The man's name is Dominick J. Rustin. He's an old friend, a twenty-year cop veteran now retired and enjoying a cushy job with a local security corp. The job comes with fringes like discounts on cosmed surgery. "You ready to put in your papers?"

Kirkland sits back in his chair, lights a cig. "I got a few more things to take care of. How you doing, Dom?"

"Let me know when you're ready. I'll have you on our payroll in twenty-four hours."

Kirkland doesn't doubt it. "What's doing?"

"You know the Seven Circles Club, Brad?"

"Naw, I live in Trenton now. I just visit Philly on weekends."

Rustin grins. "Hey, you're funny."

Anyone who's worked Philly Northeast knows the Seven Circles Club. It's a devo club, for degenerates, big on sex, chips, drugs, violence—and plenty of it. Every month a handful of straight citizens wander in there to mingle with the lowlife and are never heard from again. Several attempts to shut the place down have been overruled by one of the city's more infamous judges, a man Kirkland and others suspect to be on somebody's payroll.

"Anyway," Rustin says, "the club recently put in sec cams to monitor the action."

"Is that a fact?"

"I guess they wanna know who's doing deals on premises. Maybe they're gonna clean the place up."

"Sure, Dom. Sure."

"Anyway, you can imagine my surprise when I discovered that some decker managed to tap into the lines."

Kirkland nods rather than waste words. The drek Rustin is feeding him now comes under the heading of covering his ass. His old buddy's obviously about to feed him some data on the sly. In all likelihood, Rustin heard about the new sec cameras at Seven Circles through some contact, then got some decker who owed him a favor to penetrate the system just to see what might turn up. Once a cop, always a cop. The beauty of it of course is that data turned up by a citizen with no connection to any law enforcement agency is admissible in court, whether obtained legally or not.

"Naturally," Rustin goes on to say, "straight suit that I am, I figured I better turn the evidence over to you. I believe that tapping into secured lines is still a crime, right?"

"Last I heard."

"Too bad the perp got away. Anyhow, here's what I found."

"Scope it through."

A window opens in the upper-left corner of Kirkland's monitor, treating him to an interior view of some dingy nightclub, presumably the Seven Circles Club. The view zooms in on two people sitting in a restaurant-style booth. One is a middle-aged Anglo slag with thinning black hair, well-trimmed beard, and neat black suit. He's also wearing a pleased smile and has a walking stick propped next to him. Also seated in the booth is a slim female in red and black facepaint and synthleather to match.

The vid freezes. "Recognize anyone?" Rustin says.

"Yeah, maybe," Kirkland replies.

The vid plays on. The guy in the suit smiles and says, "Any problems?"

Striper, the one in red and black, shakes her head. Kirkland recognized her at once. What amazes him is that his old chum must have, too. Never forget a face. That was always Rustin's motto. Apparently, it still holds true.

The vid plays on. "Good. Very good," the suit in the booth remarks. "We'll have to discuss my next target."

"Now?" Striper says.

"Well, later perhaps. I have other business just now. You understand."

"Sure."

"My Leandra. Or did you have something in mind?" Striper nods.

"Such as?"

"Competition."

"Really. Someone's preparing to move against me?"

"It's possible."

"You mean they've targeted my principal weapon?" Striper nods.

"What will you do?"

"Maybe I'll go on vacation."

The man smiles, then laughs very loudly.

The vid goes on some more, but Kirkland is no longer listening. He brings up another window, opens his Exotech master file, and quickly scans the images from Exotech Personnel. The pic that catches his eye is that of a guy ID'd as Adam Malik, formerly of the Special Projects Section. Malik survived the fire at Germantown, then dropped out of sight. His personnel pic so closely resembles the image of the guy in the booth at the Seven Circles Club that the phrase "exact match" comes to Kirkland's mind.

"Brad? You there?" Rustin asks.

"Yeah, I'm here. Who's the cobber in the booth?"

"No clue, old chum. Just doing my civic duty. Hope it helps. Gotta sign off."

"Right. Thanks."

"Lemme know when you put your papers in."

"Maybe next week."

Kirkland stores the vid in memory, erases the call, then watches the vid again, enlarged to fill the screen. "Good. Very good," says the suit. "We'll have to discuss my next target." "Now?" "Well, later perhaps." he tells her. "I have other business just now . . ."

Striper nods and stands up, glances around. Practically every movement she makes brings words like *soldier* and *assassin* to Kirkland's mind. Hands free and empty, posture deceptively casual and loose. She reminds him of another killer, also a woman, one so good at behaving naturally, at blending in, that a young uniformed cop walked right by her without giving her a second look, despite having received her exact description and orders to watch for her only an hour before.

The final few moments of the vid really widen Kirkland's eyes. Malik is joined in his booth by a group of women, some devastatingly beautiful, others merely hot. All look like redheads. Kirkland stares for several moments, then hurriedly brings up another window. A quick scan of the Exotech files uncovers a pic of one Leandra Forrester, who, unlike Malik, unlike Neiman, Jorge, or Harris, died in the S.P.S. accident up in Germantown. Leandra Forrester is, or rather was, her name. A woman in her mid-thirties, stunning, and a flaming redhead.

Kirkland reverses the vid. *"Who will be my Leandra?"* Malik asks. Kirkland keys his intercom.

"Get everybody in here!"

"Lieutenant?"
"Now!"
"Yes, sir!"

Two minutes later, nearly every detective assigned to the Exotech case is crowded into Kirkland's office, along with Captain Henriquez and the lieutenant from Major Cases. Kirkland swings his telecom screen around so all the boys and girls can see. The windows on the screen show Malik and Forrester from their personnel pics as well as the scene at the Seven Circles Club, with Malik, Striper, and the redheads all present.

Kirkland runs the vid.

"Who will be my Leandra?" Malik says.

"Oh, great," Detective-Sergeant Murphy remarks. "Now we got a grade-A psycho using a pro assassin."

"What we got," Kirkland declares, "is motive."

"You mean, if Adam Malik and Leandra Forrester were sharing bed space," says Detective Shackleford.

Kirkland nods. "Anybody wanna bet?"

No one does.

44

From the start, it's more than just sex.

It's a freight train careening down a mountainside, a meteor screaming down through the atmosphere. Riveting, enthralling. Forces too powerful to control send them hurtling ahead. Once isn't enough. A dozen times isn't enough. They're at it for hours, till they're drenched in it, till the air around them reeks of it, till the only thing left to breathe is the smell of it, the thousand humid, musky scents, mingled and mixed together till the odors seem born not of two bodies but of one.

Tikki changes, assuming her four-legged form. At the start, she won't have it any other way; in the end, it doesn't matter. What matters is that she's felt his teeth gripping the back of her neck, his claws pressuring her

hide, that she's met the animal part of him, felt his power.
That's when she begins to grasp what is really happening,
it has nothing to do with whether she likes him or he
likes her, nothing to do with love or any other romantic
idea. It's something primal and fierce and wholly inexo-
rable, reaching into their animal cores as forcefully as
the moon, and yet also grazing their higher natures, their
minds, their emotions, till they feel almost welded together, two halves of a single creature.

"Nothing hurts you," Raman murmurs.

"Hurts me?" Tikki looks back over her shoulder at
him, then stretches out on her side again. A faint smile
slowly curves her lips. It feels too good to hurt.

Softly, she laughs.

As the hours wear on it goes from rough to gentle to
almost tender. After one particularly satisfying bout, she
pounds her hand against his chest, and he takes her hand,
opens it, draws it around to his back, drawing her close.
She snarls softly into his face. He covers her lips with
his mouth. To her surprise, she doesn't mind the close-
ness, the cuddling. Usually, she likes her space after sex,
from the moment the male slips out. Now, though, with
this one, this male, Raman, everything is changed. Tikki
isn't sure if that's good or bad, but there's no denying the
fact.

She's half asleep when a strange scent brings her suddenly wide-awake. She's been breathing it for who knows
how long, maybe only seconds, maybe minutes, before
she realized how starkly the odor clashed with every other
scent in the air. Instinct shouts at her so loudly she jerks,
thrusts herself up, lunges across the mattress for the
Kang, but the gun flies from her grip even as her fingers
close around it.

Then it's too late.

Standing a few steps away is a human female. She has
an extravagant mane of blonde hair, but her features are
delicate, refined. She holds a long black cloak tightly
about her body and wears boots with impossibly high
heels. Her expression hints of wry amusement.

Tikki exerts herself to maintain a façade of perfect self-
assurance. "Give me my gun."

The female smiles, a smug look. "You have no need of it at present."

Tikki struggles to control her emotions. Fear and outrage battle for supremacy. The female smells of herbs and potions, like a magician—whether mage or shaman, it makes no difference. Either means trouble. Tikki glances quickly at Raman, whose face shows displeasure.

"Her name is Eliana," Raman tells her. "We have worked together. I did not expect her here."

"That's quite true," Eliana remarks.

Tikki smells nothing of lies.

"What are you doing here?" Raman asks the magician.

"You need my help," Eliana says.

Raman hesitates, looking surprised, then says, "I do not think so."

"You are wrong."

Abruptly, Eliana tosses her cloak back from her right shoulder and thrusts out her right hand, fingers curled like claws. Tikki reacts instinctively, jerking away, banging back bodily against the wall. Eliana smiles and murmurs something under her breath. What happens then is so strange that Tikki goes rigid with alarm. What happens could only be magic.

The entire character of the room instantly changes, as if transformed from a full-color pic into a holographic negative of black and white. The bed, the low platform under it, the plastic plants, practically everything in the room *and the very substance of the room itself* become somehow insubstantial, as if mere illusions, ghosts of solid objects in a strange, deceiving dream. Eliana changes too. She becomes a figure of radiant white against a background of darkness. Her face takes on the features of a strange, ethereal cat. The hand she holds extended becomes like a paw. Traceries of a white even more brilliant than her form coil around her neck and arm, pulsing, flowing, seething to and fro like a thing alive.

Tikki struggles to get to her feet, but the very air seems to resist her, holding her in place with greater and greater force, till she is straining with all her might, quivering with the effort, and making no headway at all.

"You will stay where you are," Eliana says, her voice so resonant it smothers all other sounds. "There is something you must see. Look down, Weretigress. Look at yourself."

Now added to Tikki's fear of being caught in a magician's dream comes the frightening realization that the mage must know what she is. Tikki struggles to keep her fear hidden—and looks down. What she sees makes no sense. Her own body is like the magician's, radiant and white. Strange traceries of a white even more bright than the rest of her form lie on her breast like necklaces. They seethe and pulse just like the traceries coiling around the mage's neck and arm.

"Now look behind you."

First, Tikki struggles to lift her arm, lift one hand to her breast, and it's more like trying to lift a building from its foundations. The muscles in her arm strain to the point of agony, yet nothing happens. Her arm remains motionless. Incredibly, though, she is able to turn her head with no more effort than it takes to breathe. What she sees as she looks over her shoulder puzzles her as much as everything else. A pulsing cord of brilliant white runs from somewhere near the back of her neck to the wall.

"Do you know what you are seeing?" Eliana asks.

Tikki looks at her, says nothing.

"It's a leash," Eliana says adamantly. "An astral leash. You're in the thrall of a powerful mage."

"Liar!"

Tikki's own reply shocks her. The word carries as vibrantly through the air as every word Eliana has spoken, and yet Tikki did not open her mouth. She did not even mean to utter the word aloud. It was only a thought.

Another voice fills the air.

Raman's voice. "No . . . she does not lie. When the she speaks, she speaks truth. There is something she wants. That is why . . . why she is doing this. Showing us this."

"Listen to the he," Eliana says. "He is wise."

Tikki is almost too frightened to think, never mind

listen. Being gripped by a power she can neither fight nor escape threatens to engulf her in terror. In desperation, she wills the change.

Nothing happens.

She loses it—strains with every last drop of will and physical strength to make the change and break free of the magic, screaming until the sound deafens her. But that lasts only moments. Tikki suddenly sinks into a blackness as full and deep as sleep.

When she comes around again, she is leaning back against Raman's chest. The magician stands facing her from the steps in front of the bed. The sight sets her off. Again, she struggles to make the change, but cannot. The change just will not happen, and Tikki doesn't know why. Raman's arms grip her as if to crush her. She flails against him with her hands and arms and elbows till they're both splashed with his blood and she's panting with the effort and he's roaring into her ears, "STOP! Stop fighting!"

Then, abruptly, she slumps. The magician murmurs a word and Tikki's eyes shut and she falls asleep. When she wakes, she's leaning back against the wall behind the bed. Raman's arms hold her tightly. The air smells of blood and terror, and strangely none of it effects her.

She feels very calm.

"Do not fight me," Eliana says. "You will lose."

Tikki believes it.

"Your he is right," Eliana continues. "There is something I want. Help me get it and I will help you, but do not try my patience. There are many who are eager to serve me, many I could use. I offer you a service. Understand that. Remember it."

"She does not know you," Raman says.

"That is why I have been so tolerant." Eliana tosses her head, then looks from Raman to Tikki. "Who is the man you work for?"

Tikki wonders how this magician knows she is working for anybody. How does any magician know anything? Is there no way to escape the magician's power?

"Tell her," Raman says.

Tikki takes a deep breath. "Adama."

"His full name," Eliana says.

"Adama Ho."

It's a matter of survival. That's why she gives the name. She cannot fight and she strongly suspects that running would do no good either, even if she could run. The magician is simply too powerful. That is a frightening thing, but one Tikki can deal with now. It is a reality she absolutely *must* deal with if she is to survive.

"Adama Ho is a mage," Eliana says.

"No."

"I'm telling you that he is a mage. He has used his sorcery to veil your eyes. He has used it to control you."

Tikki considers that impossible, and opens her mouth to say so, then recalls the power Eliana has demonstrated without even breaking a sweat. Could Adama be a mage? Worse, could he be controlling her? Maybe that's possible. Anything seems possible. Some would say that her own existence is proof of that.

Tikki recalls her encounter with Hammer, who she killed, perhaps unwisely, and the news snoop and the camera-guy, who she allowed to escape, but wanted to kill, needlessly. She recalls, too, her trouble with Fat André and his underworld bank. She could swear that the money she deposited with him was the very money that Adama paid for her services. If what Eliana says is true, she might never have been paid at all. She might have been working for free. She might have spent most of her time in Philadelphia performing as Adama's puppet.

She remembers, too, how she found Adama waiting for her at her weapons cache in Chinatown.

That should not have happened.

"His power over mind and spirit is great, but limited against the power of flesh. That is why he needs you. You are his weapon."

Tikki says nothing, holds her reaction in check. Eliana's words surprise her, especially that last word. Adama always refers to her as "his weapon." His principal weapon. Does Eliana know that, does the fact prove what Eliana's saying, or is the magician's choice of words merely coincidental?

"I can counter the mage's sorcery," Eliana says. "But

to break his hold over you, the power of the spells must be attacked at their source.''

Tikki smells nothing of lies. Would a mage as powerful as Eliana even have need of lies? To strike a deal with her would be breaking one of Tikki's cardinal rules, but if Eliana is right . . .

If she's right . . .

''What do you want from us?'' Raman asks.

Eliana smiles. ''Listen closely.''

45

The alley is pitch black. The Lambourg Fiàccola rumbles smoothly, softly, lights off. From her place in the Lambourg's passenger seat, Ingrid lowers her light-intensifying shades and looks around. The interior of the car is so black that Ivette, straw-colored hair and all, is no more than a vague shape behind the Lambourg's steering wheel, barely distinguishable even though she and Ingrid are sitting side by side.

''We should get away,'' Ivette says. ''I'm sick of the city. As soon as we finish here, I want to go on vacation.''

''Where would you like to go?''

''The Carib, maybe.''

Getting away on vacation should be no problem, nothing like the effort it took for them to get away from Ohara this evening. That had turned into a major undertaking. Fortunately, their days with the covert-action staff of Fuchi security have served them well. Specifically, Ingrid's knowledge of drugs and Ivette's talent for teasing. Together, they conned the skell into jetting a large enough dose of MV-28 to put him out for a couple of hours.

''Let's go someplace where there aren't any men.''

''Sure,'' Ingrid says, smiling. ''Here's our date.''

''Yeah.''

Their date is an elf, a slim little girl with black hair

and Asian features. She comes toward the Lambourg, then deliberates for a few moments before coming around to the window on the passenger side. Ingrid draws a satin kerchief around the lower half of her face, checks that Ivette's done the same, then with a touch lowers the window, just enough to look through.

The elf girl leans toward the opening and says, "Hoi, I'm Joi Bang from WHAM! Independent News. You called me?"

"Where's your camera-guy?"

"In a bar across the street."

Good. "I've got a scoop for you," Ingrid says. "The police are sitting on a story."

"Yes!" the elf girl says. "I knew it!"

Ingrid doesn't really care. "Listen closely. Three execs from Exotech Entertainment have been assassinated. The media's only talked about one, Robert Neiman. Two others have also been killed. Steven Jorge and Thomas Harris. Jorge was killed at the Gingko Club."

"I heard about that! The police never released any names!"

Ingrid already knows that. "Harris was killed in much the same way, machine-gunned, at the Ardmore Royal Residence Plaza."

"Who ordered the hits?"

"All three of the dead men used to work in Exotech's Special Projects Section. That's the department that conducted the ritual summoning for *The Coming of Abbirleth* simsense chip."

"The hit chip's related to the killings?"

"The head of S.P.S. reported directly to Exotech's CEO, Bernard Ohara."

"Ohara killed his own people?"

Ingrid hesitates, then keys the window shut. She's said enough. Exactly what she was told to say. Presumably, the infamous Joi Bang will do the rest, all that need be done.

"Okay, hon," Ingrid says. "Drive."

Ivette does just that, taking them out onto the street and away.

46

The noodle stall is just north of Washington Avenue in the middle of the South Market. Raman stands with his back to the service counter, munching on a bowl of noodles so heavily seasoned that the smell alone is enough to make Tikki's eyes water.

Tikki stands by the telecom at the side of the stall toking on a slim Hoyo de Monterrey panatela. She isn't really expecting trouble, not right now, which is why she allows herself the indulgence of a cigar. She keeps her eyes moving anyway. The maze of passageways between the vendor stands and stalls are crowded with people, all of them jammering, walking, turning to and fro, moving their hands, reaching inside jackets and into pockets. A killing stroke could come from any one of a hundred directions.

One thing works to improve her mood: Raman's eyes move as frequently as her own.

Trusting him doesn't come easy. That he's a Were like her and moves like a pro helps. That he tried killing her hurts. That he's done nothing to rouse her suspicions since trying to kill her helps. That he's apparently worked with a mage on a routine basis hurts. Trust him? She feels like she ought to trust him, and yet that is easier said than done. She's choosey, and not in the habit of trusting. Tikki is keenly aware that the bulk of the planet's population determine their loyalties by the nuyen in the offing. For much of her life, she trusted no one but her mother. Now she trusts Castellano, and to a degree, also Black Mist. There are others she considers more reliable than not. Trust Raman? Maybe. She's trusting him right now. What happens an hour from now depends on how he handles himself between now and then.

The telecom bleeps, and Tikki picks up the handset.

The display remains dark, the visual pickup covered with gum.

"Yeah," she says.

A pause, then, "The name is not found."

She hangs up.

This concludes her final check. The message is from Black Mist, her fixer in Chiba. She's already heard from Castellano. All her sources say the same thing.

Three blocks away to the west, Tikki steps through a door into a private room at the back of a bar. She isn't expected, but that's all right. The Kang in her hand serves as an adequate invitation. She slaps it across the back of the head of the muscleguy who precedes her through the door, dropping him to the floor.

The room is swathed in burning orange synthleather. A muscleguy stands by the bar on the right. Beside him, a biff in white spandex and heels sits on a tall stool. She's either a decker or a whore, probably both. Both rent sockets. The man on the sofa at the rear of the room has slicked-back hair, a skinny little mustache, and is wearing a black tieless suit. He's called Nickels. One eyebrow flares upward as he spots the Kang. He flashes a smile as the muscleguy ahead of Tikki drops to the floor.

Tikki doesn't smile.

"Hoi, Striper," Nickels says.

Raman steps up at her right, drawing a Scorpion machine pistol from a shoulder-sling under his duster. Tikki takes a moment to screw a silencer onto the muzzle of the Kang.

"You set me up with Adama Ho," she says. "There is no Adama Ho."

The name is a lie. The suggestion that "Adama" has ties with the Green Circle Gang and Hong Kong's 999 Society was also a lie. Why she didn't investigate this till now, Tikki isn't sure, but the fact's a fact and there's no arguing with it.

Nickels opens his mouth as if to protest, but Tikki is in no mood. She was slaggered, by both Nickels and the mage masquerading as Adama Ho, and that's all that matters. She can't allow that to go unanswered. Pointing the Kang at Nickels' legs, she fires twice in quick succession. Nickels jerks and falls sideways on the couch, shouting and bleeding freely. The biff in white screams. The muscleguy at the bar makes a bad move. A quick burst from Raman's Scorpion sends him banging back against the bar, then spinning to the floor. That concludes their biz.

They're gone.

A trid screen in the Federal Street subway station shows a skinny elf female with black hair and Asian features talking about a series of killings of executives of something called Exotech Entertainment. Tikki gets a funny feeling about that. The circumstances of the killings sound very similar to certain assassinations she carried out for Adama. The names of the victims are similar, too. Almost mirror images. Robert Neiman, Ryokai Naoshi. Steven Jorge, Saigo Jozen. Thomas Harris, Tomito Haruso. She wonders if the men she killed were really yakuza. She wonders if everything Adama has told her from the beginning has been part of a calculated plan to jerk her strings.

She's very, very unhappy.

Raman follows her off the subway at Spring Garden Street. They head toward Seventh. Time for another meet with Chey, the weapons specialist.

"What do you need?" she asks.

"Ares MVR-7 demo pack with twenty-amp time-delayed igniter."

A standard model. Tikki approves. A familiar melody slips into her thoughts: Good. Very good. Where has she heard that before? She thrusts it out of mind. "What else?"

"That will do."

"You'll have to wait somewhere."

"There are some things I should do." Raman says. "Gear to collect. Before we go any further."

They'll rendezvous later.

They set a time and place.

47

The directors' meeting room is located on the fortieth floor of the KFK tower. The room is large and furnished with rich simplicity. The wall paneling looks like teak, the carpeting is plush pile. Set into gilt-edged wooden frames and dominating the tripartite paneled wall at the head of the room are hand-painted color portraits of Kono Koreyasu, Furata Morimoto, and Ko Akifusa. The conference table running up the center of the room is huge and gleams as if freshly waxed, shining like the synthleather-backed chairs lining both sides of the table.

The men seated in the chairs are junior directors of the board of KFK International, charged with presiding over the organization's North American affairs. Conspicuously absent are Bernard Ohara and the two members who sponsored Ohara's admission to the board.

Standing just beyond the head of the table is a huge trideo screen. The image on that screen makes the table before Enoshi seem to extend beyond the limits of the room, directly to the conference table inside the board room of KFK headquarters in Japan. The men seated there are the senior members of the board. At the head of the table in Japan sit the two vice-chairmen of the board of KFK, Shimazu Iwao and Torakido Buntaro. Electronic windows ranging across the top of the trid screen provide close-up views of the vice-chairmen and various of the senior members.

Then a new window appears and a pre-recorded vid begins to play, running on for almost thirty minutes. Enoshi waits patiently, standing rigidly at the foot of the table. He has testified to the accuracy of this vid because, although the vid images are utter fabrications, the video as a whole portrays only the truth.

Enoshi may have arranged for the destruction of the BTL lab used to boost Exotech's finances, as well as the elimination of the individual known as Striper, but he did these things on the direct orders of Bernard Ohara. In truth, as Enoshi sees it, Ohara arranged for these eliminations no less than if he had personally made the necessary contacts.

Enoshi merely did his corporate duty, just as he does his duty now. One's duty may require the performance of actions that are regrettable, even abhorrent, but duty is duty.

Torakido-*sama* understands that.

So would the rest of the board, were they apprised of all the unseemly details.

The vid ends. Shimazo Iwao, Vice-Chairman of the KFK International, looks down the length of the table from his place beside Vice-Chairman Torakido Buntaro in the Tokyo board room, and says, "Your assistance in this matter is greatly appreciated."

Enoshi bows, deeply, in acknowledgement.

Several moments pass. Torakido-*sama*'s already grim expression turns slowly into a dark mask of incredulity. "Enoshi-*san*," he says, "have you any idea who this person called Striper is or why a member of the board such as Bernard X. Ohara should want her assassinated?"

"*Hai*, Torakido-*sama*," Enoshi replies. "Striper is reputed to be a freelance agent of various underworld gangs. She is known variously as an assassin and also a kick-artist, which, I am told, is a term referring to those who engage in physical intimidation techniques. As to what dealings Ohara-*san* may have had with Striper in the past or what criminal gangs she represents, providing him with some motive to have her eliminated, I have no knowledge."

The point is almost irrelevant. The board will not tolerate even the suggestion of impropriety. Ohara's days are numbered.

With an expression both grave and uncompromising, Torakido-*sama* looks pointedly from one member of the senior board to the next, then finally to Enoshi, and says, "*Domo*, Enoshi-*san*. You may go now."

Enoshi bows again, first to Torakido-*sama*, then to Shimazu-*sama*, then turns and exits the board room.

In the antechamber, one of the tea-ladies in her blue corporate uniform serves tea to a pair of blonde-haired women who Enoshi recognizes, though their names elude him. They look like Swedes and are as ravishing as any Western women Enoshi has ever seen. Enoshi recalls Ohara referring to them as his "twins."

Enoshi doubts they'll be Ohara's for much longer.

If in fact they ever were.

48

"This isn't right."

The neighborhood is decrepit. Rancid garbage clogs the alleys. Burnt-out autos, building debris, and piles of junk and rotting litter line the street. The buildings themselves are three- and four-story husks, their windows smashed, façades seared by fire. There is no question she's on the right block in the right part of town, but she still can't believe what she is seeing. The four-story tenement at the middle of the block is a wreck, like every other building. That's exactly where Adama's townhouse ought to be. In front of it an ancient Lincoln American limousine sits at curbside. Battered and rusted, it isn't quite ready for the scrap heap, but it's close. That is where Adama's sleek black Nightsky ought to be, the exact spot.

Tikki shakes her head to clear it and looks again. It must be magic. She can think of no other explanation. She glances at the stocky male standing with her at the end of the alley and tries to put her confusion into words, but nothing comes out.

"You've been under the influence . . . of a powerful mage," Raman says quietly. "Your eyes were veiled, as Eliana said."

Tikki grunts.

"Perhaps this is the first time you're seeing this place
. . . the way it really is."

Maybe that's true and maybe it isn't. It doesn't mitigate Tikki's confusion or her uneasiness with Eliana's
plan. She agreed to go along with it because she had no
real choice. That doesn't help her mood.

It now seems very likely that she, rather than Fat André or anyone else, has been manipulated through magic.
That doesn't help her mood, either.

The street looks clear.

"Go," she says.

Smoothly, almost silently, Raman lopes across the
street. The black satchel dangling from his left hand
doesn't seem to affect his stride in the least. He's as agile
on two legs as he is on four, Tikki notices in passing.

She up-angles the muzzle of her shoulder-slung M22A2
assault rifle with forty-round box clip and integral grenade
launcher, preparing to give covering fire if necessary.

Raman drops to the pavement and slides under the Lincoln American limo across the street. He's under there
for about two minutes. Tikki could probably have done
this part of the job a bit faster, but there are other con-
siderations. She'd rather be doing back-up, rather than
having to rely on someone else to back her up, and Raman doesn't like guns. Raman much prefers blades,
which are fairly useless for some tactical applications,
such as providing cover.

She walks across the street, meeting Raman as he
stands up beside the limo. She still can't believe that she
could mistake a decrepit Lincoln American for a Mitsubishi Nightsky. Be that as it may. She hands Raman his
machine pistol.

The weapon seems absurdly small in his grip.

"We should leave," he says.

Tikki shakes her head.

That's what Eliana wanted them to do, fix the car, then
get out and await the next part of the plan, but that isn't
enough. For all she knows, Eliana is only fixing to get
her killed. Tikki can't just sit back and wait while a couple of mages decide her fate. She's going all the way.

Maybe that's foolish, she doesn't know. If it is, she deserves what she gets.

When people frag with her, she frags them back. That's the way it must be. That's why she did what she did to Nickels the fixer. That's why she came to Philadelphia in the first place.

She also wants to see with her own eyes if Adama is really living in a decaying wreck of a tenement rather than a luxury town house.

She could tell Raman to go ahead and leave, but she doesn't. She wants to know just how far he's willing to follow.

"It's time."

The front door opens at a touch and leads into a small room like a foyer. The walls are dirty and scrawled over with graffiti. A puddle of water fills the center of the sagging floor. Tikki runs her eyes around and breathes the damp, rank-smelling air, wondering if she's ever been here before. She remembers, clearly now, lying in the front room of Adama's town house under a hazy shaft of moonlight. Was that just a dream? a mage's fantasy? Maybe so.

They head downstairs.

This part is just as she remembers. The room of onyx. Glaring trid screens covering the right-hand wall. Adama in his intricately carved throne. The marble stand supporting the huge white gemstone at his right. The only thing that's different is the person standing at Adama's left. She's beautiful for a human. Red hair, voluptuous, and clad in a clinging black gown that bares her shoulders, arms, and a remarkable depth of cleavage. The glaring trid screens on the right-hand wall all display a full frontal image of her face and hair.

Adama smiles. "Welcome, tigress." His eyes flicker briefly over the assault rifle in Tikki's hands, pointed at him, then turn slightly aside. "You've brought your friend. I'm glad."

Raman comes up alongside Tikki.

"You owe me money," she says.

Adama smiles. "Do I?"

If her guesses are correct, and that's a big if, Adama

never paid her anything. He made her believe that she'd been paid or else he paid her in fantasies, lies, the Sixth World's equivalent of fairy gold.

Adama waves a hand in a vague gesture. A glowing orb of white briefly surrounds the hand, then dwindles. If this is proof that Adama is a mage, it's the first that Tikki can recall seeing with her own eyes. She suppresses her surprise, resists a sneering smile, and tightens her finger slightly on the trigger of the M22A2. Nothing further of a magical nature seems to happen. Adama frowns, looks at his hand, then at her, seeming puzzled. Tikki's mildly surprised about that, too.

"Ahh," Adama says, freshening his smile. "You've escaped my enchantments. Or have you?" One eyebrow slowly tilts upward. "No. Another mage. A *shaman*." Adama chuckles softly. "You wear her protection."

That's true, apparently. Under her red synthleather jacket, Tikki wears a gold medallion marked with a peculiar cat-like face. Raman wears one, too. Gifts from Eliana. The things are supposed to protect them from magic. How a pair of stupid medallions might do that Tikki doesn't know. Till this moment, she doubted that the one hanging from her neck would do anything but annoy her. She wonders how Adama detected it.

Magic, obviously.

She hates it.

The redhead at Adama's left looks directly at Tikki, moving just her eyes. It's the first time Tikki has seen her move.

"How interesting," Adama says. "The tigress dances with shamans. I only wonder . . . Did you come here to kill me?"

Tikki could deny it, but that would be stupid, counterproductive. She came here to get answers, maybe get money, maybe pay back Adama for using magic against her. She isn't exactly sure what she's going to do. She's never been in this kind of situation before. Facing a mage like this. "Killing's a possibility," she snarls quietly. "First, I want my money. *Mage*."

"You're aware of my power," Adama says, smiling as if pleased. "I was wondering when you would notice.

I've been at pains to keep it a secret. You don't like mages do you?''

"I don't like lying skells."

"Have I lied to you?"

"There is no Adama Ho. Hong Kong's never heard of the name. The only Triad gang in Philly is quietly doing biz in Chinatown."

Adama's smile broadens. He tilts his head back and laughs softly. He's some moments regaining his composure. "Forgive me," he says, still smiling broadly. "Your indignation is quite understandable. I've treated you unfairly. I admit it. You've given me more pleasure than any servant in my memory, and I've given you no reward. You must think me very ungrateful."

"I think you're due to get aced."

There's something wrong with the redhead, Tikki realizes. She doesn't smell human. She doesn't smell like anything.

Adama chuckles, smiles.

"How would you like your money?" he asks. "In weapons? Or gold perhaps?"

Tikki could swear she's heard Adama ask similar questions, not so long ago, possibly of a black-clad man or elf named Tricks or Sticks, something like that.

"What would be fair?" Adama extends a hand. On the floor before his throne appears a pile of gold coins, enough to fill a good-sized duffel bag.

"No?" Adama says, looking at Tikki. "More?" He moves his hand slightly again and a pile of platinum credsticks appears on the floor beside the coins. "Even more?" Adama moves his hand again and a pile of paper currency appears next to the credsticks. "Is that better?"

Tikki doesn't believe what she's seeing. For one thing, Adama is offering a fortune beyond anything that makes sense; for another, the credsticks and the coins and currency smell like the redhead, like nothing. Like a dream.

She risks a quick glance at Raman. He is wide-eyed and smells very tense. She looks back at Adama.

"No?" Adama says, still smiling. "You refuse my offer?"

"I want real. Real sticks."

"I have a better idea." Adama withdraws his hand. The coins, the credsticks, and the currency all disappear. "Do one last job for me and I'll forgive this little indiscretion of yours."

"Are you bulletproof?"

"I'm better than that."

Somewhere, a wind begins to rise. Tikki can hear it. In another moment, the rustling ascends into a cyclone's howling. Things begin rattling and groaning and banging as though the building is about to rise right off its foundations. Tikki glances swiftly around, then realizes Raman has vanished, is nowhere in sight. His smell is gone from the air as though he'd never been here.

Tikki growls.

She doesn't stop to think. She doesn't pause to wonder what has happened. She doesn't consider the diversity of things that Adama might have done to make Raman disappear, or seem to disappear. Her senses tell her that Raman is gone, just gone, and in her surprise she interprets that as meaning he's gone forever, that he's dead, as good as dead. Instinct and anger direct her response. She adjusts her point of aim and squeezes the trigger. The assault rifle stammers, but the thunderous noise is nothing compared to the fury rising inside her. She doesn't care if Adama is a mage, doesn't care if he's powerful enough to make her vanish, too. Were she in her natural form, she would hurl herself forward with a roar, with every intention of ripping Adama into bloody, shredded bits.

Adama tilts his head back, laughing uproariously, and fades slowly from sight. Everything else goes with him: the redhead, the wall of trid screens, the throne, the marble stand and gemstone. The roar of the cyclone fades into silence. Tikki is left standing in a dank, gloomy basement, her heart pounding like a jackhammer. The ceiling is stained and warped and dripping water. The walls are bare concrete, some missing small chunks, as from bullets. Tikki looks down to find her right foot in the shallows of a broad puddle.

Abruptly, she slaps a fresh magazine into the assault

rifle, but then looks around blankly. There's no point in shooting.

Shoot at what?

Adama's voice rises out of the empty air. "You must do one last job for me, tigress. One last job. Then our time together will be complete. You'll be free again. And if you're good, very good, I'll even return your mate to you. That will be your reward."

Tikki swallows, struggling to think amid the din of her own hammering pulse. Do one last job for this mage? She'd have to be mad to even consider it. "Suppose I *don't*!"

"Oh, but you will. You will, tigress. I choose my weapons with great care. You want your friend back. And I want the man responsible for the death of my beautiful Leandra."

"And who might that be?"

"Bennari Ohashi."

49

Without warning, the lights go out and Raman finds himself immersed in a blackness more complete than any he has ever experienced. For a moment more, he hears a howling like that of a violent storm, and then the sound fades to nothing.

It's as if he's suddenly gone blind and deaf. He can see nothing, hear nothing. A worrisome strangeness, but one he doubts. A powerful mage could easily cast such illusions. The question is, what does he do now? He looks to his right, where Striper was standing, but sees only blackness, blackness everywhere, in every direction. He can feel the gun in his hands, but cannot see it, even when he lifts it in front of his face.

He descends to a crouch. There is a hard, stable surface beneath his feet. To his hand, his left hand, it feels rough and gritty, like concrete. Is that part of the illusion, or a flaw in it? The latter, he suspects. Fooling his eyes and ears is one thing; also deceiving his sense of touch and his sense of his own body would be much more difficult. The more senses that must be fooled, the greater the magic required. A mage intent on merely neutralizing him would have no need to go to such lengths.

Briefly, he speaks into the darkness, if only in hopes of advising Striper of his situation, but hears no reply.

He wonders what to do next.

Striper may need his help.

50

When the elevator doors open, she's already in motion, tossing a Winter Systems flash-pak and a MECAR SA MP-76 riot grenade into the hallway.

The flash-pak ignites at once, firing a series of blinding micro-bursts designed to disorient any animal relying on visible light, and powerful enough to overcome the reactive flash compensators of most military-style helmets. The riot grenade bangs immediately, but takes a second or two to achieve full effect. Fragmentation damage is negligible. The MECAR MP-76's plastic shell tends to split like the skin of a fruit rather than shatter into lethal shards. The minimal explosive charge serves primarily as a propellant for the grenade's potent fumes.

Four seconds later, Tikki steps into the corridor, wearing a combat gas mask with five-stage filtration and flash-elimination faceplate. That makes the air she breathes distasteful and reduces the light in the hallway to darkness, but she's used to smelly air and working in low light.

The hallway is short, extending only a few meters to the left and right. Seven males in full body armor lay sprawled about with a variety of military-style weapons. They'll be unconscious for about an hour and too sick to move for an hour or two after that.

Tikki turns toward the door at the left end of the hall-way. Even as she turns, the doors snaps open, revealing a man in mirrorshades and a dark suit. The machine pistol in his hand makes his function apparent. He doesn't collapse because the gas from the riot grenade has already cleared from the air.

Tikki fires a three-round burst with her JAMA-5 narcoject submachine gun. The man staggers back and drops to the floor. He'll be out for about five hours. The door stays open, which is luck. Tikki follows through with another flash-pak and riot grenade.

About three seconds later, she steps into the anteroom and foyer of the condo belonging to Bennari Ohashi. The three plainclothes guards sprawled there look unconscious. Tikki pulls off the gas mask. Beneath it, she wears a balaclava pull-over face mask, a tactical assault vest, and commando-style pants and shoes, all black.

The double doors to the rest of the condo snap open, letting in a man in a white servant's uniform and carrying a tray laden with sandwiches. He gapes and stops, gazing wide-eyed at Tikki. She steps toward him, pointing the JAMA-5 at his chest.

"Put the tray down."

The man turns, hesitantly, smelling of fear, and puts the tray on a small table beside the double doors. Tikki pushes the man back against the wall and points the muzzle of the JAMA-5 at his face.

"Where is Bennari Ohashi?"

The man gapes and stares at her, then stammers in frantic Japanese, "I . . . I don't know . . . *I don't know*!"

Irritating.

She drops the muzzle of the JAMA-5 to the man's shoulder and fires a single shot. The man slumps. She's not going to stand here and argue. She'll spend less time searching the condo.

She knows the layout of the place, knows all the particulars. Adama laid it out previously, when she still believed his lies, before he took Raman captive. She isn't exactly sure how she feels about Raman, what exactly he means to her life, but she's sure he means something, and she's willing to kill—kill anyone necessary—if that's what it takes to get him back.

That Adama is compelling her to do this job is infuriating, but she can live with the anger. What she can't live with is the idea of losing what may be the chance of a lifetime.

She steps from the foyer, JAMA-5 at the ready.

Ohara wakes with a start, gripped by the realization that the ruthless demon-creature haunting his sleep is coming for him. Every night that passes without news of Striper's death is one night closer, one night closer to him that the vicious primitive gets. If she isn't killed *soon . . .*

If the assassins Enoshi has hired waste any more time . . .

The inevitable conclusion is beyond his capacity to bear. He stumbles from the bed and into his private bathroom. He grabs a handful of pills from the bottles along the expansive marble counter, hurriedly swallowing them down. He's always had a delicate constitution—just another indication of superior intellect. The pills help to stabilize his physical chemistry, and thus counter the deleterious effects of his horrifying dreams. A half-dozen bursts of DeeVine from his chromed pneumatic injector temper his emotive upset with a vague, wispy sense of euphoria. He sorts through the P-fix BTL chips scattered across the counter and slots *The Almighty*! into the datajack behind his right ear. The chip helps restore the unity of his thoughts, his clarity of vision, his objective perspective on the truth. Such aid is necessary in a world on the brink of social and economic collapse.

He returns to the bedroom and lies down on the bed.

Fortunately, almost everything is going according to plan. He already has one multinational securely in his unyielding grip: KFK International. More will follow. Before long, he will control the world's economy— corporations, banks, the orbitals, everything. Everything will be his. He will face obstacles, certainly, but with his unrivaled intellectual power he will anticipate and annihilate any and all difficulties that may arise. The world will jump at his command.

Right now his only problem—more of an irritant really—is that primitive slitch Striper. He should never have allowed her to live. He should have finished her in Seattle. He would have done it, too, except that the slitch took him by surprise. With his lofty intellect and refined sensibilities, he did not expect to be challenged, much less confronted, by a savage, something risen from the bowels of the nightmares of humanity. If he has made any mistake at all, that was it, being surprised. Now, though, he knows better. That is why he had Enoshi hire killers. Fight primitives with primitives. That's the ticket.

The fact is that he used the ignorant savage as a pawn in his mercurial rise to ultimate power. Whether every detail of his plans back in Seattle succeeded is quite irrelevant. He still used her, the slitch. He made her a servant, a slave to his will, just like he uses everybody. If he wished, he could use her in any manner he wanted. Why, if he felt so inclined, he could even arrange to have her right here on this bed, strapped down spread-eagled, a moaning abject slave to his basest physical needs . . .

The thought makes him smile, then laugh.

Other people failed him. That's why the slitch survived, why she lived to pursue him out of Seattle. She was supposed to have been killed. She was hired to kill the man whom he'd set up as a thief, the thief of a very valuable datafile. Naturally, Ohara himself had the file. The phony theft was staged merely to deflect suspicion. The death of the man was necessary to keep him from revealing the truth. Striper's own death, had she died, would simply have helped account for the disappearance of the datafile.

As it turned out, the file disappeared and Ohara got off scot-free. But for Striper's interference, her failure to cooperate by dying, the plan went exactly as intended. That ass of a police lieutenant, Kirkland, didn't know how close he was to the truth. Ohara did sell the data stolen from Seretech, as Kirkland said, but not to John Brandon Conway, the famous corporate intermediary. Rather, he used the data to buy into KFK. Like most multinationals,

KFK is highly diversified and has at least one subsidiary for which the Seretech genetic engineering data might have been tailor-made.

Just the thought of how he reamed those imbeciles at Seretech sets him off laughing again. How much more heartily he'll laugh once he's dismissed KFK's entire board of directors, including that pompous ass of a vice-chairman, Torakido Buntaro, with all his holier-than-thou jappo presumptions.

The days ahead are going to be sweet, indeed.

He lifts his head to look as the bedroom door opens and a figure in dark clothing steps through the doorway.

Tikki pauses for several moments, just staring. She feels . . . confused. She's here in a condo at the Platinum Manor Estates to eliminate a man called Bennari Ohashi. She has seen Ohashi's picture, knows that he looks Japanese. She also knows that Adama holds Ohashi responsible for the death of his *beautiful Leandra*. Yet, now, as she stands in the doorway of the condo's luxurious red-hued master bedroom, she finds herself unable to distinguish between the image in her memory, her memory of Ohashi's face, and the face of the man lying on the bed. And the man on the bed is definitely not Japanese. His features are unmistakably Anglo, and Tikki knows him, knows him from personal experience. He doesn't look exactly the same as when last she saw him, but she recognizes his smell at once, and his smell leads her to discover the familiar characteristics in his features.

His name is Bernard Ohara and she's been waiting since Seattle for the opportunity to kill him.

She only wonders how it is that she finds Ohara here.

Is this the man Adama wants dead? *Could it be anyone else?* She's at the right address. The master bedroom reeks of Ohara's odors, as if he's been living here for months. This cannot be a coincidence. Can it?

She shakes her head.

Adama always said he chooses his weapons very carefully. Now she thinks she knows what he meant. What better weapon than one which willingly seeks the target? which has personal reasons for wanting Ohara dead?

Ohara marked her for death back in Seattle. That's all
the reason she needs.

Ohara slowly sits up, wearing no more than a puzzled
frown and a pair of satiny gold shorts. "Who are you?"
he says. "And what are you doing in my bedroom?"

"Do you still dance?"

"Excuse me?"

Tikki slips the shoulder-slung JAMA-5 behind her back
and draws the Kang from the reverse-draw holster at her
left hip.

"I think you should leave," Ohara says. "Now."

Wrong.

Tikki points and fires. The Kang roars five times in
rapid sequence. The pounding reverberations are deafening. The sheets and pillows on the bed flutter and jerk.
Ohara's eyes go wide. The acid stink of his fear suddenly
floods the air. He twitches convulsively, scrambling from
the bed, falling, getting up, staggering, jumping, spinning toward the door at the right of the room.

"You get out of here!" he shouts. "GO AWAY!"

Tikki puts five more rounds into the floor around Ohara's
feet, then another five into the wall around the door as
Ohara stumbles through, exclamations rising into hyster-
ical shouts. Tikki follows him down a short hall and into
the next room, a study, popping the Kang's empty magazine and ramming home a full one. Ohara moves toward
the desk at the rear of the room. Tikki points and fires.
Slick rounds chew up the walls, the floor, the desk, and
the monitor sitting on it. Ohara's shrill shouts become
screams of terror. He staggers sideways across the room,
through another door, and into another room.

Tikki follows.

Ohara leads her through a huge room like a living
room. She rams a new clip into the Kang and opens fire
again, smashing things all around her target, lights and
lamps and expensive crystalline decorations. Why she
doesn't just put the shots into Ohara and end it she isn't
sure. She feels strangely at odds with herself. Part of her
wants Ohara to know utter terror. Another part wants to
blow him away, make her kill, have her revenge. Another
part shouts for her to make the kill personal, make the

change, assume her four-legged form and take this man as prey, shred him, then devour him. Yet another part keeps telling her, adamantly, that she's got to kill this man to obtain Raman's safe release.

And yet, she resists, She hates the idea of giving Adama what he wants, of giving into his will, serving his wishes. She despises the concept of serving another as her master. She would almost rather let Ohara escape than cooperate with a mage who has apparently been manipulating her with magic. She detests being used. It makes her feel like helpless prey, like a weak, insignificant little creature forced to turn and run at the first sight of anything like a hunter.

Feelings like that make her ill, sick with disgust, furious with outrage.

Ohara bangs through a sliding transparex door and stumbles onto a balcony, then turns and bangs back against the impact-resistant panes guarding the balcony's outer edge. Tikki follows as far as the doorway, Kang thundering. The transparent pane at Ohara's back fractures and then bursts into a shower of fragments. Ohara snivels and shrieks and begins laughing hysterically, maniacally.

"I KNOW WHO YOU ARE!" he screams, then pauses to laugh, laugh like a madman. "You're the monster . . . yes!" He laughs wildly, frantically. "You're the monster! the monster! You don't scare me! You aren't here! YOU'RE NOT REAL!"

Tikki pauses, lifting the Kang to point directly at Ohara's face. In a sense, she realizes, Ohara's right. She isn't here. Now that she's faced with the inevitability of making another kill, she remembers something, a previous kill she made for Adama. The memory comes to her clearly. It's been flitting around for days somewhere just beneath the surface of her conscious mind. She was on the back stairway of a residence tower, the Ardmore complex. A door opened and a young male came onto the stairs, and she killed him because he might sound an alarm and prevent her from reaching her target. It seems impossible now. She killed a kid, an innocent kid. The realization hurts.

She could have just clubbed him over the head.

All this effing magic has her fragged up. She's been doing things that are insane, things that don't make any sense! Here in the middle of a city, she's been acting like a creature of the wild . . .

It's all too complicated.

As she watches Ohara sniveling and shrieking and laughing, a distant part of her mind tells her that this puny nothing of a human being is not worthy of being taken as prey, that it is somehow less than prey, like a bug. The idea of even bothering to kill it is practically an insult.

On impulse, she swings the JAMA-5 out from behind her back, points and fires once. The weapon thumps. Ohara doesn't seem to notice the small dart that suddenly appears, sticking out of his midsection. Momentarily, his sniveling subsides and he goes limp. Tikki isn't sure what she will do if he sways forward; but, as it happens, she doesn't have to worry about it.

Perhaps Fate decides the matter.

Ohara sways back, back through the hole in the balcony's transparent outer wall, and topples into the night.

It's seven stories to the ground.

Tikki hesitates a moment, considering the hole in the balcony's outer wall, then turns to go. She almost doesn't care if Ohara dies in the fall, or if through some miracle he should survive. Too many other things are bothering her, questions involving her entire existence. She isn't sure who she's killing for, or why, or if she even has the right.

She has to get away.

51

There's an impact beyond comprehension, then suddenly he's tearing away, ripping free of his own flesh, shedding every last particle of humanity, everything but his animal awareness, as he hurtles down a black passage into an ocean of searing white.

The pain is beyond comprehension. He lives a billion eternities of agony in a mere instant. He lives ten billion more in the instant that follows. He senses a trillion trillion others thrashing and shrieking with a torment no less devastating than his own, and then something else, a presence, malignant and evil, a fiendish monstrosity reveling in the glorious suffering of souls uncounted. This abominable horror has caught him, along with so many others, only to feed on his agony and essence throughout all eternity.

His earthly schemes are undone. He is in the grip of one whose power exceeds all comprehension.

Then, the agony swells again, and there is nothing else.

52

It's well past midnight when Kirkland lifts his eyes from his desktop monitor. What he sees coming through the door of his office is Deputy Chief of Detectives Nanette Lemaire, accompanied by Kirkland's immediate boss, Captain Emilio Henriquez. The door swings shut behind them.

"You're to close the Exotech case," says Lemaire.

"I'm working on it," Kirkland replies.

Lemaire shakes her head. "You have till tomorrow evening to shut it down. By twenty hundred, you'll have a suspect in custody. You scan me?"

Kirkland spends a few moments watching Lemaire and Henriquez, then a few more lighting a cig. Henriquez doesn't look like he's about to make any protest about anything.

Kirkland takes a deep drag off his cig. "I'm a little thick tonight, Chief. Why don't you lay it out for me."

"Don't make trouble, Brad," Henriquez says. "Not on this one."

"I'm not making trouble. Just asking a simple question."

Lemaire compresses her lips. For a woman her size, big as an ork, she's got thin lips. They briefly disappear inside her mouth.

"This is how it reads," she says, adamantly. "The media's got it now. The mayor's ready to drop a load in his pants. By order of the board of Hetler-Shutt, our parent corporation, you've got till twenty hundred tomorrow to make an arrest, and one that'll stick."

"And the hell with justice," Kirkland remarks.

"Brad," Henriquez says darkly.

Lemaire glares.

Kirkland takes another drag off his cig. "Do I get this order in writing, Chief?"

"Spare me your drek, Lieutenant!" Lemaire shouts.

"Don't ask me to play patsy for the BOARD!" Kirkland roars.

Several moments pass. Lemaire turns several shades of red. Henriquez breaks the silence. "Why do you think I'm standing here, Brad?" he says quietly. "Nobody's looking for a patsy."

"You gonna sign off on the case, Captain?"

"You close it. I'll sign it."

That makes a difference. At least, it'll suggest, in writing, that Kirkland took advice before closing the case. That means someone to share the blame if the case comes back to haunt them. Kirkland can deal with that. He can also deal with shutting down cases prematurely, even pinning the rap on the wrong piece of dirt. There's plenty of dirt to go around and they're all guilty of something. Pinning a rap on the wrong slag bothers him, but that's the price of staying on the job, doing what little he can to actually fight crime. It's called making deals with the devil. Deals like this make him want to vomit, but somehow he manages to go on swallowing his bile. It's either that or just walk away, and just walking away isn't his style.

"You know I'll back you up," Henriquez says.

That's probably true.

Kirkland meets Lemaire's glare for several moments. "Whatever you say, Chief," he says softly.

Henriquez and Lemaire head out, passing Detective-Sergeant Paul Zanardi on his way in. Zanardi looks feverish, excited, but too bleary-eyed and tired to show it right.

"Marchese just called in. He says Bernard Ohara just fell out through a transparex wall and took a dive off his balcony."

Kirkland hesitates, then says, "He should be so lucky."

"What do you mean?"

Kirkland sips his lukewarm soykaf, drops the rest in the garbage can behind him. "Some new data's just come to light. Ohara's our perp."

Zanardi looks astounded. "You serious?"

Kirkland tokes on his cig and sits back in his chair, considering the pros and cons, then says, smiling, "Think I'd joke about a thing like that, Zanardi?"

53

Adam Malik carefully descends the stairs to the squalid foyer of the tenement, walking stick in one hand, briefcase in the other. The stick conceals a short blade like that of a sword, but one magically imbued to provide a slight edge in a fight, in the unlikely event he should ever have to participate in physical violence. The real treasure is inside the briefcase, securely cradled in plush velvet. It takes the form of a huge gemstone weighing perhaps seven or eight hundred carats. Malik does not yet understand even a fraction of the gem's potential, but he knows its value is beyond measure. It is called the Vault of Souls, and the power it contains exceeds anything he has ever encountered.

Now, as he steps into the foyer, a darkness emerges from out of the empty air in the center of the room, and swells to fill the room completely. Malik smiles, for this is the manifest form of the Master, the spirit calling itself Abbirleth. Malik holds himself still as the darkness slowly dwindles, gathering around him, filling him, becoming one with his flesh, his mind, his spirit.

"You are ready," the Master says.

Malik smiles. "Yes." Then a thought occurs. "What about the Weretiger stumbling around in the basement? My spell of confusion will fade shortly."

"Leave him," the Master says. "He is of no concern . . . We have a new servant now . . ."

"Yes," Malik says again, still smiling.

The new servant waits out front by the car. He is an ork, a blank slate as far as magic is concerned, and not particularly bright. Those two factors make him easy to control. He is physically large and powerful and has no qualms about killing. That should make him useful, a good weapon, very good. He will never be as resistant to injury as, say, a Weretiger, but in this world of violence and death, to replace him is a simple matter.

"And what of Striper?"

"We are through with her as well . . ."

"Yes, of course."

"Now, we go . . ."

As the Master wishes, so it shall be. Malik is more than pleased to be getting out of Philadelphia. More than pleased to do whatever the Master wishes. The Master has granted him many favors, given him a taste of power beyond human conception. A power enabling him to summon the spirit of his beautiful Leandra, and to bask once more in the glory of her love. The Master's power also made controlling the Weretigress Striper as easy as expressing wishes, and gave him the weapon with which to take vengeance on those responsible for the death of his beautiful one: Neiman, Jorge, Harris, and, of course, Ohara.

Bernard Ohara was the worst. It was he who ruled the Special Projects Section with an iron fist, he who insisted on the ritual summoning that led to Leandra's death. Ohara richly deserved the death he got. Malik's only disappointment was that it was not more cruel. The Master's pleasure would have been greater had Ohara's death, like that of the others, been one of exceptional violence.

The Master's pleasure is of great importance, because without the Master's power Malik would be nothing, the greater secrets of the metaplanes forever closed to him.

Now, all the knowledge of the universe awaits him.

From the foyer he steps out onto the sidewalk. He will not miss this decaying, god-forsaken neighborhood. Neither will he miss Philadelphia. Who would?

Carson, the new servant, opens the rear door of Malik's old limo. The car is a virtual antique that looks like it's falling apart, but Malik likes it, and for the moment, it suffices. Malik slides into the front-facing rear seat.

"We goin' now, boss?" Carson inquires.

"Yes," Malik replies. "On to Newark."

The Master has an affinity for places like Newark, a city like so many others that the guidebooks describe as urban hells.

Very appropriate.

Carson climbs behind the wheel of the limo and starts the engine. As the Lincoln pulls away from the curb, the world suddenly explodes into a million shards, a million fiery fragments, roaring with the monstrous searing flames of an inferno.

54

The thousand candles climbing the wall in tiers burn brightly. On the altar half a hundred incense sticks also smolder and burn. Eliana dips her thumb into a small clay pot on the altar, then dabs a spot of the gray paint of Cat on her forehead, nose, and cheeks. She uses a bowl of pure water and a fresh, clean towel to meticulously bathe her thumb and fingers and hands. That done, Eliana retreats three steps from the altar and settles slowly to her knees.

The dozens of slender bangles ringing her forearms

chime softly as she lowers her hands to the floor, and begins to softly sing.

The song is a short one, and rises from the depths of her being. The words come to her lips as if of their own will.

The room around her, her lodge, changes character, growing vibrant, potent, and pure with the energies of nature. The thousand candles gleam like stars. Her soft song echoes as if carrying throughout a gigantic cavern.

The twin doors at the front of the altar swing open, revealing the dark tunnel to the etheric. Eliana crawls into it on all fours, mindful of every movement, then she rises onto two feet as the tunnel swells in size. She emerges into an alley, a very special one known only to the very few who understand the importance of secrets.

The alley runs through the heart of a vast metropolis. Here the energies of humanity blend with the energies of nature. All is in balance. In the buildings that rise high into the night ablaze with starlight live thousands of human beings, living, dying, waking, sleeping, loving, fighting, laughing, crying.

On they go with their lives in complete ignorance of the special nature of this alley.

That is as it should be.

Eliana chooses a place to kneel and wait, a place in the middle of the alley that is free of litter and grit and dust. Examining her right hand, she finds no smudges or stains on her skin. Slowly, the brilliant stars turn across the sky. Before long, a supple form emerges from the cloak of shadows at the rear of the alley.

It is Cat-Who-Walks-Alone. She who is solitary and supreme, committed to no one but Herself and Her own Cat-Nature. She is at home with humanity and the streets and alleys of the city, but ultimately She is self-sufficient, self-satisfied, complete. If sometimes She is cruel, it is because someone has offended or betrayed Her in some way. She is anything but arbitrary.

Cat comes near, sniffs at the ground, then sits, washes her forepaw for several moments, then looks at Eliana for a time. When She speaks, it is with a voice as pure as Nature. "You have secrets."

Faintly, Eliana smiles. Cat is perceptive and wise. "I have learned many things."

"Tell me."

"Others will hear."

"Then follow."

Cat leads up the alley, then around to the rear of a building, then down a stairway, then through an open door, then down another stairway, then down a narrow hall, then into a furnace room, then around to a hidden nook behind the furnace. The floor is clean. The softly rumbling furnace makes the air warm and cozy. They sit. Eliana leans down on her elbows. Cat sniffs at her face.

"Tell me your secrets."

Eliana leans closer to whisper certain secrets into Cat's ear. Just the ones that matter now. She tells of the mage Adam Malik, and the spirit possessing him, and the great prize which the spirit keeps.

"You have learned all this on your own?"

"Yes. Through sorcery, and other ways."

"What other ways?"

"I've used others to learn things, and to prepare. They know nothing of my ultimate aim. Only that there is something I want. I have kept the greater truth hidden."

Cat hisses softly with pleasure. "What is this truth? Your true secret. Tell me."

Eliana leans closer and whispers the truth in Cat's ear. There is something she wants, a thing she must have.

"You will need help," Cat murmurs.

Eliana says nothing. To ask help of Cat is to invite rejection. Cat is vain, assured of Her power, and scornful of any who rely on others for help. Yet, She is not so foolish as to always believe the urgings of vanity.

"If you are to succeed," Cat whispers into Eliana's ear, "there is a secret you must know."

"Tell me," Eliana murmurs.

Cat gazes at her a moment, then whispers into her ear. The secret conveyed confirms her suspicions. She knows now how to proceed.

"I will go now."

"Yes," Cat's eyes gleam. She is pleased.

Eliana returns to her lodge.

Osorthonoriks, her ally, joins her.

"Prepare yourself."

Osorthonoriks replies telepathically. *I am ready, mistress . . .*

The front of the altar wavers like the surface of a pool of water, then clears. An image appears, that of an alleyway. At the end of the alley stand two Weretigers. Eliana knows them by their auras, their astral forms, and their assumed names: Ripsaw and Striper. A small patch of air shimmers in the shadows behind them, but they do not seem to notice. They speak to each other in low tones. They observe the street. Ripsaw then crosses the street and slips under a car, an old limousine. Striper follows. They meet beside the car, then go around it to the sidewalk and in through the front door of a tenement.

Eliana sneers. Her instructions to the pair were to do their work and get away. The magical defenses she prepared for them were very limited. They place everything in jeopardy—fools! Fortunately, they know nothing of Eliana's ultimate aim.

A short time passes.

Striper emerges, looks around, then walks swiftly away. Her etheric energies appear tumultuous. She deserves what she gets. Eliana wastes no sympathy on those who disobey.

Others approach the tenement, but discreetly, keeping to the alleyways, hiding within other of the abandoned tenements, just as she instructed. Eliana knows them well. They are her followers. They serve her willingly and require very little in the way of reward. They are in awe of her magic and desire to learn her secrets, to be accepted as apprentice or student. Only one or two have any real potential.

Just before the dawn, the tenement door opens again. An ork emerges. He is a servant of the mage Adam Malik. Minutes later, Malik himself steps through the door and onto the street. Within his etheric form drifts a stygian blackness. This, Eliana knows, is the etheric form of a shadow spirit. The spirit has not only possessed the man. It has hidden its life inside him.

Malik gets into the rear of the limousine, the ork enters

through the driver's door. An instant later, the limo explodes.

The street outside the tenement is engulfed in fire.

From out of the boiling flames comes the form of Adam Malik, now a human torch. The power of the shadow spirit has saved him from the force of the explosion and now protects him from the flames enveloping him.

Eliana sings a soft song of command.

The shimmering patch in the alleyway coalesces into a form like that of a man, but a man of great splendor and beauty. He is neither man nor god, but rather an animus spirit, previously bound. He steps onto the sidewalk and lifts his hands toward the street. As he tosses back his head, a devastating barrage of lightning strikes down out of the night. Within seconds, half a hundred dazzling bolts blast at the staggering, fire-blackened form of Adam Malik. As the lightning strikes, Malik falls. An instant later, a new fire erupts, a massive pillar of boiling fire, roaring toward the dark heavens, completely enveloping Malik's body.

When the flames subside, only dust remains.

With the death of Adam Malik comes the destruction of the shadow spirit that had hidden its life inside him. The spirit called itself Abbirleth, but its true name, Eliana knows, was Soul-Catcher.

Eliana retires to bathe.

Some hours later, one of her followers enters the small room at the back of her talismonger shop and offers her a metal briefcase. Eliana gestures for the boy to leave the case on a stool, and dismisses him at once. The dirty and disgusting condition of the briefcase brings a sneer of distaste to her lips, but she kneels before it anyway. The case has been twisted and seared by fire, all but melted. She whispers words of power. The briefcase squeals and swells, then snaps open. In a velvet-lined recess lies an enormous white crystal. Eliana takes it carefully into her hands.

Even from a distance, the power of the gem was obvious to her. Now, held in her hands, it is almost overwhelming. She sways with dizziness and immediately cuts out her astral perceptions. Moving with utmost care, she carries the gem downstairs to her lodge, to her velvet-draped ritual altar. There, she examines the gem once more with her astral senses. She apprehends a tenuous connection with one of the greater metaplanes of astral space, a faint, fading link with the native plane of the Soul-Catcher.

Abruptly, she assenses the gems true power. Hidden at its core, an orb of orange-gold orichalcum, infused with the essence of uncounted beings .. all victims of violent death.

The gem's power is dark, but it will earn her many secrets.

A smile slowly forms on her lips.

Cat will be pleased.

Epilogue

"Hands on heads!"

Tikki lifts her hands to the top of her head, and, peripherally, sees Raman do the same. They are standing on either side of Raman's chopper along the shoulder of a local two-lane highway flanked by heavy woods. The gruff male voice giving the orders comes from somewhere beyond the glaring colored strobes and dazzling, flashing headlights of a car stopped on the shoulder about five meters behind them.

It's a bronze and his cop car.

So much for taking so-called back roads out of Philly. Tikki didn't like the idea to begin with. Back roads lead through lightly populated regions where the police have nothing to do but drink soykaf and harass those they deem to be undesirables. She and Raman should have used the major routes of the northeast corridor. The police regulating those routes are so busy they're happy if people stop killing each other for five minutes at a time.

Tikki glances at Raman. If he feels any chagrin at hav-

ing gotten them into this, he's hiding it well. She has a
few choice things to tell him once they get clear.

If they get clear.

"Female passenger, advance!" booms the voice from
beyond the lights. "Keep your hands on your head!"

Wonderful.

She steps forward, toward the driver's side of the cop
car, from where the voice seems to be coming. Two steps
closer to the flaring lights and she has to turn her head
aside. Two steps more and she swings her elbows in front
of her face. The pain in her eyes has them full of water.
She trips and almost falls. The instant she's beyond the
front of the car, the pain is gone. But it's like stepping
from the surface of the sun straight into the bottom of a
mine shaft. For an instant, she's almost blind. Red and
blue orbs dash through a world of inky shadows. A large
hand catches her right shoulder and thrusts her against
the fender of the car.

Hands run quickly over her flanks and belly, down both
her legs, then over her back. The MK-7 gas dispenser
disappears from her left jacket pocket. The Zimmer narcoject hold-out pistol leaves her right jacket pocket. The
Civilian RX-10000 electro-stunner slips out from under
the front waistband of her trousers. The Kang slides out
of the holster at the small of her back. Various other
implements leave the sheaths inside her boot-tops. She
blinks the last of the water out of her eyes as her hands
are tugged down behind her back. The fingerless gloves
on her hands are veiled in a spiderwebbing of feminine
black lace, but that doesn't inhibit their effect. They're
called shock gloves, straight out of the Ares Winter Cat-
alog. Someone pulls them off her hands, then traps her
wrists in prisoner-restraint cuffs.

Abruptly, she realizes that there's only one bronze, one
cop. She figures that if he's going to all the trouble of
putting her in cuffs, he isn't planning to cite anyone for
traffic violations. She also supposes that if he's using both
hands to search and cuff her, then his weapon must be
in its holster.

He turns her around to face him, then presses against

her right shoulder as though he wants her to move toward the rear of the car. She stands facing him.

"Move it!" he growls.

Tikki sneers, and strains. Something hard like metal snaps. Something clinks sharply against the car. Tikki swings her hands out from behind her back. The cop looks down, then an expression of astonishment bursts across his face.

Tikki butts her head against his face, hard.

"Ra!" she shouts.

The cop staggers back, seeming stunned, bleeding from the nose, fumbling with his sidearm. Tikki snatches her electro-stunner from under his belt, puts it to his gut and fires. A brief discharge of eighty thousand volts turns the cop's legs to water. He slumps to one knee as Raman comes running up. She grabs the cop's arms and starts dragging him toward the woods. Raman helps, taking the man's legs.

"We should scrag him," Raman says.

"No." Tikki shakes her head. They put the cop down just inside the treeline, where Tikki reclaims her weapons. She's got the Kang if she needs it, but doesn't plan to use it unless her back's to the wall. The only things she intends to kill in the foreseeable future are deer and other four-legs. She's had enough of killing two-legs, humans. Maybe too much.

Out on the road, a car goes by, slowing, then abruptly speeding up. Did the driver see what happened?

A thought comes to mind.

"Get our gear."

Raman looks at her for a moment, then hustles off. Tikki gives the cop another jolt. He jerks with the shock, then grunts, acting drunk, like he can't even sit up. Tikki unloads his sidearm and tosses it deeper into the woods.

The road is empty again as she slides in behind the wheel of the officer's Nissan Police Interceptor. Raman tosses their gear into the rear seat, then slides in on the passenger side.

"What are we doing?" he says.

"Watch."

She keys the shifter, presses down hard on the accelerator. The Interceptor moves out, roaring, engine rising to a whine between gears. Another kilometer up the road and Tikki steers the car onto the entrance ramp for the interstate.

"The chopper would have been faster," Raman remarks. "And less noticeable."

"You had your turn."

Now Tikki leads.

There's a tollbooth up ahead, a few cars sitting in line. Only two of three lanes are open. Tikki steers for the empty lane with the red light over it and finds the console key for the siren, which immediately brawls out, whooping and wailing.

"Hide."

Raman bends down low.

Tikki puts the cop's hat on, just to make her silhouette more cop-like. The hat doesn't fit too well, but then she doesn't keep it on very long and no one outside the car is going to catch more than a quick glimpse of her. She steers the Interceptor through the tollbooth at something like ninety kilometers per hour, then slaps down even harder on the accelerator. There's a brief clanging of alarm bells from outside, then the tollbooth is falling rapidly behind.

Tikki keeps her foot hard to the floor. No pursuit immediately comes into view. The lanes ahead merge with the interstate. She cuts the siren, steers over to the far left lane, then cuts the emergency strobes as well. At close to two hundred kilometers per hour, they eat up pavement fast, streaking past other traffic. Tikki veers into the breakdown lane when cars ahead fail to get out of her way.

"Is it safe driving this fast?" Raman asks, now sitting up straight.

"You want to get out?"

Raman grins. "Stupid question."

"Which?"

"Both."

Probably, he's got a point.

They're north of Trenton when the voices coming over the console comm start talking about a hijacked cop car.

That was inevitable, but Tikki's idea seems to have paid off. They're a good fifty or sixty klicks north of their last-known position. True, every cop in the region will soon be looking for them, but as soon as they dump the car they'll become virtually invisible.

Tikki pulls the Interceptor off the road just short of the next rest stop. They hike through some woods to the rest stop's parking field. Raman hotwires another chopper. By morning, they're near Hartford. Two nights later, they're riding down to the end of an overgrown dirt track somewhere in a place called Maine. There's a clearing at the end of the track and an old cabin made of logs. Raman rolls the chopper straight into the cabin, where it'll be out of sight. The interior of the place is dusty and old, but it's good enough for stashing their gear, and Tikki doesn't plan to spend much time indoors, anyway.

By midnight, they're lying on a grassy bank beside what is probably the last pond in all of North America not polluted by toxic wastes. The half-devoured carcass of a deer lies nearby. The night is cool and quiet and filled with the cloying sweetness of summer, a sweetness Tikki ponders and imagines she might even come to enjoy. Her time in Philly has dampened her fascination with humans and their cities. She's glad just to have gotten out alive. She's been spending too much time with humans, too little time in the wild. She isn't sure who she is anymore. Ruthless killer? In human terms, she supposes, that's all she's ever been. She wonders if she was meant to be more. Better. A thing she'll have to think about, a thing to figure out.

Raman says he doesn't like cold weather. That makes sense for one from somewhere north of Bombay, but she'll worry about it later, like when autumn beckons.

For now, it's just the two of them, for however long it lasts. She flicks her tail lazily across his face, and he responds by growling and moving around toward her rear. The noises he makes and the smells he sheds tell her clearly how enthusiastic a response is in the offing. Tikki is more than willing to cooperate. She supposes this is what her mother meant in saying, "When your season comes, you'll know it.'' It's a time for changes. And other things . . .

Raman soon has her growling with excitement.

Roaring, even.